HOME
COMING

HOME COMING

Sixty Years of
Egyptian Short Stories

Selected and translated by
Denys Johnson-Davies

The American University in Cairo Press
Cairo New York

Some of the translations in this collection have been published previously: "Put Out Those Lights" by Yousef Gohar appeared in *Cairo Calling*, 5 February 1949; "The Mother" by Ibrahim Shukrallah in *Middle East Forum*, February 1959; "Sundown" by Shukri Ayyad, "A House for My Children" by Mahmoud Diab, "Mother of the Destitute" by Yahya Hakki, "The Lost Suitcase" by Abdel-Moneim Selim, and "The Picture" by Latifa al-Zayyat in *Modern Arabic Short Stories*, selected and translated by Denys Johnson-Davies, London: Oxford University Press, 1967; "Grandad Hasan" by Yahya Taher Abdullah, "A Place under the Dome" by Abdul Rahman Fahmy, "The Accusation" by Suleiman Fayyad, "The Man Who Saw the Sole of His Left Foot in a Cracked Mirror" by Lutfi al-Khouli, "The Whistle" by Abd al-Hakim Qasim, and "The Country Boy" by Yusuf al-Sibai in *Egyptian Short Stories*, selected and translated by Denys Johnson-Davies, London: Heinemann, 1978; "Across Three Beds in the Afternoon" by Sonallah Ibrahim in *The Smell of It* by Sonallah Ibrahim, translated by Denys Johnson-Davies, London: Heinemann, 1978; "At the Level Crossing" by Abbas Ahmed and "The Old Clothes Man" by Fathy Ghanem in *Azure* #9, 1981; "The Old Man" by Gamil Atia Ibrahim in *UR: The International Magazine of Arab Culture* #2/3, 1982; "Cairo Is a Small City" by Nabil Gorgy, "The Chair Carrier" by Yusuf Idris, "Birds' Footsteps in the Sand" by Edwar al-Kharrat, and "Another Evening at the Club" by Alifa Rifaat in *Arabic Short Stories*, translated by Denys Johnson-Davies, London: Quartet Books, 1983; "The Son, the Father, and the Donkey" by Sabri Moussa in *Al-Ahram Weekly*, 2 May 1991; "Abu Arab" by Mahmoud Teymour in *Al-Ahram Weekly*, 5 September 1991; "A Murder Long Ago" by Naguib Mahfouz in *Short Story International* #89, December 1991; "A Small White Mouse" by Salwa Bakr in *Cairo Today*, August 1992; "The Man and the Farm" by Yusuf Sharouni in *Short Story International* #96, February 1993; "The Clock" by Khairy Shalaby in *Under the Naked Sky: Short Stories from the Arab World*, selected and translated by Denys Johnson-Davies, Cairo: The American University in Cairo Press, 2000. All other stories are translated and published here for the first time. All stories appear by permission of the authors or their heirs wherever it has been possible to contact them.

First published in 2012 by
The American University in Cairo Press
113 Sharia Kasr el Aini, Cairo, Egypt
420 Fifth Avenue, New York, NY 10018
www.aucpress.com

Dar el Kutub No. 15022/10
ISBN 978 977 416 447 7

Dar el Kutub Cataloging-in-Publication Data

Johnson-Davies, Denys
          Homecoming: Sixty Years of Egyptian Short Stories/ Denys Johnson-Davies.—Cairo:
     The American University in Cairo Press, 2012
               p.   cm.
          ISBN 978 977 416 447 7
          1. Arabic fiction   I. Johnson-Davies, Denys (tr.)
          897.73

1 2 3 4 5   15 14 13 12

Designed by Jon W. Stoy
Printed in Egypt

Contents

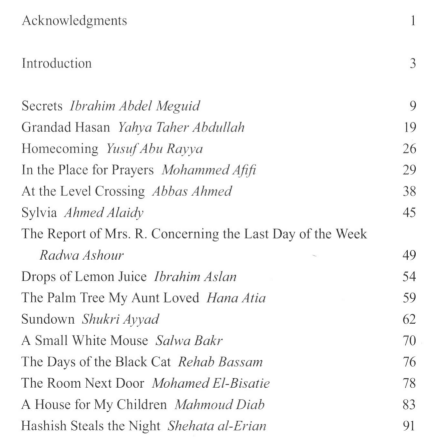

Acknowledgments

My thanks are due to all the writers who have given permission for my translations of their stories to be reproduced in the present volume, also to writers such as Said al-Kafrawi who helped me in my search for suitable material.

This selection seeks, however inadequately, to show how this genre of writing first came to be practiced in Egypt and how with time some of its practitioners were translated into different languages and came to be recognized worldwide.

I also owe thanks to several modern Egyptian publishers such as Sharqiyat, Merit, and al-Dar who have done so much to encourage younger writers, also, of course to Dar el-Shorouk.

Once again I am grateful to the artist Adel el-Siwi for providing the cover picture for this volume.

Finally, my thanks are due to Celia Alexander of the American University in Cairo Press for helping me in putting this book together, also—as usual— to its chief editor, Neil Hewison.

Introduction

This volume started off as a collection of short stories by the younger writers in Egypt who were now contributing to the Arabic short story. Gradually, however, I realized that so far no one had sought to put together a collection of stories that tried to represent the short story from the time when it first appeared in Egypt right up until today.

Having studied Arabic at both the newly set-up School of Oriental Studies at London University (it was later to have the words "and African" added to its title) and then at Cambridge University—this just before the beginning of the Second World War—I came across no one in academic circles who seemed to be aware that a revolution had occurred in Arabic literature. With scarcely anyone noticing or caring, Arabic literature had suddenly turned toward the west and adopted some of the genres of writing that were peculiar to it, such as the novel and, more particularly, the short story. It is strange that neither in the west itself nor in the Arab world did anyone show any real interest in this phenomenon, though when in 1946 I produced the first translated volume of Arabic short stories, by Mahmoud Teymour, none other than the secretary general of the newly formed Arab League, Abdul Rahman Azzam, wrote a short introduction to it. Having produced this volume, I was later to become aware that the short story was also being practiced in other Arab countries apart from Egypt and I began working on a volume of short stories that was to represent this genre as practiced in the Arab world. The stories for such a volume were available for some years before I eventually found a publisher for it in England. It is, I think, significant that the publisher that I eventually succeeded in finding, Oxford University Press, would consider putting the volume into print only if it was introduced by a top academic figure. The volume received scant attention in the English-speaking world and none at all in the Arab world. In fact, I understand that not a single Arab government or institution purchased a single copy, so the first edition of the book was remaindered and the copies were sold off to a publisher in Beirut, who turned them into a paperback edition.

Was nobody able to recognize that the volume contained stories of real worth by such writers as Naguib Mahfouz (who was later to be awarded the Nobel Prize) and such talents as Yusuf Idris and Tayeb Salih? How, too, was it that the Arab world, which now boasts some of the most lucrative prizes for writers, simply ignored the appearance of such a volume and it required a British publisher, Heinemann, to have the courage—without assistance from any Arab quarter—to produce a series of translations under the title 'Arab Authors'? In this respect it is interesting to note that in his book about Cairo the accomplished writer and journalist Max Rodenbeck stated that he had never once, when traveling daily by train from his home in the suburb of Maadi to the center of Cairo, seen an Egyptian read a book unless it be a copy of the Qur'an. There thus seemed to be little hope for any Egyptian writer who chose to take up short-story writing as a profession.

It took some time before the step was taken by the American University in Cairo (AUC) Press to start paying translators to produce English-language editions of modern Arabic writing. Today the AUC Press publishes some fifteen translations of Arabic fiction in English a year. Many of these titles then find their way into other languages such as French, Italian, and Spanish, as well as into such non-European languages as Korean and Japanese. And all this has been accomplished within the term of one lifetime.

While the first ever volume of Egyptian short stories in an English translation was published by me in 1946, and my next volume of short stories from the Arab world did not appear until 1967, in the meantime short stories in Egypt were being published in Arabic in various magazines, and the occasional volume was produced. During those early years I published English translations of short stories by several Egyptian writers such as Yusuf Gohar, Yusuf Sharouni, and Mahmoud Badawi; mostly, however, they were broadcast over Egyptian State Broadcasting radio. I still have several scripts, badly typed by myself, marked with the date and time when the story was broadcast and the name of the person who read the story and certified as "Passed by Censor," followed by a rough signature and date. Unfortunately, over the years many of these scripts have become lost among the myriad papers that I have carried around with me on my travels.

I was particularly delighted to find that I still possess a somewhat tattered copy of a volume of short stories entitled *Anwar* (Lights) by Mohammed Afifi. The volume, published in 1946, is of particular interest in that it includes an important introduction of some fifty pages dealing with the Egyptian short story as it was being written at that time. In it the author deals with the work of such writers as Ibrahim al-Mazini, Tawfiq al-Hakim, and Mahmoud Teymour. The introduction deals in the main with the important question of the language in which the Arabic short story should be written. "Logic demands that a man should write in the language he speaks," the author states, "though there are those who say the opposite, namely that the Egyptian should speak in the language in which he writes."

Reading this sentence immediately reminded me of a discussion I once had with Mahmoud Teymour on the general subject of the Arabic language and the difficulty presented by the fact of there being two separate languages, one for writing and one for speech. I remember him saying to me: "If God gives us life we shall see that in a matter of fifty years all Egyptians will be speaking the classical language." The truth, however, is that exactly the opposite has happened: more and more writers are employing the spoken language in their novels and short stories, and we see more and more advertisements in newspapers and on hoardings employing the spoken form. Let us face it: the first objective in writing an advertisement is that it should be widely understood.

Among the interesting quotations that Afifi reproduces in *Anwar* on the subject of language is one by Ahmed Zaki to the effect that the classical language must change so that it deals with the demands of this age: if it does not, then time itself will take its revenge, as has happened with all the other languages that have refused to change and adapt, the outstanding example being Latin.

Mohammed Afifi includes among his selection of stories two that were written wholly in the spoken language; one of these, "The Place of Prayer," I have translated and included in this volume. Afifi says that while these were not the first short stories to be written in the spoken language, it was the first time that such stories found their way into print. Today, most writers of fiction in Egypt feel that the classical language should be kept for the narrative and that dialog should be in the spoken vernacular.

How else has the situation changed since those early days when the Arabic short story first came into being? More stories are appearing than previously, and there are more people interested in modern Arabic literature and more people able to translate it into English. As for the quality, writers like Yusuf Idris, who died in 1991, remains to my mind as competent a writer of short stories as any of the writers of today. Freedom of expression and subject matter are wider today, and women writers of short stories—though at one time they scarcely existed—are almost as numerous as men. While my first volume of short stories, published in 1967, contained just one story by a woman writer, my last volume of stories from the Arab world, *Under the Naked Sky*, published in 2000 by the AUC Press, contained among its thirty pieces no less than eight by women.

Because in the early days the Egyptian public had little interest in the novel and the short story, Egyptian writers of fiction, if their work was published at all, could not expect to profit financially from the sales of their books. It quickly became apparent that Arabic writers, if they were to make money from their writing, would do so only if it appeared in translation. So being in those early days virtually the sole person producing translations in English of Arabic fiction, I was approached more than once by Egyptian writers with the request that I undertake a translation of one of their works. In return they offered me any profits that ensued from the book when published and that additionally they would pay me an initial fee for translating the book.

In those early days no publisher was in a position to pay out extra money to a translator. The normal practice was therefore for the writer and the translator to be paid an equal percentage of such profits as there were from the sales of the book when published. In this manner the writer gained a little extra for the work of writing the book, while the translator was rewarded for his efforts in translating it. Additionally, of course, once the book had been translated into English, it was more likely to be translated into some other language, or even into several other languages.

Happily the days when translators were scarce and when there was no money with which to pay translators are now over. Translators from the Arabic can now expect to be paid an advance fee for their work and can even bargain for a share of the royalties from the sale of the book. So the position of translations of modern Arabic literature has completely changed since the middle of the last century: it is now recognized that an Arab writer can produce a book that proves itself to be a bestseller when translated into another language.

In one other respect changes have occurred in the short story since it was first practised in Egypt in the early years of the last century: readers, writers, and critics have all become much more liberal in their outlook concerning the content of modern Arabic fiction today, especially in relation to matters of sex or bodily functions. I well remember passing on to my friend Mahmoud Teymour a short story by Yusuf Sharouni that included a description of a donkey making its way along a street while urinating, making a pattern in the sand. I was surprised to find my friend returning the story to me, expressing his opinion that this particular detail, which I found harmless enough, should be excluded from the story if it came to be published.

One can only be delighted at the way in which modern Arabic literature is today being read in translation throughout the world, and at the remarkably short time in which this has been achieved.

Secrets

Ibrahim Abdel Meguid

1

"Will you take me hunting with you?"

This was the first time Bulbul had talked to Abduh.

"Have you got any traps?"

"I bought five."

Bulbul turned to make sure his friends sitting far off under the light of the tall lamppost at the end of the lane could see him.

"Then meet me early in the morning."

Abduh rushed off as usual, carrying the wire cage filled with sparrows; in the other hand were his traps, while Bulbul, in disbelief, went back to his friends. They too didn't believe it.

The two of them met up in the morning. Abduh hurried off, Bulbul hardly able to keep up with him, till they reached the rubbish dump that stretched over the area of salt pans.

"The whole refuse of Alexandria is here," Abduh said, smiling.

Bulbul saw high mounds of garbage and a few small fires.

"Stay away from the yellow rice husks—there's fire underneath them."

Abduh said this while Bulbul was looking at the smoke rising up from between the black burning husks of rice covering a large area of the ground. The smoke was floating above it, faded blue and white. Abduh raked up the yellow rice husks with an iron rod, revealing under the surface a layer that was burning, which the smoke concealed.

He said, "More than once I've seen men and boys fall into it and have the skin stripped off their feet."

Then he branched off, walking for a short distance over the yellow rice husks, and came back laughing. Bulbul was on the point of doing likewise but he hadn't taken more than a single step when he had a sensation of burning under his foot.

"I can also lie on top of it."

Abduh threw himself down on his back on top of the yellow rice straw for a while, then got to his feet, brushing the scattered husks from his gallabiya, and walked off. For a time Bulbul was behind him, then alongside him, till the ground flattened out in front of them in a broad space of earth, white and yellow. The lakes looked to be a long way away and were shining under the sunlight. From far off there showed empty red areas; Abduh said they were shallow places that dried up in summer, leaving nothing but rough red salt that was taken off to the factory where it was rendered soft and white.

Bulbul exulted in the dazzling emptiness.

"Where will you put your traps?" he asked.

"We'll put them all together."

Abduh divided the ten traps among four imaginary circles on the ground. In the two inner circles he placed Bulbul's five traps.

"Like you, I brought five traps so that I wouldn't catch more than you," he said.

Bulbul had an extraordinary feeling of animation and pointed to the stone Abduh had placed behind each trap.

"Is it," he asked, "for the bird to stand on so it will see the bait below it?"

"Birds love things that are high-up," answered Abduh and called the stone "a warden."

Bulbul remembered the strange word.

Then Abduh asked him, "Has the war come to an end?"

Bulbul remembered that Abduh didn't go to school as he did.

"Some time ago," he said. "We returned to school and we're now in the long vacation."

Abduh smiled and said, "You see, I saw the soldiers from the national guard."

Bulbul was at a loss and made no reply. The day the men of the army and the national guard departed they destroyed their barricades and took away their guns. The children had gathered round clapping, and the women and girls had let out trilling cries of joy, and the men had shaken hands with them, and some of them had wept.

2

Abduh had pointed to the bait he was baiting the traps with.

"It brings the birds down from the sky."

There was an insect that Abduh had called "the driller" and which resembled a grasshopper. He said that each evening he would take it out of the mud of the nearby swamp and keep it in the "pot" with some mud so that it would stay alive till morning. Bulbul's eyes roved round with the sparrows that were flying and moving about over the ground.

"These are Egyptian sparrows and they know all about traps," said Abduh.

He told him that the bird that was easy to catch was a foreign one called a wagtail.

The two of them went far off and Abduh began letting out a melodious whistling as he waved his arms about in regular movements back and forth in time with the whistling.

"Do as I do."

Bulbul began copying him and saw a number of sparrows rising up from the ground in front of them. He was amazed he hadn't seen them before and Abduh said they were wagtails. Two of them went into the outer circle of traps and Abduh signaled to him to stop whistling and moving about.

A sparrow was standing atop a "warden," moving its head several times from right to left, then several times up and down, after which it flew off to stand on top of another "warden." Bulbul followed it with a heart that beat along to the fluttering of its wings, standing almost on tiptoe. Then Abduh asked him, "Is it true that Gamal Abdel Nasser visited your school?"

Dust was stirred up around one of the traps. Bulbul would have run toward it had not Abduh caught hold of him for several moments. Then the dust was stirred up around another of the traps and Bulbul realized why Abduh had taken hold of him. He discovered that the two sparrows had been caught in Abduh's traps, and he said, "Yes, he came to us more than once and he gave me a color photograph of himself."

But Abduh, who had freed the two birds and put them in the cage and had begun to re-bait the traps, said, "They won't find that girl Ahlam. Her mother says she got lost, but her father killed her, right there in front of me. I saw him but he didn't see me. He took her out in a felucca and tied a heavy stone to her and threw her in the lake."

<h1 style="text-align:center">3</h1>

Three sparrows stood together in Bulbul's traps. He was at a loss as to what to do with them. "Shall I kill them?" he inquired.

"They'll go bad. The weather's hot and we'll be out late."

"Then I'll tie them up with string."

"You'll be torturing them for the whole day. Why didn't you bring a cage with you?"

Having said this, Abduh took hold of one of the birds and folded its wings one over the other and let it fall to the ground. Then he came back to it and threw it up in the air and caught it in his hands.

"It can't fly," he said, "but its wings keep moving."

Then he put the three birds in his own cage made out of wire and said, "Don't be afraid—at the end of the day we'll sort them out. Those whose wings are free are mine, while the shackled ones are yours."

Little by little there were longer intervals between the appearance of one bird and that of the next so that Abduh would often leave Bulbul on his own and start moving around among the mounds of trash looking for something of use. Evening approached and the scattered fires grew more numerous and burnt more fiercely. The smoke from them, for no apparent reason, became thicker and the lake grew dark.

"Look," whispered Abduh and Bulbul saw a man and a woman moving away, the man's arm around the woman's waist.

Bulbul saw another man and another woman.

"They all come here at night. They hire boats and go off together on the lake. Come on, let's get going."

Bulbul became confused, but Abduh said, "They don't like anyone seeing them."

Suddenly the darkness grew dense and it became difficult for them to gather up the traps.

The Salt Lake

1

Bulbul met up with Abduh in the street and said, "Take me fishing with you."

Abduh fixed his narrow eyes on him and pulled the blue cap forward over his head by the brim. He took him to a muddy spot behind the quarter, a place that would suddenly dry up and become filled with pebbles and stones, then he came to a stop in front of a small pool thick with scrub and reeds.

"Keep well away," he said. "There are scorpions and snakes in the scrub."

Bulbul stood not far off. As he was wearing shoes made of white rubber, he couldn't keep his eyes off Abduh's bare feet. He noticed they were as wide as a man's.

"The reeds are all green, not good for fishing," said Abduh, and Bulbul didn't know what to do.

"I've got three piasters," he said.

"Then I'll take them from you and give you one of mine all prepared."

They went back, parting at the entrance to the quarter. Bulbul met his friends and they said he mustn't go off with Abduh again. He had told them how he had not started to divide up the birds with Abduh until they had covered half the distance back because after every few steps they would meet a man and a woman, and how when he began to divide them up they didn't find a single bird in the cage, and that Abduh had laughed a lot because, as he was putting in the last bird he had caught, he had forgotten to close the cage door and they'd all flown away, even those with shackled wings because, according to what Abduh had said, being so closely packed together their wings had become loosened. Bulbul had laughed, saying they'd caught more than twenty birds that day but that they'd all been lost. The traps, too, had been lost. They said that Abduh had certainly gone back at night and retrieved the traps because someone like him wasn't frightened of the night—nor of the day—and that the birds hadn't flown away but that he had hidden them some-where and that the people he had seen were a product of his imagination. But he didn't listen to them.

The next day he took the train for the first time with Abduh, from the al-Qabbari station to the Mitras station. The train was chock-full of people and luggage and merchandise, and he was squeezed up, breathing in a strange mixture of oppressive smells issuing from the sacks, crates, and bodies, and he could hear shouts that mingled with the rumble of the wheels. When he got off, he saw that the space ahead of him was white, the earth black, its soil so soft his shoes sank into it. He saw men hurrying along one of the paths; they wore lightweight trousers rolled up high above their bare feet, and dark-colored jackets with shining buttons. He saw that some of them seemed to be taller than houses. Then he burst out laughing.

"Look."

But Abduh paid no attention.

"The donkey's dragging the cart all by itself, without a driver."

Abduh gave him an unhurried look and said, "It's got a driver."

"Where?" asked Bulbul, laughing in astonishment, to which Abduh said, "In front of you, on top of the cart, but you don't see him."

2

Bulbul's eyes widened at the sight of the long, wide, glistening tongue of water that joined up with the lake in the distance. It was submerged in a space even brighter, and above it he saw a vast clear sky, and it looked to him like a lake. His eyes, relaxed, gazed at the large number of men and youths stand-ing or sitting on small chairs of wood or cane, their hands stretched in front of them above the water, with dozens of yellow and differently colored rods.

He thought about this vast, goodly universe and was surprised as he fum-bled while undoing the hair wound round his red fishing rod, to find that Abduh had already finished and had cast his hook into the water and was saying, "Look, it's dipping."

He saw the green float of Abduh's green rod bobbing about as it dipped down in successive little movements. Then Abduh quickly raised the rod and the line came out of the water and attached to it was a small white fish that gleamed in the daylight. As he released the fish, Abduh said, "I gave you a rod with two hooks. Bait them both. In the Salt Lake people bait them with prawns. This worm is better—it shines underwater like gold. I get them out of the mud of the shore here. Before I go back I put them in the pot with mud until the morning so they stay alive."

Bulbul thought: Does Abduh fish in the Salt Lake, too? Then he asked himself why Abduh should do that when mud and worms were always to be found at the place where he usually fished. However, he had hardly cast the hook into the water than the bobbing red float disappeared under the water. When he drew it in he felt it was heavy and against the sky gleamed two green fish jumping around crazily, scattering drops of water around them.

"Don't shout when you draw in the rod," said Abduh, and Bulbul was thrown into confusion, not knowing whether or not he really had shouted.

"Of course, you haven't got a net."

"I've got a feedsack."

"That's no good—it would kill the fish."

Abduh took out of the pocket of his gallabiya a large needle attached to a short piece of string and ending in a piece of wood.

He put the needle through the fish's gills and brought it out through its mouth and pushed it along to the end of the piece of string. He did the same with the other fish. Then he plunged the needle into the ground and let the string go loose in the water, and the two fish disappeared from view.

"This way the fish won't die. I'll give you the needle as a present."

It was as though the fishes could tell the difference between the two of them, for the sun was scarcely in the middle of the sky before the length of string had been filled, while Abduh had caught no more than five small fishes. These he placed in the reed basket and covered them with a piece of sacking that he would from time to time sprinkle with water.

"Let's go," said Abduh suddenly, and he saw Bulbul, who would have liked to go on, folding up his fishhooks and raising the needle and length of string from the water and placing the fish in his basket.

"The sun makes the fish go bad. We'll be returning on foot because there are no trains now."

Bulbul's dream was a simple one: to return quickly so that his mother might see what he'd caught and allow him to go about with Abduh, who wasn't liked by anyone in the quarter. But Abduh had chosen to go back on foot.

Bulbul had never previously walked such a long distance and didn't know that the sun could make you dizzy. Abduh knew strange pathways and was walking between the railway tracks, often coming to a stop to use the iron rod that never left his hand to root out some lizard from under them. Then he'd aim a stone at it and never missed. He would enter by an opening that marked the railway lines at which Bulbul saw a land filled with holes and pools of putrid water and a broad elevation of land from which surging, polluted waters fell down to land that was deeply awash, then branched out into extended and intertwined waterways.

Abduh said that the city's sewage all flowed out here and that these waters were all urine. Bulbul could actually smell the suffocating stench. He was astonished to see Abduh running after a scorpion and not stopping till he'd killed it with a stone. He watched him plunge the iron rod into its body. Then, bending one end round it and the other end over it with a curious movement, he flung the rod upward so that it became attached, with one shot, to the electric cable that stretched between giant poles alongside the wall. Bulbul could see dozens of rods hanging from the cables.

"I've killed all those scorpions and chameleons."

All of a sudden Bulbul noticed that Abduh wasn't walking but rather skipping along like a wagtail. He thought, smiling, that it would be possible for him to catch him up. He hurried after the bare-footed Abduh and wondered how it was that no thorn or nail got into his feet. Then he found himself in a wide expanse of land, cultivated and with watery shadows.

"Do you see the canal over there?" said Abduh.

"What about it?"

"I once stole the clothes of a man who was bathing in it," and he exploded into joyful laughter.

"He ran after me naked but didn't catch up with me and couldn't go on," and he laughed even more.

"Oh, if you'd only seen it!" he said.

He clapped his hands several times and Bulbul, too, burst into laughter.

"You took his clothes?" he asked him.

"I found they were too big so I returned them to him the next day."

3

Tired, Bulbul thought: Is there no end to this road? He saw Abduh sitting by some small springs from which clear water was gushing out. He was drinking and he addressed Bulbul, "My father always says that the water of these springs is pure."

Bulbul thought he was talking rubbish, for Abduh was fatherless, having no one but a mother whose chest, as grown-ups put it, had become "inhabited" by asthma, but he had drunk with Abduh because his lips had grown dry and cracked. He thought about how he could take the needle and length of string and make off, but Abduh had put his arm through the handle of the basket as though he were going to hold onto it forever. He recollected how his friends had said that Abduh no longer hunted birds so that he couldn't accompany him and discover how he'd cheated him, and that having agreed to accompany him fishing, had done so only to deceive him and go back to hunting birds. More than once he saw him standing in front of some castor-oil and mulberry trees, then climbing nimbly, with the basket on his arm, and coming down with a bird or two in his hand. He explained to Bulbul that the tree had twigs that had been gummed; the owners of the fields would put gum on the branches and the birds would stick to them if they landed on them. The birds were green and yellow, small and cowering, and Abduh called them "greens" and "yellows'" and would kill them by grasping the bird's head in one hand and the body in the other and pulling them apart. At the beginning Bulbul was terrified, then he began to laugh at it, while Abduh put them inside the basket on top of the fish and under the sacking that had dried.

"What's your father do?" Abduh asked suddenly, and Bulbul was amazed because that was something that everyone in the quarter knew. However, he said, "He's a clerk in the Public Health Ministry. Why?"

Abduh smiled and said, "Because I want to get a birth certificate made out."

They walked on without Bulbul understanding anything. There stretched before them vast fields crammed with black and white aubergines, red peppers, tomatoes, and a large kind of squash the size of a melon. Abduh said that it was being grown from seed and he began to jump between then and to gather up some of them and put them in the small basket; Bulbul was amazed at how it could hold them all. He thought about how he would separate the fishes from the bodies of the birds and their heads, and also from the vegetables. A slight shadow fell upon the world and a breeze stirred in the stagnant space, and a slight rustling could be heard advancing from across the earth toward his feet. The shadow became more static and Bulbul couldn't see a single tree around him, or a single bird flying. His eyes were incapable of following Abduh who was moving about, bent over among the plants whose leaves hung down, their stems and branches drooping onto the ground, their fruit withered like an old woman with shriveled skin over which tiny worms have worked their way, while round about them moved lizards and slim yellow and green snakes. The shadow grew yet more static, and the yellow basket, thrown down on the ground, could be made out, alone and dusty, the reeds broken in more than one place, the ends poking out, sharp and twisted. Soft objects crawled over Bulbul's feet and continued up his trousers. The buzzing increased, piercing his ears. He called out "Abduh . . . Abduh!" but there was no echo to his feeble voice and no answer. Gathering all his strength together, he yelled "Abduh . . . Abduh!" but no sound came out.

Grandad Hasan

—∽∼∽—

Yahya Taher Abdullah

It was Grandad Hasan's practice, when the holy month of Ramadan had come in and right through until its thirty glorious days had elapsed, to perform the afternoon prayer communally at the mosque of his grandfather, the late Abdullah, after which he would return and seat himself to the left of the main door, on the bench that had been built of stones taken from ancient sites.

It was nearly eighty years since this stone bench had been built and Grandad Hasan had first sat on it; since men had gone off with camels to bring back stones fallen from the wall of the ancient temple. And so the house had been constructed in less than a week: a family house in miniature but without an outer wall, a hallway, a guest-room, or a mosque, though it did have a stable for horses, also a mill and a press exclusively for Grandad Hasan's family, just as over there they were exclusively for Grandad Abdullah's family. Thus the stone that built both of them had been dragged along by two hefty oxen.

Grandad Hasan had consummated his marriage to Nashwa, the daughter of Hagg Sayyid, and he had had three sons and four daughters by her; when she died Grandad Hasan had married Hafsa, the daughter of Yusuf Abdel Karim, but she had borne him nothing but daughters, so he had married Zannouba, her younger sister, who became the mother of his boys, Abdel Mageed, Abdel Basit, and Abdel Magid, and of two daughters, Amina and Fatima.

*

On the right of Grandad Hasan the door of the house was closed. He called out, "Hey, girl!" The door made of sycomore wood gave a low, heavy creaking sound and the large stone rolling along the ground made a muffled noise. It was one of the six young daughters of Grandad Hasan's children who had done this, and now the door stood half-open, held back by the large stone. Which girl was it today? Grandad Hasan asked himself, and he called out: "Hey, girl!" Nawal, the daughter of the middle son, Abdel Hamid, came along, breathless, her small head held to one side, her thin neck twisted under a small basket filled with dates. She moved the basket from her head to her shoulder, resting it against her knee, then lowered the basket on to the bench and dragged it along till it was beside her grandfather, within reach of his right hand. Nawal went off at a run and came back with another basket containing bread, which she placed beside the basket of fruit. She remained standing without saying anything. Her grandfather did not speak to her; he merely smiled, knowing that she was happy at having done what she had. He remembered that he had not asked her about the opening of the door this time, so he did so. Nawal ran into the house then came back and said, "It's Insaf, Grandad." Her grandfather asked her with a stern frown, "And where are the rest of the girls?" "Inside, Grandad," replied Nawal. "And the boys?" asked her grandfather. "They're all at home, Grandad," said Nawal. "They're all inside, Grandad."

Grandad Hasan sees the houses stretching out on both sides of the lane. Over there, after Ahmad Rawi's house, the lane takes a turn. That large black form at the turn remains motionless: it looks like a large, black, kneeling camel.

The old men pass by, dismounting if they happen to be riding, and go up to greet him. He returns the greeting in God's name and adds joyfully: "Ramadan is noble," and hears their reply: "Noble, O son of the noble." The faces of the men are different, their expressions change, but their reply is one and unchanging: "Noble, O son of the noble." Grandad Hasan's sense of well-being increases and he jokes with the young men who come along; as they kiss his hand his body starts up in protest and he asks forgiveness of God for every great sin, then goes back to joking with them, calling each by his mother's name. "Fasting or not, O son of Husniya?" he said to Salih

Sanusi. "Fasting, thanks be to God, Grandad,' replied Salih, and Grandad
Hasan knew he was telling the truth. As for Shahhat Fikri, Grandad had withdrawn his hand from between the other's hands, which were just below his
mouth as he muttered "I ask forgiveness of God," then shouted: "You're not
fasting, you're bringing ruin to your religion," to which Shahhat answered:
"By the honor of Muhammad, I'm fasting—just as you are, Grandad." The
grandfather shouted back in rebuke: "You son of a dog, don't swear by the
Prophet's honor—you don't know his worth. Better swear by the honor of
Wadida daughter of Sakit, your mother. Off with you! It's written all over
you face you're heathen." "By God, I'm fasting this year, Grandad," said
Shahhat, smiling, knowing that Grandad Hasan would not stop joking with
him and guessing what the grandfather would say to him next. "You'll say,
don't swear by God, but, by God the almighty, I'm fasting." "Then why,"
the grandfather asked him gleefully, "is your face black?" "From anger and
the sun, Grandad," said Shahhat, "but, by God the almighty, I *am* fasting."
Half convinced and half resigned, Grandad Hasan said, "All right, off you
go. You've sworn by God. The Lord can blind you or afflict you with some
calamity if you've lied. He who has created the vast universe containing both
jinn and man, and with all the mountains and trees that are to be seen, is capable of harming you if you've lied. The name of God must not be taken in vain,
Shahhat." "Yes, by God, Grandad," said Shahhat and departed. When Mansur
the son of Sadiq passed by, he was asked by the grandfather if he was fasting;
he answered in the affirmative, and when he asked him if he used to pray he
said, "No," and Grandad Hasan exhorted him to pray and scolded him, hurling angry words at him as he went off: "You son of a donkey, it should be
known to you that His reckoning is hard and cannot be endured by a mule like
you, nor yet will ten oxen like you endure it."

And when the women pass by they have to adjust their robes around their
mortal bodies and show confusion, and Grandad Hasan will be aware of their
confusion of gait and the way their feet drag in the dust that flies up around
them. As for that stray dog with no known owner, it passes by Grandad Hasan
at this time every day and cocks its hind leg, resting it against the wall of the
house opposite, pees, then goes on its way after Grandad Hasan has screamed
at it: "Go away! Off with you, you accursed, ill-omened creature."

*

On the two mats spread out in front of the stone bench above the ground that had been sprinkled with water was a place for God's guests on earth, the needy and the deprived. From the basket Grandad Hasan gives out bread with his right hand, while from the basket of dates he scoops up with trembling hand more than can be held in one's palm. "All good is from God," he would say, "and is done in order to gain His approval." Thus the ancestors, those who had journeyed to the House of the True One, had retained the wealth and position they had inherited, so gaining the blessings of this world and Paradise in the next. I in my turn must sense my forefathers' inherited ability to give for the love of God, and it will be for my sons to know that the branch of the tree does not approach being good other than with God's permission, that this happens only to the few chosen of His worshipers, to those with full hearts.

Time passed and sunset drew near. The black camel rose with its mighty body and walked slowly toward Grandad Hasan. Gradually the houses withdrew from view, first the distant ones, then those close by, while the camel moved on, large and black, toward the grandfather. The grandfather closed his eyes. (The universe was vast, limitless, of a dark blueness, and the deserts were spacious, without bounds, the sands yellow and fiery, and from out of their belly there exploded forth hill upon hill upon hill, a whole series of hills, blood-red like the color of dusk. Everything now was at the prime virgin state of creation, and the eye of the believer could make out that black spot separating day from night, which looks so small and grows bigger as it draws nearer to the viewer.)

Grandad Hasan's heart grew dry and his failing body shook as he spoke to himself: "How puny is this human being in God's Kingdom!" and he asked himself who the guest might be? Who was that person who was wandering through the earth? The Messenger of God who appears from afar as a black spot, who could it be? Was it the Khidr, upon whom be peace, the teacher of Moses? Or could it be the Maghribi? Could it be that cunning, avid one?

The voices of the boys come through with a faint clamor. They are over there at Muhammad ibn Makiyya's shop, and over there is a mulberry tree which is still alive, while Ahmad Mabrouk who planted it died ten years ago. The boys' rowdiness means that the gun for breaking the fast has been heard on the radio of Hagg Muhammad, the eldest of Grandad Hasan's brothers, in accordance with Cairo time. The time has thus come round for breaking the fast for those living under the protection of Sayyida Zaynab and Sayyidna Hussein, and when One-eyed Yusuf gives the call to prayer from high up on the Abdullah mosque the time will have come for the people of both New and Old Karnak to break the fast. Rashad the son of Grandad Kamil, the brother of Grandad Hasan, comes along, flying like a pigeon: "The time for sunset prayers has come, Grandad," and Grandad Hasan stretches out his hand and the little boy grasps hold of it and they enter the house.

The spacious courtyard of the house has been spread with mats; the low wooden tables stand on their four legs, no large gaps between them; the brass trays on top of the tables hold dishes of vegetables and meat, also of kunafa and the other special sweets for Ramadan. The bulb hanging inside over the door-opening lets fall a cone of light on those seated and casts shadows on all sides, making the time of sunset seem nearer to that of noon.

Here you are, Grandad Hasan, amid sons and wives of sons and sons of sons, loved and held in reverence, so give thanks to God the number of times that there are beads to your silver-inlaid rosary. All await your hand to be stretched forth, the sleeve rolled up, and for you to take up your glass and say: "In the name of God the Merciful, the Compassionate" and drink the infusion of dates. Then you stretch out your hand to the food and the other hands stretch out in turn, and the many noises of mastication and swallowing of food are heard. Suddenly the shadow falls on the dishes, the shadow hides all the empty delights of the soul. You will not think long, Grandad Hasan, for you know by heart what you will say and you know too who it is who approaches.

(Come along in, Master Khidr. This is your house and this is from God's bounty. I am the servant of God, I am Grandad Hasan. O my Lord Khidr, come in and sit down.) Misgiving comes and the body shudders, O Grandad Hasan. Perhaps your guest was the Maghribi, O Grandad Hasan. Perhaps that sly one has come and you will have to bargain with him.

*

Having finished his breakfast, Grandad Hasan takes himself off to the lavatory which lies under the well of the stairway leading up to the second floor of the house. One of his granddaughters will have preceded him there and filled up the brass ewer and have left it in front of the lavatory door so that he can take it in with him, then he will come out, having rid himself of urine and excrement, to be met by a girl carrying a copper ewer and with a basin placed on the floor in which Grandad Hasan will make his ablutions. When he comes to washing his feet he takes up the ewer and pours the water over them, dismissing the girl with a muttered word, and any one of the girls takes over the spreading of one of the many prayer carpets in the house, all of which have been given to Grandad Hasan by those who have visited the holy lands of the Hijaz. On the east side, facing the open main door of the house, Grandad Hasan prays, having driven away every random thought, be it good or evil. Having finished his prayers, he recites the set part of the Quran, after which he remains seated on the soft velvety carpet, until one of the girls brings him a glass of tea and he gives himself up to some thought from which his imagination takes off.

(Each of them comes in ragged clothes, disguised as someone begging, in his hand a staff and on his shoulder a saddle-bag. Anyone meeting up with one of them cannot tell the difference. The Khidr is a great traveler and only the eye of a true believer can see him. When he comes to you in the guise of a beggar and you reject him, the grace of God that He has bestowed upon you perishes, but if you are generous to him God will be generous to you—and it is the Khidr who taught Moses about the things that are hidden in the earth, God's purest girl—and you will live happily for ever. Likewise the wily Maghribi knows what form the Khidr takes and so makes himself look like him. Then, taking you unawares, he makes his way to the house—and he is the only one who knows where lies the treasure, perhaps buried by ancestors possessed of many wiles. The vagabond takes you unawares, kills the guardian of the treasure, who is one of the jinn, and the Maghribi disappears with not a trace of him to be found. So, Grandad Hasan, you should be wary about your guest. Treat him hospitably, certainly, but keep a very close eye on his every move. He will come and you will say "Welcome" and you will offer him what you have. The guest will get up, holding in his hand a large cane. He will go round the house with it, while you keep as close to him as his shadow, as he raises and lowers the cane and counts: One . . . five . . . seven . . . then strikes the ground with the cane and it splits open by permission of its Lord and out comes the gold, the pearl and turquoise necklaces, and all the hidden things of the secret earth. Catch hold of your guest by the collar and look into his eyes. The eyes of the Khidr gleam just like two jewels, for he is a prophet. As for the Maghribi's eyes, they take on a sly look directly they see wealth. If it's the Khidr, O Grandad Hasan, say to him: "Your pardon, master," and kiss his shoulders and rain down upon them tears of remorse. If it is the Maghribi, then bargain with him. If he says "A half" say "A quarter," and if he says "A quarter" say "An eighth," and so on, Grandad Hasan, for you are a man who has struggled in the world and no one must gain the upper hand of you lightly.)

Now the time has arrived for the evening prayer. Grandad Hasan must make his ablutions anew: "God curse the stomach, it carries nothing but filth." In a low, grave voice of command Grandad Hasan says, "Hey, girl," and in the same tone: "The ewer, girl," although he has seen his granddaughter pouring the water into it.

The evening prayer and the special prayers said during the month of Ramadan have come to a close. Sheikh Kamil, the Imam of the mosque of Grandad Abdullah, is in his eighties but looks like a young man in the way he stands and sits: he was never cumbersome in the performance of his prayers. It is like a short dream that has left you, Grandad Hasan. And now you seek sleep and as on every night you are pursued by the vision of noon: three widows, three sisters, daughters of the jinn, their black robes covering them from head to foot, sitting over there under the tamarind trees amid the hillocks of the graveyards. The great mill turns, it never stops, and the stray dogs howl, the stray cats mew, blood mixes with flesh, and the tamarind trees let fall their flowers under the light strokes of wind, while the eyes of female demons gleam like hot coals.

The grinding machine throbs *tak-tak* unceasingly. Grandad Hasan rises to his feet. Death comes disguised in the garb of lengthy sleep, stealing upon a person and casting upon him an unbearable weight. No eye sees, nor ear hears, nor tongue tastes. Nothing but utter darkness, a darkness that is limitless.

Homecoming

———m———

Yusuf Abu Rayya

When the time to leave for the train approached they left the small girl at home with the neighbors and the woman of the house walked off in the lead as she adjusted the piece of muslin on her head. The young boy waited till her hand was free, then he took hold of it and began to run about once more. Behind her, the men ambled along in their clean gallabiyas, with their shawls wrapped round their faces.

At the first street the sky sent down light, sporadic rain showers that lulled into inactivity the leaves that the strong wind had been stirring up, and the group came to a stop in order to wait under the platform shelter.

When the bell of the railway signal-box rang, they looked southward and saw the train making its appearance—a mere dot on the fringe of the village—and they saw iron dripping with rainwater, as they stood submissively next to one another.

The train entered with labored breath, emitting smoke and noise.

Their eyes stared at the windows passing in succession. Faces they did not recognize leaned out of them, while the mother walked along beside the coaches till they came to a complete stop, with the wheels letting out a screeching sound that sent shivers down one's back.

She looked behind her so as not to miss a single door and saw him descending between two policemen in heavy black uniforms.

"Abduh!" she called out.

The men rushed forward with her till they had surrounded him in a tight circle.

He raised his head to them, smiling, his rosy face wrapped round in the white woolen shawl.

She went up to him and put her arm round him, "Abduh!"

He stretched out hands that were manacled and the piece of muslin fell from her as she kissed his forehead and shoulders, while the men revolved around impatiently, entering the circle one by one to embrace him.

Muhammad was far off, looking on in astonishment. He was coming forward shyly when his mother saw him and took him by the arm and presented him to his father, "It's Muhammad, Abduh. It's Muhammad—he's grown up."

"Where's Sayyid?" he asked her—and she burst into tears.

The two policemen pushed the ring of people aside. The one with two stripes said, "Have patience, everyone—there are still some steps to be gone through."

"We must get to the police station," said the other.

"Will it take long?" asked one of the men.

"An hour," said the policeman.

They took him to the stairway that led down to the wide street. He looked over his shoulder at them and moved aside the shawl to show his large white beard that joined up with the yellow, nicotine-stained mustache.

Abduh came with the men after sunset. The female neighbor who was standing at the door of his house wanted to give trilling cries of joy, but the mother pulled her by the arm and put a hand over her mouth. "Shame on you!" she shouted at her.

He entered his house passing among the women gathered in the hall, who called out, "You've filled the place with light!"

The small girl held onto him by his gallabiya and he bent over and kissed her, and they opened the door of the room for him; the room was warm and newly spread with reed matting.

The men sat against the walls, while Abduh seated himself over by the window on the striped mattress. Removing the shawl, he wiped his face with it, while Muhammad squatted down in the corner and stared at his father's face. The father's eye caught the photograph hanging in its frame beside the shelf on which stood the lamp. He caught his breath and then gazed at the faces of the men in the room. They lowered their heads. As for him, he could smell the odor of the boy, could sense his breath coming and going beside him, could see his face among the specters spread out on the wall, and his hand felt the touch of his small palm when he lifted him up so as to cross the doorway to where his mother would be sitting, as she averted her gaze and talked with the other women.

The small girl entered with glasses of cinnamon tea. As she passed them round, the men said to her, "Your father first."

He raised his hand for the glass that gave out a thin, faint thread of steam. He went on looking at the girl's face, then noticed the twin buds sprouting on her chest. "How are you, Zaynab?" he said to her, and he patted her tenderly on the shoulder.

The mother was still at the doorway talking to the women sitting near the stone base of the water jar.

"Hopefully we'll be able to congratulate you on many happy occasions," she said, and with the back of her hand she wiped away the tears from her cheek.

After they had drunk the cinnamon tea, one of the men rose to his feet as he dusted off his back, and his shadow fell, long and extended, on the opposite wall. "Goodnight," he said, and he stretched out his hand to the father. After him the other men got up. "You've filled your house with light," they said.

The father stood to say goodbye to them, and accompanyied them to the door of the house, while the women detached themselves from the circle around the grandmother and walked off with the men. One of them whispered in the mother's ear, "Be patient with him, sister—may God help him."

"May the Lord give us all patience," said the mother.

The little girl stood on tiptoe to reach the latch and locked the door. As she came back to the room, she saw Muhammad beside her father talking to him. She stood perplexed, then rushed forward to curl up on the mattress right next to her father's hand.

In the Place for Prayers

—✎—

Mohammed Afifi

The Bey, owner of the estate, was seated with his men in the place for prayers under the sycomore tree that was on the bank of the large irrigation canal, waiting for the call to the sunset prayers. The afternoon light had begun to fade, its yellowness veiled by whiteness; the sparrows were flying and chirping above the fields of corn and the white canal water gleamed like mirrors.

Opposite the place for prayers, on the other side of the agricultural path, lies an old two-story house, its windows looking down at the path, and behind it a large garden with a high surrounding wall; it's the house of Abdel Rahman Bey Lutfi. Alongside the house, facing north, is a country dwelling built, like all such dwellings, from unbaked mud brick, on the roofs of which are mounds of vegetable refuse and dung cakes. The wind comes from this direction, bringing with it the odor of corn bread, stored chopped straw, and animals tied up in the houses.

The Bey had the habit each day of collecting together the important agricultural workers and being their imam when they performed the sunset prayers. Today he was sitting surrounded by the agricultural overseer, Hagg Muhammad, the secretary, Sheikh Dessouki, an agricultural watchman, and a couple of peasants. The Bey was seated on a cane chair brought from the house, while the men were sitting cross-legged on the reed mat from the prayer room and had taken off their slippers. It was time for the peasants to return from the fields, with the children leading the water buffaloes in the direction of the peasant dwellings in long, black single-file lines, with the buffalo striking at their legs with their tails and penetrating the earth with their hooves and filling the air with dust. Some of the peasants coming back from the fields were calling out "Peace be upon you," and the Bey would return the salutation and Hagg Muhammad would say, "Join us," but the peasant would answer, "May you live long!" and wouldn't dare go and sit with the leading figures in the village. This morning they all knew that the Bey was traveling early next day to Cairo with his wife and family, but no one had the nerve to turn aside and say goodbye to him, because Abdel Rahman Bey was a man who commanded great respect and the people were shy of him. He was also a devout man and never missed a religious obligation, and would perform his Friday prayers at the small mosque at the estate. He wouldn't even curse the madman who all day long would walk around the estate with a great heavy stick saying that he was the Lord Christ and that he wasn't frightened of anyone at all, not even the Bey himself.

"It will be difficult for us to bear the Bey going away," said Hagg Muhammad. "We've had two lovely days with him and they went like the wind."

He looked around him, seeking encouragement. Those who were squatting showed their emotion by the movements of their bodies. One of them said, "By God, that's so," while the second said, "Truly, they went like the wind," while the third said, "God willing, he won't be away too long." Hagg Muhammad was a tall, broad, dark-skinned man with a thick neck and a bent nose that was like the beak of a kite. On his head he wore a heavy felt cap that he liked to crumple up when the Bey wasn't present.

The Bey set straight the gallabiya that he always wore when he went out in the village and said, "I'm really going to miss you, but what's to be done? We're fed up with your mosquitoes and your frogs—isn't that so?"

The Bey laughed at his own words, and they all followed suit.

"By God," said Hagg Muhammad, "we got used to the mosquitoes from early on. Even Sheikh Dessouki says that on the night when he doesn't get bitten to death he stays awake unable to sleep!"

They laughed even more and Sheikh Dessouki shook like a cooking pot on the boil and adjusted his spectacles that were bound together with a length of string. Then the Bey sat down and explained to them the advantages of living in Cairo and found fault with the countryside, and they all agreed with him. And all the time they were seeing the blinds of the window in the Bey's house behind the agricultural lane moving gently because the old lady used to like to sit behind the blind and amuse herself by looking down at the lane.

After a while a solitary peasant drew near to where they were; he was wearing a dirty blue gallabiya and, like all the peasants, was barefoot. Round his middle he had tied a belt made of palm fibers, while on his head he wore a felt cap blackened with sweat. The peasant went next to the sycomore and began to dawdle about like someone who wanted to say something but was too shy to do so. Hagg Muhammad saw him and got up and said to the Bey, "I see Abu Mitwalli standing and looking at Your Honor like somebody who wants something. Shall I call him over?"

The Bey looked backward and saw the man.

"Come here!" he shouted at him. "Do you want something?"

Abu Mitwalli came up to them in a state of confusion, smiling with meek shyness, his head leaning on his shoulder. He stayed silent for a while as he stood behind the Bey's chair so he couldn't see him. After a while he uttered the words, "Peace be upon you."

"And upon you be peace and the mercy of God and His blessings. What is it, Abu Mitwalli?"

Abu Mitwalli broke the piece of dried corn he was carrying and said, 'By God, Bey, I'm shy to speak to you."

"No, don't be shy! What is it?"

"The fact is, O Bey, that I'd like to ask a favor of you."

"All right, then speak. Say something."

But Abu Mitwalli didn't utter a word, he merely broke the piece of maize a second time and gave a laugh. Hagg Muhammad then bawled at him, "What's up with you? Go on and answer the Bey—it's as though you've got a vicious tongue."

Looking down at the stalk of corn in his hand, Abu Mitwalli said, "The fact, Bey, is that this year was a bit difficult—the whole crop was eaten up by the pest."

"And so what?"

"I would ask Your Honor for just a little time to pay the rent, until we cut the grain and sell the ardeb we'll get from it."

The Bey was silent for a while, then said, "How much have you rented?"

"It's just one feddan, Bey. In the southern strip, behind the canal."

"So, why is it that you want to put off payment? Aren't all the other tenants going to pay before cutting the grain?"

"The fact is, Bey, that the pest didn't leave a single healthy stalk in the ground."

"And why is it you who's complaining of the pest?"

Here Sheikh Dessouki the clerk replied, "This year the pests came a little at a time."

"It wasted my land," said Abu Mitwalli. "The whole feddan didn't give a single ardeb."

Once again the Bey was silent, then he frowned and looked at his watch.

The superintendent then said, "Go on now, Abu Mitwalli, and you can talk to the Bey some other time."

"But the Bey is traveling—safely, God willing—in the morning. I told myself that I should ask for his help before he goes, because my boy has been ill these couple of days."

The Bey interrupted him and said with a determined shake of the head, "Listen here, Abu Mitwalli, is it just your land that's had the pest, and no one else has been affected?"

"No, there are other lands that have had it."

"Then why should I not get anything from you and be paid by the rest of the peasants?"

Abu Mitwalli got up and went back, smiling and abashed. Then, bending his neck, he said, "Peasants like us, when they're in need, who should they go to but our Lord and his masters?"

The supervisor then said, "Fine, brother, so why don't you go to your Lord and spare your masters?"

Hagg Muhammad guffawed and looked around him to see the effect of his joke. He found that one of the peasants sitting there was laughing. He got up and repeated it to him, but Abu Mitwalli didn't laugh. Instead he said in a serious tone, "It's God who is kind-hearted."

Then the Bey said, "But tell me, Abu Mitwalli—say I put off the time for payment for you, isn't someone like Abu Awad going to say to me, 'Why have you put off payment for Abu Mitwalli and not for me?'"

"All of us are your servants, Bey."

The Bey looked at the peasant seated on the mat and said, "And you, Abu Awad, was your land attacked by pests or not?"

"By God, the pest didn't spare a thing in it."

"And you, Uncle Abdullah?"

"By your life, half of it didn't do any good."

"You see? Had I listened to what you said and not taken anything from you, what would I say to them?"

Sheikh Dessouki got to his feet, adjusted his glasses and said, "As the saying goes, equality in treating people unfairly is a form of justice."

But Abu Mitwalli continued in a serious vein, "God knows the situation."

The Bey laughed and said, "So your situation, Abu Mitwalli, is not like that of the rest of the peasants?"

"We're all at your command, Bey. Even I am someone who has worked with his hoe his whole life the estate. The very smell of my soul was created here. But, Bey, my son—may such a thing not happen to you—has pain in his eyes and he's nearly completely blind. If it wasn't for that I would never have behaved so boldly with you."

The overseer said to him, "Didn't you take him to the health center as I told you?"

"Yes, I did, and they told me they didn't have a place for him. I even took him to that hospital that's at the administrative center. They turned us away, and the top doctor said to me that if I was frightened about the boy's eyes I should send him to Cairo because maybe he needed an operation. I told myself that as the situation had got so bad I'd go to the Bey and ask him to wait for us to pay."

Abu Mitwalli fell silent, as they all did. But then he went back to talking, "The boy, O Bey, God protect us, can't see the difference between white and black."

"*Say: Let us not be stricken other than by what God has decreed for us,*" said Hagg Muhammad. "Put your trust in God and let Abu Mitwalli make him a poultice for his eyes. And recite for him the Throne Verse twice and he'll be fine."

"But we've recited for him a lot, Hagg Muhammad. The boy, because of what he's got, has become as thin as a stalk of grain."

Abu Mitwalli fell silent and those who were seated there looked and saw a peasant woman approaching. Her black gallabiya was trailing on the ground and she was concealing her face with her black veil. She was holding hands with a young boy, barefoot and covered in dust. He was wearing a woman's headscarf that had been drawn down over his eyes. Behind the two of them walked a thin young girl dressed in a long red gallabiya.

Umm Mitwalli advanced without hesitation toward the Bey and began speaking and gesturing with her free hand till her veil fell from her dark-complexioned face.

"By God, Bey, may our Lord keep you safe and sound, my son, who is all that I have, is going to lose his sight and we don't have the money to take him to the doctor. The hospital—may you never have to go there—isn't willing to take him and the top doctor said we should send him to Cairo. May God keep you safe, sir, my heart's hurting me because this boy is everything to me."

The woman was silent, and everyone fell silent. Then the superintendent bellowed at her, "What's going on, Umm Mitwalli? You don't like what the men are saying, so you've come here, madam, to raise your voice against them? Keep an eye on this wife of yours, Abu Mitwalli."

So Abu Mitwalli said to his wife, "Off you go, Umm Mitwalli, back to the house. Who told you to come out?"

But Umm Mitwalli wasn't listening to anyone and continued to address the Bey, "By the Holy Quran, O Bey, there's not a scrap to eat in the house, not even an ear of corn. But we're praising Him and giving thanks to Him and not asking for much. If only you'd give us time to pay the rent, until we send the boy to Cairo and we have his eyes looked at. The ardeb we get from the corn we'll not be taking into our house. We'll sell it and have the boy seen to with the price we get. By the life of Your Honor, the only time we tasted meat this year was at the Feast of Sacrifice, and our house, after being full of pigeons and chickens, has no birds in it; even the water buffalo, the only possession we had, we sold shares in it."

But Abu Mitwalli screamed, "What are you going to say next, woman? Off with you, get out of here, Fatima girl!"

Then he gave his daughter a slap that almost brought her to the ground. Weeping, she ran off to the house, tripping on her gallabiya, while her mother walked after her, dragging her son who was wearing the headscarf as he walked, tripping along on his feet and with his mouth hanging open, as silent as though he were not of this world.

At this moment there came from the direction of the house a servant boy the Bey had brought with him from Cairo. Coming up close to his master, he said to him in a low voice, "The lady wants Your Excellency."

The Bey got up, glanced at his watch, and said, "There's still ten minutes to go before sunset prayers—I'll be right back."

He entered the house, while the men got hold of Abu Mitwalli and scolded him for having annoyed the Bey and for wanting special privileges. During this time he stood silently, giving no reply. When the Bey returned, they all got up and stood on the mats of the prayer space, and the Bey said, "Come here, Abu Mitwalli. I told you that I couldn't make a difference between the way I treat you and the way I treat the others. But seeing as how your son is ill I'll put a suggestion to you. Tell me: this Fatima who was here is your daughter, isn't she?"

"She's at your service, Bey."

"The lady's just told me that she needs a young girl in Cairo to help her a bit in the house. What do you say to the idea that you let us have her and we'll train her and make you a fine girl out of her?"

"But she's still young, Bey."

"How old is she then?"

"She's not yet eight years old."

"Right, and so what? What sort of work will we be giving her? At the most she'll give a room a quick going-over, she'll bring a glass of water, go down and buy something from nearby the house. And for your sake I'll pay her two years wages in advance—four pounds will take you to Cairo and will allow you to enjoy yourself. What do you say to that?"

"O Bey, we're all at your service but . . ."

"Don't give me any 'buts.' Put your trust in God and let us have her so we can train her and make something great of her for you."

"All right, let me ask her mother."

"Don't ask and don't do anything. Aren't you her father and the man of the house?"

The Bey sat himself in the chair and took off a shoe in preparation for prayers, after which he all of a sudden looked at Abu Mitwalli and said, "I tell you what, instead of four pounds I'll make it five!"

The Bey took off the second shoe. The peasants, hearing what had been said, became noisy and called out in astonishment.

"God is great!" said Hagg Muhammad. "Long live fairness! You don't deserve it, you ugly mug! So come and kiss the Bey's hand."

Sheikh Dessouki said, "Good heavens! May our Lord keep our master the Bey safe and well. Good heavens!"

When they saw Abu Mitwalli standing there silently without showing any signs of joy, they gathered round him, prodding at him and treating him with scorn, while Hagg Muhammad lowered his felt cap over his face and said, "Why are you looking so dim-witted, you spider of a man? Stir that hulk of yours and go and kiss your master's hand," and he gave him a playful slap on the back of the neck, a slap that sent him reeling in the direction of the Bey. He bent down low in order to kiss his master's hand, but the Bey quickly drew it back as though he'd been bitten and said, "God Almighty forbid!"

Having completed the untying of his shoes he rose to his feet and took his place as imam on the matting.

Hagg Muhammad waved and called out, "You girl Fatima! Fatima girl!"

Abu Mitwalli's daughter came running. She had for a time been standing near them, her mouth open and her eyes as round as saucers, and not understanding a thing of what was going on. Once she'd come up to them, Hagg Muhammad took hold of her hand and said, "Come close, girl, and kiss the hand of your master. He's going to take you to Cairo and train you and turn you into a proper human being."

He pulled her so as to bring her close to the Bey, but she wedged her feet in the ground and screamed out, "I don't want to go! Leave me alone! I don't want to go!"

She stretched out her hand to her father for him to hold her back, but Hagg Muhammad dragged her by force as she screamed.

"Mommy, come to my rescue! Come, Mommy, protect me!"

She dropped to the ground, screaming and weeping, with Hagg Muhammad still holding her by the hand.

"Let her go for now, Hagg Muhammad. Come along, folks, it's time for the sunset prayers."

Hagg Muhammad gave her a blow to the head and released her, and she went off at a run in the direction of the house, with her hand over her eyes, tripping on her gallabiya and weeping.

Abu Mitwalli remained standing where he was for a while, smiling to himself and looking preoccupied as though he were making a calculation. The world had whitened and the canal water was the color of milk, while the dogs had begun barking in the fields.

Finally Abu Mitwalli came to himself and moved toward the house, still giving out a heavy, calm smile, like the sunset prayers. On his way to the house he was met by a peasant who gave him a slap on the shoulder and said, "Congratulations, Abu Mitwalli. It came to you like a gift from our Lord."

"Yes, by God."

Before entering through the narrow black door he heard from the direction of the sycamore the voices of the men, loud and awesome as they repeated the words, "God is great," after the Bey. After that he heard a low, serene hushing sound as the men knelt and said, "May the Almighty God be praised."

At the Level Crossing

―~m―

Abbas Ahmed

D r. Magdi Suweilim was driving along the narrow country road to Mit Yazid where, as he had been informed that afternoon, his father lay dangerously ill.

His wife Inayat sat beside him. Night had set in and so had the rain. The speedometer, lit up on the dashboard, did not vary between twenty and twenty-five kilometers an hour. Only occasional words were exchanged between them.

"Shall I light you a cigarette?"

"No."

Most of the conversation took place within them. Inayat felt her body tense with irritation. There was something that shut her off into a frightening isolation, cutting all contact between her and Magdi. What's all this to me? What have I got to do with this old man who's lying in Mit Yazid, even if he is in fact dying?

As she crossed her legs her dress rose up slightly from her thighs.

"The weather tonight," she said, "is colder than it's been so far this winter."

Dr. Magdi Suweilim did not speak, contenting himself with closing the window to the full. The half-circle made by the windscreen wipers was like a door that kept approaching. The headlights transformed the eucalyptus trees along the edge of the canal into towering genies, delighting—as they stood there everlastingly—in being washed by the rain and rocked by the winds.

Magdi was thinking about his father, Hagg Suweilim, who had now reached the age of death. Might it not be a crisis that would pass? The man often exaggerated the pain he was in, in the manner of the very old and the very young, who do it in order to draw attention to themselves. Despite himself, Magdi smiled as he remembered his father the last time he had visited him two months ago, when taking hold of Inayat's hand as she greeted him, he had said, "It's like velvet—not like the hands of those sons of bitches"—and he had pointed to the young peasant wife he had married only two years ago. Magdi himself didn't know whether she was his fourth or fifth wife since the death of his mother. In fact he wasn't able to accurately distinguish between his young brothers and sisters that his father had produced after his grown-up brother who now lived in America.

Inayat put on the inside light and looked at her watch.

"It's eight but it's as though we were in the depths of night." When Inayat turned off the light darkness reigned again inside the car.

"Things are always like that in the country." Inayat felt as though he was forcing himself to be silent and withdrawing himself from her. Maybe he wanted to torture her, to leave her on her own to suffer fear, shame, and misery. She had not given him a single child. During the twenty-five years she had lived with him she had done everything possible to give him a child. But was it her fault? Yet she didn't once recollect Magdi reproaching her for this. This was perhaps the most terrible thing about him. His clinic, his research work, and his patients were his world. Why was it that Inayat felt that this night, tonight in particular, had a strange importance for her? There was a sudden outburst of thunder, a flash of lightning, and Inayat, in an instinctive movement of fright, touched her husband's chest. Quickly she drew back—it was as though she were groping at the chest of some stranger.

The road had begun to climb slightly toward the distant level-crossing, after which it would dip for two or three kilometers when the group of villages, with Mit Yazid in their center, would make their appearance.

"It seems we've arrived," said Magdi.

Memories of his childhood enveloped him with an overwhelming sense of joy. Nothing here had changed one iota in these vast plains with the huts sticking out of the ground here and there. The level-crossing alone had changed. At first it was like a shadoof, the trunk of a large tree that was pulled down with a rope, shutting off the track so that the train could pass through, puffing and blowing out its smoke with its rhythmic beat against the rails.

"I hope Hagg Suweilim will be all right," said Inayat in a final attempt at making contact with her husband.

But Magdi was busy with his thoughts and didn't hear. Inayat was fighting against a feeling of unbounded distress. She hadn't forgotten when he had approached her father, the Pasha, to ask for her in marriage, the effect the name Magdi Suweilim had had on her. She wished she could be taken back to the times when she was a child playing in the garden of their old house, to the times when, like a queen at her father's parties, she had been surrounded by young men; young men who imagined that she bathed only in rose water and drank nothing but fruit juice.

The level crossing appeared to be closed; in the middle of it there was a faint light.

"This isn't the time for the trains to pass," said Inayat, once again looking at her watch by the inside light of the car.

"We'll see."

The small shed was lit by a brazier. The rain had almost stopped and the road was at its highest point, the trees no longer visible. All around them the earth stretched out into endless space. Magdi parked his car alongside the shed, switched off the engine and called out:

"Abdel Ghani . . . Abdel Ghani."

Opening the door, he got out, walked a step or two and stretched his body, filling his lungs with the air. Once again he called to the man who operated the level crossing as he approached the shed.

"Perhaps he's on the other side," said Magdi from afar. "I'll go and look for him."

Inayat almost shrieked at him: Are you going to leave me on my own?— but her pride prevented her. She remained in the car. The clouds had begun to clear and the stars seemed to light up the plains that stretched around her. All this, though, only increased her sense of alienation and isolation. If only she'd put an end to this matter at the beginning. Twenty-five years ago things weren't as they were now. What were these invisible shackles that prevented

her from setting herself free? Does one live twice over? Why does man continue to preserve something that doesn't exist? Does he love me? Shall I, at the
end of the road, find that what I was holding, imagining it to be a pearl or a diamond, was nothing but a pebble like any other, strewn on the ground? Inayat
threw the stub of her cigarette into a nearby patch of water. When she heard
the hiss of the fire dying she started. "It's over," she said angrily. "It's over."

Abdel Ghani had appeared from a direction other than that taken by her
husband. Inayat took him in with a quick glance. The man was tall and slender,
his gallabiya tucked into tattered trousers; he also wore a leather waistcoat
and heavy boots covered with mud and grass. Having become aware of the
presence of the car, he came to a stop far off.

"Who's there?"

It was as though he were a tree rooted in the ground. Inayat did not answer.
This was her husband's childhood friend. The space Abdel Ghani was crossing
toward the car was as flat as a tennis court, its surface gleaming like a mirror,
and the man strode across it with the unhurried confidence of a god. Quickly
realizing to whom the car belonged, he broke into a run. "Welcome, Doctor.
Welcome, Doctor." Suddenly he came to a stop as he saw Inayat on her own.

"Welcome, lady. Thanks be to God for your safe journey."

"The doctor's looking for you on the other side of the level crossing."

The man hurried off, passing the level crossing, but Inayat, in almost a
shout, called to him: "Wait, Abdel Ghani."

The man became nailed to the spot. Inayat got out of the car and took a
step or two toward him, then realized that she didn't know what she wanted.

"Yes, lady," said Abdel Ghani, still where he was.

"Wait, Abdel Ghani," she repeated.

The man came up to pay his respects.

"May God be good to you, lady."

With his thick mustache, his frank, strong face and great body, it was as
if he were the owner of all these plains, as if he were some legendary king
living with his people, the trees and birds and wild plants. After the man had
taken a cigarette from her, Inayat said, "Aren't you going to light it?"

Stretching out her hand with the lighter, she clicked it alight and the man
took her hand between the palms of his own and brought his mouth close

to the flame. Inayat did not understand exactly what she was doing except that, with her hand between his rough palms, she felt herself trembling deep inside her, being carried away. Perhaps she was challenging Magdi, perhaps wanting to destroy this silence at one stroke and so find the world around her boisterous with life, perhaps pushing this man into the car and fleeing away with him, perhaps throwing herself into his embrace, allowing her body to be squeezed in his arms, her lips to be filled with that thick, unruly mustache.

The man was soon leaning backward with the cigarette, the light from the flame still dancing. She saw nothing on his face but an expression of gratitude and sadness.

"The land's cut off, lady. You can't go to Mit Yazid. The waters have cut the road."

Dr. Magdi Suweilim made his appearance and Abdel Ghani hurried over to embrace him.

"Welcome, Doctor. Hagg Suweilim's all right. He had a slight attack but he's got over it."

Laughing, he went on: "And he had his dinner—a chicken and seven oranges."

Inayat came up. "What do we do now?"

Abdel Ghani noticed how tense and nervous the lady was. "It would really be a great honor for us," he said, "if you were to accept to spend the night at my place. Morning's best for traveling. As the Doctor knows, the house is close by, right by the railway line."

"We have to go back," said Inayat.

"Thank you, Abdel Ghani," said Magdi. "You've always been a generous man."

"I've long enjoyed your kindness, Doctor, but it wouldn't be right for you to go back when my house is available."

Abdel Ghani brought out the brazier from the shed and Magdi went up to it to warm himself.

"Please go ahead, lady," Abdel Ghani called out to her.

As she came up to them Magdi was laughing at the top of his voice, recalling with Abdel Ghani the story of how they'd stolen mangoes from Abdel Ghaffar Pasha's mansion.

"Magdi," she shouted—"won't you stop that? I want to go back at once."

The two men came to a sudden stop. Abdel Ghani was deeply embarrassed and Magdi, only a few paces from her, looked at her face and found it a mask fixed in senseless anger. He felt her savage insolent shout like a harsh slap in the face. He was amazed at her behavior and recollected that it was she who had insisted on coming with him to do her duty by her husband's family. Many times he had told her not to come but she had insisted. What, then, was the good man's fault in offering them his house? Abdel Ghani had taken himself far away from the husband and wife.

"Give me the car keys," said Inayat, and he immediately gave them to her.

"So you're not coming back with me?"

"No, I'm not going back."

Abdel Ghani rushed forward:

"I hope to God I haven't done anything to make the lady angry."

"No, Abdel Ghani, what's happening has nothing to do with you."

Ingenuously the man went on, "You see, lady, when we stole the mangoes from Abdel Ghaffar Pasha's mansion, we didn't really mean to steal. We'd got tons of mangoes—it was just childish naughtiness."

This ingenuousness inflamed Inayat's anger still further. Her husband looked at her from under his thick glasses and for the first time in her life she felt frightened of him and realized that there was nothing to prevent him from slapping her. A heavy moment of silence, tense and awkward, took over, broken by the voice of a young peasant girl of about twenty who came toward them, calling, "Father, Father."

Everyone looked round at the girl. Her face shone, her cheeks were rosy as ripe apples. Drawing closer, she quickly recognized the doctor. Falteringly she said, "Welcome, Bey. How are you, Doctor?"

Magdi smiled.

"And how are you, Hafeeza? Everything all right now?"

"Thanks be to God, Doctor. After the operation everything's fine."

The girl flung out her arms as though showing herself off. Inayat was conscious of having become utterly isolated. Hafeeza, though, quickly put things to right by saying, as she advanced to kiss her hand, "The lady's your wife, doctor. Welcome, it's an honor for us."

Inayat was on the point of collapse. Quickly she stepped back a little, then suddenly turned and began running toward the car. Moments later, as the sound of the motor broke the silence, Magdi said to Hafeeza, who had been stricken with a feeling of having done something wrong, "Never mind, Hafeeza. The wife's got an important appointment in Cairo. Now tell us what you've got in this bundle."

As the car drew away Magdi was looking round himself quietly with affection at the earth, the trees, the sky, while Hafeeza sat herself close to the fire in front of the shed. She opened the bundle and took out some cheese, beans, honey, and flat loaves of bread.

"We owe all this to you, Doctor."

Looking at Abdel Ghani, who was standing there like a statue, Magdi said, "What's up, Abdel Ghani? Aren't you going to invite me to have dinner with you?"

Abdel Ghani recovered himself, though he did not return to his former cheerfulness until the two of them were devouring their food. In the meantime Hafeeza had run to the house to bring them some hard-boiled eggs and a couple of sticks of sugar cane, along with a promise that a duck was already grilling over the fire.

Sylvia

———❦———

Ahmed Alaidy

Now I know what happened.

If the palm of your hand is as big as mine, clench your fist, then wipe your sticky brow with it.

It's the first, second, and third drop to fall on my face. I look up to the top of the building; I hear the snoring sound of the air conditioning and read "Union Air" in green and blue.

I waited for her to announce to me, "Stars F.M."

She exits from the door of the building. His soft voice vibrates across the radio receiver, across my ear, to say, "A woman is with you, she's a woman who is being unfaithful to another person."

She approaches with her two buttocks and a smile. When there's less than my arm's length between us, her face changes. "What's this?" she asks.

"What?"

She stretches out her fingers to feel my face, like a girl in an advertisement. She rubs her thumb between the middle and the ring finger. She draws near with her nose and frowns.

They are the fourth, fifth, and sixth drops.

"Blood?"

I look to the top of the building and the seventh drop comes down right in the middle of my left eye, and then the body plunges down.

He moves, he whose name we won't know, toward her right away, and we, upright, do likewise. She gives me her hand. She buries her face in my shoulder, then screams, "No. Nooooo!"

If the palm of your hand is as big as mine, clench your fist, go downward, and press gently.

"For God's sake, O Lord."

He whose name we don't know says this, then pulls out the newspaper from under his armpit and spreads out the symbol of the three pyramids with a slow upward movement.

The directives of the president go down and the bilateral relations between two countries go to the bottom. They come to rest on the shuddering body so that the viscid red can drink up the efforts expended on containing the crisis.

He folds over the edge of the paper rectangle, stealing a glance with his tilted head.

"For heaven's sake . . ."

"Her name was Sylvia . . . she's been murdered."

Across my ear the gentle voice whispers, "Imagine her as she was when she was with you, but instead in the arms of another about whom you know neither name nor origin."

"Are you sure?"

Sylvia doesn't say that she shivers when having a moaning crash with her spinal column. Sylvia doesn't mention my fingers passing behind her ears. Sylvia looks for someone who won't mind shoving her intoxicated into bed, without her wiping away his dried cum from her thigh in the morning . . . someone, just anyone.

I open my left eye. The narrow field of vision grows red, and a thread of dirty water flows along my cheek.

If the palm of your hand is as big as mine, clench your fist, then rub harder.

The "buttocks" girl says that the distance between the middle of a sword and its hilt is the best area to use for amputation, and that it has a name she can't remember. She takes out the Japanese sword from its scabbard. She displays it to the neon light and the whiteness fuses along the expanse of the sharp blade, while I run through an album of photos of the two of them together in different poses.

"What do you think?" she asks.

"And who are you?"

"Her mum."

I obstruct "her daughter's" path with my foot.

"What's your name, sweetheart?" I ask the girl.

She looks toward me for an instant then continues on her leisurely way.

Her "Mum" follows up with, "She doesn't hear and she doesn't speak." Then she concludes hastily, "But she understands through signs."

She makes a snapping noise with her thumb and the middle one toward her, as though asking for the bill, and calls out, "Sylvia."

Sylvia is alerted. She paces along the red velvet "cat walk" with her slim backside. She turns round, to retrace her steps with the same feminine nimbleness, while the buttocks girl leans toward me to say, "Where are you spending the night?"

"Here," I say, pointing to her suspended bed.

"She's still on her diet. Yes, and something else . . . You must put a nip of brandy in her warm milk."

"Brandy?"

"So she can sleep . . . she suffers from insomnia."

If the palm of your hand is as big as mine, clench your fist, then touch the wall. We have come to the end of the photography test. I pour the rest of the brandy into the white cube fixed at the bottom of the camera.

I light the cigar while giving her her mixture. I administer it to her and after seven minutes she'd drunk it and was in the suspended bed. This is the permitted range. The cigar ash falls on her back.

"Good heavens. I'm sorry."

I say the words while my fingers go after the ash, behind her ears. She shivers at my breath making contact with her spine. Sylvia. The best performance in town.

I kiss her forehead, then wish her goodnight, like anybody, just anybody.

Her mum says she needs to pee. I point to the bathroom. The cell phone in my pocket rings: "I want to do one . . . I want to do one . . . one, one tea . . ."

I answer the call at the moment when there comes from inside it a stupid laugh. I call out to the one with the buttocks, "Get going and close the door after you, I'm down below," and into the mobile, "All right? Yes? Oh, at work. Who am I talking to?"

I move outside.

"I'm talking to the maid? Really? No, not at all."

I take the stairs three at a time.

"Are we on the air?!"

I put the radio receiver in my other ear with my free hand. I move the dial to a hundred-point-six, while moving out of the door of the building.

"By the Prophet, peace is integral to the program, and by this flimsy link."

Now I know what happened.

"You're divorced. I divorce you."

The girl with the buttocks puts Sylvia on top of the hanging bed. She returns the sword to the wooden holder clamp without a scabbard. She leaves the window—above the air-conditioning—open.

She slams the door closed and, when doing so, the special light switch shakes the bolt of the door, thus making shapes move on the ceiling. Sylvia notices.

If the palm of your hand is as big as mine, clench your fist. This is the range it has.

Sylvia walks the "cat walk" dizzily on her suspended bed up to the edge. She falls from its height above the sharp blade. Perhaps in the area whose name I don't know between the middle of the sword and its hilt. The tap of blood in her neck is opened. It strikes the open window, again and again and again. It becomes dizzy for my advertisement "Staaars F.M." It crashes for the fifth, sixth, and seventh time. Quivering, she turns over onto her side to pass across the window, above the snoring of the air-conditioner, and she falls, across the earpiece, across my ear; weeping, weeping, weeping.

I imagine her twisting between my arms. Another one I call a son of a bitch despite the fact that I don't know his name or where he's from. You won't understand that there's a woman with you, she's a woman who is being unfaithful to another person who doesn't know my name or where I'm from and who calls me a son of a bitch. You can imagine her twisting and turning under you just as she was with me.

The Report of Mrs. R. Concerning the Last Day of the Week

—⟋⟍⟍—

Radwa Ashour

It's a lake. In olden times a Romantic poet would picture himself sitting on its banks, and behind him, or perhaps to one side, would be a willow tree whose branches hung down like the plaited hair of a despondent woman. He stares into the lake and sees the face of Narcissus on the surface, beautiful and miserable, matching his own. He is preoccupied by his face. He feels sorry for himself and mutters, "Who'll mourn for you, you poor thing?" Then he begins his elegy.

There's no willow tree, no face of Narcissus, just my car in which I drive to my job. A passing driver, as he overtakes me, hurls an insult at me; I give one back and continue on my way. At work it's all a mess; I face up to him as though I'm stronger, then I get in my car to return home. The traffic light shows red, giving me the opportunity to answer this question: I appear as fragile as an autumn leaf that has surrendered itself to the wind before it settles on the ground. How, then, had I faced up to him? In the evening I'm used to going out in the street. My shoes have got wet and I must buy another pair. I move between the display windows of shops selling shoes, then I go into one of them and buy a pair. As I walk in the street I mumble to myself, "What happens to a dream that's postponed?" The question remains suspended in front of me as I drive the car slowly, hindered by the heavy traffic on Gala' Street. Once again there's a traffic light and I come to a stop. I spot a large rat hurriedly crossing the road. "Is its smell diffused like rotten meat?" I wonder. The dream, not the rat. Maybe we drag it along like a heavy weight. Eventually, I arrive at the house. I park my car. I climb the stairs and turn the key in the lock. I make myself coffee and a cheese sandwich and put on the television. I watch the news, and some of the commercials, which are interrupted by a telephone call from a colleague at the office who gives me a free lesson in office etiquette: "Common sense dictates that you treat those younger than yourself harshly and those older gently. To clash with your boss at work is stupid. His venom must be dealt with by tact, flattery, and cunning. Confrontation is always hopeless. Do whatever you like with those you're in charge of and stand up to them as you think best; put to right any deviation they are guilty of, if necessary with a blow to the head with a stick. I see that you're doing the opposite of this and that's a grave mistake." I thanked him for his advice and terminated the conversation. "What happens to a dream that is postponed?" I turned off the television and called my friend. She told me about her day and I told her about mine. We had a long chat, then I said, "I've got an idea for a story."

"Don't talk about it," she said. "Write it."

But I wanted to go on talking, "A woman in the prime of life prepares to meet the man she loves. Having made herself up, she leaves her house, buys a bouquet of flowers and goes to the station where she waits. A train arrives. She looks around, she searches: he hasn't come. Another train arrives. More and more trains arrive. The flowers wilt. The hours go by, the days, the weeks, the years. The woman becomes middle-aged, then reaches old age."

My friend interrupts me, "And she dies, and they walked in her funeral procession from the Omar Makram Mosque, and the film ends with the National Anthem. The old maids weep their hearts out, while the audience in the cheap seats whistle and call out 'The movie's nonsense, so give us our money back.' The two sides get caught up in a fight and the riot police come along to break up the disturbance. Two people are killed, one from each group. The one who'd been in the cheap seats has his picture published in the paper, with the caption "The terrorist who caused the disturbance and fell a victim to it." As for the picture of the old maid who was killed, the national press ignored her, though the Egyptian Organization for the Rights of Women hastened to send her picture to Europe and America where it was decided by all the women's groups to consider the day on which the film was shown and the woman was killed as an international day for spinsters."

I didn't laugh and moments of silence went by. Then, "Are you angry?"

"I didn't imagine that the project for the story was all that bad."

"Melodramatic!"

I decided to change the subject. I told her about the book I'd finished reading and about the woman who had refused to look at her newborn child after giving birth to him: "For several days she remained in this state, sleeping in her bed on her right side, with her face to the wall and her eyes staring into its whiteness. They carried the child to her and placed him alongside her. They talked to her about him, but she didn't budge an inch."

"And what happened after that?"

"I don't know."

"Didn't you say you'd finished reading the book?"

"Yes, but the book wasn't about her. It tells her story in a mere three lines."

Before we finished the conversation she said, "Can you write your story along the lines of Charlie Chaplin's silent films?"

"How?"

"As a comedy, with broad characters and a fast pace."

"I don't understand."

"Like cartoons—would it be possible for you to do that?"

"I don't know. I don't think so."

Having put down the phone, I sat down to write.

The First Project: The Melodramatic Story

Her image in the mirror astonished me. She had taken a bath and made herself up well and paid attention to arranging her hair, and had put on her best clothes, yet all that did not explain the sudden change from a girl with pleasant features to the beautiful woman she was looking at in the mirror. She left the house to go to the flower shop. She chose scarlet roses with long stems. The florist wrapped them in cellophane after having added some greenery with leaves like those of the evergreen cypress but with tiny white flowers. The florist was about to tie the bunch of flowers up with a white ribbon but she quickly informed her that she wanted a pink one. Having handed over the money, she went to the station, the bouquet in her hand and a song on her lips. In the station she looked up at the large clock fixed to the wall and at the small watch she was wearing round her wrist. The time on both was identical. It was possible for her to sit in the café for the twenty-five minutes that remained before the train's arrival. She asked for a cup of coffee, which she forgot to drink. She went off to stand on the platform.

The train approaches its destination. Her body trembles at its uproar and her heart beats. She chooses a position that makes it possible for her to observe all those arriving. They pass by her. They all pass by. He hasn't come. She inquired about the time of arrival of the next train.

Seven trains arrived.

It was midnight.

The stationmaster said that the next train would arrive in the morning. As luck would have it they didn't close the station café at night.

The Second Project: The Story as a Comedy

She put on her clothes with lightning speed, then left the house at a run. In the elevator her neighbor looked at her in astonishment, noticing that she was holding a pair of shoes in her hand. She put them on and sped out of the elevator to the flower seller. She bumped into a man, then into a woman, then into a tree, and she apologized to the tree. She bought a flower and flew with it to the station. The train arrived. She poked her head into its windows. She climbed up into all the carriages. She peered into people's faces. She got down on her knees and searched under the seats. She climbed onto the seats and explored with her hands the luggage racks on either side. She jumped down from the train just as it was leaving. She waited for the next train. The platform was on the other side. She darted off to it, tripping over luggage and colliding with passengers. She asked. She described. She employed her hands to reinforce her words with gestures. They shook their heads. She rushed off to a bookshop close to the station. She bought some cardboard and a pen. In thick black letters she wrote his name and a description of him and took up her position on a side of the platform, holding up the board. No one stopped. She ran to the outside of the station. She bought a bell. She came back to the platform. She stood ringing the bell trying to attract the attention of passersby to the board. The trains kept on coming, arriving and departing. The sun comes out. The sun sets. The wind whistles. The rain pours down. The summer heat intensifies. She's seized with pangs of hunger. She eats the flower.

She hasn't noticed that the ink she'd written with on the board has been dampened by the rain and is no longer legible and that her hair, made wet by the rain and then dried by the sun, then made wet yet again by the rain, has become disheveled, and that her dress has become shabby and faded and is hanging down loosely on her skinny body. She is also not aware that the passersby were placing a few small coins alongside her before hurriedly moving on.

My friend was right about the melodramatic story. I took a tranquillizer and got into bed. Once again I attempted to think about the story, but my thoughts were cut short as I fell into a deep sleep.

Drops of Lemon Juice

———∽∿∿∿∽———

Ibrahim Aslan

When I spotted him walking ahead of me in Fadlallah Uthman Lane I slowed down so as not to catch up with him.

After a while I feared that, were I to walk at this slow pace of mine right to the end of the street, it would draw the attention of someone who happened to see me, as this wasn't my usual way of walking, while his leisurely pace was only natural for anyone seeing him, since he was a sick man. Therefore, I went back to walking at my usual pace until I had drawn alongside him and he had seen me.

"Are you here or what?" he said.

"For ages," I said.

After that we didn't talk until we reached the corner of the narrow lane.

"Let's go and see Abdel Khaliq."

"Which Abdel Khaliq?"

"Abdel Khaliq the undertaker."

"Abdel Khaliq the undertaker?"

"Yes, sir."

"Why?"

"Why not—isn't he ill?"

"But I don't know him."

"So what?"

I explained to him that of course I knew him like anyone else, but that I'd never spoken a word to him and had never entered his house.

"Did anyone tell you not to go?" he said with a smile.

I smiled back but felt greatly exasperated because I didn't want to see Abdel Khaliq the undertaker, nor indeed anyone else. All I wanted to do was to buy a packet of cigarettes and sit in the café for a while and then go back home. He then patted me on the shoulder with his soft hand and turned to me and said, "Come along."

I followed him into the lane I used to pass by every day without ever entering. It was quiet, the earth soft and cleanly swept, with the front blocked up by a red brick wall with a solitary window low down; it had an old wooden frame and was closed by bars, behind which was a sheet of cardboard. I was surprised to come across a bare trunk where, in the days of my childhood, I would find a tree; I had forgotten it, though I used to catch a glimpse of it from afar from time to time. It was dried out and part of it had been sawn away, and at the very center of it was a brown navel, punctured and cracked. Stretching out my hand I touched its bare wood as I went down the low step to the house on the side where there was a damp passageway and the open entrance to the flat.

"Peace be upon you," he shouted out.

The woman who was sitting there jumped to her feet with the words, "In the name of God the Merciful, the Beneficent."

She gazed at us till she had calmed down, then said, "Welcome, sir. Bring me the headscarf, girl, that you've got there."

"Hi! How are things, Abdel Khaliq?" said the gentleman in a normal tone.

Abdel Khaliq made no answer.

He was lying down on the mat spread out on the floor of the living room. The room was lit with a weak bulb suspended from the dark ceiling by a twisted wire. The man had his back leaning against the chest of the woman who was sitting behind him wearing a black gallabiya. He was lying between her thighs, while she held in her hands a half-full cup and a spoon. There was a bundle of freshly washed clothes on the couch, with a handful of wooden pegs. Above the couch was the closed window, on the other side; the closed window with the sheet of cardboard that I had previously seen blocking it up from outside. What had been used as the result of the wall and the paper stuck to it had seen its last days long ago and in its place there was left an ugly patch on the milky polished surface.

A young girl came along with a light black headscarf with which she covered her mother's bare head, after which she stood by watching us.

The gentleman said, "No, you're a lot better today."

"Thanks be to Him," said the woman. "Where were we?"

She pushed Abdel Khaliq's head backward as she filled the spoon from the cup.

"What's he drinking?" asked the gentleman.

"He's drinking lemon."

The girl said, "Lemon juice boiled with sugar."

I looked at her and saw her beautiful eyes done with local kohl and her unusually large breasts. He saw me doing so and looked annoyed. He turned to the woman and asked her if Abdel Khaliq was taking any medicine, and she said, "He is," and she told him that the doctor had prescribed him a suppository.

When he asked her if he was taking it at the right times, she said that he was refusing to do so.

"We have a hard time with him—I take a shift and then the girl does one."

She was talking with her hand raised in front of Abdel Khaleq's face, the spoon filled with lemon juice, and I noticed that as she talked the spoon was leaning over and drops of juice were falling onto his nose and mustache. When she wasn't talking but listening to the gentleman, the spoon wouldn't lean over but would shake slightly and the juice would collect down below in the bottom of the spoon and would form a drop that wouldn't fall on his nose or mustache but on his cheek or eye. During all this time Abdel Khaleq would be opening his lips and rolling them about in time with the movement of the spoon above him so as to be able to get a drop inside his mouth, but in this he was never successful. After that I saw him putting out his tongue and sucking up the juice from his moistened mustache and moving his cheeks with evident delight. While he was doing this our eyes met and he realized I'd seen him, so he immediately drew in his tongue and closed tight his lips.

"Then where's the suppository?" said the gentleman.

"Abdel Khaleq's?"

"Yes."

"Why?"

"I would like to see it."

"We took it back to the pharmacy. The trouble was it was melting in the heat."

"And he agreed to take it back?"

"We exchanged it for some cough syrup for the boy Morsi," said the girl.

I turned to her again and she gave me a smile with those beautiful eyes of hers—a well-mannered smile—and I saw that the size of her breasts was really reasonable and they weren't as big as I'd thought. The gentleman gave me a look and told the woman to give Abdel Khaleq the suppository at the proper time. I was about to remind him that there was no longer any suppository, but he immediately looked at Abdel Khaleq and said, "Don't talk rubbish—you're not a child or anything."

The woman placed the cup beside her on the rug and dragged Abdel Khaleq by the top of the head because she had rolled to one side and had it squeezed between her folded thigh and large breast, after which she took the cup in order to fill the empty spoon.

"In any case, try to sleep a bit. Peace be upon you."

With these words he moved toward the open door of the flat, walking ahead of me, when the girl, from behind us, said, "Heavens, what about the tea?"

Leaning forward toward me, he said, "Give it a miss."

In the lane he took out his handkerchief and dried his eyes.

When we got out into Fadlallah Uthman, we found ourselves walking among people and he asked me, "So, what do you think?"

"About what?"

"What do you think it's about? About Abdel Khaleq of course."

"Well, it seems to me he's all right."

He came to a stop and turned to me, "Abdel Khaleq's all right?"

"So it seemed to me."

"Fine, just so you know, Abdel Khaleq the undertaker is dying."

I told him I'd seen Abdel Khaleq putting out his tongue and licking up lemon juice from his mustache.

"And it doesn't make sense that someone who's dying would do such a thing."

"What lemon juice?'

"The lemon juice that was on the spoon."

"What lemon juice and spoon? What are you talking about?"

Before I replied we heard a sharp scream and, turning to me, he said, "There you are—he's died."

Placing the handkerchief in his pocket, he made off back to the house.

I followed him for a while, then came to a stop.

Turning around, I walked off, looking down at my feet so that any of the neighbors seeing me would think I hadn't heard the scream and that I hadn't gone there because I was busy looking for something I'd lost in Fadlallah Uthman Lane.

The Palm Tree
My Aunt Loved

—⦿—

Hana Atia

She looked at me from high up in the palm tree that stood erect among the graves. She was holding the end of her gallabiya that was curled around the dates. "This year," she said, "it's given the best dates ever."

Looking hard at her bleeding feet, I said, "Come down. That's enough, Auntie."

They were gathered around us: the young boys with their rowdiness, and the women whispering among themselves and making sucking noises with their lips. I heard one of them say about my aunt that she loved the blood of the dead upon which the date-palm fed.

My aunt went on smiling at me, her body swaying with the wind. The rope circling her waist was pressed up against her swollen stomach.

"There are only a few left," she said.

"The sun will be setting."

Their eyes were fixed unwaveringly despite the orange-colored rays that fell upon them. They warned their children not to eat the dates that had fallen to the ground, while invoking the name of God with verses from the Quran and asking for His mercy on the dead.

She began the task of climbing down, one hand grasping her gallabiya filled with dates, the other clinging to the date palm. When I wiped the blood from her feet with my handkerchief, I could hear—despite the noise being made by the boys—her heavy, labored breathing.

"Your legs are hurt."

Her wide, sweet smile returned to her thin brown face which had been invaded by a delightful redness. Then she looked at the women who were staring at her. "I'll give to those who are ill," she said.

"God is the Healer," said one of them, an old woman whose black head-scarf did not succeed in concealing her baldness.

My aunt approached her as she twirled a ripe date around in her fingers. "Look, it is God who has brought it to life."

They looked hard at my aunt, muttering vague words. One of the boys picked up a stone from the ground and threw it in her direction, then went and disappeared behind the graves, with the other boys chasing after him.

She averted her face as she bent over to pack the dates inside a large cloth bag. With trembling hand, I grasped one side of the bag, and I saw her giving that mysterious smile of hers that would escape from her whenever she was assailed by sadness.

The fields were swaying and she went walking through them with uneasy strides, with me at her side. When she began to walk slightly ahead of me, I found that my eyes were fixed firmly on her stomach, while I thought vaguely of the doctor's report and of a liver that could become so enlarged.

Their whispering continued unabated from behind us, their gaze directed at us, their black gallabiyas being struck by the wind and standing out against the stifling gray light that had quickly unfolded.

"Don't look at them," she said.

Then she came to stop and opened the cloth bag and gave me some dates. "Eat," she said.

She began swallowing the dates, one by one, as she asked of God to have mercy on the dead and muttered Quranic verses. She was looking at me out of the corner of her eye. In the palm of my hand I was grasping some dates.

"They have ripened a lot this year," I said, feeling awkward.

She looked toward the sea which was entering in to blackness.

"Yes," she whispered. "They've ripened."

The forms advancing behind us were little by little disappearing from view, and that strange oppressive sound, screamed out from afar in notes that proceeded step by step from high to low until the final note was lost mid the emptiness of the open sky, returned again and again.

"Is it a hawk?" I said.

"Yes. Don't I tell you so every day?"

"Why does it scream like that?"

She looked at my hand clenched round the dates and she smiled. It seemed to me that she was crying, so I took hold of her hand, while I quickly swallowed a date. Then I plunged my hand into the cloth bag to take another.

When my fingers touched the dates inside, I was seized by a trembling that wracked my body. I didn't know why it was that my hand nevertheless continued to grasp hold of the dates.

In the darkness, we went on walking slowly, with the women behind us dividing up into groups as they headed toward the houses amid the dense shadows.

Sundown

———ᨁᨁ———

Shukri Ayyad

For the twentieth, the seventieth, the hundredth time, he read through the same piece of news. This time the letters drilled themselves into position with superb precision, some moving forward, others taking a step back, while yet others had disappeared completely, had fled the field; some were as big as walking sticks, others as small as ants; some a mere whisper, others a bugle blast. The item of news, scattered over the page of the newspaper, now read approximately as follows:

Tawfiq Hussein Baligh
one of the passengers of the ill-fated plane
on a mission connected
with the organization he represents
had put forward the time of his departure in order
to be beside his eldest daughter
who is expecting a happy event

The sun was flooding the balcony. A beautiful warm day. His wife appeared, wearing a pink-colored knitted housecoat. Her body looked as though it had been stuffed with numerous articles of clothing; on her feet she wore a pair of his old socks and shabby slippers. He almost let out a short childish laugh but managed to stifle it. What did it matter? She sat down beside him on the other cane chair, the one with arms, and busied herself with her knitting-needles, without saying anything. Her face was still, still as a tranquil pool, though wrinkles had begun to make their incursions upon it. She was followed by the maid who placed the tray on the table, and then passed him his unsugared cup of tea. The newspaper was now on the table in front of him; the words had disappeared, had sneaked away in indifference between the lines of the newspaper as though some secret pact existed between them and him. She thrust the needles into the ball of wool, put it on the table and took up her tea which had become tepid. This was what she always did. He felt his heart thumping. These were the minutes during which she would take up the newspaper and start commenting. He was longing for the secret to come to light. It had to do so. He would have to speak. If only she remembered the name! If only she would prompt him into speaking!

"Good heavens, what a terrible accident! Sixty-three passengers. The plane must have been full—did you read about the accident?

"I wonder how it crashed. They say here that the exact reason isn't known. These airplanes are really frightful. This poor family—the husband, wife, and three sons. God bring comfort to their relatives."

She put the paper down on her lap and went into a daydream. Perhaps she had read enough, perhaps the tranquil pool had been sufficiently disturbed. He almost despaired. She glanced at the paper once more before throwing it on to the table.

"Did you read the story of this man? He put forward his departure so as to be with his daughter when she was having her child. What an ill-omened birth! Look how they wrote up the news in the paper: 'Because his daughter was expecting a happy event.' Happy!?"

"Don't you know this man?"

Again she gazed at the name, then looked up at him perplexed.

"I mean—don't you remember the name?"

She shook her head and he experienced a feeling of resentment toward her. He felt obscurely that her having forgotten the name was a neglect of himself. In exasperation he muttered:

"Tawfiq Hussein Baligh—don't you remember him?"

A certain worried irritation, as though the surface of a pond had become muddied, appeared in her eyes. It was of no avail, though.

"Don't you remember the case I once brought, the case I brought in the Supreme Administrative Court, because they promoted someone over my head?"

She bit her lower lip.

"Of course. You wore yourself to shreds over it; for years you wore us all out too, and then you lost it."

He gave a wan smile.

"This Tawfiq was the colleague of mine they promoted over my head. God rest his soul. He was hasty in everything."

"Even in death."

"Even in catching the plane."

His eyes suddenly sparkled.

"Can you imagine, it might have been I who died in that blazing plane. Didn't we compete for one and the same place our whole lives? Do you see where this haste has taken him? To the seat in the airplane. Don't be alarmed. Always it seemed to me that he took my place, so much so that many a time I forgot that there was a place for me apart from the one Tawfiq occupied. Yet here I am sunning myself on this balcony, while Tawfiq is over there, a charred corpse on the mountain."

She pursed her lips and returned nervously to her knitting. No doubt she was remembering bitter conversations that had taken place in the middle of the night and had brought him to early diabetes and blood pressure.

"I haven't told you much about Tawfiq," he said with sudden tenderness. "We were fellow students at secondary school. He wasn't my friend. No, he was never once my friend, though we were always mentioned in the same breath. As for him, no one knows where he came from. His father was a government official or something of the sort. He was a lovable, soft person who after a while made friends with all his classmates. As for myself, I was always accused of being a bit snobbish and mixed with the boys from my own village, a few of whom were my particular friends. He and I were rivals, in continual competition in the various subjects we were taking."

He was silent for a moment; his face was slightly flushed and he looked younger. She placed the two knitting needles and the wool in her lap, tilting her head slightly as she listened to him.

"We joined the College of Engineering together and were in the same class. We went up together year by year, remaining rivals at the top of our year. Coming out first was now regarded by the students as of more importance, not like at secondary school, where leadership generally went to the tallest student or to the captain of the basketball team. The rivalry between us became sharp and bitter though we were polite enough when meeting face to face. Though he remained pleasantly friendly, he now began to employ his talents with the teaching staff; he made himself known to them from the very first day, after which he went on to ingratiate himself with them. Even so, though, I often beat him to first place. And so came the year for taking our finals.

"The country was boiling with revolution and among those who met their deaths in the streets were colleagues of ours. Even so an English lecturer ventured, within the hearing of us all, to make a remark insulting to Egypt. Finding myself unable to disregard it, I insulted him back. The man kept silent and didn't react at all. The emotional coldness of the English! At the end of the year, though, I found that I had failed in his subject. This was unbelievable. Who knows, I might well have been failed again had not the lecturer left the Faculty and returned home. This put me a year behind Tawfiq and he was therefore ahead of me, both in being sent abroad to complete his studies and in taking up his first appointment. Yet I still did everything I could to establish my superiority over him by putting more into my work."

She gave a deep sigh; she tried to return to her knitting but found that she had miscounted. She knew well what had happened after that. He had no longer tried to talk to her about his work and achievements, which meant his having to use long English words which had been meaningless to her; instead he talked about his work in a bitter, resentful manner. Later, when the other man was chosen for the important post, his zeal had cooled of completely. And what post a it was! From what he had to say it had seemed to her that the person occupying it was all-powerful. And so the legal case had been brought and replaced work as a subject of conversation. She had listened and had then tried to amuse him, to distract him with other things.

He looked at her. Her face had begun to fade with age, yet it gazed at him imploringly, like the face of a child. Had she gazed at him like this in the old days?

"But he was always smooth as a snake. I never knew how he managed to twist his bosses round his little finger. I used to hear about some frightful things, though, some filthy things that went on between them. I wasn't able to mention everything when the case was brought as I lacked evidence."

Was he able to mention everything to her now? Had he ever talked to anyone about his dreams, strange dreams that he still remembered whenever he looked at his wife? When he remembered them he would turn away his head to escape from himself. But what dreams were these? Dreams without meaning, nightmares. Was it possible that these dreams were at all connected with those 'filthy things' he had heard? But what connection had these dreams got with his wife? Why, for nights on end, did he dream that Tawfiq had come and taken his wife away from him, his wife who was still a bride, sweet and good, and whom he loved most dearly? He had heard people saying behind his back that she was the most marvelous choice he'd made in his life, and the funny thing was that after these dreams of his he found himself incapable of loving her as he should. He would also feel fear of Tawfiq, together with extreme hatred. No, Tawfiq had not known Hana, had perhaps never seen her in his life. But this was not at all the crux of the matter. Besides, he had never doubted his wife. Yet, even in his waking hours the dream did, sometimes, appear possible, and he would release his closely guarded secret to twist about like a worm in his bosom, careful to appear outwardly calm and strong.

"Five years you wasted on that case. How you burnt yourself up over it and lost it in the end!"

Yes, he had lost the case, as well as the work which he loved. He had lost life itself because he had been unable to stand his colleagues seeing him defeated and had therefore asked to be transferred. Eventually he had come to rest at his present desk, where he would sit through the morning hours scarcely doing any work. The case had become his one amusement all these years, a bitter amusement of which his wife was not aware, nor yet his colleagues in the office; it was like an addiction, a fell disease. He would search through the papers for news of Tawfiq, reading and re-reading each item till he found that its words and letters often became so engraved upon his mind that when he was sitting by himself on the balcony or lying stretched out on his bed he was able to recall it. At first this had happened by chance; he had not been looking for news of Tawfiq when, amusing himself as was his wont by reading the newspaper at the office, his eye had alighted on the name. It was nothing of any importance, merely the reporter asking him, among a number of other people, about some project, and the space given to what he had to say occupied no more than a few lines following on from a brief description of who he was. But reporters, as is their wont, once having got to know someone, begin writing more and more about him for no apparent reason. Also there was no doubt that Tawfiq was past master at making reporters welcome. In any event, the items of news became both longer and more frequent. At first the reading of them had been a bitter, joyless experience and had stirred up feelings of resentment and opened old wounds. Soon, though, it no longer did so; the bitterness became pleasurable in the same way as when one gets used to bitter sugarless coffee and finds any other sort completely insipid. And so he began to look around for news and stories about Tawfiq, and when he found them he would feel as though he had read something of real interest.

Year after year he followed Tawfiq on his upward path. When he left government service and became a director of an important organization there was a noticeable shift in the attention accorded to him in the press: his name no longer appeared in items of news and stories but in paid announcements. Such announcements, however, had an advantage, which was that his picture would appear in them so that it was possible to ruminate over his expensive clothes, his body which had filled out slightly, and his shining hair now gray around the temples. Apart from this, though, he did not differ greatly from the young Tawfiq returned from abroad, or Tawfiq the student at college, or even Tawfiq the secondary schoolboy.

One day he found himself feeling he would like to meet him again. It was a strange wish, for he didn't imagine that he would really enjoy the meeting, neither did he know how he would behave at such a moment. Anyway, where could they meet? His activities had dwindled considerably and he no longer went to his professional association, even on election day. But conjuring up pictures of this encounter had become something else on which to spend time at his office, or when sitting on the balcony, or stretched out on his bed.

"What hours I spent with him," he thought. "All this will now come to an end." Perhaps a news item or two—the fortieth day after his death and the first anniversary, on that back page. Tawfiq would move from the front page to the back before finally withdrawing. The newspaper would lose its interest and flavor.

"Aren't you going inside? It gets cold on this balcony, I tell you."

"H'm, h'm. I'll be coming in soon."

The sun had grown decidedly pale as though it had become chilly; its rays gave out light without heat, and from time to time it was covered over by a small cloud seeking warmth. A slight wind rustled the dry leaves. Now he was alone on the balcony. Though he had begun to feel the cold he put off the moment for getting up. He was at the climax of his discussion with himself and didn't want to abandon it without reaching a conclusion. It was as though his eyes had looked down on a minute, wondrous spot which would be lost to him if he shifted to either right or left; as though he were balanced precariously on the side of a ship: he had only to move a hair's breadth and he would fall.

Admit it! Admit it! What were you doing all these years? This man ruined your life, and now that he is dead, what will you do? Nothing, of course, your life will merely become more empty. Why don't you admit it? As time went on he became your main concern, and life seems wholly trivial without him. What irony! Some people have a love story in their lives, others a story of strife, while your whole life has been made up of a story of hatred.

The girl handed him a blanket. "Madam says you should put this round your feet."

"Where is she?"

"In her room, sir."

"Listen, Hamida—tell your mistress—or—never mind."

His was a love story he had failed to make anything of, like a book that has fallen apart before its pages are cut. How sweet and full of vitality she had been as a young woman! Now nothing mattered to her at all: her two children had grown up and gone away and nothing remained but the two of them face to face and the long lonely nights of winter.

The time for love had passed. Had he tried to inspire any feelings in her now she would have experienced nothing but distress. Such affection as existed between them was shown by the blanket she had sent to him on the balcony to protect him from the cold.

If only he could see his children now!

Tawfiq came so as to be with his daughter while she was having her baby. What an affectionate father he was! We regard our children as being what we have made them; we do not know what life will make of them later.

Could his son become like him, he asked himself, and his daughter like her mother? God forbid! Were his children beside him now he would give them some sound advice. He would have so much to say to them.

Are you happy or sad at Tawfiq's death? I find you neither happy nor sad. The time for happiness and sadness has passed too. But do you think that he was happier than me? It's funny that I should never have thought about this question before. I had imagined that it required no thought. I always imagined him as being happy—merely because I was miserable. Yet I know nothing of his life. I wish I had met him, if only just once during all these years. Oh, how bound up our lives were! More than with a wife or children! Is it possible for us to love our enemies so? Strange! It seems to me now that we were never enemies. If only Tawfiq hadn't been so hasty, if only he hadn't put forward the time of his departure—God rest his soul, he was a pleasant fellow. Do you remember how you used to tease him with:

"Tawfiq they called you, a flop you are,
Who named you thus from truth was far"?

Had he been *tawfiq*—success—or a flop? When the sun sets all colors are reduced to the same level. I feel something pressing down on my chest. I am calling to them but they don't seem to hear . . .

His wife called to him to come inside so that she could close the balcony door, but he didn't answer. When she went out to him she found he was dead, his eyes staring out at the setting sun while the sparrows still chirruped noisily among the trees.

A Small White Mouse

—∞∞—

Salwa Bakr

The lights turned to red and the insane uninterrupted deluge of traffic came to a halt, allowing a surge of people to rush forward and hurriedly cross the street. This caused Husniya to stand up straighter and raise her voice in a shout, "Have a go and see your luck for a shilling."

Over and over she repeated the call. When no one stopped by her, she threw a piece of dry bread into the cage of the mouse, who was looking on expectantly, then began once again to gaze at the traffic lights in anticipation of probable customers. Meanwhile her attention was taken up with the very same thoughts that had begun several days ago to harass her, and which up until this very moment still spoilt her life for her: "Just suppose, my girl, Uncle Hasan recovered and was up and about, hale and hearty, it would be as if all your efforts had been for nothing. And what if Uncle Hasan agreed to bring you a work kit, when he's convinced you're intending to make your living in some place away off the map, the problem's still there, the same knot in the wood the saw can't deal with. Because the work kit costs money, it can be very expensive, and he'd take it out on you because you know he'd give his life for a piaster and can't easily part with money."

She sighed with annoyance and extreme anger at her husband, feelings so intense that she imagined that, were he to appear before her at that instant, she would pick up the largest stone and hurl it at him to smash his head in and would also give him a good beating, because all the hardship she was living through was caused by him, he having left her in the position of some charitable endowment that can never be changed, neither divorcing her nor returning to her to take up her worries and make her feel she was someone living in the world like everyone else.

She felt that the world in her sight was narrower than the eye of a needle. She left the mouse in its cage on the cardboard box she used as a table and walked a few steps until she reached the boy sitting in front of a mat on which were scattered shoelaces, boxes of matches, and plastic combs. Suppressing her feelings of exasperation, she said to him, Abdul Rahim, "Let's have a couple of puffs, by the Prophet." With a flamboyant gesture, which made him look like a miniature man, the boy took a long pull at the cigarette between his lips that bore as yet no trace of a mustache, then he raised his head and handed her the cigarette, while his eyes roamed over the details of her body under the gallabiya, which appeared somewhat transparent due to the morning sunlight. Busying himself with arranging some small mirrors on the mat, he said to her, "It's all yours."

She thanked him, after having filled her chest with a long draught of smoke, and went back to the mouse. When she felt she had calmed down a little, she began calling out again, "Have a go and see your luck for a shilling."

Within a matter of seconds—she didn't know what happened exactly—all hell broke loose. A huge gray van came to an abrupt stop by the pavement and with lightning speed policemen and officers descended from it, after which boxes of matches and tins of shoe polish, metal keys and plastic shoes, nails and shoelaces, all went flying about, and blows were mingled with shouts and with people rushing about and screaming. The policemen were scooping up the wares of the vendors with dazzling speed and hurling them into the back of the huge gray van. When Husniya saw the white mouse making a complete somersault in the air, complete with cage, then disappearing into the van, she was quite sure they must be the authorities police. She slapped her breast and screamed at the top of her voice. "What a calamity!"

Madly she rushed off in the direction of the van in an attempt to rescue the mouse, but all she got was a slap on the face from a well-practiced hand, which set her head spinning. She began swearing and cursing, the tears streaming from her eyes. Once again she tried to retrieve the mouse, dashing forward and covering the hand of the sergeant with both of hers, trying to stop him so she could tell him that the mouse had been left in her safekeeping and that she was working with it for an old man, like himself, who was ill. "O God, may He keep you safe for your children, sergeant, and protect you from the evils of the highways. Give me back the mouse because it cost a lot and it will be difficult to find another one like it." She told him she'd be forced to pay its price to its owner because it was his only capital.

But the sergeant turned a deaf ear and violently withdrew his hand from between hers. "Get away or I'll throw you into the van to join your mouse," he told her. He busied himself collecting up the rest of the things left by the vendors who had fled.

She stood watching and hitting herself on the head in desperation but before long, when she saw him lighting a cigarette and putting his hand in his pocket, an idea occurred to her. She went up to him and pushed ten piasters furtively into his hand, at the same time adjusting her headscarf and whispering, "May God keep you safe in every step you take. . . . By the Prophet, let me have back the cardboard box."

She stood waiting when he told her that he would do so when the officer had moved away a little so that he wouldn't be noticed. She tried to look unconcerned whenever an officer or a policeman passed in front of her, thinking about the people's things that the government had taken, things that were all they possessed and that they worked with in order to keep body and soul together. She was extremely surprised at how the government never stopped lying in wait for poor miserable folk, always picking on them over every blessed thing, and having no mercy on them and not even letting God's mercy descend on them, making problems because people may be standing around looking for charity, despite the fact that the road's plenty wide enough and people are going about as they wish, and the vendors haven't trodden on the government's toes in any way—not like shopkeepers who fill up the streets and the pavement with their goods and their cars. She smacked her lips in disgust and brought to mind the proverb that says that he who doesn't have someone to back him will be beaten about the ears. Suddenly it was as though an electric current had passed through her face: she had seen the sergeant returning from the van quite empty-handed. She hurried toward him inquiringly. "The cage broke and the mouse escaped," he told her. All the joints of her body went slack and the blood in her veins ran cold. Again she began striking her chest. "Woe is me, mother!" she shrieked.

Then she sat down on the ground, crying and wailing, at which the sergeant advised her to leave the place quickly and make herself scarce because if the officer were to see her making such a fuss he'd get annoyed and would perhaps collect her up in the van with those who were being detained for not having identity cards, and perhaps he'd think up some charge to make against her and she'd be in a real mess. She leapt up in fright, looking like someone who's just had somebody die, and she went off dragging her feet, thinking about the disaster that had come to her from God knows where and which she'd never dreamt would happen, and wondering what she'd say to Uncle Hasan, her neighbor and owner of the mouse. She was the only one, from among all the neighbors who lived in the rooms of the house, whom he had trusted with the mouse, and with his money. When he had got ill and become bedridden, it was she he had asked to go out and seek her livelihood in the street with the mouse, as he had done, by telling people's fortunes through it. Things would be even more difficult for her when he learnt that she had gone against his instructions and hadn't stood with the mouse somewhere along the outer wall of the university, but had got greedy and taken her stand on the pavement of the big street with the rest of the vendors. It was the boy Abdul Rahim who had recommended this to her and had given her the impression she'd do better business in the new location because it was near the main road. Also, Uncle Hasan wouldn't believe the truth because only three days ago he had asked her about the month that was coming and, when she had told him that it was February, he had urged her to take courage and get a move on in the work because that meant the season had begun and the students' exams were approaching, which would result in their asking more and more to have their fortunes told.

She wept bitterly. She felt that the Lord had taken vengeance on her for having deducted for herself a little of the takings—during the days that had just passed she had hidden a quarter of a pound each time for herself and hadn't told Uncle Hasan about it. But this thought quickly flew from her head when she remembered how stingy and tight he was with her, and that, despite the fact that she had to stand the whole day, in the end all he would stretch out in his hand to her was fifty piasters—though he knew perfectly well that she wouldn't stint him in his demands. On returning late at night she would do his washing and would cook for him and feed him with her own hand, because his own had begun to shake and he had grown very weak, and, over and above that, she would put up with the things the women in the rest of the house said about her, because of her going in and out of his room. She kept silent because the position with Uncle Hasan was a thousand times better than previously when she used to go around on the buses peddling chewing gum and combs. At least she was now standing in one and the same place with the mouse and no longer heard dirty talk directed against her by the driver or ticket collector, poisoning her body every other minute, and was no longer exposed all day long to curses and harsh treatment.

A furnace was raging in her head as she made her way toward the house. Her sorrows seemed to be endless, and if she had happened to meet her wretch of a husband at that moment she would have cut him into bits, would have made mincemeat of him, for it was he who had caused her all this torment she had lived through since he left her and disappeared. He had separated her from her family when he married her in the village years ago and brought her to this city in which one didn't know whether one was coming or going and where there wasn't a soul prepared to raise his eyes and look into the face of the person in front of him in the street. Her mother had died ages ago and it hadn't occurred to her husband even to ask about her because he hated her in the same way as she had hated him. As for Uncle Hasan, who was so kind to her and was the only person she had in this world, she would lose him forever from the moment she reached the house and told him she had lost his means of earning his daily bread and had allowed the government to make off with the mouse. Perhaps he would believe her when she swore to him by her mother's grave and told him that the mouse had escaped from the government but that the policeman hadn't found it. The trouble was that she had invested high hopes in Uncle Hasan and so put up with his bossing her about and endured patiently his many demands although they made her absolutely furious sometimes. She was dreaming one day of his conscience pricking him and his saying, "If I die, Husniya my girl, take everything I have because I've got no family and everything's in your hands, and you've got a better right to it than any other creature in the world—to the mattress and the blanket, and the chair and the rest of the things—because you're a good girl and you've been at my disposal and service just as though you were my own daughter, my own flesh and blood. As for the few piasters in the pocket of the gallabiya, you can have them to buy yourself a nice gallabiya and a new nylon nightgown."

The tears streamed down even more as she remembered all that and she chewed at her lips in bitterness as she approached the door of the house. She thought about how she would open the conversation with Uncle Hasan, and she pictured to herself how he would look when he got to know and flew into a rage and would say to her, "Get out of my sight, you accursed girl, you who spoil everything, you thief, you bringer of disasters. Your man left you because your face brings bad luck."

She had reached the courtyard of the house and was crying more and more. She found a throng of people in front of Uncle Hasan's room, with the owner of the house standing and barring the door with her vast body. "No one's to go near him," she was saying, "till the health inspector comes and writes the paper for him."

When she saw Husniya approach, the tears filling her eyes, she said to her in astonishment, "Did you hear the news, Husniya? You're a good sort, by the Prophet, coming so quickly. Give me the money you got so we can prepare what's required for the burial and take part in the funeral procession early tomorrow morning, God willing." Then she returned to the rest of the neighbors and said, "Not a soul is to touch anything belonging to Uncle Hasan, for we intend to sell his belongings, God willing, to pay off the months of rent he's owing me."

The Days of the Black Cat

———ᴍ———

Rehab Bassam

I live an extremely simple life. On most days I wake up some minutes before the alarm clock goes off and prepare for meeting the world. I go down to the street. I meet the black cat and my heart sinks. I begin my day. The black cat continues to be the first thing I see in the street on the morning of each day, whether it be in Cairo or Alexandria, inside Egypt or outside, whether it be in Medinat Nasr or Maadi or Mohandiseen. On the days when I work in Heliopolis, if I don't meet up with him in the morning in front of my building, I find him walking along the garden wall that my office window overlooks, the same black cat, with the same green eyes, and the same indifferent expression. If he had come close to me on any day throughout these past years, I'd have said he was a spirit that was protecting me, or some person I know imprisoned in the body of a cat. But not at all—the black cat never attempted to say anything to me. With time I came to look around each morning and be upset if I didn't find him. And when I did find him, my heart would sink and I'd try to look into his eyes, but he'd ignore me and walk off.

I have continued this regularity for the last ten years until I entered my phase of loving cats. Since then I give a nod of the head to the black cat as a morning greeting each day, while he, as haughty as the statues of pharaonic cats, takes no notice of my greeting and takes himself off to matters of greater moment.

After deep thought I realized that the best solution for getting rid of the black cat was to own him. It seemed to me that perhaps if I succeeded in making him my property he would come to love me and to open his heart to me and clarify his role in my life. I started off on a secret quest (for my mother dislikes cats) for my black cat with green eyes. I decided that his name would be Gaafar, and I began talking about him with my friends and placing pictures of him everywhere. While seeing many black cats, Gaafar was never one of them. It occurred to me to run after him one morning when I met up with him, and to seize hold of him, but I felt that such an action would give him the wrong impression of me and would make me out to be a cat-napper, and who would want to open his heart to a person who had chased him around the streets, scaring him in front of all the ginger and gray cats?

But today I woke up having come to a definite decision: I don't ever want to own Gaafar. Gaafar will live in my imagination as a destination, a symbol, as a reminder to me of all the dreams that slip from my hands when I chase them and that come to me when I renounce them. I don't want him to be held in confinement, but to remain as free and wild as my thoughts, even if he has ignored me, even if I never know the reason for his presence in my life.

I got out of bed, happy with my decision. I prepared myself for the morning and went down to the street. I had to walk a bit to get to where my car was. I looked alongside me and found a white cat jumping most elegantly across a large puddle of water, landing on the other side of it without so much as touching the water, and then sitting himself with confident certainty as though this giant leap of his was the very least of the brilliant feats he could perform. I laughed and said to myself, "How extraordinary! So that's it. Is it all that important not to get your leg wet?" The cat turned to me and said, "Meow," to which I said, "Meow," giving a nod of my head in greeting, and got out my keys. Before I set about opening the car, I realized what had occurred. Standing firmly where I was, I turned slowly. Yes, it's a cat, and he's white, and he said meow to me. I looked around myself in the street. Not a sign of Gaafar. I looked at the white cat. Taking my time, I approached the cat and said "Meow" to him. He came closer and I stroked him on the head and rubbed him under the chin. He gave a longer "Meow" than the first time and moved his head from right to left in my hand in order to achieve maximum warmth.

Turning, I got into the car. I started it up, knowing that after today I wouldn't be seeing Gaafar again. Not ever.

The Room Next Door

—⁓—

Mohamed El-Bisatie

The two rooms on the top floor are next door to each other. I can hear the talk that's going on in the other room, which is occupied by a mother and her son. The sound intrudes on my privacy. The boy is no more than eight years old and the mother, thin and emaciated, is in her forties. It is always she who is talking, with not a sound to be heard from the boy. She has to persuade him to eat or to change his clothes, and to stop cutting up the paper that covers the floor of the room, with the boy not wanting to listen to her. She asks him what he does at school and about his lessons, then goes back to trying to persuade him to have his lunch before it gets cold. In a trembling voice she says, "Just tell me what food you'd like and I'll make it for you."

Sometimes the boy answers in such a soft voice that I can't hear it. Then I hear her saying, "Just a minute and I'll go down and buy the sesame paste," and I hear her steps as she hurries toward the stairs.

The building has four floors, yet she's not gone for long and I soon hear her panting as she approaches. Seeing me standing by the door of my room, she mutters, "Just so he eats."

She sometimes seeks my help when faced by his stubbornness in not eating. I find her standing in front of her room waiting for me.

"He's not eaten a mouthful for lunch, and he doesn't want to have any supper. You speak to him, perhaps he'll listen to you."

There's a plateful of rice with mulukhiya and a bit of chicken on the low, round table resting on the mat, and I see him squatting in a corner, as he gives me a fleeting look, with his thin neck slightly extended and a small frown on his face.

I ask him why he's not eating.

He eyes me casually for a moment, then silently crawls toward the table and bends over the food.

I am surprised at his obeying me. My voice wasn't angry, and it occurs to me that he refrains from opposing me lest he opens up an argument he doesn't want to have.

There's an empty space in front of the top of the stairway where we sometimes meet in the morning. She will be dressed in her clothes for going out, while he'll be in his school uniform with the bag of books on his back. He goes down the stairs without a word, while his mother stays alongside me, casting a look into the stairwell until the sound of his footsteps dies away. Then she arranges her head covering with the words, "He doesn't want me to go down with him—his friends are standing in front of the house. They walk together to the school."

She fixes her faded jacket around her shoulders.

"It's cold." Then she says, "Keep an eye on him—I may be late. The key's on the space by the window—he knows. Maybe I told you before about where it was, one forgets."

A moment later she says, "So, I'll be off to work."

I hang around for a while so she'll be ahead of me.

She was a housekeeper. Every day except for Fridays she'd be at a house. She had her clients, who were happy with her. She'd arrive early, before they left for work, and they'd leave her the flat. After cleaning and cooking she'd close the front door behind her. She doesn't eat what she has cooked even though the people try to insist, preferring to eat with her son. Many of them ask her to come to them on Fridays, offering her more money, but she never agrees. She keeps it free so that she can go out with her son. They go to public gardens and the zoo or they take a boat on the Nile: a large motorboat. It's just as he wants, she always asks him what he'd like to see before they go out, even the Pyramids, though she didn't know where they were. She asked about them and they went there. She asks me if I've seen them and I say that I have.

They bring their lunch in a bundle that he insists on carrying.

"He doesn't frown or get annoyed or bother me by refusing to carry it. He reminds me of the old days when his father was with us in the other flat and how he would pay attention to what I said."

She talks away as she sits on the doorstep by my room, while I'm inside finishing off the remainder of the work I'd brought with me from the office. The time spent there, with so few employees, doesn't help. I note down dozens of orders in the notebook with the numbers of receipts of fees, orders for installing water meters despite their not being available in the office's storerooms.

She stops talking for a while, then goes on, "Only once did I do so," and she asks me if she's distracting me from my work, and I reply, "Not at all."

I notice her craning her head inside, perhaps to make sure that she is not distracting me.

And she goes on talking.

"It was the only time—I never did it again. There was food left over, a great amount of it. The owner of the flat, who hadn't gone to work that day, insisted that I take it with me. There was meat and vegetables and rice, also some things for dessert. There was a big package I brought back with me to the room. If only you'd seen him as I was opening the parcel on the table, while I called out to him to come and see the lovely food I'd brought. The sound of his groaning made me pay attention to him: his face was turning from red to yellow and he was shivering. He scared me and I called out, 'What's wrong?' He kicked at the table, while I grabbed hold of the parcel of food. He stretched out on the mattress with his face to the wall. I talked to him about the food, saying this and that, and that it was I who had cooked it and that he should eat. Not a bit of it, and he wouldn't even turn his face and talk to me. Nothing. That day I took the parcel to the doorman who was down below, and this went on for a couple of days, with him not eating or speaking to me. That's how it was."

She lapsed into silence, scratching with her fingernail at the dirt that had collected in the gap in front of the doorstep, craning her head inside so she could see me and inquiring, "Do you have a lot of work?"

"Some."

"All right, so I'll get going."

But she doesn't go anywhere. She stays for a while staring into space, with her head on her drawn-up knees.

She said that he was inside but didn't want her sitting with him or seeing what he was drawing. He had a slate board she had bought him from the scrap merchant, and some colored chalk. He'd draw something then rub it out—animals. She said, "I don't know what he liked about them: dogs and donkeys and mice. Once I stood up to see what he was drawing, but he no sooner felt me there than he turned the slate over, saying that he didn't like anyone seeing what he's drawing. I said to him, 'You draw beautifully. Why not draw people and houses?' I stretched out my hand to touch his head and he pushed it aside. When he saw me still standing there, he wiped out what he'd drawn and went to the mattress. After that I didn't go near him. As soon as I saw him take hold of the slate I'd finish what I had in hand and go out to the roof."

That day, as she was sitting at the threshold of my room, I asked her, "And where's his father?"

"Who knows?"

She was mending a tear in her son's shirt. Cutting the thread with her teeth, she spread out the shirt in front of her, then folded it into her lap.

"It's been several months now that no one knows where he is."

"And his family? His father, his mother, and brothers and sisters?"

"His father and mother died years ago, and I don't know the rest of them. They're right down in Upper Egypt. He once told me the name of the village, but I've forgotten it. Not one of them ever paid us a visit, nor us them. Even his friends—that's if he had any. I never saw him greet anyone in the street. He'd be on his own, looking neither right nor left."

She took up the shirt from her lap and once again spread it out. There was a hole at the armpit. She put her finger inside it, then began to mend it.

She said that they had been living in a room in a flat that was made up of three rooms, and each room was occupied by a family, with everyone living on their own and keeping their door closed. The lavatory was communal. It was quite a lifestyle. There was no place for any visitor in their room. It was just enough for them, with a bed and a mattress for the boy and two boxes for their clothes, and the pots and pans in a corner all higgledy-piggledy. No chairs or anything else. What did they need chairs for? She still doesn't know the reason why he left. It was on a day like any other. He woke up early as usual to go to his work. He was a carpenter at a workshop not far away making windows, doors, and chairs. The lavatory was occupied, one of her neighbors was taking a shower and had decided to rinse out her undies while she was at it. The woman was a bit long in the bathroom, while the husband was clasping his stomach and twisting about in the narrow space of the room. From time to time she'd open the door and glance toward the lavatory, not knowing what to do. Embarrassed, she hurried to the lavatory and asked her neighbor to vacate it as her husband was late for work. Finally the woman came out and her husband, having relieved himself, went off to the workshop. There was nothing to suggest there was anything wrong. She took the boy to the school and, on her return, found that while she was away he had come back and had collected up his clothes and his belongings into a bundle and taken off. He had left her some money on the pillow to cover their expenses for a month. He hadn't done this before, usually paying their way day by day. One of her neighbors told her that he was carrying a bundle with him as he left. She hurried off to the workshop to find out what she could and was told by the owner that, having paid him his due, he had left them.

"Where to?"

"The owner of the workshop doesn't know."

She waited around for a whole month, but there was no news of him. She couldn't wait any longer. The money he had left had been used up. Finding work in people's houses was easy enough and so she looked around for a separate room with its own bathroom.

I take a short walk at the end of the night on the roof, having finished writing down the applications in the notebook. There is a gentle breeze and the pale light of the moon. I look down from the wall: the streets are just as I am used to seeing them every night. For some time the light in the other room has been extinguished, and the woman's slippers and those of the boy are right by the door. I enter my room to sleep.

A House for My Children

—◆—

Mahmoud Diab

I t isn't possible that the idea occurred to me suddenly, for I had always dreamed of having a house. Though in my dreams its features were not sharply defined, it was characterized by a general enveloping air of warmth and serenity. When, therefore, the chance presented itself I grasped it as though my life depended on it.

While the idea was not a sudden one to me, it came as a surprise to my wife, who was unable to hold back her tears of excitement. I didn't in fact surprise her with it as an idea, which would not have caused her such excitement, but in the form of an actual contract for a vacant plot of land on a new housing estate in the eastern part of the city.

This was on the birthday of my children, Hala and Hisham. The former was four years old and the latter three. Born in the same month, though not on the same day, we used to celebrate their birthdays together.

On returning home that day my wife asked me:

"Have you forgotten that today's the children's birthday?"

"No, I haven't forgotten," I said softly, attempting to conceal my restlessness.

"Don't tell me you're broke," she said slyly.

"No, I'm not broke."

"They've been waiting for you and yet I see you've come back without even troubling to buy them a piaster's worth of sweets," she said, indicating my empty hands.

"I'm fed up with getting them only toys and sweets."

Unable to prepare the way for the surprise any better than this, I produced a large envelope from under my arm and handed it to her.

"My present's in this envelope," I said, and she took out the contract and ran her eyes over it while I watched her in an ecstasy of pride. Failing to understand what it was about at first glance, she raised her beautiful face inquiringly.

"What's this?" she cried.

"It's a house for them," I said, smiling.

Hisham crept out from behind, and buried his face between my legs and gave a soft laugh. I bent over, picked him up and began kissing him, oblivious of the unexpected results my surprise had wrought in my wife.

From that moment great changes came over her. No longer did she bring up the old story of my love affair which she had found out about some days ago. Whether she had forgotten about it or merely pretended to have done so I don't know. She also became more tender and gay and there wasn't a relative or friend of hers to whom she didn't announce the news of the house we'd be building. In fact she no longer enjoyed talking to me about anything else.

We went, the four of us, to the plot of land the following day, in order, as she put it, "to give it the once over." We stood by one corner of it, she beside me, radiant with smiles, while Hala and Hisham ran races nearby, shouting and stirring up little eddies of dust.

My wife was outlining what the house would be like and went on unconsciously repeating herself, "It'll be a single story, won't it? But when the children get bigger we'll add another one. We'll surround it with a large garden. I'd love a house of mine to have a garden. I'll look after it myself. I'll fill it with flowers. What sort of flowers do you like, darling? Isn't it funny that for five whole years I've never known what flowers you liked?"

"I like jasmine," I said.

"We'll cover the garden with jasmine," she cried. Then: "Living in a house like this far away from the smoke and din of the city is beautifully healthy for the children. My grandfather used to have a lovely house in Mansoura—it had an acre of garden. Imagine! By the way, you must make provision for a laundry room on the roof, also a servants' room—"

"What do you mean by a servants' room?" I cut her short. "I've spent precious years of my life turning a dream into reality and I'd ask you not to turn it into a nonsense!"

"All right—and the garage, the house must have a garage."

"But I don't own a car."

"You'll have a car some time and where would you put it if the house didn't have a garage?"

She called out to Hala to bring back her brother, then she let out a shrill laugh and raced after her children with the gaiety of a young girl.

My thoughts wandered far afield as I watched the three of them in the middle of the plot of land. Only when my wife returned and was standing by me did I come to. She repeated what she had told me before, embroidering on it, while I replied to her in between my thoughts with "yes" or "no," without paying any attention to what she was saying.

I remembered an old house, far away in both time and place. The place was the town of Ismailiya; as to the time, I am able to fix it in terms of my age, for at that time I was eight or nine years old. We owned a house in that town, a modest single-story house surrounded by a small but beautiful garden. It did, not, however, possess a servants' room, for we had no servants; nor did it have a garage, for my father had never been in a private motorcar in his life. I remember that there was a trellis of vines in our garden, and two mango trees, a lemon tree, and a large hen house. I also remember that my father would not be in the house for a minute before he'd take up the hoe and wield it in the garden, the fence of which was covered in strands of jasmine. I don't remember when it was that we came to own that house or when we moved into it. I do remember, though that my father was extremely proud of it, while my mother regarded our coming into possession of it was a stupendous and historic event. She had thus made of it a set date by which she fixed the events of her life and those of the whole family. Many is the time I have heard her say:

"When we moved to the house I was pregnant with so-and-so—" or "when we bought the house my husband's salary was so much—" and similar expressions which I still smile at when I recollect them.

I don't remember any particular happenings that occurred at home during that period other than the birth of one of my brothers, the fifth of us all and the third male child. No doubt the other incidents were all so commonplace that they have left no special impression on my mind. I do remember, though, that when evening came a group of our neighbors would turn up to see my father and they'd gather out in the garden and converse on various topics, while we children would play around them, and the breezes of spring would blow drowsily, made sluggish with the aroma of jasmine. It must be that it was forever spring in our house in those days, for I can scarcely imagine it now without games in the garden and the smell of jasmine.

Then some events occurred which did not immediately break the monotony of life. For this reason I can scarcely remember them now in detail though I do remember vague echoes of them, as for instance that I began hearing the word "war," a word new to me, being repeated at home far more frequently than the word "bread;" it was also constantly used by the grown-ups in our street without my understanding its meaning to begin with. There were other words I learned by heart despite their difficulty and strangeness because of the way they were repeated: "The Allies—the Axis—the Germans—the Maginot Line" and others, all of which were mere words that I chanced to hear.

My father and our neighbors gathered in the garden would talk only about such matters. They would divide up into two opposing factions, one wanting victory for the English and the other praying that the Germans would win. My father belonged to the latter faction, and I, in my turn, prayed for a German victory. Often I would hear my father say, "A German victory means that the English would get out of Egypt," though Uncle Hassan, our nearest neighbor, believed that if the English got out of Egypt it would mean the Germans entering it. The grown-ups would carry on long animated discussions which would end on one night, only to begin again on another, while we children, in our games, would divide ourselves up into two groups, one "the English" and the other "the Germans." I naturally belonged to the latter. We would then indulge in childish warfare which left us puffing and blowing to the point of exhaustion.

When it was time to go to sleep I would slip into bed and lie there for a time listening to the voices of the grown-ups in the garden. I would single out my father's voice among them and would then try to conjure up a picture of the Germans. I did not picture the Germans as being the same size as the English or as looking like them, but saw them as both larger and more magnificent.

One night the air raid warning sounded. That, too, was something new and exciting in those days. The lights in the street and the houses went out and darkness, weighted down with tense silence, ruled. Ghostly forms gathered at the doorways and the scent of jasmine was diffused more strongly than on any previous night.

"German airplanes!" shouted my father. Gazing up at the sky and listening intently, I was able to make out a disjointed humming that cut through the solid darkness at the horizon's end and drew nearer.

"Will they bomb the town?" I asked my mother in terror. "No," my father answered here in the tones of someone well-informed on such matters. "Hitler wouldn't do that. They're merely making for the English camps."

English camps surrounded our small town on all sides, indeed were almost touching it. We heard terrible explosions which I don't remember ceasing for an instant. An airplane burst into flames in the sky; then ghostly forms with a heavy tread passed by announcing to the rushing people that the planes were laying waste the town and advising them to keep away from the houses.

Bands of phantom figures rushed out, running and stumbling in the street. Our parents got up and hurried us off with the terrified crowds toward the desert which stretched to the northeast of the city; there was no other place of escape.

That night seemed like nothing so much as the gathering of the dead at the end of the world. This was how father expressed it and my mother later repeated his words. People were pushing one another about crazily, barefoot in their nightgowns, calling out to one another in the midst of that solid darkness. "Where are you, Muhsin? Where are the children? Did you close the door? Let the house go to hell! Hurry up, Lawahiz! Wait for me, father," while the barking of dogs rang out in every direction. I cried as I ran, with three of my brothers and sisters—many were the children that cried in the midst of that solid darkness.

I am unable to say exactly how many people took refuge in the desert on that confused night. All I know is that the black desert was filled with them so that we were like people "at an anniversary feast of some saint—at the anniversary feast of Sheikh Hitler," as Uncle Hassan said ironically.

"Help me dig," said my father to my mother in the voice of an expert on these matters. "Dig, children! Hassan Effendi, make a hole for your children to protect them from the shrapnel."

We dug a large hole in which my father fitted us tightly together, while explosions thundered in the town and the disjointed humming filled the sky and sudden flashes of light burst forth like lightning from time to time. Then the airplanes were circling above us.

"They're right over our heads," shouted my father. My mother gave an anguished scream and threw herself on to us to cover us with her body. My father did likewise. Voices were raised throughout the desert ordering the people to be silent, followed by other voices telling them to shut up. I craned my neck, thrust up my head, and took a look, over my father's shoulder, at the sky in the hope of seeing a German in his airplane so that I might verify the picture I had stored up in my head of the Germans. However, my father violently pushed my head back into the sand.

"Why are they bombing us if it's the English they're fighting?" whispered my mother.

My father answered not a word.

"Aren't we their friends?" I asked.

"God's curse be on both of them!" my father shouted angrily.

The airplanes came so close to the ground that I could feel the reverberation of their engines shaking my body. Then sudden, fearful lights that whistled stripped bare the desert and were followed by shots that "sprayed the people like rain" as Uncle Hassan's wife said the day we met her for the first time two years after that night.

The shouts that rose up from the ground mingled with the explosions coming from the sky, forming an inferno of clamor that still echoes in my ears despite the passage of years. When morning came my mother gave herself up to a fit of hysterics, as did all the women around us, and it was in vain that my father attempted to bring her back to her senses.

Eventually the slaughter came to an end, the airplanes dissolved from our skies and the explosions and all the other noises from the heavens ceased, making way for the crazed noises of the earth, until the blackness of night melted away before the first thread of daylight.

We got up out of our hole and followed our parents in utter exhaustion, our eyes tight closed as ordered by them lest we should see the carnage around us. We made our way to our house but didn't find it; nor did we find Uncle Hassan's house, nor a third house and half a fourth in the same street: they had all become heaps of rubble. On the heap that had been our house one of our geese roamed around in bewilderment; she was followed by one of her young of whom there had been five. There was not a trace of the scent of jasmine in the air.

Like someone in a daze my father stood looking first at the ruins, then at my mother who had been rendered speechless by the unexpected sight. The final and ghastly event of that day was to see my father crying, something I had never seen in all my life.

"A whole life's hard work gone in an instant," my mother muttered through her tears.

"Thanks be to God," mumbled my father, drying his tears, "we weren't inside it." Silence enveloped us for a while, then he said. "You must emigrate into the country—" and in "emigrate" I learned a new word that day.

"Let's go now to your aunt's house," my father resumed, "if it too hasn't been destroyed, until we arrange our affairs."

The melancholy procession re-formed and off we went with miserable gait, "as though at a funeral"—as I used to say whenever I recounted the story to my friends when I had grown up. Before moving away from the ruins of our house I saw my father pick up a protruding piece of stone and hurl it at the big heap of rubble.

"When the war ends," I heard him say, "we'll return and build it again."

And the war ended . . .

My reverie was broken by a jog at my shoulder and my wife's voice saying, "What's wrong with you? Aren't you listening? When shall we start building?"

The specter of the ruins of our house still filled my head.

"Those people who invented all these terrible means of destruction," I said, "why didn't they think of inventing something to protect houses against them?"

Surprise appeared on my wife's face. She stared into mine with questioning tenderness. I smiled and added, sighing and waving my hand as though to chase away my thoughts, "It doesn't matter, because I don't believe there'll be another war."

Which only increased the signs of surprise on my dear wife's face.

Hashish Steals the Night

—⚏—

Shehata al-Erian

'd crossed Cairo from one end to the other so as to arrive at that distant
spot in al-Muqattam. All the while I was going along parallel to the
mountain after coming out of Helwan and going right along the auto-
strade to Sayyida Aisha, where I took the microbus to Duweiqa. I got off at
the end of the route and took another microbus, ending my journey along
the narrow, twisting, snake-like road that takes one to the highest point in
that part of the mountain, among the dwellings of the craftsmen that look
down on Old Cairo. At that time Duweiqa was only known because of the
people who lived there, before it became famous for the disastrous pre-dawn
collapse of a portion of the Muqattam range on top of some of its sleeping
inhabitants, killing more than the Israeli bombardment of Gaza. In general,
it seems that the popular quarters only achieve fame through some disaster.
However, the present story occurred some time before that particular disaster. The broken down microbuses that made the journey up the mountain
were of course unlicensed and were driven by crazy men who were only
half aware of the effect of the stimulants and drugs which had such a market
here—and that is precisely what brought me there.

Just a few steps and I'd be in the flat with all the boys and the primus
stove that had been lit in the living room and placed between the thighs of
the woman with kohl on her eyes who was preparing tea for us, while I and
her husband, my friend, would take turns with a hand-rolled cigarette and

discuss how best to get some hashish. It only took a few minutes for him to get what I required from the hashish seller in the building opposite us.

"By the time you've drunk your tea I'll be back," he said.

"Fine, but let's have something good—not like the last time!"

"That's not fair—after all, the cigarette you've got in your hand is from that lot."

"The smell's all right but it does nothing for one's brain."

The lady whose yawning voice blended with the noise of the Primus intervened, "You haven't really smoked a thing yet. Yesterday a single cigarette sent me all in a whirl and I spent around an hour wandering between the bedroom, the living room, and the kitchen, not knowing who I was, while your friend smoked his cigarette and went into a deep sleep."

I smiled at her and muttered, "We'll see," while saying to myself, "This ass smokes hashish and goes off to sleep and lets a woman like this wander round the flat!" and I told myself that I should urge him to find himself another situation.

"Come along then, man, so we'll be able to smoke a couple of cigarettes together. After that, how about you pass by the butcher to bring us a piece of meat that Umm Tamer can boil for us with some rice and then I'll have dinner with you."

Ragab's features widened into a smile at the mention of meat and rice, and the trip to the butcher at the top of the street gave me a few extra minutes alone with Samia. There had already been skirmishes between us and there was a time when I would have kissed her had it not been for the girl screaming from the nearby room. But where were the boys? Since I had come in I hadn't heard a sound from them, and it was with difficulty that I stopped my tongue from inquiring about them as this would only delay Ragab, who was lazy at the best of times, from setting off. I was in a hurry for him to leave the remaining cigarette in the plate so that I could add the hashish to it and then smoke it with Samia by blowing the smoke from mouth to mouth. The last time we were together she had talked about smoking a cigarette with Ragab in this manner, and I was expecting she would have no objection to doing so, considering what had previously passed between us. Anyway, I would start off our conversation by suggesting we do that.

I handed Ragab a goodly sum of money and said, "So leave this cigarette and when you get back we'll roll into it some of the stuff you bring."

"All right." Having finished his tea, he rose to his feet and Samia said,
"Also get some black pepper 'cos it's finished, and a bag of salt, and a packet
of Cleopatra cigarettes."

He gave her a look of annoyance. "With all that there won't be
enough money."

So I handed him an extra ten pounds, and she said, "Also some cigarette
papers—there are no more than two or three left."

I ignored the remark as the ten pounds was quite enough for the pepper,
the salt, the Cleopatras, and the cigarette papers.

Ragab stood, rocking on his feet slightly before making for the door,
where he turned around to me and said, "I won't be long."

With the closing of the door behind him Samia's face flushed under my
defiant gaze, and her kohl-rimmed eyes flashed a playful look of caution,
while my hands were working with remarkable speed at rolling the cigarette.
When I stood up and made my way to her I realized that I was high. She
laughed at the way I was staggering about. Slipping myself alongside her on
the ground, I stretched out my hand with the cigarette above the fire from the
burning primus stove, its hissing sound prevailing over my whispered, "Good
evening—we'll smoke this cigarette together."

"What do you mean 'together'?" she said coyly.

"Meaning we'll puff the smoke into each other's mouth."

"We'll waste the cigarette and I'll get nothing from you but rudeness."

"Is there anything better than rudeness?"

"You should have come yesterday, my dear."

"When Ragab had gone to sleep?"

"Like the dead."

"Fine, so let's put him to sleep again today."

"How?"

"We'll give him a sleeping pill?"

"You have any?"

"Yes, I do."

"Don't tell me! And how do we give it to him?"

"Dissolve it in his tea."

"No, man? What if it does for him?"

"This is a good chance with the children not being here. By the way, where are they?"

"At my mother's and Mona's with Sameera our neighbor. Mona slept over there at sunset and I'll go get her later."

"And the older boy?"

"Tamer? He's with his father."

"Your first husband?"

"Yes."

I'd lit the cigarette from the burner and had taken a deep puff, bringing my face close to hers. I drew nearer and placed my lips on hers, blowing in the smoke which she imbibed, while I continued to keep her mouth closed playfully until she would push me so as to let out the smoke from her mouth, as she coughed and choked, her face suffused with blood. Speech between us fragmented into intermittent mumblings as we exchanged gulps of smoke from the cigarette, drawing it in through the mouth and exhaling it from the nose as we kissed and groped at each other's bodies. When the cigarette came to an end, it became difficult because we were close to having sex, but expected Ragab back any minute. Hearing his voice raised in returning someone's greeting below the window, Samia jumped to her feet, while I went back to the chair in the corner where I had been sitting. She adjusted her clothing and whispered hurriedly, "Where's this pill?" and I searched around in my pocket for the pill wrapped in cellophane and handed it to her. She stuffed it between her breasts, while saying, "Yes, you leave now and return after he's gone to sleep."

I pointed out to her that the taste of the pill might really change the flavor of the tea and she laughed at my naiveté.

When Ragab opened the door everything was just like it had been the moment he left us. He handed her the parcel of meat and the package of odds and ends, placing the cigarette papers in the dish that lay between him and me. Carefully he extracted the hashish wrapped in cellophane, saying as he pressed it in my hand, "It's the right weight this time."

I weighed it in my hand. "Not all that good," I said, "but what's important is that it's the same as we smoked, because that was really great." He said that it was the same, and Samia got up and went to the kitchen to prepare supper, while Ragab made another round of tea on the Primus, and I prepared the cigarettes we would be smoking with the tea. Afterward I set about hassling him by saying how was it that somebody like him, a frequenter of hashish dens, didn't have a waterpipe that was functioning in his house, so he reluctantly got to his feet to prepare the shisha. He pointed out that there was no coal and no molasses tobacco, which meant providing a further ten pounds and his going down to get them. Meanwhile Samia came from the kitchen with the suggestion that she should put his sleeping pill into the soup. She had already placed the meat on the fire and was rinsing the rice and putting it into a bowl while I was agreeing with her and proposing that she shouldn't add too much pepper as I believed it to be a stimulant and would work against the sleeping pill. But she objected that it was the one thing that would conceal the taste of the pill.

Then in a conspiratorial tone she said, "After supper and the two pipefuls of tobacco, you go and stay away for an hour or so, by which time he'll have gone to sleep, and when you come back don't ring the bell. Just give one knock so he doesn't wake up and I'll be listening out by the door. But if I don't open, it means he's still awake, so you go down again and stay away for a while before coming back."

"Fine."

"And if I don't open the second time it means it hasn't worked. You keep away for today and we make another arrangement."

"There's no question of it not working," I said, rejecting such a possibility. "The pill must work."

"I'm saying just suppose it doesn't, perhaps this one won't affect him."

"Believe me . . ."

I was about to explain to her that a sleeping pill is not like narcotics, but I was interrupted by Ragab's return with the coal and the molasses tobacco. She then went off to the kitchen to wash the rice, taking the meat with her to finish, preparing it in the kitchen, leaving the Primus stove alight for the coal Ragab had brought back with him. Meanwhile, he had begun getting the bits of tobacco ready while I was cutting round pieces of hashish, which I was arranging on the edge of the plate. The piece of hashish had reacted to the warmth of my hand and had become pliable and easy to cut. During this time we were passing round one of the joints I had prepared and talking about the hashish that had been made ready for smoking in the waterpipe. It was my belief that what had caused us to smoke joints instead of shisha was the widespread use of bango, which undermines the sovereignty of hashish; in every quarter dens were crammed full of laughter and intoxicated people, with some dens operating at night and others during the daytime, while some operated all day and all night.

I was looking back nostalgically to those gorgeous far-off days in the mid-1980s when we got to know each other in the den he had in al-Darrasa under the old house that later collapsed and became a ruin. Ragab lived in the rubble for a time before marrying Samia and the two of them then moved to Duweiqa. When he gave up his job as the boss of a really top-class den and went to being the owner of an ordinary den in the hut he'd set up in the ruins—before the authorities got wind of it and did away with it—he changed from being Boss Ragab with a lofty standing, into a coffee-maker working for a daily wage in a café in al-Azhar. He would put in an appearance for a day and absent himself for ten, relying for his livelihood on good fortune coming his way by leading someone from among his old clients, someone like myself, to spend an evening with him in the house, to be repeated two or three times a month. Such evenings would be interspersed by visits from others like Hasan the mechanic, the owner of the repair shop at the beginning of the road and who is regarded as being in charge of supplying bango when hashish is scarce, and Bakr Bayoumi, the employee at the Ministry of Religious Endowments who makes a good living, a man 'with whom God is pleased' and has provided with an excellent job, the blessings from which are unceasing. He turns up with a packet of prepared cigarettes and a kilo of grilled meat and kofta, because God likes to see His favors being bestowed on His servants. There is also Shawki the fruit vendor, who brings along fruit in lavish quantities, and Ragab buys him a great amount of hashish. None of these guys likes the other and I don't like a single one of them, and they all are on the look out for Samia's laughter and comments and her eyes done up with kohl, and they all get high and go off—or that's what I think—but no doubt every one of them has his own arrangement with her.

Whatever happens I must concentrate now on my own arrangements, which look as if they are going to come to fruition tonight. We had finished two pipefuls of the shisha when Samia brought the low, round table and placed it in the middle of the living room, then she gave each of us a bowl of soup in one hand and a spoon in the other before arranging the plates on the table. I was monitoring Ragab's drinking and was drinking myself with a loud sound to encourage him to finish his bowl, praising the tasty soup that had been spiced with a lot of pepper, contrary to my advice to Samia. I was trying to catch her eye to blame her for doing so but her eyes were evading mine and there was a devious smile on her face. Having finished eating, Ragab prepared another pipeful for us to smoke with the tea that was about to be served. I noticed that he was looking sleepy, which he put down to the heavy meal, and he seized the opportunity of Samia being away in the kitchen washing the plates to ask me for a stimulant pill. I had a couple on me just in case, so I gave him one, keeping the other for myself to take in the café where I would be waiting till he fell asleep. In any case, it was convenient for me to go now, having finished the tea and smoked the last pipeful, leaving Ragab with a piece of hashish.

On the road I encountered a breeze that was cold after the warmth of the living room, adulterated as it was with a spray of water. I pulled my sweater around my body and found myself a place in an inner corner of the café, keeping well away from the winds outside. I occupied my time with tea and coffee and a pipeful of molasses tobacco and concentrated on what had happened up till now and on the many possibilities that might yet occur, and ended up concentrating all my thoughts on Samia. She was the woman I'd been after for the last quarter of a century, ever since she became a dressed-up new bride crossing the street in front of Ragab's hashish den in Darrasa on her way to her husband's house on the opposite sidewalk. She was as thin as a young child and didn't know how to make up her face, so it looked comic under the vivid make-up and the heavy kohl. She then became plumper and more skilled at making herself up, but it had taken her a long time before she became pregnant with her first child from her previous husband, and since she was on the short side, with pregnancy she took on the appearance of a woman always about to give birth, with full thighs, buttocks, and breasts.

Though rounded of stomach, she always had attractive features with shining black eyes that sparkled with liveliness and a sexual attractiveness that bore a whiff of black magic. Ten peaceful years of her life went by before anything occurred between her and Ragab. She had given birth to two girls, both of whom had died after the first child, a boy, had been born with Down's syndrome, something that had spoiled her relationship with her husband who owned the haberdashery store in the Muski. And so she became of necessity the girlfriend of Ragab, whose own situation had deteriorated after the hashish den was destroyed and it became a shed in the ruins with a limited number of clients and a small income. He would go to her when she was replacing her husband in the shop, who had gone to have lunch and take an afternoon nap at home, and take the money she'd made from her sales. Then he would go to visit her in the house when her husband went back to the shop after his afternoon nap. This went on till the husband discovered the ruined state of the shop shortly after he had become aware of the ruined state of the house. He then held her responsible for the money made from the goods, so she screamed out and the people gathered round. She said that he had behaved dishonestly toward her and that she wouldn't live with him after what had happened, so she collected the boy and went back to her father's house in Qurtum Lane. All attempts at reconciling them failed, so they divorced on condition that she would leave the boy with him and would see him at intervals. She did this, with Ragab promising to marry her, and that was how things ended up.

When the government removed Ragab's hut from among the ruins, he and Samia took her savings, alimony, and the gold that she possessed and bought this flat in Duweiqa. The government, when removing the hut, had also arrested Ragab on a charge of dealing drugs, a charge he escaped thanks to a lawyer who was related to her father, who discovered some errors in the legal proceedings. And so it was that Ragab found himself on the street and was taken in by the owner of the café in al-Azhar to work half a shift without any pay, having to rely on the generosity of the clients who discovered that he was working without pay. He continued at the job reluctantly until the situation improved a bit for him, after which things never improved again. In fact, things only got worse when Samia had twins twice so that he now had two girls and two boys from only two births. He was saved from having a third lot of twins by a miracle when Samia had a miscarriage after getting a good thrashing, following which she was advised not to get pregnant again for a while so as to preserve her future fertility. During this time Ragab's brothers had sold the ruined lot and had given him his share, while Samia emerged from the experience of having a miscarriage to join her opium-smoking father in selling vegetables in the al-Azhar market. Her life with Ragab temporarily improved after a reconciliation, though it ended up with the loss of their remaining capital. She said that her father conned her and stole her money, so she went back to Duweiqa, without a bean to her name, to join Ragab in his struggle. He had doubts about her, believing she had conspired with her father to strip him of his inheritance so as to secure her authority over him. Ragab only went off to his job in order to satisfy himself by meeting his old clients with a taste for drugs, and to achieve some small earnings from selling hashish now and then "outside the house" as Samia demanded; she now harbored distrust for the modern times, the neighbors, and even Ragab himself. And so it was that life went on its way.

Having spent an hour there, I paid the man at the café, feeling that the stimulant was doing its job adequately, and gave the door that single knock we'd agreed on. When I heard nothing from inside, I stood listening for a while. Then I went off for the second time to the only café that was still open, but which was on the verge of closing down, the night's coldness having emptied it of all clients apart from myself and four people who were playing cards in the opposite corner, and an Upper Egyptian vendor who was selling men's underpants. It looked as though he had nowhere to go and that he was coming to some arrangement with the owner of the café so that he could stay there till the morning. I found myself obliged to witness the negotiations between them whereby the Upper Egyptian regarded the payment of one pound to the owner of the café, in addition to his being an unpaid guard, as quite adequate, though the owner was insisting on no less than five pounds and that he should keep the man's identity card as security. They ended up by agreeing to three pounds, with the café owner taking the television set with him because the television at home had conked out; he also took the precaution of rolling down the metal shutter and locking it from the outside after he'd given the Upper Egyptian the chance of relieving himself in a dark area outside. These negotiations, the departure of the men who had been gambling, and the tidying up of the café took another half an hour, during which time I felt embarrassed and fed up since there was no longer any reason for my being there. The café owner had carried away the television set and placed it on the pavement and his young assistant had lowered the metal shutter halfway down and the Upper Egyptian was preparing himself to stretch out and go to sleep. I paid the bill and did my best to avoid the café owner's inquiries: where was I from, and where was I going, and what was I doing here at this late hour, and he hadn't seen me before tonight, not even passing by in the street. I escaped from the man's cross-examination, saying that I was in a hurry, and I set off walking aimlessly in the empty streets where the homes of craftsmen were, with the cold wind slapping at my face and with hashish in my pocket which would be difficult to explain away if I happened to be stopped by one of the police patrols going about on foot or in vehicles. I went up to Ragab's flat, determined to knock on the door till Samia opened it, and if she woke up Ragab I could say that maybe I'd forgotten the keys and had come back to look for them after having reached Sayyida Aisha. I knocked on the door and waited. I knocked a second time with force and waited. Then I rang the bell insistently. After some moments Ragab opened the door. He was dishevelled and in his pajamas. He was surprised to see me and I quickly said to him, "Haven't I forgotten my keys here?"

He stood at a loss, not finding anything to say, and it didn't seem as though he wanted to invite me in. But I entered and went to the chair on which I had been sitting and asked him to turn on the light so that I could look for my keys. When I didn't find them on the chair or the sofa, or under either of them, I asked him to wake up Samia as she had perhaps found them after he had gone to sleep. He went in and came out to tell me that Samia wasn't there, explaining that when she found him going off to sleep she had gone upstairs to Sameera to bring back the daughter who was sleeping up there, and maybe she had stayed there for a while, saying that of course I was aware how women loved to chatter. I asked him to sprinkle a bit of water on his face and to go up to Sameera to ask Samia about the keys. He mumbled something in protest saying that Sameera was living on her own after her divorce and that it wasn't proper for a man to knock at her door at such an hour, also that he didn't even know which flat was hers and he was afraid he might be knocking at the neighbors' door, so he asked for me to sit and wait for Samia who wouldn't be long. I was at a loss and didn't know what to do, having completely forgotten that my keys were in my pocket, so I found myself saying that if I didn't find them I would most likely break down the door of my flat as there was no one living with me and no copy of these keys to be found anywhere. Ragab went off to bring the primus stove from the kitchen so that he could make us tea till Samia turned up.

He lighted the fire redolent with kerosene, lighting up the darkness of my mind. I said to myself: This woman must have a boyfriend and she's taken advantage of my ruse to put her husband to sleep and has gone off to join him, betting on my shyness and irresolution which she had reckoned would prevent me from waking up her husband.

But what about Ragab being so untroubled at her absence?

I told him to prepare us a couple of pipefuls of tobacco with the tea, and he placed two pieces of coal alongside the tea. I took out the cellophane of hashish, having lit the kettle, which had started its humming sound. The warmth rose up inside me and prepared me to stay on until morning or so that I could find out her secret.

We had finished the set of pipefuls and Ragab had gone off to change the water of the goza when I found the door being opened and Samia entering, carrying her sleeping child covered up on her shoulder. She was surprised at finding me there so I explained to her in a loud voice so that Ragab, who was in the kitchen, might hear, and she said that she hadn't seen any keys and went inside to put the child to sleep. Her eyes and mine met up in two big questions: What had induced her to say, directing her words to Ragab in a loud voice, that she had gone to bring the girl from Sameera's? I was at a loss to understand why she had made all these arrangements with me, but I now had an excuse for staying on till the morning: it was now late and I wouldn't find anyone to help me to open the door and I couldn't disturb my neighbors at such an hour, so let's sleep on it.

Ragab put down the now-clean goza between us as he mumbled, "That's fine, sir." He looked disappointed, waiting for Samia to reply. He then went inside and I heard a whispered conversation between them, after which he came out looking joyful because Samia allowed me to stay till the morning, making it possible for me to stretch out on the sofa in the living room "after we have our evening together."

"No question of sleeping or anything like it," I answered. "We'll spend the evening together and at the first glimmer of morning light I'll take off."

In preparation for the rest of the evening, which would be a long one, I put the bit of opium I had under my tongue, while Ragab was occupied with pouring out the tea and sweetening it. I had a vague hope that Ragab, by some miracle, would go to sleep, but he didn't seem to have reacted to the sleeping pill—if Samia really had put it in his soup.

This bitch of a woman came back from outside looking even more beautiful than she had earlier in the night. I cursed the cold that had chased away the customers and had closed the café down, as well as my fear of the authorities brought about by the hashish in my pocket. Had I stayed outside a little longer everything would have gone as I had planned.

I became aware of Ragab's voice asking me to take a drag on the pipe, as the mouth-reed of the waterpipe was between my lips. I took such a strong pull that it lit up the pipeful of tobacco with an explosive noise that brought a laughing Samia from inside, giving vent to one of her unforgettable remarks.

"What's up with you? You're smoking like someone whose house has gone to ruins. Be careful the piece doesn't get into your throat."

I burst out laughing and passed her the mouthpiece, while she demanded Ragab fetch her a fresh pipeful of tobacco, pointing out that someone who smoked like me couldn't have someone smoking after him.

For an hour or two the pipe was passed around followed by glasses of tea until the two of them began yawning and Samia, first of all, went off and handed Ragab a blanket for me, for I had made up my mind to stretch out on the sofa. She thought it was a good idea, especially as there were only two or three hours to go till daylight. Ragab encouraged me to get some sleep and blew out the fire, leaving me the light to put out when I wanted and off he went.

I lit a cigarette and finished it; then I went off to have a pee before getting ready for sleep.

While walking through the corridor on my return to the living room I was brought to a halt by the screaming sounds of a woman in intercourse coming through from the other side of the closed door. I put out the living room light and stretched out as I listened with all my attention to the convulsive screaming becoming louder and louder, and I naturally realized, despite my heavy state of intoxication, that they were having sex.

This went on for several minutes before the sounds quieted down, while I myself attained a climax of excitement. I then heard their door opening and, most likely, the sound of Ragab's feet as he made his way to the bathroom, because I could still hear the quick breathing of Samia coming through from the room. He then came back and the door was closed again and silence reigned. This time it went on for a long time until my hopes that Ragab would go to sleep and that Samia would come out died, and I too, in the end, entered a troubled sleep.

When I was woken by Ragab, the sun was flooding a square on the floor of the living room the size of the shutters of the window whose glass had been shut so as to keep out the morning cold of the month of Amsheer. He needed some money to buy breakfast and cigarettes. I went off to the bathroom to wash my face and found that Samia was in the kitchen making tea.

"So what happened?" I said to her with a laugh.

"What happened?"

"Weren't we agreed?"

"All right. Couldn't you have been a bit more patient? I was at Sameera's getting ready for you."

"My goodness!"

"Honestly. She has a bath and hot water, also the girl was sleeping over there and I had to bring her back."

"And Ragab—it seems he wasn't sleeping or anything of the sort and the man was in fine form, so that was it."

"You heard?" and then she laughed before saying, "Ah, I forgot. Believe me it didn't last more than that—bing bang. Two or three minutes and that was it. He has left me to myself till the coming Friday."

"Is that really true?"

"Also last night he was doing his very best."

Then, sadly, she adds, "He wasn't like that in the beginning."

I recollected that I had given him an upper. I told her about it and how I now regretted it. She was laughing, while I was trying to get hold of her, but she'd slip from my grasp. She had rolled up her hair and she looked extremely attractive in her house clothes. But she brushed me off saying that Ragab might be back at any moment, and there would be plenty of times to come.

"When?" I say to her.

"Next Thursday. It's my cousin's wedding and I shan't be going because I've quarreled with the bride's family and afterward Ragab will be taking the children with him, which means that you can come and I'll be on my own."

She pushed me into the living room, and she came after me to ask for twenty pounds as a loan.

"I'll repay you on Thursday."

I gave her the money, telling myself in a low tone, "You'll never see that again," but Sayyid Ahmad Abdel Gawad got a Zubayda in the end and it doesn't seem as if my state of affairs is anything like his, and of course I have no ambition to be like Kamal, for he, like me, was unlucky in love and all that is left to me is Yasin and there's nothing wrong with him except for impetuosity and extravagance to the extent of causing problems for himself.

Samia stood openmouthed listening to that strange talk but she was used to me sometimes saying things she didn't understand. Now, Ragab returned with beans and bread, so she hastened to say to him with a smile, "Your friend's been talking gibberish first thing in the morning."

"Let him be—the Lord will put him right."

After breakfast the two of them were going down to al-Azhar, so I accompanied them for the first part of the way.

Eyes Staring into Space

Mansoura Ez Eldin

Did he really exist—that boy whom I met five times at the most and with whom I talked on the telephone once a week?

I am careful to place him in a far corner of my memory and to talk about him as though I'm talking about a fictional character, and I tremble with fear when someone I know reminds me of his actual existence.

I gaze at the bare walls of my sparsely furnished room, stealing troubled looks at the mirror, after which my hand moves automatically to the telephone. I raise it and press with my finger on the seven numerals I have memorized so well. I satisfy myself that there is no voice replying, but then my smile disappears and I almost stop breathing when his voice, barely, comes through to me:

"Hullo."

I don't say anything.

"Hullo. Hullo."

" . . ."

"Speak, you ass."

In a hotel from the forties in central downtown I saw him with a group of my friends. He said that he knew of me from an extremely long way back and that he had been waiting for me ever since he heard my name, then he gave a vague smile. I knew that there was some weird story being woven and I was intimidated by the confident way he talked of it, the sort of confidence that appears to derive from a knowledge of the unknown.

The boy who had waited for me for so long informed me that I have the eyes of a wild tiger and the mentality of a hunter, and I brought to mind the picture of the tiger that my father had given me on my ninth birthday and the target practice I took with the old rifle.

After some minutes the boy and I took off. We walked along streets, with me carrying a bunch of red roses he had bought me, while he told me of the marvelous moments he had lived through and others that awaited him. I sensed an endless lightness and yearned to dance under the lights in a vast empty square. But when I went to sleep on my own at the end of the night, I dreamed of him and woke up screaming, and didn't divulge to a soul what I had seen.

In my dream I'm in a street I know well. I'm sitting at an old café and sipping my coffee. My hand is stained with blood, and in a flat in the building opposite I see him lying immersed in his own blood, while, with the coldness of a professional killer, I await the coming of the police. On another occasion I saw a thick rope encircling my neck and men dressed in black gazing at me with hatred, while his eyes, quite without any expression, were following me.

He was standing in the space halfway between me and sleep: between me and a girl I know, with his vague looks and satisfied smile that I hadn't previously seen on him. He comes to me in dreams with a shout and drops of blood that widen and daggers that fly toward me in the space between us.

After I had dreamed of myself several times in that old café, I decided to look for it, and I actually found it on 26th July Street in Bulaq Abu al-Ila, and I was struck by the similarity between it and how I had pictured it in my dreams.

I was in the habit of going to it daily after finishing at work and then examining a particular balcony on the third floor of the building opposite. I was certain that the boy was not to be found there, for the simple reason that he lives in Helwan. This was the only thing that kept me from the brink of madness. Many times I decided to stop calling him, but for some unknown reason I was unable to put my decision into practice. It was as though there was some hidden force that was pushing me to him and there was nothing for me to do but obey and go along with my inevitable fate.

I hear his sleepy voice and I make up ordinary conversations like those that occur between friends. He answers me gently and I repeat to myself that there is nothing unnatural about it and that it is nothing more than a normal relationship like those that bind me to other people.

The boy talks about his mother and his sister and about his quarrels with his father, and when I feel that I am on the point of feeling sympathy for him, he brings the conversation to a close with some banal words as an escape from a possible emotional entanglement.

Often I would ring him up only to find that no one was answering, and I would smile at having scored a victory and would tell myself that what had happened previously were merely illusions. In order to make sure that I was right, I would go on trying to contact him till he would destroy my feeling of joy at hearing his still-sleepy voice. He would pronounce my name before I spoke which caused me to believe that I was the sole woman who was in contact with him; this being a way of escaping from another belief that was dogging me, namely that he knew when I would be contacting him even before I myself had decided on it, and that he knew everything I was thinking, that perhaps even it was he who was pushing such thoughts into my mind.

In the middle of a conversation I was having, I said, without any preamble, "Do you know Umm Quwaiq?"

"Yes, it's a sort of owl."

"My grandmother used to say that when Umm Quwaiq hoots at night, it's because it wants to see the blood of a human being, and when it does so it stays silent and leaves the place for somewhere else. Do you know that there's an Umm Quwaiq living in a tree alongside the window of my room, and every night, from one o'clock till two it begins to hoot."

"Is that really so?"

"Indeed, it's exactly five months ago, just when I got to know you."

"What are you saying? Are you saying that it'd like to see my blood or yours?"

He said this final phrase with a deep and frightening calm, so I answered him back, "Did you believe what I was saying?"

"I was asking myself what had happened to you—you were so sensible."

I learned never to speak of what was going through my mind for fear it would increase my terror at words that might have been said offhandedly and unintentionally.

Despite our long telephone conversations we met only occasionally, meetings that occurred by chance during which we would behave with great caution and anxiety, each of us striving to end it quickly as though we were two other people or there was some agreement between us about set rules for the game.

I was fleeing from the fact of his actual existence in front of me; thus through the telephone it was possible for me to rely on the illusion that he did not exist. As for when I did see him, this belief would then be regarded as a kind of madness.

The last time I met him was also by chance, downtown in Mustafa Kamel Square. I merely greeted him and he went off at speed as though he was being chased by ghosts.

I stood for a moment in the square facing several streets from which I chose one to cross. All of a sudden I found myself in a street that was unfamiliar to me and empty of passersby; also its buildings looked larger than they should.

At once an image of his face sprang into my mind and for the first time I thought that there was something inhuman in the way he looked at me. My heart was racing and I ran off as fast as I could. I had the sensation that fearsome eyes were staring into me from behind. The street had become so long that it was only after more than an hour that I reached the end of it, and—contrary to logic—I found myself in front of the statue of Mustafa Kamel, from where I had begun my journey.

At exactly one o'clock at night I reached the Abdel Moneim Riyad bus stop. My eyes scanned the people waiting there but I didn't spot him. Having boarded the microbus, I looked out of the window. I came to myself only when my neighbor prodded me as a request that I should pay my fare. I handed the money to him without seeing him. After some minutes I glanced in his direction and found myself looking at extremely sharp features and frightening eyes that were staring at me. I collected what little courage still remained within me lest my glance be broken in front of my eyes so strongly and deeply concentrated.

Suddenly he shouted at the driver, "On your right," and he got off the bus at great speed and walked off in the opposite direction, while I began to tremble all over. While I slept I dreamed of many flaming eyes aimed at me while I lay naked in my bed, quite unable to get up despite my desperate efforts.

The next morning I didn't go to work. Having placed in my handbag a sharp knife I had bought a while ago, I went out.

The Dancer

Shawqi Faheem

There were five of us in the Peugeot. Not one of us uttered so much as a word during the two hours the journey took from the village to the mountain where the family graveyard was. It was a heavy, conspiratorial silence that was pervaded by the sound of the engine and the ringlets of smoke and dust.

There was no one more present in the car than Madeeha.

Madeeha, my cousin, just twenty-one years old. Last night had been the night of her eldest sister's marriage, with Madeeha being the most beautiful girl I'd seen in my whole life. Last night she had been even more beautiful.

In the middle of a licentious song that the girls were intoning, suddenly the sound of drumbeats rang out, beats of dance music that pervaded the bodies of the young girls like a bolt of electricity. Madeeha rushed into the middle of the dance floor as if drawn by some magical power. She tied a scarf round her slim hips and loosened the long tresses of hair that then flew about to the rhythm of the drums and the undulations of her body as she danced with flowing tenderness. Then, with the rhythm becoming more intense, her body, with all its vigor, harmonized with it, while I stood alongside my older uncle, who is also Madeeha's uncle, and when she spun toward us, I noticed that her lips were open and her peacefully enchanting smile was directed toward me and my elderly uncle—and for some moments I saw on his face a mixture of obscure passion behind his bushy mustache and white turban.

(I see Madeeha every day on the morning train, with all of us, the youth of the village, making for the university and the higher educational institutions in the capital of the governorate. She treats me as the youngest of her cousins, but I would always look at her, in the company of her colleagues, as being replete with vigor and gaiety.)

The drumbeats slowed down and to the slower rhythm Madeeha began to extemporize a dance like modified strokes on a violin, employing the suppleness of her body in a way that overwhelmed those present so that silence reigned over them all.

In a corner of the hall sat a woman some sixty years of age. She was dressed in black and had a silver ring piercing the left side of her nose and a green tattoo under her mouth. She hadn't lifted her gaze from Madeeha.

The woman in black said, "May God preserve your youthfulness, my little girl! How is it that you're pregnant and can dance like that? What would your dancing be like if you weren't pregnant? Be careful, my girl, of what you have in your stomach!"

The drumbeats were silent and Madeeha stood still, clinging to the arms of the girls until she was seated and they were drying her sweat. Madeeha's mother broke through the silence with a resounding voice directed at the face of the woman in black.

"Shut up, you whore. My daughter's a virgin and more respectable than all your people!"

The woman didn't reply, her lips merely opened into a smile that revealed a front tooth covered with gold.

The girls carried Madeeha up to the top floor where they laid her down on her bed, in a state of exhaustion and pale of face.

Madeeha's mother ordered the women to go on with their singing and dancing and demanded the woman in black leave the place. As she left she muttered, "I came only to get what I'm owed."

The bridegroom's relatives said that they didn't know her and that she hadn't come with them and that they thought that she was a relative of the bride.

No one knows when this woman arrived or how she got in.

Some said that she was a gypsy, one of those who roamed the villages telling people's fortunes by throwing down shells.

Madeeha having left, the air of joyfulness also departed, and the attempt to go back to dancing and singing failed. It was as if everyone in the house had been struck dumb, though the echo of the words of the gypsy woman still rang in the ears of them all, and like lightning had flown into the streets of the village and its houses.

The elderly uncle came up to the woman and took her away by the hand. Before leaving the hall he signed to me to go with him. He took her to a room that was used for storage in the back courtyard of the house. We entered and he locked the door. I looked into the woman's face and she returned my gaze with penetrating black eyes.

From behind one of the sacks my uncle brought out a large knife, which he unsheathed in the face of the woman.

"I'll sever your head from your body right now if you don't explain what you've said about our daughter."

She didn't bat an eyelid. Staring into my uncle's face, she said, "Let the doctor decide between us! If I'm lying, then chop off my head. I'm quite capable of putting my head back on my body!"

My uncle looked really scared, but he quickly took control of the situation and shouted at me, "Take this gypsy woman and lock her up until God decides about the matter."

I took her by the hand and moved toward the door. Before we left the gypsy woman turned toward my uncle and addressed him in a deep, penetrating voice, "The fair girl that you intend to marry in place of your wife will be the ruin of you."

He drew away from her.

"And the man who took the bribe from you for him to play around with the papers so that your son wouldn't have to go into the army, that man's a crook so be careful that not a soul knows about this matter!"

My uncle was alarmed and his large mustache was trembling.

"Sit down, Hagga," he said to her in trembling tones. Then addressing me, he said, "Go and bring a plateful of meat and rice for the Hagga."

"I don't want anything to eat or drink. Take me to the bus stop so I can leave your village—I've got a lot of work to do."

My uncle offered her a large sum of money, but she refused. I accompanied her to the bus stop.

The wedding came to an end in silence. The bride cried when she learnt that her sister Madeeha was ill and confined to bed.

The next morning, before sunrise, my uncle went up to the top floor and made his way to the room where Madeeha was sleeping.

Madeeha's mother was aware that he was there. Jumping out of bed, she stood in his path and screamed at him at the top of her voice, "Don't go near her! My daughter is virtue itself!"

"Then go inside and tell her to come with us to the doctor."

The mother was silent for a moment before rushing into Madeeha's room and shutting the door behind her.

A few minutes later she came out and faced the head of the family.

"Not a soul is going to touch my daughter—not you or the doctor!"

He pushed her and she fell to the ground. He made his way to Madeeha's room and opened the door. She was sitting quietly on the bed.

"I'm ready," she said in a normal tone of voice.

One of her brothers took hold of the mother, while my uncle dragged Madeeha down to the ground floor. I was walking behind them, with the reverberating sound of funeral drumbeats in my ears.

I knew what was going to happen, while she was pale and beautiful like a sheep in front of its butcher.

A Place under the Dome

—⟋⟍⟍⟋—

Abdul Rahman Fahmy

I got to know him when I was working at the Municipality of Kafr Dawwar. At that time I was a bachelor and divided my day between working at the Municipality and sitting in the station buffet. At first glance he didn't attract my notice for he was one of those Sufi sheikhs with a green turban, a gown made up of all the seven colors of the spectrum and a long, whittled stick, a man in no way different from other dervishes except for his excessive shabbiness and his disregard to the dirt stains on his gown and his white matted beard that had never been trimmed or combed.

I was sitting in the café the first time I saw him. He stood in front of me for a long time, then pointed his stick at me.

"Don't trouble yourself," he shouted at me. "It's no use."

On looking at him I immediately realized that I was in front of a man who was living in a different world from mine and that his conversation should not be taken too seriously.

"What's no use?"

"The matter you're troubling yourself about. I'm telling you it's no use. Leave things to God and get me a glass of cinnamon."

He threw himself into the chair on the opposite side of the table, and leaning his stick against his thigh, began mumbling things to himself which I couldn't make out but which I took to be verses from the Quran. I clapped my hands and Abduh the waiter hurried across and I ordered the cinnamon.

"For Sheikh Sabir?" he asked, pointing at the man sitting with me.

Before I could answer Sheikh Sabir had shouted:

"Yes, for Sheikh Sabir—a fiery cinnamon with Sidi Utaiti's blessings."

When Abduh brought the cinnamon Sheikh Sabir sipped at it with a noise that roared in the ears of everyone sitting in the café, then he rose hastily to his feet and hurried off, shouting:

"Sidi Utaiti—my beloved, my quest!"

He hadn't thought of thanking me for the cinnamon or even of saying goodbye.

"Do you know him?" I asked Abduh the waiter.

"That's Sidi Utaiti's beloved. Haven't you see him before?"

He then related to me his story.

No one in the town knew where he'd come from. They had woken up one day to find him among them, having taken Sidi Utaiti's tomb as his home. This particular tomb lay on the outskirts of the town amid surrounding fields; it was a small domed shrine in a state of dilapidation, several of the stones having fallen from its walls and its wooden window having been smashed so that it lay on the ground under the opening. No one thought of renovating it until one morning Sheikh Sabir appeared. He began doing up the tumbledown walls, replaced the wooden window and repaired the cracked door, then he went off to the house of one of the rich merchants and rapped on his door with his stick.

"O you who are rich," he shouted at him, "God is richer than you. Don't set yourself up falsely against God—and send a mat to Sidi Utaiti's shrine."

In this way he was able to spread mats on the ground round the tomb and to get himself a kerosene lamp with which to light the place at night. Then he took up residence alongside the tomb where he would spend the night praying and holding discourse with Sidi Utaiti in a voice that could be heard out in the road. When morning came he would wander through the streets of Kafr Dawwar uttering the name of God and calling upon Sidi Utaiti.

I used to see him from time to time. Sometimes he would ask me for a glass of cinnamon, at others he would refuse it if I offered, but always he would seat himself in the chair opposite me, across the table, and speak disjointedly of things I did not understand. Then, one day, he stood in front of me, pointed his stick at me, and shouted:

"Why are you annoying your father? Go and make it up with him and kiss his hand."

My father having died several years before, I said to him:

"And from whom did you learn I had annoyed my father? Did he tell you?"

"Sidi Utaiti told me. He came to me in a dream and said to me: 'Sabir, go and advise your café friend that he should make it up with his father.'"

"I myself can't go to him. Let Sidi Utaiti give him my greetings. When will you be seeing him?"

"When will I be seeing him?" he shouted angrily. "Every night he's with me—I perform the dawn prayer behind him. O my beloved, my quest, O Sidi Utaiti. Come on—get me the cinnamon."

Then he threw himself into the chair and began muttering verses from the Quran.

"Have you known Sidi Utaiti long?" I asked him as he sipped at his cinnamon.

"I'm his servant, his slave. O Sidi Utaiti. O . . ."

"And who," I interrupted him, "gave you the job of being his servant?"

"He—my beloved and my master."

Then, taking a reverberating sip from his glass of cinnamon, he went on:

"I was living like you—one of the dogs of this world. I was preoccupied with my belly until Sidi Utaiti came to me in a dream and said: 'O Sabir, have shame and turn to God in repentance. Come to my sanctuary, I want you.' And he began to rain down blow on me, and when I awoke I found that his stick had left marks on my shoulders. I gave up the world and all it contains and came to his sanctuary. I read the Fatiha for him—O my beloved, O Sidi Utaiti."

Then calling out to him, he hurried off.

The days passed and I learnt that a large company in Kafr Dawwar had bought a big tract of land on which to build a club for its employees and Sidi Utaiti's shrine was within it. Seeing Sheikh Sabir one night in the café, I asked:

"Is the company intending to destroy Sidi Utaiti's shrine?"

Letting go the glass of cinnamon, he seized his stick and waved it about in the air, shouting, "Sidi Utaiti's power for good will destroy every slanderous tyrant."

"But they'll have to destroy the shrine," I said, "or at least move it."

"I'm telling you, Sidi Utaiti is stronger than them—tomorrow you'll see."
He returned to his cinnamon and when he had finished it he hurried off.

The following days proved that Sidi Utaiti's power for good was in truth 'stronger than them' for the company that was going to build on the land decided to rebuild the shrine and to construct round it a mosque for those employees who wished to perform their prayers.

One night Sheikh Sabir came to me, ordered his cinnamon, and said, "Do you see Sheikh Utaiti's power for good?"

"That they'll build him a new shrine?"

"The hand of the man who wanted to destroy the shrine became paralyzed."

"God's greatness, O Sidi Utaiti."

"Every time he raised the pick to strike at the wall his hand stayed suspended in the air. Didn't I tell you?"

Two months passed during which Sheikh Sabir supervised the building of the new shrine and the mosque. He would spend his day with the workmen, shouting and calling upon Sidi Utaiti, and at night he would sleep alongside the tomb among the piled-up stones, until the building was completed in all its glory: windows of worked iron, the floor of white marble, the walls painted in rich colors and decorated in gold, the broken-down door changed for a fine carved one. The floor was strewn with elegant carpets, while a massive electric chandelier hung from the ceiling, its pure crystal beads sparkling. Sheikh Sabir began wandering through the town's streets calling out at everyone, "Sidi Utaiti's got himself a palace. Sidi Utaiti has become the best holy man in the district. O my beloved, my quest, O Sidi Utaiti!"

The company finished setting up the club and fixed a day for the opening. A party was held in the evening so that people could get to know one another. It lasted till midnight and when Sheikh Sabir went to Sidi Utaiti's shrine to spend the night in prayer as usual, the company's manager was leaving the party with his family and met up with Sheikh Sabir at the front door. Sheikh Sabir endeavored to pass by him and to make his way through the groups of employees who had gone out to say goodbye to him. The manager's notice was attracted by his shabby, patched clothes and thick, unkempt beard, so he called the doorman and asked, "Who's that?"

"That's Sidi Utaiti's servant."

"And who's this Sidi Utaiti?"

"The sheikh who's inside."

"And that's the man who's looking after his tomb? Looking as filthy as that?"

"Yes."

"No. Get rid of him. Tomorrow I'll go to Cairo and bring you another sheikh who's a bit cleaner-looking."

And so Sheikh Sabir was turned out of Sidi Utaiti's palace.

When I saw him one night in the café he was sad and glum.

"How did they turn you out of Sidi Utaiti's shrine when it was he who ordered you to be his servant?"

He lowered his stick to the ground and said, "It's not they who turned me out; it was Sidi Utaiti himself who turned me out."

"It was he who turned you out?"

"Yes, he came to me at night in a dream and said to me, 'I don't want you, Sabir—I've got myself someone better than you.'"

There was a ring of grief in his voice that shook me to my depths.

"And what will you do now?" I asked him.

"Your Lord is more powerful than all."

"Where will you go? With whom will you spend your nights?"

"I'll go off and look around for a sheikh of my own size, someone whose circumstances are as wretched as mine, seeing as how Sidi Utaiti has become too exalted for us."

The Story of Black Knight

———✠———

Hosam Fakhr

I was riding my beautiful black horse, with its long mane billowing in the wind, and I was riding really fast in the corridor, while Granny Amina, with an aluminum dish in front of her, was sitting at the dinner table topping the okra. She'd take off the neck of the okra with the knife and then remove the black threads from the sides, letting them remain sticking to her fingers. When we arrived at the mountain peak, I found that my horse was tired, in a sweat and panting for breath because of the long distance we'd traveled. So I dismounted and we went into the dining room. When I tied him to the arm of the sofa he neighed, and it was as though he was thanking me. Without raising her head or pushing up her glasses, I found my granny asking me, "Does this horse of yours fly?"

"Yes, of course."

"And he drinks nothing but drops of dew?"

"Yes, that's right."

"And he eats nothing but sugar and peeled almonds?"

"That's it exactly."

"Then it must be him."

"Who's he?"

"The son of the filly I had when I was your age—or perhaps he's her grandson. What's his name?"

"I haven't given him a name."

"What a thing to say! Of course he must have a name. What color is he?"

"He's black."

"Then what do you think about calling him 'Black Knight'?"

"That's a really beautiful name—agreed."

"All right, then come and sit beside me while I tell you about 'White Mane,' the filly I had. I was at boarding school and I was sitting there really fed up with my life and saying, 'O God, get me out of here in any way possible, right away if you please.' Before finishing my supplication, I found she had come down to me from the sky—as white as cream and her mane so long and just like silk billowing in the wind. She landed on the balcony and I found she'd got a velvet saddle on her, while the stirrups were of silver, so I mounted her. I tell you frankly I was scared. How could I ride a filly that wasn't known to me and when I didn't know where she'd take me? I just told myself that it was an outing and I'd amuse myself and then go back to the school very discreetly. She flew off with me higher and higher. Do you know where she took me? She took me to the moon. All the horses of this family are very fond of going to the moon because of the gardens there that produce nothing but peeled almonds. Yes, the almonds come out on the trees already peeled and ready for eating. Also, my dear sir, up there are rivers of dew drops, so the horses go there and eat and drink and enjoy themselves and while they're at it they see their friends and relatives. Black Knight hasn't taken you there yet? Never mind, God willing he'll take you tomorrow. Now, where were we? Oh yes, on the moon. After she'd taken me for an outing and had shown me what no eye had seen, nor ear heard, nor single human experienced, she took me back to the school. Before leaving me on the balcony, she asked me, 'Amina, do you want us to speak to each other in Arabic or in English?' I said to her, 'In Arabic of course, for heaven's sake! Isn't it enough that I'm forbidden to speak it at school?' So she said, 'All right, go off to sleep now and tomorrow night think about where you'd like to go. Good night to you.'

"Naturally the following day there I was standing like a sentry on the balcony after the sunset prayer. She didn't come till after the evening prayer and I was almost in tears fearing she wouldn't come at all. As soon as she landed she said to me, 'Where do you want to go today?' What I said to myself was that I'd really like to see the Taj Mahal. 'Nothing easier,' she said. 'Jump on.'

Of course you know where that place is? It's in India—it's a beautiful building, like a palace in heaven, with lakes and rivers and gardens full of flowers in front of it. It was built by a king called Shah Jehan who was married to a very beautiful, very pleasant, and very good-hearted lady who was called Mumtaz Mahal. He was madly in love with her so he had no concubines like the kings of that time and wasn't prepared to have any other wife. They lived happily together for ever after and had several children, boys and girls. But what disappointments life brings! One day Mumtaz Mahal woke up tired, her face all pale. They brought her doctors from all over the place but there was nothing to be done. When God took her, Shah Jehan wept and wailed in grief and later decided that he must make the most beautiful building in the world and make it like a sort of paradise for her to be buried in, and when his time came he would be there alongside her. He told the architect that he should position it so that he could see it from any of the palace's windows. Just imagine what faithful love he had!

"If only you'd seen the Taj Mahal with its white marble and red roses. It's so beautiful. But even more beautiful is the love that built it. As soon as I got there I recited the Fatiha for the two of them. Then I went out for a walk in the gardens to have a look at their beauty. After a while my filly was saying to me that I must go and have a look at . . ."

Then all of a sudden, raising her head and pushing up her glasses, she breathed in the air and slapped herself on the chest with the words, "For God's sake—I forgot I'd put the rice on!"

Red and White

—∽∽—

Ibrahim Farghali

We really couldn't believe your crazy stories, Muhammadi. Each time you came along with some new amazing tale. And always we'd believe you. Was that due to the very spontaneous and convincing way you told them? Honestly, I don't know.

At first I marveled at your fertile imagination, at your ability to clothe your lies with a sense of reality and with minute details that didn't complicate the story. You surpassed all other liars by having an extraordinary storehouse of lies and the ability to repeat them with the very same details, without adding to or subtracting from them. So, with the passage of time, I asked myself: Why don't I believe you, Muhammadi? What you're telling me is wonderful and perhaps odd. Yes, yet it seems ordinary at an extraordinary time.

You once swore to us that you'd met a man who had the foot of a goat, also a dog that talked to you, and that you'd had a conversation with it before it took on human shape. Then, one day you came up to us all of a tremble, with a pale and haggard face, and recounted to us the strangest ever of all your stories. Do you remember it, Muhammadi? How a beautiful mermaid called to you one day; the top half of her was female and of an indescribable beauty, while the bottom half was nothing but the tail of a fish. She took you down into the depths of the sea for a whole night. When you kissed her you had a feeling that you couldn't explain, and you were also able to breathe under the water just like the mermaid.

But here you transported me from the depths of the seas right up to the skies. Didn't you also ask me about the extent of my knowledge of the language of birds? Do you recollect that, Muhammadi?

I told you that that was not beyond many people. I informed you that pigeons constantly repeat, "Declare that your Lord is One . . . Declare that your Lord is One." I also told you—if my memory hasn't failed me—about the plover bird I love passionately and which keeps on repeating "Power is Yours . . . Yours . . . Yours . . ." or that bird that I send to my loved one with the words I select for her. It goes to her and returns, repeating in the stillness of the night her reply: "I love you . . . I love you . . . I love you," so that I am in raptures.

That greatly delighted you, Muhammadi, and it seems that it was this that made you abandon your reticence about letting me know the secret of your comprehensive knowledge of the language of the birds, particularly that of pigeons. You began making that strange sound that resembled their melodious cooing, followed by a childish smile as you detailed the different meanings for the cooing sounds. You were in a state of ecstasy, so you kept pushing me into that pigeon coop on the roof of your house.

I was met by the birds, which were jumping about, and the place was filled with the flapping of wings, while you went on crazily enumerating their different varieties and specifications: the "black roller" with its tail resembling a fan and its haughtiness like that of a peacock, and the angelic "white roller," and the "somersaulter" that hovers high up before letting itself fall down as it twists and turns in the air and the tiny Kashakuwwa with its coffee-colored wings and the Abla'a with its red and blue color, and the multi-colored Australian, and the Murasila, which is derived from the carrier pigeon. After that you went on relating to me in detail your sightings of the birds on their daily journeys.

O Muhammadi, you can be anything except speechless. So what occurred? Why all this melancholy? Speak—say something, Muhammadi, and I swear we'll believe you—at least I'll believe you.

In the end I decided that you should tell me what was occupying your mind: that beautiful white pigeon. Its slender neck and its grace and mind-boggling haughtiness and its streamlined form that is so miraculous it shatters everything you have seen of the laws of flying in all its modes. But don't swear that it's true because I believe all you've said, just as I believe all you said about the charm of its voice and the music of its cooing.

But, Muhammadi, what's the secret of your sudden disappearance? Where have you gone? What has happened? Where can we search for you?

When I opened the door of the coop, I found you lying on your stomach. But where are the birds? So this is your beloved white pigeon at rest in a far corner. But, O God, what's this? It's no longer white: the white has become colored with bright red. Right in the very place of its fertility it is completely torn apart. As for you, O Muhammadi, you haven't answered my call. I came closer to you, while still calling to you, and when I pulled you by the shirt so as to see your face, I leapt backward as though I had been stung, and shouted out in terror. Your face was all deformed and I could see some of the bones of your skull, colored with blood: it was as though the birds had completely mangled you. What had you done, O Muhammadi?

The Accusation

Suleiman Fayyad

Free Time

In the morning he awoke from his second snooze. The time was still before noon. He stretched, yawning, lazily rose to his feet, made the bed and opened the window on to the light of day. The calls of vendors and the shrieks of children flowed in. Leaning on the windowsill, he took delight in the blue autumnal sky, the flat roofs of the houses, the windows. From where he was he could see, through an open window on the ground floor of the house opposite, his fellow-student Abdel Wahhab: sitting in semi-darkness, he was painting a portrait of a girl on minutely squared paper, copying from a photograph stuck with a pin to the top of the picture. On the wall behind it were his clothes on a hanger, the nail from which it hung being covered by his turban.

He drew away from the window and left the room. He went down the stairs. Crossing the walled courtyard of the house, he knelt down to wash his face. He dried his face with the end of his gown and sprinkled a few drops of water on his hair, rubbing it with his hands, and went up again to his room. He went through the hallway door and, standing before the shelf and mirror, began combing his hair. Entering the room, he took off two lids from the remains of yesterday's supper and sat down to his breakfast. He then quenched his thirst with water and wondered what he should do.

He returned to the window and leaned on it. All too soon he was bored by the spectacle: the bright light, the empty roofs, women sitting by the doors picking over rice, blowing away the particles of dirt, the calling of vendors, the shrieks of children.

He left the window and gazed about him in the room, searching for something to entertain him, to keep him occupied. His school books were ranged along the floor on an old newspaper. Beside them were the books of his colleague and a number of literary books by al-Rafiʻi, al-Manfaluti, al-Zayyat, and Ali Adham, also some numbers of the magazine *al-Risala*. He felt no desire to read any of the prescribed books. Of the other books and magazines, he had finished reading the last of them yesterday by the dim light of the lamp. His mind was blank, incapable at present of giving itself over either to past memories or to daydreaming.

What, then, should he do? He thought about the cafés, about visiting fellow-students who occupied rooms scattered about the quarter. He told himself that today was Friday, the time noon. The cafés would be almost empty of customers and his fellow-students would be busy preparing, on their stoves, the lunches they had bought themselves in the market. He would not find himself welcome. He wished he could go to sleep again; he wished his fellow-student Farag would come back quickly from his trip to the village and bring back with him some of the tasty country foods, some of its fruits, its news, stories about who had married and who had died and who had quarreled. His eye happened to alight on his turban and that of his fellow-student hanging on their nails. He saw the two pure white, newly washed shawls. Here, he thought, was something he could do. He felt animated, full of enthusiasm.

He brought the two shawls and, one after the other, sprinkled them with water and rolled them up beside him on the bed so that the moist dampness of the drops of water would work its way into the whole of the fine, soft threads.

He brought the two turbans and began brushing the dust from them, restoring to the dark red plush its normal brilliance and splendor.

He took hold of one of the shawls and spread it out fully. Drawing it tight from each direction, he smoothed out its silken creases with the palm of his hand. He pulled it from opposite ends and made a triangle of it. He folded the head of the triangle over on to its base, then again, drew up his leg to his thigh, and fitted it on his knee.

Lifting the end of the sheet on the bed, he extracted several pins from the mattress by their tiny heads and placed them in his mouth; he held them between his lips, the heads facing his teeth and tongue.

He combed through the black tassel with his hand, making sure its silken plaited strands were smoothed out into a single tidy line. The tassel lay toward his chest. Placing the end of the shawl by the corner of the tarboosh opposite the tassel, he began going round it leftwards, the shawl held taut by the thumb of his right hand, gently and precisely until the tip of the beginning had been hidden under the winding of the shawl. The fingers of his left hand began smoothing out the wrinkles and making the fringe show near the end, standing up straight and neat. Then he began putting the pins in with great dexterity: one he put in from top to bottom, a second sideways, while a third he inserted from below, then turned round upward and pressed downward.

Finally, he concealed the end of the shawl between itself and the tarboosh in the right-hand corner so that when the tassel was standing upright on the head it would be in line with the neck and back. He then made fast the final movement with three pins, the very number he had estimated from the start. Using spittle, he paid yet more attention to the fringes till they were like needles.

He removed the turban from his knee, put his left hand inside it and twirled it round his left index finger with his right hand. It went around twice, spinning evenly. He smiled at it, at his skill which so few people could equal. Placing it alongside him gently and cautiously, he began doing the other turban.

Having finished both turbans, he placed them carefully alongside each other on top of the books. He covered them over with an old shawl to protect them from invisible specks of dust. Wiping away beads of sweat from his forehead, he seated himself on the edge of the bed.

What should he do now? He thought again. He got up and brought the short-handled palm-fiber broom and began sweeping out the bedroom and hallway. He went downstairs and washed up yesterday's plates. He wiped the sweat from his face with the end of his indoor gown, with its black, red and white stripes, then leaned on the window sill, hoping to find a fresh breeze, but there was none. The feeling of loneliness came back to him, with its boring, weary emptiness. He thought about his favorite pastime: the dagger and the target.

On the cinema screen stands the girl, her back to the wall. The man with the dagger, when aiming at the wooden wall right behind her, takes hold of the tip of the dagger, its handle pointing downward, brings it up to the top of his chest and hurls it. It plunges into the wood above her head, perhaps severing a stray hair. The daggers follow in quick succession from his hand until her head, shoulders and arms are all ringed round. The girl leaves her place, the daggers remaining in the wall, and there is applause for this dangerous act successfully accomplished.

From behind the window the villain comes into view: a secret agent or spy, a hired killer. He forces the point of the dagger between the two halves of the window. The sounds of the party spill out. He looks around for the man who is fated to die by his hand. He spots him. Quickly he hurls the dagger with the same unerring accuracy. The poisoned dagger plunges into its target. A loud scream, then silence. The villain who has thrown the dagger disappears and the window remains empty before appalled eyes.

He brought out a knife. Its blade was of black, unwrought, inflexible steel. Its wooden handle was light and out of balance with the heavy blade. It would not work for knife-throwing. He went into the hallway and slammed the door. He tried it out. His assumption was confirmed: the knife fell to the ground. Then he took it by the handle and hurled it. It fell. He retrieved it. He went a couple of steps near to the door and hurled it. It plunged into the door, ripping the long fibers. With difficulty he wrenched it out; its tip had gone through to the other side.

He came to the conclusion that this knife caused too much damage, so he returned it to its place in the bedroom and brought the brass pair of compasses. He opened them as wide as they would go. They had a strong, sharp, tapered point. The grooved wheel on the other side, which opened up and held the pencil, was stiff, as was the arm where the place for the pencil was. It would work—he had tried it before—for knife-throwing.

Holding the pair of compasses by the tip, he brought them up and threw them. They plunged into the door. The whole of the point penetrated into the door. He should have stood a little farther away.

He went to retrieve them. Getting them out was a troublesome job. The point snapped off. The main body of the pair of compasses remained in his hand, which had struck back against his chest. He regretted what he had done. He spat at the door and flung the pair of compasses from the bedroom window into the street.

He brought a stone from the courtyard and went on knocking the end of the point from the outer side of the hallway door till it was even with the wood and its other end stuck out inwards. He tried to extract it with his teeth but failed. He knocked at it with the knife till he had flattened it against the wood of the door. Once again he went back to leaning on the window, panting and in a state of angry dejection.

The Visit

As he was returning from the mosque he felt himself as light as a bird, as empty as a strip of bamboo. Traces of dust still lay on the palms of his hands and there was matting on the center of his forehead. He thought about what the person giving the Friday sermon had said in his first sermon. He tried to remember, but the monotonous voice in which the second sermon had been recited, memorized by heart from far east to far west, chased away every word contained in the first. He thought: Perhaps it has settled in my soul. He assured himself: The important thing is to live in innocence, without spite or malice or envy, "cleansed of heart" as the Prophet Muhammad had said. The priests of ancient Egypt had also said nothing but this. Zarathustra, Buddha, Christ. What, then, was the difference between them? All say to you: Do not be wrong-doing. Wronged against? There is no harm in being wronged against. Christ said: "Turn the other cheek." God said to Muhammad: "He who attacks you, attack him." But He also said: "He who desists and makes amends, his reward is with God. Do not act wrongly." There is no objection to being acted wrongly against. He told himself that tomorrow he would ask his sheikh at the Institute.

Nearing his home, he again thought: What could he perhaps do? In the afternoon Farag would come. Until the afternoon he should not eat, for he had slept a lot last night and into the morning. He thought about Hindawi's visit. He thought that such a person would not stay alone in his room; every moment he must be doing something. He was vicious, ever-rebellious, ever-irate, with a vitality that was inexhaustible. His sarcasm was never-ending; his eyes gleamed with ill-temper. He had never seen him calm from the time he had first known him. He was in the class at the Institute when the sheikh was giving a lesson on grammar, on the verb *kana* and its sisters, devoting himself wholeheartedly to it. He had put one of the students as a guard by the door. The guard would shut the door on him, then open it as the sheikh said, "Open the door for Kana that he may enter."

The guard opened the door. The student Kana entered.

"What do you do?"

"I make the subject go into the nominative case and the predicate into the accusative."

"*O Amsa, enter. O Zalla, O Bata, O Asbaha.*"

Hindawi's turn came. He entered and gave his answer.

"Give an example," demanded the sheikh.

"Hindawi continued running," shouted Hindawi.

The class laughed at the mention of his name in the example. The sheikh flew into a rage so as to quieten the class. Suddenly Hindawi began leaping over the desks, returning to his own by an unfamiliar route. The sheikh screamed curses at him, rushing after him to hit him, but he did not catch up with him.

"Make way, boy," yelled Hindawi as he jumped.

As Hindawi's feet approached, the boys ducked. The sheikh was running up and down the aisle between the desks, but Hindawi was always at the other end. He would run after him, beating about with his stick to land him a blow. The stick, though, always caught someone other than Hindawi. Eventually the sheikh was panting and gasping for breath, puce in the face. He coughed because of the asthma he was always on his guard against. He coughed and coughed till the tears ran down from his eyes, while he cursed the young generation, present times, and the end of the world which was at hand.

He turned off at the street junction to Hindawi's house. He was aware that he was drawn to him by the magic of his biting viciousness, which was both delightful and hurtful. He passed in front of one house, then two more on the right, keeping the door of Hindawi's house to his left. Finding the door open, he entered the dark narrow hallway. The door of his room to the left being open, he stepped down over the threshold.

He found Hindawi unexpectedly asleep at noon. His snoring indicated he had been asleep for some time. The smell of his sweat filled the room with a fecund, nauseating stench. His crinkly hair was rumpled from tossing about in his sleep. He was sleeping in his woolen gallabiya with the country-style neck-opening and his silk, striped waistcoat. His Upper Egyptian face was dark brown, sharp-featured, with thick mustache and eyebrows. As he regarded him he thought: if he were not a student he would be a railway porter, a night prowler on village farms, a crooked merchant.

It occurred to him that the other's world was closed to him, that he had never entered it. He would have liked to wake him up, to talk to him. He was on the point of doing so. He hesitated: sleep has its own sanctity, is a temporary respite.

He saw the end of his wallet protruding from his waistcoat pocket through the opening in his gown, as though about to fall, as though some hand had been pulling it out, had then hesitated or changed its mind suddenly. He approached it: its thick leather was dark brown and it bulged with the pieces of paper it carried. God alone—and its owner—knew what good things and secrets it had hidden inside it. He thought of stretching out his hand and seeing what was in it. He thought of taking a small note from the money it contained. He stretched out his hand and touched it. For a fleeting moment his hand stopped there, while his heart thumped. A fleeting moment, no more. This isn't taking, it's stealing. He did not have the right to spy on someone's personal affairs. He pushed the wallet down, covering it over carefully, cautiously, with the end of the opening of the gown decorated with black thread.

As he was walking round the room away from Hindawi, it seemed to him that he saw two half-open eyes, so slightly open as to be scarcely perceptible, fluttering to the suddenly calm rhythm of his breathing. He stared at him for a moment. His breathing was once again heavy and labored. He reckoned he was completely asleep, now that his eyes were again closed tight. He felt a tenderness toward the sleeping man, a sympathy and affection.

The two wooden halves of the window were open. He closed them gently, taking care to make no noise. He walked on tip-toe. Taking a light coverlet, he covered him up to the chest with it. He arranged the end of the sheet of his own camp bed. On an ashtray he saw a packet of Gold Flake. He opened it. He felt a desire for a cigarette, to smoke it at his leisure. He took one. He remembered he had some matches at home. He withdrew from the room, stepping over the threshold and up into the hallway. He drew the door to behind him.

As he was leaving the room he saw the landlady sitting in the darkness in another small, narrow hallway, watching him with half-closed eyes. Momentarily uneasy, he left the house.

The Trial

When he awoke to the call of the high-pitched, sarcastic nasal voice, and the movements of Farag's hands shaking him, it was evening. A bewildering surprise was in wait for him: Hindawi was sitting, a short cane in his hand and his elbows resting on his knees, in the only chair in the room. On his face was a scowling, glowering silence and a gaze that was directed toward him with impatient hate. Farag was standing up, with his fair, oval face, his huge nose, narrow forehead and differently colored eyes; his woolen peasant skull-cap, the color of cooking butter, was tilted backward, pressed down upon light, honey-colored hair, the ends of which showed on his forehead in a triangle; his ears were as large as baskets. He rose to his feet, then sat down again. His inner self told him that something unpleasant was going to happen. The light from the fully opened room looked yellow, mournful and depressing. He felt a sensation of sadness and anxiety for which he knew no reason. He reckoned he was ill. Without wanting to, he smiled at Farag:

"Thanks be to God for your safe return. When did you arrive?"

"What safety does someone like you give?" the other yelled with nasal sarcasm.

He looked at Farag once, at Hindawi once. He was sure about the unpleasantness. He got to his feet. He was surprised at not finding a newspaper spread out as was usual whenever Farag came back from a trip, with dishes of stuffed vegetables and pigeons on it, and boiled eggs and loaves of bread that were still hot, retaining the smell of the oven, of burning and fire. Farag's hand was inside the left-hand opening of his gown, by his pelvis, idly playing.

He went to the window. He looked out, to his left, at the far horizon, broken by lines of roofs. A twilight cloud was reddened by the rays of the facing sun. A thought leapt into his head: Hindawi has been robbed; Hindawi has come to accuse me of the theft.

At the very moment he turned, tense and uneasy, angry and chat challenging, Farag pulled him by the shoulder. Except for anger there was no other emotion on his face: he had been accused, his punishment had been determined, and nothing remained but the formalities. Despite himself he made the mistake of asking:

"What's happened?"

Hindawi got up with explosive laughter. Putting the stick under his arm, he brought the palms of his hands together. He guessed Hindawi was thinking of the saying: He kills and walks in the murdered man's funeral.

"That's really great, man."

"What's happened?"

"Hand over the wallet."

"Wallet? What wallet?"

It was just what he had expected. He told himself that he must be careful. Any word would be held against him.

"What wallet?" he repeated hotly. "I don't understand. What's happened?"

"Hand over the money. It doesn't matter about the wallet."

"Farag, I don't understand."

Hindawi sprang at him and got hold of him by his gown, at the chest, with both hands. Shaking him, he screamed, "Hand over the money—a hundred and thirty piasters. I'm not the person to be cheated or robbed."

He stammered, shrinking into himself. Hindawi was twice his size and stronger than ten like him. Farag was six school years ahead of him. Even if he was capable of putting up a fight, what would be the point? He had now become a thief. The matter had been decided and was at an end. He should nevertheless try. Farag had pushed him away. He quieted him down, reassured him with a sign from bunched fingers, which also bore a threat.

"Hand over the money," said Farag, "and we won't punish you. We'll keep the secret between us as deep down as in a well. No one will know. You're from my village and what brings disgrace upon you brings disgrace upon me. God curse the devil who put you up to it—confess. I'll tell you what: there's no point in confessing, just hand over the money and the matter will be at an end."

Tears of anger gushed from his eyes.

"I didn't steal," he screamed. "Search my belongings, all my books. I took one cigarette from the packet, I took it as a friend."

"Then you did come into my room while I was asleep," shouted Hindawi triumphantly. "He's confessing, Farag."

"I only took a cigarette," he said pleadingly. "Believe me."

He thought: This too he shouldn't have mentioned. He thought: But the woman had seen him and Hindawi's eyes had been partly open; he had certainly seen him for a fleeting moment.

"You took a cigarette from me?" said Hindawi. "So you did come to my room. I definitely found a cigarette missing from the packet. Oh yes, he who steals an egg will steal a camel."

"Hindawi, Sheikh Hindawi, believe me—just the cigarette."

Farag seated himself on the edge of their two beds that had been brought together under a single mattress. To one side of the room the mattress of his own bed was rolled up and covered with sacking.

"Then we'll hold an interrogation." He put the question to him: "have you any evidence?"

"Evidence? I? Why?"

"Evidence showing you didn't steal."

"I swear I didn't."

"Evidence comes after swearing."

"It is from him I demand evidence to the effect that I stole." He quoted: "Evidence is for him who accuses and the oath is for him who denies."

Hindawi sat himself down in the chair.

"The evidence," said Farag, "is that the landlady saw you when you were entering the room and when you left it, and that you admit you stole."

"Farag, I took … as a friend."

Hindawi laughed. "Without my knowledge!" he said.

"I thought of you as a friend," he told himself.

"Don't be annoyed," said Farag. "You took a cigarette—from Hindawi's packet."

"It was on the ashtray," said Hindawi in affirmation.

"But I didn't steal," he said desperately—"neither a wallet nor money. I swear. God is my witness."

"So you did take something," said Farag. "Confess. Hurry up, I want to change my clothes and for us to get Hindawi his food. We'll bribe him so he'll hide your shame and mine."

"Farag, I told you, I took nothing but the cigarette."

"And the landlady?" said Hindawi.

"She's a liar, a liar—she's lying."

He thought. He remembered. A wallet was sticking out from his pocket as though it was going to fall. A hand was extracting it, was surprised by a step, a push at the door. Fleeing away in haste, the landlady had returned and taken it after he had gone out. Perhaps she had not been there before him. She might, for instance, have gone in after him. His going to Hindawi possibly had given her the opportunity for stealing from Hindawi and then accusing him. He wished he had not admitted taking the cigarette. Up till then it had been possible for him also to deny he had paid Hindawi a visit. Yet his eyes, for a fleeting instant when his breathing had grown calm, had appeared partly open. At that instant Hindawi had seen him. He thought: Why doesn't Hindawi mention this fact now? Maybe he was mistaken about what he had seen. Were this true, he would, by his denial, be more likely to be believed that it was the landlady who was the thief. Her husband was a seller of animal fodder and Hindawi used to sleep with her when he was away.

"Why are you silent? Speak."

"Hindawi," he said, earnestly. "Believe me, I didn't steal either the wallet or the money."

"Where are they then? Listen—I'll skin you alive." He turned to Farag. "I don't want any questioning—he's the thief."

"Listen, Hindawi," he said. "The landlady, your landlady, it's she who stole from you."

"I've lived in her house for two years and she's never stolen from me, not even when I've been away."

"But she stole from you this time."

"Impossible. She's not a thief. She never stole from me before."

He was on the point of saying something that would cause an explosion but thought better of it. He feared the other's violence, his savage anger. He was somebody who stood up to the sheikh and the local toughs of the district. Were it not for Farag he would not have been as amenable as he now was.

"There's no point in discussing it," said Farag to Hindawi. "I'm hungry and I want to change my clothes. We'll eat first, then . . ."

"And my money?" Hindawi said to him, his tone reflecting his former composure which he expected and reckoned would be justified.

"You'll get it."

"How?"

"Listen, Hindawi. Though I've taken nothing from you, I'll pay you the money."

"And the wallet?"

"I know nothing about it."

Farag looked amazed. His astonishment passed to Hindawi, who suddenly said:

"I'm demanding back what you took from me."

"I didn't take anything."

"Do you think you're doing me a favor?"

"No," he hastened to say, "but there's nothing else I can do. You two have pronounced me to be the thief and there's nothing else I can do."

Hindawi fell silent and his anger increased with his silence. At the same time, though, his mind was on Farag's basket and the food it contained, as Farag took out the dishes from it and spread out a newspaper.

"Wash the plates," Hindawi said to him.

He carried off the plates and washed them. When he returned he found they were already eating. He saw the pigeons and knew where they were from, the eggs too. In them lay the skill of his mother, the munificence of his father. He wanted to eat. He was held back by shame and having capitulated to what he could not help, to what was inevitable. Farag laughed with delight.

"Sit down," said Farag in a malicious, tormenting tone. "It's from your home. Eat."

He sat down and began to eat. He lowered his eyes to the food, to he movement of his hands. He did not dare raise his eyes.

Ordinarily, they would have been laughing: they would have made jokes and he would have listened and laughed. Unable to resist the desire, he stole a glance at them. He saw their eyes speaking, the sparkle in them charged with warning. Deep within his head he saw the world's light as a sickly yellow, the horizon drowning, during the few instants preceding sunset, in the redness of blood.

The Punishment

He returned from below, having washed up the plates. He entered the room and put them down. He bent down to dry them. He heard, "Take it—here's your money."

The voice added, "He'll have seventy piasters left. His monthly messing is forty and the rest he'll have for himself."

He thought about the schoolbook he had to buy for fifty piasters and the price of the cigarettes he used to smoke on the quiet from time to time. He assured himself that his father would believe him. He would tell him what had happened. His father would send him what he wanted—but if he did not question his story he would come and take him away from sharing digs with Farag. As though talking to himself, he said to the others out loud:

"I'll ask my father for a pound. He'll send it."

He turned to them nonchalantly. This confident gesture set off and pre-cipitated the moment that had been planned. Farag gave the signal to Hindawi with a wink. Farag's father worked as a servant with the village omda. His own father was a teacher, well provided for, a man of position and influence in the village. Hindawi was offended by having the sum of money handed over to him. Perhaps he too had doubts about his having stolen it from him. Hindawi leapt at him. The metal dish fell from his hand and spun round and round before coming to rest, while Hindawi threw him to the ground on his face and seated himself with his full weight on his back, his own back toward his head. Hindawi savagely twisted up his legs, grasping each foot in a powerful grip.

It was as though some sudden catastrophe had befallen him. He did not utter. Not a muscle stirred in resistance. Farag rained down blows with Hindawi's thick, solid yet supple stick on the soles of his feet that had been brought close together. He struggled, with desperate movements of his legs, against the powerful grip on them in an attempt to stop the stick from falling on the veins of the soles of his feet. In a fearful inner silence his tears flowed. He wanted to scream out in protest, in assurance, in entreaty. He made up his mind not to do so. His younger brother never did so when his father was angry with him. He would not say "Ow," though he knew what the result would be: further blows until he did say it, this placating "Ow" that brings deliverance. He abandoned his resolution. He moaned. A few more blows rained down, then the beating stopped without a word. Hindawi rose to his feet, picked up the stick, and examined its end which had split and become frayed. He immediately left the room.

Getting up, he tried to stand on his feet. They hurt him. He shuffled across to his own mattress in the corner. He sat down on its sacking. He hid his face between his forearm and upper arm. His resistance collapsed into sudden, hysterical weeping. He heard, through his weeping, the labored breathing of Farag, tired from the beating he had given him and seated relaxing on the edge of the bed. He sensed that darkness was on the march, that the sun was dropping behind the horizon, the blood-redness tarnished by black night. He sensed Farag's movements, heard them, anticipated them. Farag got up and took off his clothes, changing them for his house gown which was on the clothes hanger.

The pain had stopped but the swelling in his feet remained. He pressed down on them so as to be able, though with the utmost difficulty, to walk. Scowling, he dried his tears. He thought. He found no word on his lips, discovered no course of action in his head. He sat down again, gravely silent. It came to his mind that as he was taking the cigarette he had had a sensation of stealing. The sensation had flowed out from the tips of his fingers to the wallet, to the waistcoat, to Hindawi, and thus it was that he had looked as though he had had his eyes half-open. The sensation had flowed out into the air of the room. It had transmitted itself to the landlady, and she had come along after him and had stolen, as the saying goes, the camel and its load.

But you, Farag, what has all this got to do with you? Your father and mine are the reason. Were this not so you would not have sided with Hindawi against me. It's who your father is, and who's mine. Or is it that you're as frightened of Hindawi's vicious nature as I am?

Raising his head, he looked at Farag. He was sitting with his shoulders and back supported against the edge of the bed. He was smoking with greedy enjoyment and eyeing him with a sly smile. He belched contentedly.

Everything he saw depressed him. Making an effort, he got to his feet and walked in the direction of the corner where the books and turbans were. He threw aside the old shawl and began to demolish Farag's turban. First of all he unwound it, then removed the tarboosh from the middle of the shawl, and then the pins; he even straightened out the special folds in the shawl.

Farag laughed, "So what . . ."

He answered not a word, so Farag added, "You'll do it up again by yourself."

"Never. It won't happen."

Farag laughed. "We'll see," he stated.

He turned his back so as to sleep for a while. He remained alone, isolated, humiliated to his very marrow. He went and stood by the window, watching flocks of pigeons circling in the air and fluttering their wings in formations that danced, formations of farewell to the light of day.

A Dog

Hamdy el-Gazzar

I celebrated my birthday alone at my office.

Thursday, midnight, is almost the moment at which I was born thirty years ago. Thursday night is a glorious night in our quarter: in the alleyways, lanes, and streets of Tulun the women now take to their beds, they sprawl out on the sheets, with their legs raised high in the air, while the men push their way into them, entering the welcoming bodies and coming out, happy and delighted. The beds creak and screech, and the voices of the women are raised in screams of sexual excitement and ecstasy, while the spirits of the men are stimulated with joy at their masculine potency. A fleeting summer furnishes the quarter with a comforting warmth throughout this cold winter night; then, at dawn, in delight the satisfied women throw down from the windows and balconies of their homes the water in which they and their husbands have bathed, thus cleansing the streets of dirt.

In our house it was the same, and on a night such as this my father and mother did it thirty years ago. They didn't content themselves with this. In fact, my mother was continually reminding me of the merit of Thursdays, for she became devoted to me on a radiant night of passion and she brought me into the world while people around her were making love all over Tulun. My mother was very cruel, a stranger to nature and temperament, and unfeelingly she would remind me of my function as a man; it was as though she were saying to me, "A real man is not afraid of murderers and dogs, and isn't scared of women, my dear sir."

In the bedroom I put on my heavy wool suit with the red tie as I hummed to myself and danced where I stood. I put on some sexy Gucci cologne as I gave myself a broad smile in the mirror, saying softly, "Many happy returns, man."

While I was crossing the drawing room to the office Salwa was in the bathroom, drenched in shampoo, soap, hot water, and steam, and she was singing to herself. I went into the room and locked myself in. I sat at my small wooden desk on the revolving leather chair and took out from the drawer in the desk a bottle of Polonaki 84. Opening it with my teeth, I began to gulp down my first glassful, slowly, taking my time. I was clasping the glass in the palms of my hands and drinking. I could hear the mumbled crooning that came to me from the bathroom. I was staring at the shelves of books that covered most of the walls of the room, while whispering to myself, "You're now old enough to become a real man. You mustn't wait for anything or anyone."

I slowly gulped down more of the cheap wine, having nothing particular in mind. I opened the study window that overlooked the square and the Tulun Mosque. Despite the darkness I could clearly make out the tall, ancient minaret, strongly erect, a giant stake cleaving the emptiness of the sky. The vast square surrounding the mosque was empty, with the wind whistling inside it. Gently it began to rain in Tulun, nobody was outside. I raised my face to the sky and smiled at the rain, while Salwa's snoring began to come to me from our bedroom, like accompanying music. Her snoring grew louder and in time and harmony with my progressive drinking. Closing the window, I went back to staring at the shelves of books. I realized that I was happy being on my own and celebrating by myself, feeling good that she had forgotten me and had gone to sleep.

After three or four hours—I don't know which—I finished off the bottle. Having filled my body with alcohol, my head was spinning. With difficulty I rose from where I was and staggered toward the door and opened it. I fell to my knees in the sitting room, but eventually reached the bedroom. I stumbled about in the darkness till I reached the large bed. I pulled off my tie and lay down in the double bed, still wearing my suit, my cologne, and my drunkenness, stretching myself out alongside her like a happy man killed in battle.

We hadn't had sex for a long time. We would merely stretch out in the bed together side by side, touching only by chance, each of us sleeping in our own clearly defined space and domain. Slipping under the blanket, I had a sensation of warmth flowing through my body.

Suddenly it occurred to me that it would be good for me to begin my new year with an enjoyable bit of sex. She was sleeping on her side and had her back to me. Her body was plump and fully stretched out, her breathing warm. From behind I stretched out my hand toward the two pomegranates resting on her chest. Her skin was warm and she was—unusually for her—completely naked under the blanket. Her chest rose and fell; her breathing was regular and I understood from the way she was completely naked, without even her nightdress, that it was a celebration, an invitation, and an expression of desire. Slowly, gently, I touched her torso with the palms of my hands, then the roundness of her buttocks. From inside her dreams she shouted out angrily, "That man's a good-for-nothing—he's not a man at all." She continued her regular breathing and went back into a deep sleep. I no longer felt like doing anything, so I didn't try again with her.

I was stretched out on my back, my eyes staring up at the ceiling with my thing dead between my thighs.

I placed a long pillow between my arms and went on rocking myself like a mother talking gently to her baby so as to send it to sleep.

I didn't sleep.

Scenes from the past, scenes I thought I had forgotten forever, assailed me.

I see myself now: I am this pale boy whose mother, delighted at the sight of him, said to him, "God protect you. When you were in your swaddling clothes, he who feared God wouldn't look into your face." She used to comb my hair and gaze at me admiringly as I put on my new school uniform for the first time.

He is me, a boy of a pale complexion rare among the boys of the quarter, with the exception of Abdel Rahman, the cousin of Fawzi the grocer. He was of the same height as me and was similarly fair complexioned, both in his features and the color of his hair. People couldn't tell us apart. They would call out to me, "We'll say to your father, 'What have you to do with dogs, O Abdel Rahman, you dog," And I'd flee from their angry, annoyed faces. Out of breath, I'd run to our house.

Abdel Rahman had a strange passion for dogs and a tremendous passion for wandering around the alleys, lanes, and empty lots of Tulun at night without the fears the rest of us had. He had a large, ugly black dog that would pick quarrels with the other male dogs in the quarter, biting them and scaring them, and would leap onto the backs of the females. One day the dog returned from his usual daily run around, bleeding from his nose, and with wounds to his chest and a fractured skull. Abdel Rahman didn't cry as we used to about many things. He merely grasped hold of the dog, clasping it to his chest and covered up the wound with his hands until his mother came along with some coffee grounds, at which he left the dog with her. He stood on his feet like a grown-up man and stared down at the blood from his dog that was spreading across his white gallabiya. He told the gang of kids who were gathered around him that the criminal who had tried to kill his beloved dog was just a dog himself and that he'd take revenge on all aggressive dogs, and on evil people too.

The lads say that grown-ups only swear at Abdel Rahman by calling him a son of a bitch because his mother in her youth loved a large black dog and was intimate with it behind Fawzi's back.

When I recounted this in front of her, my mother said "Shame on you, she's a poor woman and she's not all that well." When she'd given birth to Abdel Rahman she had no milk in her breasts and he refused to drink processed milk and would vomit it out until she saw him crawling toward their female dog, which was lying down on the tiles of the lounge. He pushed his way among the puppies that were suckling from the mother dog. The dog didn't reject him but looked at him with tender affection. Abdel Rahman's mother resigned herself to God's will and started to pay attention to the dog's diet, providing it with milk, meat, and oily foods, foods that Fawzi the grocer doesn't eat. Abdel Rahman was well fed and grew up loving dogs, especially black ones that had a resemblance to the bitch they owned.

Three days after disappearing from the streets of Tulun and staying in the house of Fawzi the grocer, with all of us thinking that we had seen the last of it forever, the black dog made its appearance once again, being led along by Abdel Rahman. It looked to me as though it had recovered from its wounds and had got back its frightening appearance and its viciousness.

In front of his father's shop Abdel Rahman had given his dog a bath with rose water and scented soap, all this under the gaze of the children who had gathered around him to watch the spectacle. He placed a new red leather collar around its neck and covered its back with a piece of white cloth decorated with flowers and trees. He had also placed under its belly a shiny yellow piece of tape, after which he had led his dog very gently by its lead to its usual place in the mosque's square. He embraced his dog, patting it affectionately, kissing it on the head and saying to it, "Praise be to God for your well-being, you bridegroom. Just a minute and I'll be back."

Abdel Rahman went into his father's storeroom and brought out one of the many empty sheet metal barrels that used to hold oil. He rolled it along the ground and set it up in the square alongside the dog, which was squatting grandly on its hindquarters. Abdel Rahman poured two buckets of water, bottles of rose water, and two blocks of ice into the barrel, and the news of all this quickly spread throughout the quarters, lanes, and alleyways.

People ran to the square in hordes.

Abdel Rahman tied the ends of his gallabiya around his waist and began ladling the rose water out of the barrel with a tin mug and giving a long file of young boys and girls, women and old men something to drink. He would say to each one, "Drink. Drink. By the Holy Quran, in the name of all the dogs of the quarter. Enjoy it."

If someone asked for another mug of the drink he'd hand it over with the words, "Good health to you. By my mother's life I'll not leave a single dog, the son of a dog, in this place. Drink. Drink."

In a mere two days Abdel Rahman had performed what he had sworn he would do; not a single one of the twenty dogs in the quarter was left alive: they were all stretched out in the various alleys and lanes groaning and twisting about in pain till they passed out, while we looked on, delighting in playing about with their bodies. One of the good men in our quarter made his appearance and started swearing at us and chasing us away as he clapped his hands together, saying, "There is no god but God," and he'd remove the new corpse to the vast square in front of the mosque and pour kerosene over the dog and set it alight.

The square became a great crematorium with smoke and the smell of burning corpses rising up from it.

When people accused me of poisoning the dogs I cried and ran away from the square in terror. I called to my mother, who had come out to the window and was shouting out to God to change the devil of a boy, Abdel Rahman, into a monkey, as I bounded up the stairs. She was still angry as she leaned out of the window and heaped curses on Abdel Rahman and the good-for-nothing kids and the dogs. I embraced her from behind, sobbing and trembling. She turned around and took me into a warm embrace, and went on patting me on the back, saying, "For shame the man has no fear—he doesn't even cry."

Abdel Rahman was always viciously frightening.

At this moment I see him, with the eye of memory and imagination, standing in his place in the large square in front of the mosque; in his right hand he has a short rope with which he holds the black dog; on his fair face there's an awesomely sly smile, a smile that can only issue from a heart that is dead and black. He is making his way to where the boys and girls are so as to amuse himself with them. Because of the terror I had for him and his dog, I would avoid him by going around the high wall of the Tulun mosque. I would hurry along, looking around me, my body trembling in fear, my hand resting on the piasters in the side pocket of my gallabiya. I'd scurry around, running the long distance till I reached the bakery. Having bought the loaves for my family, I'd hide them under my gallabiya and return to my mother, happy that I had escaped the insolence of Abdel Rahman.

Many years later Abdel Rahman narrowly escaped the hangman's noose when his lawyer was able to prove that he was defending himself when he fatally stabbed the butcher, Awad, in a quarrel over money—ten pounds to be exact.

I didn't hate anyone as much as I hated Abdel Rahman and his black dog. Abdel Rahman was a murderer and his dog was unclean and scary.

Were you a real man if you were still worried about Abdel Rahman and his dog, while lying stretched out alongside your wife's naked body?

I woke up because of the sunlight that had suddenly filled the room as Salwa drew the curtains to the bedroom, deliberately making a noise as she called out, "Wake up . . . wake up. It's afternoon—it's three o'clock, you blockhead!"

I mumbled in exasperation. Turning my back on her, I moved about in the bed until I became warm, with my head on a small pillow, my knees up against my chest, and my body in my preferred fetal position. At that moment I wished that I could just go back into the womb I'd come from.

The Old Clothes Man

—— ⟋⟍ ——

Fathy Ghanem

T he incidents of this odd story started exactly three years ago. I remember the date: we were at the end of June. It was a Saturday, the time, five in the afternoon, the weather hot and the sweat pouring from us. The two of us were moving from shoeshop to shoeshop, from one shop window of shoes to another shop window of shoes. In the end Ibrahim bought a pair of shoes, light black and white leather shoes. He paid two pounds and fifty-four piasters. He was happy. I, though, had been thinking of the shoes I had wanted to buy, the handbag, the summer dresses, and the swimsuits for the children.

Anyway, we left the shop and returned home. The next morning Ibrahim put on the new shoes and went off to the Ministry. A couple of hours later, at eleven o'clock, I was surprised to find him returning with a colleague, one of the employees working with him at the Ministry. Ibrahim was leaning on the employee's shoulder and his face was sallow. The two of them entered the bedroom with me behind them. We called the doctor, who came and gave Ibrahim an injection in the arm and applied artificial respiration. The room was dark and my little daughter Aida was crying, the employee was wringing his hands, and froth was issuing from Ibrahim's mouth; I was pulling at my hair, the doctor's mouth was pinched in distress and Ibrahim died.

Then came the obsequies, the funeral ceremony and the burial in the Imam al-Shafi'i cemetery, the weeping and the mourning and the black clothes.

Ibrahim no longer occupied the house and I was left with nothing but pictures of him, his clothes, and his new shoes.

They were sad, cruel days. I would sit alone on the bed in which he had died and look at the cupboard that contained his clothes. Hours would pass; I wouldn't be thinking or crying or feeling anything. Sometimes I'd open the cupboard and touch the sleeve of his suit, then look at the new shoes and hold them in my gaze. He had been happy the day he'd bought them. He'd only worn them for a couple of hours; they had been unlucky shoes and yet they reminded me of the last happiness I'd known. I had wanted to buy shoes and a handbag and colorful dresses for myself, and I had wanted to buy swimsuits for the children. Now everything had come to an end.

It was then that I began to be aware of a voice calling in the street, one of many such voices that reached me from the street. This was the strongest of them and was drowning the noise of the tram and the cars, the vegetable sellers, the children's screams, and the servants' cursings.

"Old clothes . . . clothes . . . clothes."

I asked myself: Will the day come when I'll sell Ibrahim's clothes? Sell his new shoes? Impossible.

But the voice was reaching me with clamorous clarity and I fortified myself against it, bracing myself. I fled to a far room, went to the cupboard and opened it, handling Ibrahim's clothes and new shoes. I looked at the bed and recalled the whole of my life. The day Ibrahim had come to ask my father for my hand in marriage my heart had pounded with fear, longing, and hope.

Our wedding night: Ibrahim and I surrounded by the bridesmaids, Khadiga dancing and Sana' giving out trilling cries of joy; Ibrahim lifting the tulle and kissing me on the cheek with trembling lips, his mustache large and black, his eyes strong.

Our house in Shubra and our eldest son Mustafa. Our house in Aguza and our second son Mahmoud. Squabbling and making up, tenderness and cruelty, contentment and anxiety.

Where did our old clothes used to go? Our old shoes?

Did they fall to pieces? Did they get lost? Were they turned into dusters? Did we give them to the servants?

I had not sold a single old thing to that man who called out for old clothes. I had never had any dealings with him. The old is not for sale, is not to be converted into money for buying new things. I think that's wrong, quite wrong.

One morning I ventured out onto the balcony and looked down at the man as he called out: "Old clothes . . . clothes . . . clothes."

I wanted to see him. He was tall and thin with black trousers and a dirty white shirt. On his head he had a wooden box which had glass sides. He was walking slowly, his eyes raised. Our eyes met and the man shouted, "Clothes . . . clothes."

It was as though he were stabbing me. I left the balcony in flight from him, his voice pursuing me, urgently insistent, hurtful and forceful.

"Clothes . . . clothes."

Have I gone mad?

I'm giving this voice unwarranted importance. He's merely a man calling in the street. I don't want to have any dealings with him—and I shan't do so.

The old brings back memories. We fondle it, we love it, we mourn it.

I mourn Ibrahim and I shall continue to do so. The children have forgotten. I alone do not forget.

At sunset the children gather around me, laughing and shouting joyfully. When they play hide and seek they turn the house upside down, bursting into his room and hiding under his bed. Once Aida hid herself in the cupboard, and when they found her she came out holding the new shoes. Mahmoud put his feet in the shoes and stomped around on the tiled floor. I was upset and almost scolded him, but I concealed my anger, smiled and gently took the shoes from him and returned them to the cupboard. They don't understand. They're little children. How could they understand?

While I was in the kitchen I heard the voice making its violent intrusion: "Old clothes . . . clothes."

I wonder how much those clothes and new shoes would be worth?

God forbid. How did such a question enter my head?

God forgive me. May the Lord confound you, Satan. It's an unforgivable sin. To think of how much the clothes would fetch? I, who am in mourning? Tomorrow I'll visit him and recite the Fatiha and ask God's mercy for him.

This accursed man, why doesn't he go off to some other street? It's as though he's waiting, as though he's confident he'll get what he wants. I hate him.

It was three days ago exactly. I remember the date, it was at the end of December. It was a Wednesday, the time: one in the afternoon, the weather so cold it cut through to one's bones.

The man called out, "Old clothes . . . clothes . . . clothes."

I called to him.

He came up the stairs and before he had knocked at the door I had opened the cupboard and had taken out the new shoes.

It's an odd story, it really is.

A Visit

Gamal al-Ghitani

It was a long street with hardly a soul on it. Every now and again a squall of wind would blow in from the direction of the mountain and would raise small whirlpools of dust. Dirt and straw would crash against the walls of the houses, the silver-colored lampposts, and the legs of the few passersby. The wind was dry and full of tiny particles of sand, while the sky was clothed in a dark yellowness. Along the street, trees emanated from the earth at equal distances from one another. Their leaves had fallen, leaving the branches bare. I'm still some distance from the tram stop and I'm drawing close to the Abbasiya Fever Hospital, after which stands the asylum.

After a short distance I arrive there. The smell of dry earth is fiery. It fills my nostrils and has the same pungency as the smell that had been there that night.

I lay down on the bed, my eyes staring up at the ceiling. Darkness shrouded the whole town; the night, long and dense, breathed calmly. In my ears there was a faint but continual buzzing noise. I didn't know where it was coming from. Also, there were vague nocturnal noises: the faraway bark of a dog, a child crying, a mother's voice ringing out. Then, utter silence. The clock struck and my mother came. Her face was pale, filled with bewilderment.

"Your father."

"What about him?"

"He's not his usual self."

"Is it like what happened last week?"

"No, worse than that."

I felt anxious, and mysterious, trembling sounds were sneaking into my ears. At first I didn't know what they were, but when I was able to see better in the dark I found him sitting on the bed wearing the yellow suit of clothes that he refused to discard when he came back from work. He was raising his face to the ceiling and staring at it with protruding eyes. Then he counted on his fingers and said, "Fifteen . . . fourteen . . . thirteen. There aren't many more days to go in the month. Debts to be paid . . . the first of the month . . . the first of the month."

"His debts? What debts, Ma?"

"He's doing what he used to do when you were without a job. Do you remember?"

"Yes, I do. He used to spend the night calculating the debts that were piling up."

At that time I had no work and his salary was tiny.

Propping his head against his hands, he wept softly, then muttered, "It's lost . . . lost . . . ."

"Shall I go to his room?"

"Come, my boy—I only came here for this."

The smell of dry dust increased in my nostrils. I didn't think about where it was from. From the dark corner—the scratching of a rat, doubtless, a rat. I entered the room and the darkness seemed to slap at me. I stood still, looking in the direction of the bed.

"Father, why are you still awake?"

"Huh . . . . Yes . . . . Ah."

"Father, I'm asking why you're still awake?"

"Debts . . . I'm reckoning up my debts, my son . . . three, four . . . five . . . Abdel Moneim the grocer . . . Ali the butcher . . . ."

"But there aren't any debts left for you to calculate, so what is it you're calculating?"

He leapt up with a scream, waving his arm about. "Get away from me— I'll get my calculations wrong. Isn't it enough that you're out of work? You got the certificate and then you didn't get a job. What is it that you want?"

"Father?"

"Get away from me . . . I told you to get away. I'll get the sums wrong: the . . . the butcher . . . the grocer . . . the landlady . . . ."

"There are no debts, Father, and I'm no longer unemployed."

"Get away from me. You're plotting against me. You want them to kill me—the butcher . . . the grocer . . . the landlady . . . the . . . the . . . the . . . ."

His voice dissolves the silence of the night. The houses of our quarter are close together. The slightest noise makes the windows come open, the lights flash on, and heads peer out and inquire, "What's over there? Who's having a squabble? Who . . . ?"

The comments continue, then silence returns and I back away. I have heard the sound of my mother's weeping. Her corpulent body is shaking.

"What a pity for me!"

"Don't cry, Mother."

"Why shouldn't I cry, my boy? Is this the end of your father? Poor thing . . . poor thing . . . Life is so hard! So hard!"

I was almost at the end of my studies. I had just a few months more to go and I'd get my intermediate certificate. All of a sudden my sister came to me from Upper Egypt. She had been divorced and there were her children. Our expenses increased and my father's salary was so meagre we couldn't manage. Previously he had had many debts. Really rough months went by, and every other month he'd take himself off to the distant village.

There, in the depths of Upper Egypt, he sold what little was left of the land. Then, one day, he returned and said that there was no more land to be sold. He looked homeless and bewildered the whole day. He'd return from his work carrying paper and pen, with his lips mumbling all sorts of numbers. They are piasters and pounds for the creditors. I had graduated but I hadn't found any work. I was unemployed, with my sister and her four sons still with us. My poor father!

Once, he went out and after a while I followed him. I reached al-Hussein Square. I stood not knowing where he'd gone. Then I spotted him. He was putting the tattered end of his gallabiya in his mouth, while wandering round the square, his forehead furrowed, his eyes roaming around as he gestured to the people with his hand. He was at a loss.

My poor father. On that day I went up to him.

"What is it, Father?"

He looked at me but gave no answer.

"You're walking around in the square, but you didn't go to work."

Once again he gave me a look. Wind blew in from the direction of Darrasa Mountain. Those crossing the square were doing so at greater speed: their work awaited them. My father stared into my face. All of a sudden he dashed off away from me and I hurried after him. Then, suddenly, he disappeared, swallowed up by the vast crowd. My poor father.

No more than a week later I got myself a modestly paid job and I paid off his debts. Then one afternoon I was sitting at home. I was exhausted; suddenly my mother rushed in, screaming and wailing.

"Mother, what's wrong?"

"Your father. Your father."

"What's happened to him?"

"A messenger from the ministry where he works is outside. He refuses to say anything and is asking to see you. Something's happened. Something's happened."

"Where is he? Where? Where?"

I hurried outside. The sky was gloomy, blanketed in dark clouds. The day was reaching its end. The terrace on which we lived looked dismal. My mother wailed and screamed.

The slightly built messenger said, "Are you Imad, the son of Hagg Hassan?"

"Yes, I am."

The screaming didn't stop. The neighbors gathered round. My sister's screaming began.

"Prepare yourself for the worst—your father . . ."

The screaming grew louder and the boys burst out crying. My mother continued to thump the wooden wall of the room.

"Your father was sitting in the Ministry," continued the messenger, "mumbling obscure words. I don't know what they were. Then all at once he jumped to his feet, raising his fist threateningly to the skies, and called out, 'It's hopeless . . . hopeless! Four, five. Nine, seven. Abdel Moneim the grocer, he wants me to pay, but I haven't got anything. Four children and

she's divorced.' He was raving and shrieking as we struggled against him."
Then there was more screaming, this time coming from the rotund body
of my mother who was shaking all over. My sister was wailing, while the
neighbors exchanged whispered comments as the news spread and the wind
became dry, with its smell filling my nostrils.

My poor father.

From far off the building could be seen. All was dust and dirt. My sick
mother is now in the house. The dust is dry.

My poor father.

From far off the large building appears once again, more clearly, surrounded by the silent, bleak trees. Imad's footsteps quickened as he
approached the large door in front of which people and dealers were jostling.

Good—there was still plenty of time.

Put Out Those Lights

—✹—

Yousef Gohar

H asan Effendi's life was darkened by the continual shadow of boredom and weariness. A so-called musician in a band that performed
at wedding celebrations in the poorer quarters, he was more often
idle than working and would spend his days sitting and yawning on his chair
in front of the shop in Muhammad Ali Street where the band hung out.

All day long he would sit staring at the women passing by, at the trams,
at the carts bearing professional women mourners going along behind some
'dear departed' toward the cemetery of the Imam Shafi'i.

Biting his nails or pulling at his mustache nervously, his tarboosh, the edge
blackened with sweat and dirt, pushed back from his forehead, he would sit
and stare. Though he appeared to stare long and searchingly, yet in actual fact
they were but the casual, passing glances of a man distracted by memories,
the worries of life, the contemplation of the past and the future. In this manner
he spent his free time, immersed in sadness and regret for a life that had been
wasted—yes, and alarm at the misery and privation that was in store for him.

He was now in his forties. In his youth he had worked as an assistant at
a barber's shop, but success had not been decreed to him—the razor had the
habit of slipping and drawing blood from the customer's chin, and once a
man had had his hair cut by him he never put his foot inside the shop again.
It was soon noticed by the bosses that Hasan was scaring away customers,
the result of which was that he found himself out of work. He took on various

types of jobs before ending up with the band. The job was a wretched one, providing him with scarcely enough to keep starvation at bay, for the times when people used to have weddings in the grand style had long ago passed: now they preferred spending the money on a dowry or other essentials. So it was that the band used to wait for work without any real hope, like an undertaker in a town where the people enjoy perfect health and whose relations with the Angel of Death are few and far between.

Hasan Effendi used to live in Bulaq in a house of a seamstress. The woman was a widow and had a daughter, named Nafusa, who was not bad looking.

Hasan thought about marrying her, for the row of gold teeth that glittered in the mouth of Nafusa's mother indicated that she was comfortably off. Apart from which, Nafusa herself possessed a pair of heavy earrings, a dozen gold bangles on her arms, and round her neck a large pendant. The two of them obviously made a good thing out of their business—thanks to the Singer sewing machine which was never silent.

Marriage, he told himself, would do away with a lot of his present worries. He would no longer find himself at the end of the month being asked for the rent, would not be faced with having the bailiff in to remove his bed because of the past months that hadn't been paid or because he owed money to the baker and the grocer.

He would return home to find something clean and decently cooked waiting for him; he would be freed from the slavery of the little shop that sold dishes of beans, from the butcher who sold offal.

Nafusa's mother was encouraging him, hinting that he would be happy, that he would have no worry in the world. . . .

When still in his thirties, Hasan Effendi had married Nafusa. He had now been with her for ten years and had four children by her. Yes, through marriage he had insured his future and his daily bread, but in return he had given up his personality and self-respect. His whole life had become humility and submission. At his work he had to obey Gaber Effendi, the head of band, for fear of losing the five piasters he took at the end of the day, while at home he obeyed his mother-in-law, handing over to her the five piasters to help with house.

It was from this moment that his life became oppressive, darkened by the shadow of boredom and weariness. The whole world now seemed to gaze on him with contempt. In his filthy yellow shoes, his black trousers, his yellow coat and faded tarboosh, his cheeks puffed out from all the blowing he'd done, he was like a clown moving about in the midst of life; coming and going under glances of contempt from his fellow creatures. In the quarter he was known, not as Hasan Effendi, but as "the husband of the daughter of Umm Nafusa." At the local café he sat with head lowered, for seldom did Umm Nafusa give him any pocket money, so that he would spend night after night yearning to smoke a pipe of tobacco or to gamble a little at cards. A friend would pass, and he wouldn't be able to invite him to a pot of tea.

At home he commanded no respect whatsoever. His miserable wage scarcely sufficing to provide them with bread, his children regarded their grandmother as the mistress of the house. His own wife came and went as she liked, refusing to tell him where she'd been.

To escape from all this Hasan Effendi volunteered as an air-raid warden. Having learnt something about the job, the government provided him with a helmet and uniform.

Cairo was plunged into darkness and Hasan Effendi went out on inspection, and was astounded to find out that everyone in the district obeyed his least word. He only had to raise his head toward the stately houses of the rich and shout "put out those lights" for them to be put out instantly. Even the local constable would call him "Sir."

Hasan Effendi was amazed and overjoyed. Once, seeing a light at one of the windows of a villa, he had gone up, and rapped boldly at the door. Only as he was doing so did he notice the name on the brass plate—it was the house of the head of the local police station. Before he could take to his heels an elegant young girl had come out to inquire who it was. On seeing his uniform she was full of apologies and rushed off immediately to see about the window. Another time he spotted a car whose headlights hadn't been blacked out properly. He stopped it, but when he began to tell off the driver, the man answered him haughtily: "The Pasha's in a hurry. He's got a meeting at the Chamber of Delegates." But, nothing abashed, Hasan Effendi shouted back at him: "Orders are orders. I'm telling you; you've got to black out those headlights of yours." The Pasha took Hasan Effendi's side and began apologizing to him in a loud voice—no doubt in the hope that some journalist would hear of the discussion and would bring out in the morning papers an article under the title "The Democratic Pasha."

His mother-in-law had not yet got up by the time Hasan Effendi arrived back home. "Hasan, me lad, go up on the roof. All the chickens . . . ," she called at him from her bed. "'Lad' be damned, you shameless wench," he shouted back at her. "Get up yourself."

"Don't you shout at me like that," she screamed at him, taken completely aback by the way he had dared to speak to her.

"Shut up," he said, drowning her voice. "Shut up if you know what's good for you."

She took one look at the glint in his eyes—and she shut up.

Hasan Effendi went out and returned at noon. Not finding his wife at home he inquired where she was. "Nothing to do with you," answered his mother-in-law, at which Hasan Effendi calmly removed one shoe and gave her a good beating. Only then, begging for mercy, did she provide him with the information.

"That's better," he answered her, haughtily.

He then proceeded to inform the children that he was going to take a nap and that if he heard a sound from any of them he'd wring their neck. Generally they took no notice of him, but this time they too saw the glint in his eyes.

On awaking he ordered a cup of coffee, though previously he had always prepared it for himself. His mother-in-law brought it along to him. She was surprised and perplexed. "Perhaps," she told herself, "he's won the first prize in a lottery." Hasan Effendi tested the coffee, then flung it across the room, shouting at her that it was far too sweet. "I want things done as I like them."

Umm Nafusa's astonishment was redoubled.

That evening he rounded off his day bringing back some bananas for the children. His mother-in-law, on furtively searching his pockets, discovered only two piasters but could not find the courage to say anything.

The following morning he greeted his boss casually, seated himself on his chair, crossed his legs and began watching the passersby. The boss, in his turn, was amazed. None of his employees had ever shown him such disrespect; the man's manner and tone of voice were nothing less than arrogant. "Perhaps he's won the first prize in the lottery," said the boss to himself.

At the end of the day Hasan Effendi tackled him.

"Look here, Gaber. The money you're paying is no good to me. It's either ten piasters or goodbye and I'll find my living somewhere else."

The other agreed and changed his opinion about Hasan Effendi.

That night Hasan Effendi called out in his sleep "Put out those lights . . . put out those lights." His wife jumped out, thinking the order was addressed to her, and put out the light in the room; she then went out into the hall where she encountered her mother who had also heard the order.

Meanwhile Hasan Effendi snored contentedly, dreaming about authority, about a man named Hasan Effendi whose every word commanded blind obedience.

Cairo Is a Small City

———∿∿∿———

Nabil Gorgy

On the balcony of his luxury flat Engineer Adel Salim stood watching some workmen putting up a new building across the wide street along the center of which was a spacious garden. The building was at the foundations stage, only the concrete foundations and some of the first-floor columns having been completed. A young ironworker with long hair was engaged on bending iron rods of various dimensions. Adel noticed that the young man had carefully leant his Jawa motorcycle against a giant crane that crouched at rest awaiting its future tasks. "How the scene has changed!" Adel could still remember the picture of old-time master craftsmen, and of the workers who used to carry large bowls of mixed cement on their calloused shoulders.

The sun was about to set and the concrete columns of a number of new constructions showed up as dark frameworks against the light in this quiet district at the end of Heliopolis.

As on every day at this time there came down into the garden dividing the street a flock of sheep and goats that grazed on its grass, behind them two Bedouin women, one of whom rode a donkey, while the younger one walked beside her. As was his habit each day, Adel fixed his gaze on the woman walking in her black gown that not so much hid as emphasized the attractions of her body, her waist being tied round with a red band. It could be seen that she wore green plastic slippers on her feet. He wished that she would catch sight of him on the balcony of his luxurious flat; even if she did so, Adel was thinking, those Bedouin had a special code of behavior that differed greatly from what he was used to and rendered it difficult to make contact with them. What, then, was the reason, the motive, for wanting to think up some way of talking to her? It was thus that he was thinking, following her with his gaze as she occasionally chased after a lamb that was going to be run over by a car or a goat left far behind the flock.

Adel, who was experienced in attracting society women, was aware of his spirit being enthralled: days would pass with him on the balcony, sunset after sunset, as he watched her without her even knowing of his existence.

Had it not been for that day on which he had been buying some fruit and vegetables from one of the shopkeepers on Metro Street, and had not the shop-keeper seen another Bedouin woman walking behind another flock, and had he not called out to her by name, and had she not come; and had he not thrown her a huge bundle of waste from the shop, after having flirted with her and fondled her body—had it not been for that day, Adel's mind would not have given birth to the plan he was determined, whatever the cost, to put through, because of that woman who had bewitched his heart.

As every man, according to Adel's philosophy of life, had within him a devil, it was sometimes better to follow this devil in order to placate him and avoid his tyranny. Therefore Engineer Adel Salim finally decided to embark upon the terrible, the unthinkable. He remembered from his personal history during the past forty years that such a temporary alliance with this devil of his had gained him a courage that had set him apart from the rest of his col-leagues, and through it he had succeeded in attaining this social position that had enabled him to become the owner of this flat whose value had reached a figure which he avoided mentioning even in front of his family lest they might be upset or feel envy.

Thus, from his balcony on the second floor in Tirmidhi Street, Engineer Adel Salim called out in a loud voice "Hey, girl!" as he summoned the one who was walking at the rear of the convoy. When the flock continued on its way without paying any attention, he shouted again: "Hey, girl—you who sell sheep," and before the girl moved far away he repeated the word 'sheep.' Adel paid no attention to the astonishment of the doorman, who had risen from the place where he had been sitting at the entrance, thinking that he was being called. In fact he quietly told him to run after the two Bedouin women and to let them know that he had some bread left over which he wanted to give them for their sheep.

From the balcony Adel listened to the doorman calling to the two women in his authoritative Upper Egyptian accent, at which they came to a stop and the one who was riding the donkey looked back at him. Very quickly Adel was able to make out her face as she looked toward him, seeking to discover what the matter was. As for the young girl, she continued on behind the flock. The woman was no longer young and had a corpulent body and a commanding look which she did not seek to hide from him. Turning her donkey round, she crossed the street separating the garden from his building and waited in front of the gate for some new development. Adel collected up all the bread in the house and hurried down with it on a brass tray. Having descended to the street, he went straight up to the woman and looked at her. When she opened a saddlebag close by her leg, he emptied all the bread into it.

"Thanks," said the woman as she made off without turning toward him. He, though, raising his voice so that she would hear, called out, "And tomorrow too."

During a period that extended to a month Adel began to buy bread which he did not eat. Even on those days when he had to travel away or to spend the whole day far from the house, he would leave a large paper parcel with the doorman for him give to the Bedouin woman who rode the donkey and behind whom walked she for whom the engineer's heart craved.

Because Adel had a special sense of the expected and the probable, and after the passing of one lunar month, and in his place in front of the building, with bread on the brass tray, there occurred that which he had been wishing would happen, for the woman riding the donkey had continued on her way and he saw the other, looking around her carefully before crossing the road, ahead of him, walking toward him. She was the most beautiful thing he had set eyes on. The speed of his pulse almost brought his heart to a stop. How was it that such beauty was to be found without it feeling embarrassed at ugliness? For after it any and every thing must needs be so described. When she was directly in front of him, and her kohl-painted eyes were scrutinizing him, he sensed a danger which he attributed to her age, which was no more than twenty. How was it that she was so tall, her waist so slim, her breasts so full, and how was it that her buttocks swayed so enticingly as she turned away and went off with bread, having thanked him? His imagination became frozen even though she was still close to him: her pretty face with the high cheekbones, the fine nose and delicate lips, the silver, crescent-shaped earrings, and the necklace that graced her bosom? Because such beauty was "beyond the permissible," Adel went on thinking about Salma—for he had got to know her name, her mother having called her by it in order to hurry her back lest the meeting between the lovers be prolonged.

Adel was no longer troubled by the whistles of the workers who had now risen floor by floor in the building opposite him. He was in a state of infatuation, his heart captured by this moonlike creature. After the affair, in relation to himself, having been one of boldness, to end in seeing or greeting her, it now became a matter of necessity that she turn up before sunset at the house so that he might not be deprived of the chance of seeing her. So it was that Engineer Adel Salim fell in love with the beautiful Bedouin girl Salma. And just as history is written by historians, so it was that Adel and his engineering work determined the history of this passion in the form of a building each of whose columns represented a day and each of whose floors was a month. He noted that, at the completion of twenty-eight days and exactly at full moon, Salma would come to him in place of her mother to take the bread. And so, being a structural engineer, he began to observe the moon, his yearning increasing when it was waning and his spirits sparkling as its fullness drew near till, at full moon, the happiness of the lover was completed by seeing the beloved's face.

During seven months he saw her seven times, each time seeing in her the same look she had given him the first time: his heart would melt, all resolution would be squeezed out of him and that fear for which he knew no reason would be awakened. She alone was now capable of granting him his antidote. After the seventh month Salma, without any preamble, had talked to him at length, informing him that she lived with her parents around a spring at a distance of an hour's walk to the north of the airport, and that it consisted of a brackish spring alongside which was a sweet one, so that she would bathe in the first and rinse herself clean in the other, and that there were date palms around the two springs, also grass and pasturage. Her father, the owner of the springs and the land around them, had decided to invite him and so tomorrow, "He'll pass by you and invite you to our place, for tomorrow we attend to the shearing of the sheep."

Adel gave the lie to what he was hearing, for it was more than any stretch of the imagination could conceive might happen.

The following day Adel arrived at a number of beautifully made tents where a vast area of sand was spread out below date palms that stretched to the edge of a spring. Around the spring was gathered a large herd of camels, sheep and goats that spoke of the great wealth of the father. It was difficult to believe that such a place existed so close to the city of Cairo. If Adel's astonishment was great when Salma's father passed by him driving a new Peugeot, he was yet further amazed at the beauty of the area surrounding this spring. "It's the land of the future," thought Adel to himself. If he were able to buy a few feddans now he'd become a millionaire in a flash, for this was the Cairo of the future. "This is the deal of a lifetime," he told himself.

On the way the father asked a lot of questions about Adel's work and where he had previously lived and about his knowledge of the desert and its people. Though Adel noticed in the father's tone something more than curiosity, he attributed this to the nature of the Bedouin and their traditions.

As the car approached the tents Adel noticed that a number of men were gathered under a tent whose sides were open, and as the father and his guest got out of the car the men turned round, seated in the form of a horse-shoe. With the father sitting down and seating Engineer Adel Salim alongside him, one of the sides of the horse-shoe was completed. In front of them sat three men on whose faces could be seen the marks of time in the form of interlaced wrinkles.

The situation so held Adel's attention that he was unaware of Salma except when she passed from one tent to another in the direction he was looking and he caught sight of her gazing toward him.

The man who was sitting in a squatting position among the three others spoke. Adel heard him talking about the desert, water and sheep, about the roads that went between oases and the wadi, the towns and the springs of water, about the Bedouin tribes and blood ties; he heard him talking about the importance of protecting these roads and springs, and the palm trees and the dates, the goats and the milk upon which the suckling child would be fed; he also heard him talk about how small the *wadi* was in comparison to this desert that stretched out endlessly.

In the same way as Adel had previously built the seven-story building that represented the seven months, each month containing twenty-eight days, till he would see Salma's face whenever it was full moon, he likewise sensed that this was the tribunal which had been set up to make an inquiry with him into the killing of the man whom he had one day come across on the tracks between the oases of Kharga and Farshut. It had been shortly after sunset when he and a friend, having visited the iron ore mines in the oases of Kharga had, instead of taking the asphalt road to Asyut, proceeded along a rough track that took them down toward Farshut near to Qena, as his friend had to make a report about the possibility of repairing the road and of extending the railway line to the oases. Going down from the high land toward the wadi, the land at a distance showing up green, two armed men had appeared before them. Adel remembered how, in a spasm of fear and astonishment, of belief and disbelief, and with a speed that at the time he thought was imposed upon him, a shot had been fired as he pressed his finger on the trigger of the revolver which he was using for the first time. A man had fallen to the ground in front of him and, as happens in films, the other had fled. As for him and his friend, they had rushed off to their car in order to put and end to the memory of the incident by reaching the wadi. It was perhaps because Adel had once killed a man that he had found the courage to accept Salma's father's invitation.

"That day," Adel heard the man address him, "with a friend in a car, you killed Mubarak bin Rabi'a when he went out to you. Ziyad al-Mihrab being with him."

This was the manner in which Engineer Adel Salim was executed in the desert northwest of the city of Cairo: one of the men held back his head across a marble-like piece of stone, then another man plunged the point of a tapered dagger into the spot that lies at the bottom of the neck between the two bones of the clavicle.

The Girls and the Rooster

~~~

Abdou Gubeir

D on't hit black cats at night."
This was said by Sheikh Yasin in his Friday sermon in the
village mosque about nine years ago, and it was the same appeal
voiced by the young boys, on the recommendation of the mother Sayyida
and her mother-in-law Sakina after the triplets were born: Three girls whose
father found nothing in which to seek refuge from grief other than to laugh
crazily. From that day on he began to mock everything, though in the end he
accepted the matter as his destiny.

With the passing of the years, and as a sort of self-defense, the three daughters had become famed for their high-pitched voices: a loud screaming that
pierces one's forehead, or into "my heart" as Auntie Huda repeatedly put it.

As a solution requiring no careful deliberation by the father Barakat as he
was standing in front of the recording official, he named them all at one go:
Sayyida, Sakina, and Huda.

Some moments before, the voices of the three girls had been raised in
such a way as actually to pierce one's heart all at once, even though their
father Barakat had done what was necessary—as was intimated by Auntie
Huda and confirmed by the mother Sakina—by bringing from the Thursday
market three red blouses and three dresses with frills of cloth decorated
with bright red fuchsia.

Dresses with puffed up frills.

Each of the three girls slept with her frock: each had it clasped to her and was submerged in deep sleep till the morning; it was a long night and everyone in the village had made up their minds not to run off the three black cats that roamed round the roofs of the houses at night. In fact, the grandmother Sakina had placed for them, on the wall of the roof, three pieces of boiled meat in a clean container, also drinking water in a white enamel bowl, and had sworn on the morning of the following day that she had found small pieces of henna that had fallen from the girls' hands into the white bowl: they had definitely eaten the boiled meat, eaten it for certain.

Thus, when they had woken up, the mixture of henna had all but disappeared from their hands and feet. How can a girl wander around at night with her hand all bound up without at least some quantity of the henna coming off?

But, quite naturally, you can't remind the triplets that at night they changed into black cats and had then gone back once again to being what they were: girls happy with the henna on their feet and the palms of their hands, happy with the decorated fuchsia dresses, and happy with the singing begun for them by the other girls of the village, and aided by the mother, the grandmother, and the aunt. The three of them were confronting a memorable day in their lives. A day that would not end before they sat, one after the other, on the wooden bathroom chair in front of the midwife Umm Hamad, who had no sooner entered, with the call to the afternoon prayers having burst forth, than the girls screamed all at once.

"I'm always met by screams like this," Umm Hamad said to herself as she clenched her teeth, took off her black dress, and threw her head-covering to one side, then untied the cloth bundle and took out the razor that had just been sharpened at the knife-grinder's, the bottle of surgical spirit, and the wad of cotton wool.

Who was to be the first one whose clitoris Umm Hamad would cut? This was the terrifying question revolving in the girls' minds, each one separately, as each of them pushed forward one of the others.

"Come along," said Umm Hamad, rolling up her sleeves and enquiring in her loud voice, "Where's the chair? Where are the girls?"

They were screaming in the dark inner room, all piled up together in the corner.

The grandmother had boiled up the water and the mother had brought the red blouses, but they continued to scream and it became necessary for the father to come and settle things.

"Blood . . . blood . . . blood . . . ," said the girl Aisha, daughter of their maternal aunt, as she rushed out in terror.

"Everything will end now," said the father Barakat as he stretched out his legs on the couch outside the house, while the men, arriving together, seated themselves alongside him on the couch placed alongside the wall of the house.

The screaming had in fact ceased and the three girls, in a dazed state, were carried to the bed where the grandmother, with the help of the mother, stretched them out one beside the other, with their blouses pulled up from their thighs and the wad of cotton wool, oozing red, planted in the middle.

"Don't let in any old maid or woman wearing gold to see them," said Umm Hamad. Drying her hand, she replaced the razor in the wrapper. Then she sat down in the empty room at the low, round table to eat the roast male duck that had been specially prepared for her.

The singing grew louder to the sound of cooking pots and plates while places were laid out on the round tables where the men sat eating the dish of hot broth with rice and goat's meat.

Inside, the mother Sayyida was cooking for the three girls the big rooster that only that morning had been proudly showing off its scarlet comb.

Mother of the Destitute

—∿∿—

Yahya Hakki

Praised be He whose dominion extends over all creatures and Who knows no opposition to His rule. Here I have no wish but to recount the story of Ibrahim Abu Khalil as he made his way down the steps of life, like the leaves of spring, which, though lifted a little by the wind, contain, even at their height, their ineluctable descent until at last they are cushioned and trampled down into the earth. I was a witness to his descending the last steps of the ladder, but I only learnt later that he was an orphan and had been cast out upon the world at an early age; as to whether he came from the town or the country I know not, though my belief is that he was a city creature born and bred. His life of misery started with being a servant, and then a vendor of lupine on a handcart hung round with earthenware water-coolers from Qena, their necks decorated with flowers and sweet basil. I heard that later he had opened a small herbalist's, after which he had gone back again to being a street-vendor, jumping from tram to tram with his pins, needles for Primus stoves, and clothes-pegs. His life contained sporadic periods about which I have no information, though I am inclined to think that during his roving existence he must at times have known the sting of asphalt in the Kora Maidan penitentiary.

Just before I got to know him he used to occupy the triangular corner of pavement in the Square facing the shop of the Turk who sold halvah. There he would sit with a basket containing radishes, watercress, and leeks. His cry was

170

simply, "Tender radishes, fine watercress!" His face told of none of the various upheavals he'd been through or the buffetings he had had in his innumerable occupations. Such people take life as it comes; each day has its individual destiny, each day passes away and dies—like them—without legacy. They enter life's arena with their sensitivity already dead—has it died from ignorance, from stupidity, or from contentment and acceptance? Their eyes do not even blink at the abuse showered down at them. Yet you must not be too hasty in judging in case you should be unfair; had you known him as I did you would have found him a simple-hearted person—genial, polite, and generous.

In spite of the efforts he expended in his search for sufficient food to keep himself alive, his heart knew neither envy nor rancor. His rheumy eyes hinted that in his heart there was a latent propensity for joking and being gay. He had a most captivating way of looking at you; his smile seemed to emerge through veil after veil—just like watching a slow-motion picture of a smile of the eyes being born. When he raised his face, sheltering his eyes with his hand, it would seem to me as if the world had shrunk to this small frame containing just the two of us and that his words were a communion, subdued and private.

Abu Khalil would take up his accustomed place shortly before noon. When afternoon came and the morning basket was sold out, or almost so, he would get up and walk off in his languid way; wandering round the square, he would pass by many of the shopkeepers, lingering with this one and that as they asked each other how they were getting on, and swapping anecdotes and jokes with some of them. He had a friend from whom he would buy a loaf stuffed with taamiya and carry it off tucked under his arm, and another friend from whom he bought the cheapest kind of cigarettes, which he kept in a metal tin above his belt, between his naked body and his outer garment. Then he would leave his friends for the pavement outside the mosque where, as he put it, he'd enjoy a breath of fresh air—and meet the newcomers of the day. When the novelty had worn off he would return to his place, seat himself, mutter a grace, and eat his meal. Having finished it he would kiss the palm and back of his hand in gratitude, give thanks to God and, settling his body into a relaxed position, light up a cigarette and smoke it with great delight, for he was a man who took his pleasures seriously. Then he would disappear from the Square and not return until just before sunset when he would lay out the evening basket. As for his supper, it consisted of a loaf of bread and a piece of halvah which he would buy from his neighbor whose shop lay north of his pitch; after which he would vanish from the Square as it became empty of passersby. I don't know where he slept, though I did hear that he shared a mat with a toothless, bedridden hag in a small room under the curve of some steps at the furthermost end of a steep lane.

Had he ever married? Did he have any children or relations? I don't know. Because of my liking for Abu Khalil I have no wish to talk here of the things I've heard about his strange relationship with that bedridden, evil-smelling old woman—Ibrahim has a kindly heart—nor do I want to talk about the way he was unfaithful to her from time to time, when God provided him with the necessary money and vigor on a hill close by Sayyida, for there is nothing I am more reluctant to do than speak evil of this holy quarter and its inhabitants.

One clear, radiant day Abu Khalil arrived at his customary place on the pavement to find that the far corner was occupied by a woman surrounded by three young children, with a fourth at her breast, its eyes closed in swooning ecstasy as though it were imbibing wine. The catastrophic thing about it was that she was sitting in front of a basket filled with radishes, watercress, and leeks, and when she began calling out, "Sun-kissed radishes, a millieme the bundle!" her piercing voice rang out through the whole square. O Provider, O Omniscient! For a while Abu Khalil sat watching her in silence, then he sighed and took himself a little way off. He, too, began to call his wares, trying to raise his voice above hers, but he could not do it and broke into a fit of coughing. He wanted to speak to her, to ask her where she came from and why she had chosen this particular place, but she paid no attention to him. With one hand she sold her wares, with the other she managed her children: transferring the drugged infant with a mere bend of her knee from one breast to the other, and then moving toward her water-cooler like a cripple, so that a little of her thigh showed naked. This had no effect—Abu Khalil's heart was so incensed against her that he was not in an affectionate mood. No doubt, he assured himself, this was but a fleeting intrusion and everything would be all right the next day.

But the following morning he found her there before him as large as life. He began turning his gaze toward her, toward the passersby and his neighbors, getting up and sitting down again, leaving his basket and going off to tell his friends this depressing piece of news. Then he would return only to find her voice ringing through the square as though calling together her kin on the fateful Day of Resurrection.

During these days Abu Khalil bought five cigarettes instead of his usual ten.

He was at his wit's end and sought to dispel his anxiety by watching this brazen woman who had trespassed on his pitch and was competing with him in the earning of his daily bread. The strange thing was that he started to become interested in her and tried to exchange smiles with her on one occasion. Days went by and his basket crept closer to Badr's; it was as though he wanted to say to her, "Come, let's go into partnership together," but he didn't do it.

Badr felt that she was firmly established and that Ibrahim was powerless against her; she realized that she had gained some sort of hold over him. So, one day, she deigned to reply to him and it was not long before she was bidding him keep an eye on the children when, at a call from nature, she had to go off to the plot of waste land close by the public fountain.

For a long time Abu Khalil neglected his own basket and gave up loafing round with his friends or standing at the door of the Mosque, whether a breeze was blowing or not. A secret hope lay in his heart. Perhaps Badr would prove to be his share of good fortune, rained down unexpectedly upon him by the heavens. Nothing would he love better than to hand over the leading-rein of his life to this resolute woman and to live under her protective wing. She was a woman (although so much like a man) of whom he would have every reason to boast to all and sundry. He would ingratiate himself with her, would make her laugh so that he might laugh with her, and would wait till she first bit off a mouthful or two from the loaf before she passed it to him and he would eat from where her mouth had been, possibly receiving a taste of her spittle; she it would be who would wake him in the morning and cover him up at night; and when he behaved badly and stayed on with his friends and the shopkeepers, she would search him out and drag him back to where he ought to be. It was thus that he talked to himself. But would he ever broach the matter to her? He wouldn't dare, for he knew nothing about her and there was no one in the square who knew her.

At this time Abu Khalil bought the taamiya for his lunch on credit.

One evening when his basket had drawn so close to hers that they were touching, Badr—without being asked—told him about her life. And thus it was that she too became one of the problems which it had been decreed should fall to Ibrahim's lot in this world. She told him that she was free yet not divorced, married yet living as a widow, for she had a husband of whose whereabouts she was ignorant, a man from Upper Egypt who used to carry a large bundle of vests, socks, and towels on his back, hawking them round the cafés. He would stay with her for a time and then suddenly disappear; on one occasion she had heard that he had gone to Lower Egypt, on another to the south, not knowing whether he was running away from her or from the fear of an old blood-feud, or whether he himself had a blood-feud which honor forced him to pursue. Almost a year and a half having passed since his last disappearance, she did not know whether he was dead or alive—though the odds were that he was alive and well, because the news of his death would have reached her, as he had his name and that of his village tattooed on his arm. Or had they perhaps skinned his body? Was he a murderer lingering in prison, or had he been murdered and was lying in some grave unknown to her? He had just disappeared, leaving her with her children. She had gone out in search of her daily bread and chance had led her to a good man like Ibrahim Abu Khalil.

More days passed and they grew closer. Badr began to feel tenderly for Ibrahim and would buy him food without asking for money, for she had amalgamated their baskets, while both their earnings had ended up in her pocket. She felt that her life had finally taken on this particular form. One day, accepting her position (and don't ask if it was from choice or necessity, it being no easy matter to find another Upper Egyptian to replace the absent man), she said to Ibrahim, "Your gallabiya is dirty. Come with me tonight and I'll wash it for you."

Abu Khalil was sitting in front of her, his back to the road. He began talking to her, oblivious of the passing of people and of time. Could he believe his eyes or were they playing him tricks? It seemed to him that her lips suddenly trembled, her teeth gleamed and her eyes, wide open, were sparkling. Her glance was glued to a spot behind him. He turned and found an Upper

Egyptian, his back bowed under a large bundle, coming toward them with measured gait. It needed but one glance to tell him that this was a hard and merciless man, one who couldn't be trifled with. The man lowered his burden, squatted down, and wiped away the sweat from his brow.

"How are you?" was all he had to say to Badr.

"Everything is well," she answered. "Thank God for your safe return!"

The young Upper Egyptian was silent for a while. Then, turning his head, he directed but one glance at Abu Khalil. Reassured, he turned to his wife and said, "Everything comes to pass in time, but patience is good."

Poor Ibrahim rose, shaking the dust from his backside, and disappeared from their sight, swallowed up by the crowds in the square.

Many days passed during which I didn't see him. Some say that he was taken ill with fever, others that the old bedridden woman had learnt about Badr and had put something into his food—something which she had had to wait for till nature took its course with a woman younger than herself—and that this had caused him grievous harm.

For a long time I was absent from the square and its inhabitants. When I returned and passed by the pavement facing the Turk who sold halvah, I found neither Badr of the many offspring, nor Ibrahim.

Then one day it chanced that I went out early on some business or other and entered the square before the shops had opened. My teeth were chattering with the cold, for we were then in the Coptic month of Touba, which is proverbially the peak of winter. Barefooted beings thrust their swollen fingers under their armpits and walked as though treading on thorns; from time to time a harsh, raucous cough rang through the square, followed by silence; then muttered scraps of conversation could be clearly heard from voices still heavy with sleep and phlegm. In spite of all the people to be seen coming and going, one couldn't help having the sensation of being in a deserted city, which neither knew, nor was known by, those passersby. Suddenly I bumped into Ibrahim Abu Khalil: his clothes were tattered and torn, his head and feet bare, his walk a sort of totter, though his somber manner of looking at one was the same as ever, and his smile unchanged.

He had gone out at this early hour to do his job, which had to be finished before traffic unfolded in the square. He had a new occupation: providing incense—a job requiring no more than a pair of old scales, a thick chain, sawdust, and a few bits of frankincense and wormwood. These, together with chunks of bread, he would put into a nose-bag slung round his shoulder, into which some millieme and half-millieme pieces had perhaps also been thrown.

The moment I saw him I realized that this was the occupation to which Abu Khalil had been born. I should have expected him to have ended up in it, for it suited his temperament admirably, being an easy job that provides its practitioners with the pleasures of loafing about and coming across all kinds and descriptions of people. Besides which the earnings were steady— being in the form of subscriptions—and there was no fixed price. He was his own master and there was no fear of his goods spoiling in case business was bad. While a man in such an occupation would admit that he does not attain the status of those pedlars who gain their livelihood with the sweat of their brow, he cannot on the other hand be accused of mendicancy, for there he is in front of you, going off to work with the tools of his trade in his hand.

If this was how this occupation was regarded by the majority of those practicing it, it was something altogether different in Abu Khalil's view. He had tired of trade in its various forms, having found it to be a tug-of-war of deceit, calculation, and endless haggling over milliemes. The incense business, however, was based solely on emotion, and he was confident that his greeting, with which shopkeepers would begin their day, was bound to be auspicious, emanating from a heart which was pure, devout, and affectionate. Poor Abu Khalil! He understood neither life nor the nature of human beings.

For many days after this I was often in his company, and saw with my own eyes Master Hasan the barber (who was no simpleton!) unwilling to pay him his millieme until he'd dragged him into the shop to fumigate the chair, the mirror, and the small brass basin with its edge cut away to allow for the customer's neck; I also saw the owner of The National Restaurant pick him out a single taamiya left over from yesterday or the day before; as for the Turk he would give him a millieme, irritated and resentful, and send him packing. When most of the shopkeepers had got used to him, they would give him the millieme whether there was any incense floating upwards or not, and so Abu Khalil became negligent about his business and his coals were dead for the

greater part of the morning; or, if there was a faint glow, all that issued forth
was an evil-smelling black smoke repellent to the nostrils.

One clear, radiant day I was walking beside Ibrahim when I felt a sudden
hush descend on the Square, just as the weather grows calm before the advent
of a cyclone and the eye imagines that the sky is quivering like a bat's wing.
Then a man with hawklike eyes approached from Marasina Street, wearing
a garment made up of seventy patches, a green turban on his head, and with
a brisk, determined, indefatigable gait; his body erect, his tongue unceasingly chanting prayers and supplications, holding a brazier from which rose
beautifully fragrant smoke, the brazier's chain sparkling yellow. O Provider,
O Omniscient!

On the first day the shopkeepers sharply repulsed this newcomer, for
they were Abu Khalil's customers and it wasn't reasonable to buy two blessings, one of which might spoil the other, on the same morning. But when
he returned on the second, the third, and the fourth day, he received his first
milliemes. Then he did the rounds of all the shops once again, whether the
owner had had pity on him or not. I was fascinated by this man's persever-
ance and strength of purpose. Leaving my bleary-eyed friend, I went off
after this extraordinary newcomer and found myself being dragged along
at a brisk pace from Sayyida Zaynab to Bab al-Khalq Square, to the Citadel
and thence to Sayyida Aisha and across the Cemetery to Sayyida Nafisa and
so to Suyufiya and Khayamiya and Mitwalli Gate. Then he went to a small
café in Sayyidna Hussein where he took off his green turban and sat down to
smoke a shisha. Breathless and dripping with sweat, I sat down beside him,
having seen how he had walked for a whole hour to get one customer. Never
in my life have I met anyone who strove to earn his living with the persever-
ance, patience, and energy of that man.

Poor Ibrahim left his brazier and began to content himself with passing
by the shopkeepers empty-handed, in the hope that they would remember
him and dispense their usual charity. His income decreased and he was
sometimes forced to stand in the middle of the Square, or at the Sayyida
Zaynab Gate, so that some visitors might press their charity into his hand,
taking him for a beggar too shy to ask for alms. The strange thing was that
after a while Abu Khalil worked up a clientele of a few faithful customers

who would search him out to give him what they could. Poor Abu Khalil! He understood neither life nor the nature of human beings.

One clear, radiant day as poor Ibrahim sat in his accustomed place, a loud shout rang out close by him which echoed through the whole Square: "The Everliving! The Eternal!" People gathered round a man who had fallen down in a trance, seized by religious ecstasy. A woman, dressed in a black gown, yellow mules, and a necklace of large amber beads, stood at his head and broke out into trilling cries. The stricken man came to, but his mouth was closed and he uttered not a word; his squinting eyes, darkened with kohl, stared round at the faces of those gathered about him and filled with tears. Then he raised his hands, loaded with blue, green, and red rings, wiped his face, and prepared to gather up the money.

When Abu Khalil heard that very same scream at the very same hour on the second and third day, he left his place and turned toward the mosque, mumbling, "O Mother of the Destitute! Give me succor!"

He had tired of life; illness and weakness held him in their grip. The film on his eyes had grown worse, and his back was bowed. With heavy steps he moved toward the shrine of the Mother of the Destitute; around it were ranks of squatting beggars—it seemed as though they had been created like that, their backs propped against its wall, making a circle like lice round a poor man's collar. Little hope for him to find himself a place in the 'first-class' by the door! So he left and went round the mosque till he came to the place of ablution, where he sat himself down by its door. Those who had come before him and had seniority turned and gave him a withering look: nobody hates a beggar like a beggar.

Here I left Abu Khalil and dissociated myself from him, for he had joined the people of a world which is not our world. He was in a world from which there was no exit; it had but one entrance and above it was written—"The Gate of Farewell."

The Old Man

Gamil Atia Ibrahim

The old man is in the corner of the room. His period of service in the government has come to an end and the procedures and papers for retirement are being completed. While in the service and at an age of over fifty he had graduated in law, but in regard to promotion he had not benefitted greatly from the qualification. Without uttering a word, the man runs his eyes over the men and women working there.

When he had entered the faculty of law he had been preoccupied by the question of justice. Why should his wife have died when she was still young? Why had she not given him any children? Would he have been entitled to divorce her? Why did she die during the air raids of Cairo in 1956?

The doctor had told him that the war had frightened her and had affected her weak heart. He was, however, not entirely sure about that because in the last two weeks her state of health had been extremely bad.

The burial grounds of Imam Shafi'i in Cairo are full of the living, who have taken up residence in the rooms specially built for those visiting the dead. At the time he told himself that directly the war ended he would move her body to the burial grounds of Port Said, but till now he had not carried out his promise.

He had learnt during his long life in government service that nothing was so harmful to an employee as becoming attached to a young girl at work.

He speaks to himself, addressing the depths of his soul, and sees himself standing on a high rock in a wasteland and talking to a group of people, declaiming them and shouting for justice. He would have liked to have donned a judge's robes and have dispensed justice among people. He keeps control of himself, paying particular attention to his hands lest he wave them about in the air as he shouts silently and draw to himself the gaze of those sitting in the room. One hand he puts in a pocket and the other under his chin as he sits relaxed, gazing ahead of him and leaning back against the chair.

He too had been a young man. His wife had been in her prime when he had married her. Later on everyone would say: An old man whose wife had died and who remained a widower the rest of his life, then he went mad during the few hours before he was to go on pension. Let him go off to the lavatory and talk to himself there to his heart's content.

The woman who was deputy head of the department suddenly said to him in a voice that betrayed a dislike of him, "Mr. Abdel Azeem, you can leave. You are now on pension."

The man realized what was going on in her mind. He decided to ignore her invitation to go, to be driven away from the office. He took refuge in silence and, as usual, did not turn his face to her. Everyone was sitting and looking at him. They all knew that today he would be going back home and would not again put in an appearance. He had retired on pension—and Leila too knew that.

The man began asking himself why he hadn't yet moved his wife's body to the burial grounds in Port Said. Leila wished him good health and a long and happy life, and he said to her, "That's life." He wasn't, though, altogether sure that he had said anything to her or whether he had contented himself with looking at her, with staring into her ever-radiant face.

Before leaving the room and saying goodbye to the others he told himself that he hadn't failed his wife, for after the 1956 war there'd been the 1967 war in which both the dwellings of Port Said and its burial grounds had been laid waste, then had come the war of 1973 which had ended with the liberation of part of Sinai, and it hadn't been possible for him throughout these wars to move the body. He also told himself that it was just as well, for there were still many wars to come.

Across Three Beds
in the Afternoon

Sonallah Ibrahim

H e was hungry. The alarm clock placed above the television set
pointed to eight o'clock. There were still twenty minutes to go
before Sayyid returned, and then they would all start to eat.

He inclined his head slightly, listening to her moving about in the kitchen.
He knew that she was now walking about energetically between the sink, the
gas stove, and the table with the thin sheet-iron top, despite her sixty-five years,
and that everything would be scattered round about her in utter confusion.

When she had almost finished she would call to him from the kitchen,
"Isn't it yet time for Sayyid to come back?"

He would look at the alarm clock, carefully examining it from behind his
thick spectacles, and would then say to her, "He must be on his way now."

From the place he had chosen for himself on the bed he was able to
see the door of the flat when Sayyid would put his key into it, and with the
familiar movement push against it to open it, and he would walk inside
saying, "Peace be upon you."

Despite the fact that his wife never stopped complaining that this position of his exposed him to drafts, he had continued to retain it ever since
his recurrent illness had forced him to take to his bed, so that he might, as
he put it, "be in touch with events." The room had three beds in it, two of
which stood close to each side of the balcony door; the third joined up with
one of them to make a straight line. When he lay down on it he was facing

the balcony, and if he turned round and sat across the bed, leaning his back against the wall as was his wont, the door of the room was facing him, followed by the hallway, and then the front door of the flat.

Because of the drafts the balcony door was always kept closed night and day, summer and winter, so that those who visited them, in particular their daughter Fadia, always complained that the smell in the flat was unbearable.

According to the alarm clock Sayyid should now be at the top of the street, approaching with long, easy strides, the day's newspaper folded under his arm. On reaching the bread shop, he would stop and buy ten loaves, which he would wrap up in his newspaper, and then once again continue on his way to the Cooperative to see what new things they had on sale. If he were lucky . . .

He sucked in his lips, hoping that Sayyid would bring with him some of those Ummahat dates which, besides being cheap, were easy to munch up and swallow, and had a sweet taste if dipped into white sesame oil; the latter, however, was not at present on the market.

He gave a characteristic shake of his head and, stretching out his fingers under his vest, he began scratching his chest violently to rub away the accumulated dirt. By reason of his illness he was excused from having a bath, a practice he had had no taste for since his youth, not so much through a dislike of cleanliness as through laziness. Thus, when young, he used to go to sleep in his outdoor clothes in order to save the time required for putting them on in the morning before going off to school—a habit he had been forced to abandon when he had taken his Primary examination and had joined the Ministry.

He interlaced his hands on his stomach and once again looked at the alarm clock. After ten minutes it would be time for the news bulletin. Sayyid would certainly come in before then and would turn on the radio which was placed in the hallway.

Before he was able to smell it, the spluttering sound of frying came to him from the kitchen. Seating himself up straight, he blinked behind his thick glasses as he strove to keep the front door of the flat in view so that he would not miss it being opened and Sayyid entering.

The mother's voice was raised from the kitchen: "Sayyid? Have you come, darling?"

Having closed the door behind him, Sayyid crossed the hall. He put the bread on the dining-table, then moving to the room in the forefront of which his father was seated, said in a loud voice so that it might reach his mother as well, "Peace be upon you."

The old man repressed his disappointment when he perceived that Sayyid had not brought any fruit with him; he stretched out his hand and took the newspaper from him, saying, "What's the news?"

Sayyid pursed his lips as he seated himself on the edge of the bed beside his father, and put his fingers up to his tie to undo it.

"Nothing."

Then casually: "Just a military communiqué."

Suddenly the old man became so animated that Sayyid added, "Ten minutes' exchange of fire."

"But war will break out," said the old man, struggling against his feeling of disappointment.

Carrying his shoes in his hand, Sayyid looked round for his slippers. Not finding them, he called out, "Mummy—where are my slippers?"

At forty-two Sayyid was still unable to remember where he left his various belongings before going out in the morning.

"You've got them, darling," the mother answered from the kitchen. "They're where you left them this morning."

"Perhaps they're in your room," said the old man, spreading out the newspaper and gazing at the headlines.

Barefoot, Sayyid went off to his room, where he found the slippers beside the door. He stood taking off the rest of his clothes in front of the large wardrobe mirror, which as usual reflected his face distorted. However, the softness of his skin and the lack of a trace of a single hair on his chin showed up on its surface. Were it not for a slight pallidity, somebody seeing him might mistakenly think he was in his twenties—and this would often occur.

He pulled open the flap of the wardrobe to put his clothes on the hanger, then he took up the pajamas he had thrown on the chair that morning without folding them and began putting them on.

Sayyid used this room solely for the purpose of changing his clothes, and would spend all his time in the other room. When the mother had been ill for a long time, he had started to sleep in the third bed facing her, the bed which had belonged to his sister Fadia before she had married. Scarcely had the mother recovered than the father became ill, and thus Sayyid had stayed on in the third bed.

When he had finished putting on his pajamas he heard his mother's voice from the kitchen, "Sayyid. The plates, darling."

He left the room. His father caught sight of him crossing the hall and called out, "Put the radio on for Daddy."

He went to the old radio and turned it on, waiting until it gave out a noise like the intermittent coughing of an old man; satisfied that the radio was working, he took himself off to the kitchen.

His mother was bent over the food on the stove. She turned to him and asked,

"Have you bought the cooking butter?" Several beads of sweat had collected above her conspicuous mustache.

"There was a great crush at the door of the Cooperative," said Sayyid, "and I couldn't get in."

He began collecting up the plates from the rack and carried them in to his father's room.

In the past they usually ate in the hall. Of late, however, they had, because of illness, come to eat in the same room as they slept, on a small table at the end of which the television was placed. The hall table was used only when guests came, which was rare now.

When Sayyid had brought the salt cellar, the spoons and knives, the mother appeared with her slightly bent back and flabby body, which shook as she moved to right and left. She was carrying a large bowl of potatoes cooked with tomatoes, which she placed in the middle of the table. Sayyid went to the kitchen and returned with a wide dish filled with rice.

The father made sniffing noises as he got out of bed with difficulty and took his place at the table. In comparison with the picture of him hanging on the wall he looked as though his body had shrunk to half its size.

"A glass of water for my medicine, Sayyid," he said.

There was no need for him to have asked because Sayyid was, by force of habit, already in the process of bringing two glasses, not one, because both the father and the mother used to take a number of medicines, in the form of both pills and drops, before and after meals.

Breathing heavily, the mother filled a large plate with rice and potatoes to which she added salad, and gave it to her husband. She did it with
the aplomb of someone performing an act that would go down in history.
He started turning over and mixing up the food, then he attacked it with
prodigious appetite, having forgotten about the news bulletin which the
announcer was reading out in a grave voice. The mother piled up a similar
plate for herself after having swallowed her medicine. As for Sayyid, he had
started off with the potatoes on their own. There was no longer any sound
except that of their mouths as they munched at the food, interspersed by the
mother's heavy breathing.

"Hasn't Fadia phoned?" asked Sayyid.

"Not a word," she said. Her preoccupation with the food prevented her
from speaking at greater length, so she contented herself by adding, "Perhaps
she'll phone in the afternoon."

The question and answer had been repeated at the same time for the last
fortnight, for on that date Fadia had given birth to her first child. A month
previously the mother had sworn that she wouldn't put a foot inside her
daughter's house, while the girl's husband had likewise sworn that he would
break her foot it she did so; thus neither the father, the mother, nor Sayyid had
paid Fadia a visit when she had given birth, or afterwards. This had caused
the husband to swear anew that he would divorce his wife were she to take
her child to see its grandparents.

The mother and daughter, however, remained in touch by telephone. The
latter would often place the receiver by her child's mouth so that his grandmother could hear his screaming or gurgling, although mostly he made no
sound whatsoever.

The father having finished everything that was on his plate, the mother
gave him another helping, which he attacked with the same gusto. The mother
took the opportunity of a moment's break from eating to ask him, "How does
Daddy like the food?"

Ever since their marriage more than forty years ago they had been addressing each other as 'Daddy' and 'Mummy.'

"Bless you," said the father through a full mouth, and several grains of
rice fell on to his pajama front.

The mother turned to Sayyid, who was eating with no less good an appetite than his father.

"Don't you yet know when your inquiry will take place?"

"No," said Sayyid.

"It was in the power of the Head of the Department to finalize the matter himself without the need for an inquiry or anything of that sort," she continued.

Sayyid shrugged his shoulders and did not reply.

Putting a large spoonful of the mixture of rice, potatoes, and salad into his mouth, the father asked, "Was it necessary to change the universe?"

It was a comment that came as a surprise to Sayyid in that it was a harbinger of a change occurring in his father's attitude. Up until now he had believed that his father and mother were on his side, as they had always been. Were they not the only people who always gave him looks of admiration when, for instance, he announced to them the linguistic and grammatical mistakes he discovered in the newspapers, whereas at the firm he was met with looks of boredom and scorn, especially from Suleiman?

This was quite apart from the fact that he had no desire to change either the universe or anything else: all it amounted to was that he wanted to put matters right.

What, after all, was the sense of an Arab firm in an Arab country dating its letters to other Arab firms in figures rather than in letters?

"But Sayyid's right," said the mother, looking at him with pride.

"What will we gain by writing the date in letters?" said the father whose faith in his son had been shaken by the prospect of the awaited inquiry.

Sayyid bent his head over his plate and began thinking about the matter despondently. Was there not a certain music pleasing to a trained ear about a sentence such as this: Written on the third of November of the year one thousand, nine hundred and sixty-nine? Or—the fourteenth of December of the year one thousand, nine hundred and sixty-eight. Ninety per cent of people today would not notice the difference in the grammatical inflections of the two sentences, brought about by the fact that in Arabic there are two words for 'year' of different genders. Are there many people capable of distinguishing the correct form in which to write 1912, for example, in letters, there being no less than four different ways of writing 'twelve'?

Had Suleiman not objected and taken the matter to the Head of the Department, no difficulty would have arisen. Many such matters occurred every day that were open to the sort of change Sayyid had wrought in the dating of letters, matters that would normally pass unnoticed. But Suleiman—someone without any subject of daily conversation except his innumerable amatory conquests— had wanted to make an issue of the matter, and an occasion for exhibiting his talent for ingratiating himself. What would the firm do when writing to other firms in Arab countries that used different names for the months? Would it date its letters with two different words for the months, sometimes three?

Sayyid was at no loss for words to defend his views to the Head of the Department. Numbers are always liable to error, and for this reason cheques, for example, are written both in figures and words. There was also the basic argument that the figures used were alien to the Arabic language. Had the head of the Department been somebody more serious-minded, the matter would have ended with his suggestion being accepted and that would have been the end of it.

The father had finished what was on his plate and had left his spoon balanced on the side of it. He sat back in his chair and placed his hand on his stomach.

A whole plateful of food took him no more than a few minutes to get through because, having lost all his teeth long ago, he masticated none of it.

"Shall I give you some more?" his wife asked.

"Thanks be to God, but I've had enough," he said. He took two of the pills to be taken after meals and swallowed them with the rest of the water in his glass. Then, getting up from the chair, he went to the bed and stretched himself out on his back, interlocking his hands over his chest.

Lassitude had overcome him and he felt a strong desire for sleep. In a state of semi-doze he watched his wife and son as they removed the food that was left over and hurried off to their beds, their two heads placed in a line with his own. The three made a triangle with six eyes looking in one direction, which was the balcony door.

In the past a nap after lunch would last for a long time, after which the father would wake up refreshed and active. But in recent years it had become extremely short, so that he would soon wake up and remain stretched out looking at the ceiling without clearly distinguishing its details. Meanwhile, the sun outside would fall away on its path to its final disappearance, and the light in the room would gradually diminish. Then, raising his head from time to time, he would scrutinize the other two beds from behind his thick spectacles. Generally the mother too would wake up. What usually happened was that one of them would start up a conversation across the two beds at the time when the other had, in fact, just woken from sleep.

This conversation would usually begin by one of them—generally the father—mentioning that such-and-such a relative of his had not visited them for a long time. He would mention this in a matter-of-fact voice that outwardly suggested nothing. The other—generally the mother—would then do a swift calculation as to the last time this relative had visited them. At which the father would say, pretending indifference, "Perhaps he's too busy or he's ill—or it's somebody in his family. Who knows?"

The mother would immediately retort that this relative had been seen at so-and-so's last week, for, without leaving the house, she was fully informed via the telephone about what was going on in their small world.

This being the reply the father was awaiting, he would give a sigh. The conversation would then take one of two courses: either a review of all the information available about the personal life of this relative, or an enumeration of the other relatives and friends who had also not done their duty for some time by visiting them.

Today, however, the conversation took a different turn by reason of the fact that Fadia had announced over the telephone yesterday that her husband had got himself a contract to work in Kuwait and that they'd be going away just as soon as the child's health permitted.

"I'll die without seeing the boy," said the father in his usual matter-of-fact voice.

His wife immediately answered, "Don't say such a thing." Then:

"May God take vengeance on whoever may be the cause!" little knowing that she was exposing herself to this heavenly vengeance.

There was a great deal of truth in what the father said after a while: "Were it not for your romance with his father we wouldn't have given him Fadia."

It was an accusation which the mother continued to deny. She merely answered, "Let him and his father go to Hell."

This, however, did not alter the fact that she was once in love with the father of her daughter's husband, to whom they were related. This was found out by her husband one night when they were in bed together and she, in a moment of abandon, had called out the name of the relative instead of that of the person in whose embrace she lay.

"Who do you think he looks like?" he asked for the hundredth time.

"I swear he doesn't resemble his father at all," she answered, also for the hundredth time.

Then, remembering: "Would you like me to make you a cup of coffee, Daddy?"

Without averting his eyes from the ceiling, Daddy asked, "Hasn't Sayyid woken up yet?"

Sayyid was the only one who derived full benefit from the afternoon nap. He would sleep deeply for an hour or more, and on getting up would begin the evening's program by drinking some coffee—an uninterrupted habit ever since he had taken his licentiate and joined the firm which had later become a governmental organization.

What would happen was that Sayyid would choose this moment to turn over on his bed and stretch out his legs to the full; he would then fling out his arms in a deep yawn, at which the father and the mother would intone with one voice, "Had a good sleep, darling?"

Sayyid would mutter, "Bless you," directed to the two of them.

"Did you sleep well?' the mother would ask.

"Not bad," he would answer.

On this day, at the moment that Sayyid awoke from sleep, there immediately came to him the picture of the Head of the Department's room as he rose to his feet with flushed face to announce in a peremptory voice: "An inquiry must be held."

But it was the Head of the Department who was responsible for everything that had occurred. No sooner had he disdainfully announced that the question of dating letters was of extreme triviality and did not require all this discussion than Sayyid had jumped to his feet—perhaps for the first time in his career—to insist that many things depended on this trivial matter and that anyway it was an attempt to combat ignorance and indifference. This was an allusion which Suleiman regarded as an insult to himself, so he replied with a reference to Sayyid's chin on which no hair had until now appeared. And so Sayyid had raised his hand, certainly for the first time in his life, and slapped Suleiman on the face.

He was snatched away from the room of the Head of the Department by his father's voice saying, "What do you say about Sayyid going off on his own and bringing the child back with him?"

He had for a long time past, owing to the affirmations of doctors, lost hope in having his name perpetuated on earth through Sayyid. Despite the fact that Fadia's child would not bear his name, he would, of course, carry a large part of his own blood—and here he was, at death's door, being deprived of seeing him.

When thinking about the new suggestion, the mother felt that complete victory over her daughter's husband would not be realized. He had a sort of assurance about their weakness and the best thing would be for them to find a way of forcing him to bring the child submissively—or at least to allow Fadia to do so.

"And will he accept?" she said without enthusiasm. "In any case I'll tell Fadia if she rings."

They were all thinking about the same subject when the father said in an unconcerned tone, "I wonder what will happen to the flat?"

The flat was a large one, consisting of the first floor of an old house with a garden, though its furnishings were all new.

"Perhaps they'll let it off furnished," said the mother, "or leave it for one of his brothers."

"And when they return they'll find all the furniture ruined," said the father anxiously.

They had known the furniture well, piece by piece, ever since the father and mother themselves had bought it—all except the massive American refrigerator which their daughter's husband had bought from God knows where.

"Perhaps he'll only stay a year in Kuwait," she said, "and then there'll be no point in letting it out."

"In that event," said Sayyid, translating into words the thought that had appeared on the horizon, "they can give us the refrigerator instead of leaving it in a closed-up flat."

Over the past fifteen years the father had managed, from his meager pension and Sayyid's salary, to provide his household, consecutively, with a gas oven, a water-heater, a hand shower, and a telephone—and finally a television, the installments on which he was still paying off.

Every time they decided to buy a refrigerator he would stand beside the old wooden ice-box and, patting its surface, would say that it could carry on for the next summer and the best thing was to buy something else.

It was Sayyid who used to buy the ice for it twice a day in the summer, which they would place above its pipes; in the winter it was left unused for the cockroaches to sport about in.

"Fridges in Kuwait are dirt cheap," said the father, "and they could bring a new one back with them."

"Everyone there owns a car," said Sayyid.

The mother imagined Sayyid in a fast red car before the door of the house.

Sayyid was thinking about the clippers of the electric shaver which had gone wrong some time ago. It was one of the three gadgets he had bought from Gaza during one of the trips the organization used to arrange for its employees before June 1967. When the clippers had broken he had put the shaver away because there were no spare parts for it available on the market. (The other two gadgets he had also bought for twice their proper price.)

"Shall we have some coffee now?" said the mother with a sigh.

"By all means," said the two of them together.

Sayyid left his bed and passed his fingers through his hair, then he went to the bathroom. When he returned to the room his mother had prepared the pot of coffee and had poured out three glasses; Sayyid distributed them round and each settled down anew on their bed.

"Perhaps they'll like it there and settle down in Kuwait," the father continued the conversation.

Immediately the matter took on a new dimension in their minds. No one, however, dared to translate this dimension into words. Each one merely began to imagine summer afternoons in the garden, seated outside on rush chairs with a gentle breeze blowing whose coolness increased as the night advanced; or winter mornings on the other side of the house with the sun falling hesitatingly at first, then becoming increasingly warm as the day wore on.

It was the father who after a while said, "Why don't we get in touch with Fadia and enquire how she and the child are? After all, he is our child."

"I couldn't bear it if he answered," replied his wife.

Her voice, though, was gentle when she added, "If she hasn't rung within an hour I'll do so."

Sayyid finished his cup of coffee and lit a cigarette. "Aren't you thinking of going out, child?" his father asked him.

Sayyid did not usually go out in the afternoon, yet his father used to address this same question to him every day, and every day Sayyid would answer, "No. I'll stay at home."

For fifteen years this answer had filled the father's heart with sadness, for while other young men of his age would dress and spruce themselves up and run after girls, then marry and have children, Sayyid had suddenly begun, while still at school and university, to lose the great vitality which had distinguished him, and would lounge around the house silently drinking coffee and smoking while he read novels and watched television.

With the passage of time the father had forgotten these old feelings and now, when he said to Sayyid, "Go out, son, for a while instead of shutting yourself up here," he had come to feel a sense of contentment and happiness when the other replied, "And where shall I go? There's nothing I like better than sitting at home."

Thereby, both the father and the mother were assured that at the appropriate time they would obtain the necessary medical aid if they were to have one of the attacks that had begun to afflict them of late. It was truly strange that these attacks did not occur during the morning period when Sayyid was at the organization, but invariably came on after noon, and in particular at night after Sayyid had gone off to bed.

Then one of them would shout out "Oh my!" and the next second Sayyid would be at the bedside asking what was wrong, dispensing medicine, and hurrying off to the telephone to get in touch with the doctor, who would make light of the matter in a bored voice and order a repeat of the same medicine on the prescription.

Sayyid's role did not end there. At the earliest opportunity, and on the instructions of the father and mother who generally took to their beds at one and the same time, he would start contacting the members of the family, one after another, to announce the news in that usual matter-of-fact voice: "Actually, they're both a little unwell," or "They've both been in bed since yesterday." In order to rebut the suspicion of having exaggerated he'd add, "The doctor says . . . ," then, "What? Yesterday while we were asleep," and would mention in detail what had happened.

Then the three of them would lounge about on their beds awaiting the reaction.

The father had turned over on to his left side and was facing the hall. "See what's on the television tonight," he said.

Sayyid searched around for the morning paper and found that it had fallen down behind his father's bed; he took it to his own bed, spread it out on the sheet, and began reading out aloud the evening's programs.

The father was hoping that one of the old films the television had taken to showing of late would be on. How marvelous the young Abdel Wahhab was when he would button up his jacket, set his tarboosh on his head tipped slightly to the left, then, passing the palm of his hand across the hair along the right edge of the tarboosh, begin to sing; or Yusuf Wahbi when he gathered the ends of his robe around him, stood up to his full height, and roared out in his magnificent voice that a girl's honor was like a matchstick that could only be lit once!

Then, leaving his bed, he would seat himself directly in front of the television in order to be able to see properly, with Mummy on his right and Sayyid on his left, having put out the light, all three of them would lean on the table with their elbows until the evening's viewing was over.

Outside the darkness gathered quickly. Sayyid got up and put on the light and went back to poring over the newspaper.

"Fadia hasn't rung yet," said the mother.

The father lay out straight on his back, his eyes once again coming to rest on the ceiling without distinguishing its features. "We'll get in touch with her if she hasn't rung up in an hour's time," he said.

Then: "What are you giving us to eat this evening?"

The Chair Carrier

—ↄↄↄ—

Yusuf Idris

You can believe it or not, but excuse me for saying that your opinion is of no concern at all to me. It's enough for me that I saw him, met him, talked to him and observed the chair with my own eyes. Thus I considered that I had been witness to a miracle. But even more miraculous, indeed more disastrous, was that neither the man, the chair, nor the incident caused a single passerby in Opera Square, in Gumhuriya Street, or in Cairo, or maybe in the whole wide world, to come to a stop at that moment.

It was a vast chair. Looking at it you'd think it had come from some other world, or that it had been constructed for some festival, such a colossal chair, as though it were an institution all on its own, its seat immense and softly covered with leopard skin and silken cushions. Once you'd seen it your great dream was to sit in it, be it just the once, just for a moment. A moving chair, it moved forward with stately gait as though it were in some religious procession. You'd think it was moving of its own accord. In awe and amazement you almost prostrated yourself before it in worship and offered up sacrifices to it.

Eventually, however, I made out, between the four massive legs that ended in glistening gilded hooves, a fifth leg. It was skinny and looked strange amid all that bulk and splendor; it was, though, no leg but a thin, gaunt human being upon whose body the sweat had formed runnels and rivulets and had caused woods and groves of hair to sprout. Believe me, by all that's holy, I'm neither lying nor exaggerating, simply relating, be it ever so inadequately, what I saw. How was it that such a thin, frail man was carrying a chair like this one, a chair that weighed at least a ton, and maybe several? That was the proposition that was presented to one's mind, it was like some conjuring trick. But you had only to look longer and more closely to find that there was no deception, that the man really was carrying the chair all on his own and moving along with it.

What was even more extraordinary and more weird, something that was truly alarming, was that none of the passersby in Opera Square, in Gumhuriya Street or maybe in the whole of Cairo, was at all astonished or treated the matter as if it was anything untoward, but rather as something quite normal and unremarkable, as if the chair were as light as a butterfly and was being carried around by a young lad. I looked at the people and at the chair and at the man, thinking that I would spot the raising of an eyebrow, or lips sucked back in alarm, or hear a cry of amazement, but there was absolutely no reaction.

I began to feel that the whole thing was too ghastly to contemplate any longer. At this very moment the man with his burden was no more than a step or two away from me and I was able to see his good-natured face, despite its many wrinkles. Even so it was impossible to determine his age. I then saw something more about him: he was naked except for a stout waistband from which hung, in front and behind, a covering made of sailcloth. Yet you would surely have to come to a stop, conscious that your mind had, like an empty room, begun to set off echoes telling you that, dressed as he was, he was a stranger not only to Cairo but to our whole era. You had the sensation of having seen his like in books about history or archaeology. And so I was surprised by the smile he gave, the kind of meek smile a beggar gives, and by a voice that mouthed words:

"May God have mercy on your parents, my son. You wouldn't have seen Uncle Ptah Ra'?"

Was he speaking hieroglyphics pronounced as Arabic, or Arabic pronounced as hieroglyphics? Could the man be an ancient Egyptian? I rounded on him:

"Listen here—don't start telling me you're an ancient Egyptian?"

"And are there ancient and modern? I'm simply an Egyptian."

"And what's this chair?"

"It's what I'm carrying. Why do you think I'm going around looking for Uncle Ptah Ra'? It's so that he may order me to put it down just as he ordered me to carry it. I'm done in."

"You've been carrying it for long?"

'For a very long time, you can't imagine.'

"A year?"

"What do you mean by a year, my son? Tell anyone who asks—a year and then a few thousand."

"Thousand what?"

"Years."

"From the time of the Pyramids, for example?"

"From before that. From the time of the Nile."

"What do you mean: from the time of the Nile?"

"From the time when the Nile wasn't called the Nile, and they moved the capital from the mountain to the river bank, Uncle Ptah brought me along and said 'Porter, take it up.' I took it up and ever since I've been wandering all over the place looking for him to tell me to put it down, but from that day to this I've not found him."

All ability or inclination to feel astonishment had completely ended for me. Anyone capable of carrying a chair of such dimensions and weight for a single moment could equally have been carrying it for thousands of years. There was no occasion for surprise or protest; all that was required was a question:

"And suppose you don't find Uncle Ptah Ra', are you going to go on carrying it around?"

"What else shall I do? I'm carrying it and it's been deposited in trust with me. I was ordered to carry it, so how can I put it down without being ordered to?"

Perhaps it was anger that made me say, "Put it down. Aren't you fed up, man? Aren't you tired? Throw it away, break it up, burn it. Chairs are made to carry people, not for people to carry them."

"I can't. Do you think I'm carrying it for fun? I'm carrying it because that's the way I earn my living."

"So what? Seeing that it's wearing you out and breaking your back, you should throw it down—you should have done so ages ago."

"That's how you look at things because you're safely out of it; you're not carrying it, so you don't care. I'm carrying it and it's been deposited in trust with me, so I'm responsible for it."

"Until when, for God's sake?"

"Till the order comes from Ptah Ra'."

"He couldn't be more dead."

"Then from his successor, his deputy, from one of his descendants, from anyone with a token of authorization from him."

"All right then, I'm ordering you right now to put it down."

"Your order will be obeyed—and thank you for your kindness—but are you related to him?"

"Unfortunately not."

"Do you have a token of authorization from him?"

"No, I don't."

"Then allow me to be on my way."

He had begun to move off, but I shouted out to him to stop, for I had noticed something that looked like an announcement or sign fixed to the front of the chair. In actual fact it was a piece of gazelle-hide with ancient writing on it, looking as though it was from the earliest copies of the Revealed Books. It was with difficulty that I read:

O chair carrier,
You have carried enough
And the time has come for you to be carried in a chair.
This great chair,
The like of which has not been made,
Is for you alone,
Carry it
And take it to your home
Put it in the place of honor
And seat yourself upon it your whole life along,
And when you die
It shall belong to your sons.

"This, Mr. Chair Carrier, is the order of Ptah Raʿ, an order that is precise and was issued at the same moment in which he ordered you to carry the chair. It is sealed with his signature and cartouche."

All this I told him with great joy, a joy that exploded as from someone who had been almost stifled. Ever since I had seen the chair and known the story I had felt as though it were I who was carrying it and had done so for thousands of years; it was as though it were my back that was being broken, and as though the joy that now came to me were my own joy at being released at long last.

The man listened to me with head lowered, without a tremor of emotion: just waited with head lowered for me to finish, and no sooner had I done so than he raised his head. I had been expecting a joy similar to my own, even an expression of delight, but I found no reaction.

"The order's written right there above your head—written ages ago."

"But I don't know how to read."

"But I've just read it out to you."

"I'll believe it only if there's a token of authorization. Have you such a token?"

When I made no reply he muttered angrily as he turned away, "All I get from you people is obstruction. Man, it's a heavy load and the day's scarcely long enough for making just the one round."

I stood watching him. The chair had started to move at its slow, steady pace, making one think that it moved by itself. Once again the man had become its thin fifth leg, capable on its own of setting it in motion.

I stood watching him as he moved away, panting and groaning and with the sweat pouring off him.

I stood there at a loss, asking myself whether I shouldn't catch him up and kill him and thus give vent to my exasperation. Should I rush forward and topple the chair forcibly from his shoulders and make him take a rest? Or should I content myself with the sensation of enraged irritation I had for him? Or should I calm down and feel sorry for him?

Or should I blame myself for not knowing what the token of authorization was?

Undoing the Spell

—∽∽—

Said al-Kafrawi

I was listening to the loudspeaker while playing in the lighted space in front of the cloth pavilion that had been set up for paying condolences. By the electric light I could see the loudspeaker hanging on Uncle Abdel Ghani Badr's sycomore tree. The Quran reciter was repeating the words of the Beneficent God, may He be praised, "Wherever you are death will reach you." At the time I said the usual response to myself, "Death follows the son of Adam even to the mouth of the grave." Later, I ran toward the boy Shaaban, the son of Shalabiya, the woman selling fruit laid out at the entrance to the village on the seaside. Shaaban was sitting on the steps leading to the house of Abu Mousa, and before sitting down with him I saw my uncle Ahmad coming along, ignoring the distant pale light. I don't know why, but at that moment I saw him as being tall and thin.

I looked at Shaaban and pointed in the direction of my uncle, saying, "My uncle Ahmad." After a moment's reflection, with his eye fixed on my approaching uncle, the boy answered me, saying, as though talking to himself, "Brother, your uncle's an odd guy, always walking on his own, never talking to anyone, as silent as an abandoned house." I kept silent, not encouraging him, nevertheless he leaned over to me and whispered in my ear, "Couldn't it be, boy, that his spirit's broken because he doesn't have children?"

I stood up; going down the steps, I crossed Uncle Ahmad's path. I surprised him and he placed his hand on my head, saying to me, "Good God, are you here?" He asked me about my father, then plunged his hand into his pocket and took out his wallet and gave me five pounds with the words, "You can bring me a packet of Super cigarettes and keep the change." Then he took a step and came to a stop. "Come to the pavilion," he said. My uncle went off, while I made my way to Uncle Abdel Aziz Zayid's grocery shop to get the cigarettes. I was preoccupied with the recital of Sheikh Sayyid Gabir. When I was young, upon hearing the Quran, I used to feel sad and think about the people who had departed, especially my grandmother Hanim, God have mercy on her soul. Whenever she saw me looking absent-minded while hearing the Quran, would shout out at my father, "Your son, keep him safe, has some demons and you must find him some help."

From early youth I had been concerned about my uncle Ahmad whom I loved as much as my father. I was aware of what was being said in the house about children and about the spells that were made against him that had caused his impotence, and about his wife who used to be the object of many insults. When she heard about the wives of uncles being made pregnant, she would say, "Whose spells and what spells? It is she who's not functioning." If she came along they kept quiet and changed the subject. My grandfather Abdel Ghaffar, who was sitting on the sill alongside the wall, sunk in his mumbling and continued mental absence, used to ask me, "Did I go to sleep, Ali, or have I been awake from the very early morning?"

I would put his mind at ease about my uncle and I'd inform him that my uncle had moved from our place to the old house by the fields. When I used to see my uncle's wife Fathiya coming down early in the morning from the second-floor room all blossoming and clean, with her clothes emanating light, and I'd see her two plaits of hair protruding from under her silk veil and the gold necklace gleaming on her chest, she would be looking in my direction and I'd see the gleaming of her eyes done up with kohl; and when she passed alongside me I would breathe in a sweet smell like that of scented soap. I would get annoyed when I heard the women of the house asking her if there was anyone having baths or not. She would avoid sitting with them and would make her way in the direction of the lotus fruit tree on the river. After a while I'd see that the kohl on her eyes had flowed down onto her cheek, while she stood looking across the river at the beginning of the day when the banks were far apart.

I recollect that at that time I saw my uncle Ahmad inviting my father and my uncles in, and they sat in the reception room that faced the street, and I heard their voices being raised and my uncle demanding his share of the estate of my grandfather—land, a house, and livestock—and my father, who appreciated his circumstances saying to him, "So, Ahmad, it all comes down to your wanting to divide things up and for you to live on your own!" My uncle was holding his throat and was pulling at his garment and shouting at the top of his voice, "I've had enough, I'm at the end of my rope!" I was sitting beside the old cupboard that had a mirror that reflects the picture of the family, from where I could spot the tears in my uncle's eye and hear the choked sound of my father saying, "That's enough, man—take it easy."

I think he dismantled his furniture and got his belongings together, and put them on a horse-drawn cart. He and his wife then walked behind the cart in the direction of the old house by the fields, while I was walking far back behind the cart, which was drawing out of sight, and I was crying at my uncle and his wife Fathiya leaving. When my wails became louder, the cart stopped until I caught up to them. My uncle's wife embraced me, while wiping away her tears. "After all, where will we be going? Here we are in the village and we'll take you to live with us." I heard the sound of the wheels moving along the road as they went in the direction of the old house, and I decided, while returning to the family house, that I'd go to my uncle's and live over there. When I arrived at the house I saw my father giving water to the animals from the river. Noticing that I'd had a bout of weeping, he raised his head and spoke to me, "Weep away, then, like a woman. Was there anyone annoying him? After all, he went off at his own free will." My father's face was all inflamed and he had turned his back to the house and was pouring water over the body of the animal he was providing with water to drink.

I returned to the cloth pavilion set up for receiving condolences. The electric lights were on. As I was entering from the door of the vast tent I took a look at the people sitting on the chairs, while making my way toward where my uncle was. I had come near to the row in which he was sitting. I began looking at the cloth of the pavilion decorated with circles bearing the names of the Prophet, upon whom be peace, and the Companions, God bless them, and the chandelier hanging down from the roof, putting out light and radiating its resplendence along with the fine voice of the Quran reciter. My uncle was sitting near the door of the pavilion that was open onto the fields, with the village elders around him. I heard the coughing and mutterings being repeated whenever the reciter's voice penetrated the meanings hidden within the verses of the Holy Book, and I'd hear the scattered prayers said for the gracious departed.

My uncle asked me, "Have you brought the cigarettes?" I held out my hand with them, also with the rest of the five pounds. He took the packet of cigarettes and said, "The cigarettes are for me and the change is for you. Enjoy them, my lad," and give me a pat on the back.

The whole pavilion saw Elwan entering by the vast door; he was holding his ivory stick, his tall body fully extended, with his best quality blue broadcloth aba around his shoulders. He was grasping the silver pommel of his stick and had fixed on his head a woollen skullcap of the same color as the aba. He stood showing off his imposing presence in front of everyone, raising high his arms while his voice reverberated in the space, "May God repay your efforts." Everyone answered, "God make great your recompense!" The shadow of a smile that knows no sadness projected itself for a second onto the faces of these offspring of Turks who, for a while, had been overtaken by a time of poverty, but who had dealt deftly with life and had brought it round to their benefit, gaining wealth and social standing.

Elwan looked down from his high position at the people at the condolence ceremony, and the people there knew him well: a sack filled with injustices and ruthless acts against big and small. From my hiding-place beside the chair I watched the people of the village in the light who appeared as though they were at a Sufi ceremony inside the mosque.

Elwan cut across the recital and in a loud voice called out, "May it be the last of mournings." All offered condolences and replied to him with proper respect. My uncle uttered not a word and occupied himself with listening to the verses of the Quran being recited.

Elwan took my uncle by surprise by saying to him, "Answer the condolence, O Ahmad, O Abdel Ghaffar."

"May God repay your effort," said my uncle.

Elwan sat in front of him, clutching the pommel of his stick and staring into my uncle's face with his eye, which resembled that of a hawk, blue and gleaming, shining in the brightness of the electric lights like a piece of glass. My uncle had often told me that they were a family of wrongdoers who had lived by taking money illicitly and humiliating people.

At the moment when the reciter had finished the second quarter of one of the sixty parts of the Quran, Elwan leaned across to my uncle and whispered, "You'll stay your whole life, O Ahmad, O Abdel Ghaffar, finicky and not brought up properly."

"I'll tell you what—just cut it short and let your night go by. We're at a condolence ceremony," replied my uncle.

"Brother, it's the likes of you who make my blood boil. You're a beggar, yet you've got your head high up in the sky. From the day you were born you've been claiming how big you were and thinking of yourself as Antar, though what disasters are hidden under your clothes?"

It was as though my uncle had been bitten by a snake, so he busied himself with talking to his neighbor, as if Elwan didn't exist.

I was annoyed and wished that my uncle would rise to his feet and shut him up and teach him some manners. I knew of the ancient enmity that had existed between them, a lifetime of hostility. Often I had seen things Elwan had done against my uncle.

Silence descended on the condolence pavilion.

The electric lights hissed and the reciter was having a hot drink of aniseed, and the people sitting on the chairs were talking in whispers and smoking. The first winter's wind blowing in from the fields struck at my bones with the first cold and the fears it brought, while I looked out from the door of the pavilion at the encompassing darkness.

He banged the pommel of his stick and spread out his aba and folded it. It looked to me as if a thousand demons were riding on his back, with his glass eye radiating anger and hatred.

I am at a loss about his hatred for my uncle. For days and years things had grown ever more complicated, with my uncle gesticulating in my father's face with the words, "What a pack of dogs, with corruption a natural part of them, and buying people's integrity and making loans while charging illegal interest."

I remember that Fathiya, my uncle's wife, if she saw Elwan coming along the bridge at a pace, would return to the house and bolt the door.

Elwan, directing his words at my uncle, said, "If only you had children you'd be in better shape."

The world flashed in front of my uncle's eyes and it was as if he'd had a seizure. For him, talking about not having children was worse than talking about death. Anything but talking about having children.

My uncle answered, "Don't talk so much, Elwan, and let your night go by in peace."

Elwan raised his voice so that it reached the far end of the pavilion, "All right, I irrevocably divorce my wife if it wasn't I who deprived you of having children and the enjoyment of the world."

My uncle was surprised at what he said and didn't reply. At the same time a voice from the far end of the pavilion said, "Leave it, Hagg Elwan, we're paying condolences."

Elwan pressed on the wound, with his voice going off into the night, bearing secrets and the pains of mankind.

"I swear by God it's I who cast a spell on you so you were impotent on the first night of your marriage to your wife. I went to Raghib al-Saftawi who made the spell by magic. You drank it with the food you both ate on the night of your wedding, and by it I cut off the chance of your having children forever."

He laughed in a voice that resounded above the heads of the people, who said, "There is no power or strength but with God." My uncle's brain had taken flight, while the ignorant man was laughing loudly and pressing down on the wound till it exuded pus.

"I swear by God I remember that day as if it was today. Years have passed yet I remember it like today," he continued.

I stayed near to my uncle, trying not to cry as I saw him jump to his feet amid the crowd of people paying their condolences as though it were a spectacle at a religious festival. I saw him as though he's naked, standing on his own in the village market and I saw his whole life suspended before his eyes, with the wind convulsing and pushing the shade of the trees, as they swayed, into the light, producing that sound that scares me.

With complete calm and without any warning, everyone as quiet as someone with a bird sitting on his head, at the moment when to touch cold steel is to touch death itself, at that propitious moment my uncle discovered the reasons for his torment of thirty years. Within his chest his heart shuddered, freeing the imprisoned bird and, despite himself, his voice emerged, "The whole of this life! You bastard!"

My uncle drew out from the pocket of his gallabiya his German style weapon. He aimed and pressed the trigger. Nine bullets were fired as Elwan sat on the chair. All at once shots reverberated in the condolence pavilion, piercing the flesh of the Deity's sky. Bullet after bullet resounded like screams, and the faithless man's body shuddered and was silenced. He fell to the ground clothed in blood like a slaughtered animal.

I stood behind my uncle Ahmad not knowing what to do.

My uncle left the pavilion with his weapon in his hand and with the wind blowing through the village. No one stopped him and he walked along the bridge across the river, while I followed him at a distance, thinking about my father and my uncles and Fathiya, the wife of my uncle, in her house at the end of the edge of the village.

My uncle is walking in a mysterious world, the lightning increasing over there at the margin of the sky.

I was walking behind my uncle, unbeknownst to him. He was making his way to his home, erect as though smashing his shackles.

On reaching the house, he kicked the door with his foot and it opened wide with a screech. Entering, he left the door open, while I snuck in cautiously and hid myself in an old cabinet in the middle of the house.

Fathiya, his wife, was alarmed at his appearance and I saw her trying to hide within the house. "O God, let it be all right! What is it? What is it, Ahmad?"

I saw my uncle ripping off her nightgown, and I saw her flesh, bare in its paleness under the light. I saw, too, her breasts that had never been known to have milk, spilling out onto her chest and my uncle seizing them in his hand and rubbing his face against them. He pushed her violently toward the bedroom, having stripped off his clothes. From my hiding place I saw my uncle naked, his manhood in view.

He disappeared with his wife, composed and with the resolution of a man who is right inside his own house on the boundaries of the village where the night held tales to frighten.

Birds' Footsteps
in the Sand

—⟋⟋⟋⟍—

Edwar al-Kharrat

The world was in its first dawn, devoid of anyone. The virgin air, cloudless and of the desert, had at one and the same time the sea's moisture and a particular dryness.

The time was noon, quiet and utterly still.

The silence was not a solid one; it was a soft silence. Everything was soft and limpid.

I had returned to this world that never comes to an end, and yet I am a stranger in it; I know that I am not there.

My mother takes me by the hand as we get down from the train at the station in Abu Kir. We are alone: no one but us on the train or at the station.

The platforms are raised, standing directly on the clean yellow sand, their surfaces black, the paving stones glistening.

The station structure with its cool shaded entrance open to the sands on the other side—its triangular roof covered in red tiles—the solitary ticket office with its writing in Arabic and English, and the face of the stationmaster, motionless in the half-darkness behind the iron bars, looked like some enchanted building.

The great black hose, hanging down by its ribbed iron nozzle from the tank, is firmly muscled; its outer skin is damp and hot, with a cohesive stream of water spouting from it, striking the platform, then falling abruptly as though it were something solid, writhing and hunching itself and giving out a foam that is translucent, thick and white and that descends into the rectangular space between the two high platforms and runs along the wooden sleepers, between the iron rails that stretch out confidently to the anvil-shaped iron buffers.

The driver got down from the strong, round-bellied locomotive, wholly black except for the gold-colored writing on it, which was still spitting out thick gusts of white steam into the noon light. He bent down with his whole body and turned, with effort, a great horizontal wheel on the large tap that stood on the platform, at which the flow of water was cut off and changed into a thin trickle that came on and then stopped, dripping from the two sides of the platform on to the coarse sands that lay under the gravel, pebbles and coal dust and quickly and thirstily drank it up.

The man was silent as he worked; the water was silent, the station silent. There was no sound, no one.

I saw a solitary cart beside the station. The horse, clad in a broad brass collar that sparkled in the light, was alone, abandoned, thrusting its head deeply into the sack of straw, and suddenly the little brass bells that hung round its neck gave out a tinkling sound, their echoes quivering in the vast quietness, sharp and high-pitched, tiny and consecutive.

Escaping from my mother's hand, I set off at a run, with difficulty extracting my feet from the damp sand into which my shoes sank; the canvas shoes that I had cleaned very early that morning with Blanco and a piece of flannel dipped into a coffee saucer full of water.

"In the name of the cross and the sign of the cross," exclaimed my mother, but she didn't call me to her. She let me run off and I entered, on my own, into the broad, desert passageways between the huts and the cabins and the few one-story stone houses, from behind their fences that were made of reeds implanted in the sand and tied together with rough, faded twine. As I ran with difficulty along the sands, I would touch them with my hand and the fencing would sway slightly. There were thin openings lengthwise between the reed supports that were scorchingly hot from the sun. The pathways rose and fell, all sandy and clean; the air rose in little eddies of fine sand, making a rustling noise in the brittle reed canes.

The decorations, perforated in geometrical and ornamental patterns in the wood of the closed cabins and the empty, sloping balconies whose paintwork was peeling, faced the light of noon with a special intimate darkness from within.

Between the cabins were random; irregular gaps, small and narrow and ever shady, and on the sand were thin dry sheets of newspaper covered with grains of sand. The tops of lemonade bottles, rusty tins, and sharp dry bits of refuse were submerged in the sand; and rising out of it, between the cabin walls, were tilted date palms, their bark firm and ribbed, with the wind soughing in their tops that swayed with gracefully tremulous fronds.

From behind the huts I heard the dull, lilting call in the vast empty space: Kerosene . . . kerosene; the call had an echo that was full of a warning and a nostalgic desire that had no explanation.

Suddenly the kerosene cart appeared before me, very close, at the broad intersection, with its small, cylindrical body colored red, on it the drawing of an open half of a shell and the writing extending along its belly, being pulled by a solitary slow bay horse, its head lowered, its eyes blinkered. The cart had large round wheels reaching up to its swollen middle, slowly turning and leaving in their wake two lines that bit deeply into the sand as it moved along on its way, encountering no one, no one responding to its call.

I told myself that we must be in early summer, very early in summer, perhaps just after Easter.

Our going to Sheikh Makar's cabin at Abu Kir was, on each occasion, a recurrent festive event about which there was no guarantee that it would come round again. There was, first of all, the exciting train journey, after which we would spend the whole day on the beach and in the cabin. While I would remain on the shore, my mother would go out to the last of the barrels in the sea, and beyond them, till I could see no more of her than a black dot. She would be wearing a swimsuit with long legs that showed no more of her than her two arms and was rounded at the throat. She would go down into the sea with her friend whom she called "my darling Victoria," the daughter of the Protestant minister from Upper Egypt, with the square face and the eyes that were both tender and sly.

Tall and thin, Victoria's face was smooth and elongated and ended in a chin that appeared as sculpted, angular and delicate; her eyes, tapering to the sides of her face, possessed a very calm and silent look; her voice was always soft, even her laugh was low and had a steady, even rhythm to it. With the short black swimming trunks stretched tight across my thighs, I put on the old white silk shirt which I wore when we went to the sea. I could hear her laugh from behind the wood of the adjoining room as she, together with my mother, took off her clothes.

I loved Victoria and would flee from her in shyness. I never wearied of gazing at her and I yearned deeply for her.

Upon this face has been deposited layers of love whose stormy waves bore forward time and time again and then drew back, I looked at her with clear love of a young man, in which , nevertheless, I was aware of all life's cracks and flaws.

Did my mother want to go alone and leave me with my sisters in the crowded house in Gheit al-Enab? And had I cried that day with those burning tears of disappointment that fall as the world itself falls? Had I forgotten this recurring drama which was so cruel for the child who has never grown up? Had I forgotten it as soon as the events had gone full circle? Had I run off to drag out my canvas shoes from amid the jumble of things under the bed and to clean them with a coating of the Blanco in the middle of which had been hollowed out a hole made smooth by the rag soaked in water? And had I put on my short black velvet trousers that I wore at celebrations and on feast days?

The floor of the shaded wooden corridor of the upper story of the hut would shake under my feet and sway slightly, between the railing of the balcony that looked down on the street on the one side and the doors of the closed rooms on the other. The long thin cracks between the wooden floorboards would fascinate me: hot lines of noonday light below which, if I bent over and put my eyes to the, I could see the sand of the road.

When I went into the bathroom I was at a loss as to how the water came to the tap and the porcelain basin fixed to the wooden wall, and as to where the flush water went, suddenly gushing forth, then stopping and then once again bursting out, surging and of variable color.

I descended the fragile, steep, dark-colored steps, feeling their cool wood against the soles of my bare feet, and when I looked up I saw Victoria wrapping round her waist the belt of the soft, fluffy blue bathrobe, with slippers of a very old dark brown leather on her feet, and with her thin brown thighs rising up under the clinging robe and ending in the mysterious, magical darkness. Her breasts in the dark blue swimsuit with the high neck, faded by sun and water, were small, cone-shaped, and delicate; they showed directly under the cloth of the swimsuit that clung to them and gently enfolded them, with nothing in between, so that the nipples took shape, rounded and protruding. She descended toward me slowly, as though not heeding. I saw her eyes smiling. We went down, racing each other. We were side by side on the narrow staircase, running.

She said to me, "I've beaten you—first there eats the pear."

She gave her mysterious laugh that was slightly husky. I lowered my face as the blood rushed to it in embarrassment and ran to the sands and was stung by their heat.

Had we gone down to the sea, and returned and eaten, and was I now alone in the afternoon in the utter silence, in the shady, humid gap between the sand of the road and the floor of the cabin, turning my hand around in the sand and feeling its dampness under the granular surface and thinking about the elongated body that the waters had taken far away from me, while I was on the sea shore in the middle of a small bay filled with translucent waters of a crystalline clarity in which wavy lines, as though drawn by a fine moving pen, fluttered, coming and going gently between the small glistening rocks which quickly dried and were again wetted?

How quickly the faded blue swimsuit was changed into a far-away dot in the vast sea! My mother had outstripped her to beyond the barrels, and I could hardly see her amid the slight spray raised by the waves.

I was standing in the clear, shallow water and looking at the wooden bridge extending into the sea on short, circular columns of slimy cement on which quivered diaphanous green seaweed, sporting in the water and trembling like living creatures, then emerging wet from the surface of the water, the fibers intermingled, then suddenly drying and growing yellow, crisp and motionless as older paper.

Now, at noon, there was no one standing on the bridge with cane rods and pails of shrimps and small worms. The bridge, with its dry wood, stretched out far into the sea, unending.

The desolation on the shore was absolute. There was not a single bather on that calm noonday. The sunshades, scattered far apart and of aging colors, threw their shade on to the empty, opened-out deck chairs; even the lifeguard, with his shrill whistle, was not there.

I was alone, not knowing how to enter the vast, frightening, deep, magical sea, not knowing how to turn back from it.

On the surface of the white sands were the untouched tracks of birds, small and clearly defined, following one another in a single curving line, then suddenly coming to an end.

I bowed my head slightly so as not to bump against the cabin floor and went in between the short, square, gray stone pillars. I had to bend down and crawl along the sand on my bare hands and knees. Old yellow pages of newspaper, buried in the sand, were rustled by a secret wind that came in a hot blast from the sun outside. The garbage can at the corner of the cabin in the narrow passageway gave out a dry, slightly putrid smell, unfamiliar yet not disquieting. I could feel the movement of the floor above me as it shook slightly under footsteps, and I would be excited by a clear picture of delicate thighs stripped of clothing and moving about naked in a closed room with wooden walls, radiant with light stealing in from behind the cracked wood of the boards.

As my hands rummaged in the sand they came across a small blue bottle with a rounded body, embossed with tiny letters I couldn't make out. I knew it was a bottle of perfume like those I would find at home on the marble slab of the dressing-table in front of the mirror alongside the silver kohl container with the thin stick at the mere sight of which my eyelids would quiver, and a brass box of powder with its small mirror, and yellow hairpins with two tightly contiguous prongs.

The bottle was filled with sand which I emptied out, cleaning it carefully yet impatiently with my hands. Then I crawled out quickly, my head lowered and my knees scraping against the moist sand.

I went up the steps at a run and rushed into the living-room where my mother was stretched out on the ottoman with colored cushions, I came to an abrupt stop when I saw Victoria sitting at the end of the couch, alongside my mother's feet, her back resting against a soft pillow, her arms raised as she combed her hair with rhythmic movements, gentle and feminine; the look in her eyes was far-away and had in it neither sadness nor silence: it was as though she had left us all and didn't know where she was.

I rushed to my mother, saying: "Look what I've found." I stretched out my hand to her with the magical blue bottle that now shone with the sweat of my hands that had been grasping it like some treasure. My mother smiled and said without anger, "What things the crow brings to its mother!" She didn't take the bottle from me and I didn't cry.

I walked by the edge of the water on the sea shore, with the world deserted, inside my body a pleasing a sense of exhaustion, the awakening blood of youth and a slight burning from the sea's sun, with the water not yet dried, I could see it gleaming on my skin, which glowed and pulsated in regular throbs of heat.

The limpid blue waters under my feet were shallow. They were almost motionless except for a slow ripple. They contained the expanse of the imprisoned, upturned sky, slightly deeper in its blueness than the vast emptiness lit up by the sun, an expanse that mingled with the bed of soft sand, smooth and sleek, on whose surface my feet scarcely left any tracks. Once again I extracted my legs from this under-sky and put my wet feet on the first of the marble steps, which swayed with a gentle trembling as though broken and rose suddenly from the skin of the translucent waters that could hardly be seen. The rich, white marble was as old and smooth as vintage wine. The edges of the steps that rose in a scarcely perceptible curve entered anew, in the direction of the sea, into a wide sweep as they ascended toward the scorching sky, step by step, towering and unhurried, with their smooth marble, delicate yet firm, the pores on the outer skin rendering it even smoother. It had been dried by the sun, and the little water left on it by my feet was evaporating, a coating that was soon dispersed and scarcely left any trace other than a dark patch in the tone of the marble, which became more sparkling. I would feel its heat under my feet as I climbed up further and as, little by little, the last drops of water wetting my feet dried away.

In my ascent of these endless stairs there was an eagerness, a lively expectancy; it was as though I would be finding something I didn't know about but which I yearned for deeply, something that excited me, over there in the heart of the pale blueness of the sky.

I arrived at the last step in the stairway without effort; it was as though something were bearing me along, rather was it that I didn't even feel that something was bearing me along, some power that was outside me yet which, at the same time, emanated from within me. The sea was below me, far away, ever so remote, and the waves were clashing together soundlessly, excessively distant, and the foam, tossed about in a zigzag, slightly frothy line, was melting away in a greeny blueness close to the shore.

The final step was wide and unsupported, creating the impression that one could easily slip and fall, yet it held no danger, not the least threat, as if the descent from it to the surface of the sea that sparkled, deep and unfathomable underneath, would be more like a weightless landing without gravity or shock. Its marble was polished and rounded and contained no little pores, which had gradually decreased the further I climbed, until its full bloom was restored to it, new, warm and utterly smooth.

The sensation of the hot marble had an enjoyment about it; it was as though it were responding, merely through this tender heat, to a particular demand in the body clinging to it, transferring its grateful heat and deferring to its silent, feminine gentleness with a discreet and engrossed enjoyment; an enjoyment that ripples and tumesces and takes in the sky, the distant waters of the sea and the great blaze of the sun quietly burning, cleaving to contours that are easy and pliant, then swirling and massing and swelling till it explodes. The burning disc of the sun flies apart into shreds that are immersed in the belly of the blueness in scattered stabbings with extended echoes and melt away. And the light of noon returns sober, white and silent-colored.

I came to the end of the street and left behind me the last of the huts. I had the sensation that the blood of youth was still flowing in me for a few final years. From behind the church the railway station appeared small and distant and still, as though it were a toy, and on the other side I could see the topmost tips of a narrow grove of date palms spread out in a curving line, drowning and almost submerged between two undulating dunes of white sand, only the tops of the palm leaves, scarcely stirring, showing above them.

I stood in an expanse of sand that appeared to be unclean: piles of heaped-up litter were scattered about at random, having a smell only of a slightly sickly sweetness. I told myself that where we are concerned our garbage easily disintegrates, for what do we throw away as garbage? And yet I saw red Coca-Cola cans that were flaking, newly imported blue cans of Seven-Up, torn nylon bags with faded advertisements for whisky and cigarettes, the spiky tips of splinters of glass projecting from pages of newspapers and an old torn woman's swimsuit and bits of tattered rags.

At the beginning of the empty space overlooking the stretch of desert, behind the railway lines, stood the huge ten-ton lorries, their enormous wheels of thick black rubber so solidly heavy that a part of them had sunk into the hard sand. Their engines were turning over with a rhythmic rumbling sound. The drivers had left them and were gathered in a small circle, with their imported leather jackets and with their scarves round their powerful necks. One of them was wearing a round white skullcap over his long hair. They were smoking and from their cigarettes there rose up in the stillness of the wintry summer resort a slightly blue, fragrant smoke. They were not talking.

The lorries were weighed down with mixed loads of cement and books and paper and bricks and iron rods piled up with their ends unevenly stacked; they were of differing lengths and the ends of the thin rods protruded, arching upwards and giving warning of how easily they could pierce and rend. Though I was very far away, I turned my head aside as though to avoid them, and came to a stop.

Not far distant I saw a young police sergeant with a thin athletic body, a cap on his shaved head, his revolver in its dark brown holster. He was standing in a bored attitude, his face motionless with suppressed anger, his eyes not looking at anything. Behind him were two plainclothes men with long overcoats and high regulation boots; they were bareheaded and each one held a thin cane which he struck against the side of his overcoat with regular movements.

Behind me all the huts were locked; along their fronts had been let down coverings of intertwined matting, fixed to the ground by great iron rings, coarse and rusty, while the wintry setting sun cast long shadows on to the deserted sandy pathways. As I stood there without moving, I looked around me anxiously. There was no longer anyone but myself at the end of this sandy world; anxiously I waited for someone to come, as though to save me from some danger I didn't know of, for someone to appear and to bring with him— merely by making his appearance—companionship, affection, and security, for a voice to be raised, for a cry or a scream. And no one comes.

There is nothing there but the murmur of the sea waves, their relentless rhythm ever repeated, so far away.

The workers from Upper Egypt were circling round the lorries in small groups. They were unloading the stacked-up piles of iron bars, and the iron would fall with a muffled thud, immediately scoring long lines on the sandy ground. Sacks of cement, covered on the outside with their own white dust which had erased the writing on them so that all that showed were the faint letters 'Portland' in English, were being lifted by an Upper Egyptian with a powerful back, who had got into the lorry and had placed an old piece of sacking over himself to protect his head and body. He would let the sacks slide down from his braced back to be snatched up by his fellow workers from below, their arms raised, strained, and they would throw them on to the iron, and from underneath them he would gather up motley piles of books and magazines, and pieces of paper of various shapes and sizes, which he would throw to them, and the books would fall from their hands on to the sand, and the covers, their colors faded, would be ripped apart. In among them would fly in all directions sheets of paper, new and shiny and old and yellowed, printed and written in strange handwritings, and on typewriters, as if they were governmental communications or love letters or rough notes taken of lectures, and I saw old numbers of the magazines *al-Fukaha, al-Hilal, Kullu shay'*, and *al-Muqtataf* and *al-Lata'if al-musawwara,* and *al-Magalla, al-Katib,* and *al-Kawakib,* with their differently sized and variously colored covers and their nostalgic pictures and drawings. The workers were throwing one pile on top of another so that the books and papers were being crumpled. I had the sensation of the red bricks scraping against their rough hands as they quickly transferred them, four at a time, throwing them on to the books and the cement and the sand and the iron so that thin, brittle chips would break off from their symmetrical edges.

They were all silent. The only sound was that of the iron grating against the side of the lorries as it slid down and hit the sand, the rustling of the papers, and the sound of the sacks of cement rasping against the dryness of the bricks. No one was talking.

I said to myself, "Where is the joyful singing of the Upper Egyptians with echoes of faraway sadness, when they take up and put down the loads of the world?"

I did not hear the sound of what I had said to myself.

With a burning, irrepressible urge I wanted to approach the circle of drivers. I knew with a knowledge of utter despair that they would not see me, and that if I addressed them they would not hear me. And yet I wanted to move toward them, while my bare feet, wet with seawater, shifted around on the sands, digging, with their slowed, heavy turning, a deep, determined hole, and yet they did not move.

The first tongues of fire rose up from amid the debris. In the pure air there was an acrid, penetrating smell. The flames advanced slowly, with timorous wariness at first, then writhing with greater confidence and all at once plunging down until they disappeared and no trace was to be seen of them among the iron and cement, then suddenly bursting forth, as though from deep within my anxious self, from the other side of the piles, above the bricks whose color I saw was blackening slightly. And I saw the fires take on their full glory, robustly in command, and there was the sound of them babbling with quick, successive cracking and popping, with the smoke from the paper giving out a smell of burnt lime.

I saw the red covers of *Hours of Pride* growing white between the flaming tongues, their white pages folding in upon themselves, curling and falling as the fire consumed them. I heard the voices of old friends I hadn't seen for a long time; among them were some who were now living in London, in Paris and Harvard, and among them was a friend I had loved dearly who had died a short while ago of cancer of the brain, also a friend who had drowned twenty years ago in Agami, and Victoria was running with them in the faded blue fluffy bathrobe. There were many of them and they were running after things that are not easily attained. They were running toward me, toward the fire, and calling out for help, to telephone the fire brigade, and for buckets of seawater, while other voices were saying there was nothing to be done about it. Then the fires exploded into a roar of radiant light.

The Man Who Saw
the Sole of His Left Foot
in a Cracked Mirror

—⟋⟋⟋⟍—

Lutfi al-Khouli

At a quarter to five on Sunday afternoon—as shown by his wrist-
watch the hands of which lit up when night fell—the weather was
unbearably hot, but what was he to do? The weather—captive—
was doomed to be as hot as hell-fire, while he—free—was doomed to live
in such weather. Each of them, for some reason or other he did not know
and had no desire to pursue, hated the other but they were at the same time
shackled to each other like the blacks and the whites in New York. There is
no escaping one's doom.

The most absurd thing about this heat was that it imitated the cold: it pierced
the skin with feverish pricks when, instead of the burning stings that caused
the body to retreat hedgehog-wise into itself, springs of viscid water oozed
out of it. A week ago he had discovered by chance that Nadia—who was
more or less his wife—had been unfaithful to him with Hamid, his handsome friend with the blond mustache and the laugh that hung with surprising
persistence between the elongated nose, as though borrowed from Cyrano
de Bergerac, and the slightly drooping lower lip, thus providing his evenly
spaced teeth with the chance of showing off their sparkle. It had occurred
to him more than once to ask him the name of the toothpaste he used, but
when he was about to utter the words he finally renounced the idea. Of what
importance was it? Had his brother Waleed been in his place, he would have

asked Hamid the very moment the question-mark passed through his mind. He was constantly sowing question-marks around himself so that the world might seem to him a garden verdant with questions. No. The matter was not one of doubts alone. Why doubt or not doubt when he possessed enough bits of evidence to keep his certainty warm? And because certainty is comforting, he felt nothing out of the ordinary about the matter. To be exact, he was not concerned with feeling anything, either ordinary or out of the ordinary. During this week, he had twice caught himself in the act of flagrantly asking, "Is there still the possibility of feeling something—anything?" He awaited the answer. But nothing in him gave utterance. Within him silence had for long been howling, as though it were an unknown wind in a lost desert. Was there some new epidemic that had spread through the world extinguishing the lights and gagging the feelings inside those born of Adam and Eve? Well and good, the head has landed on the axe—or the axe on the head. He knows not how they say it exactly, this phrase as oddly constructed as one of Salvador Dali's pictures, utterly abstract. Everything in the world has a function, a role, yet even so it is something abstract. A world complete in itself in which is to be found beauty, the square, sex, the straight line, fire and death. Cigarettes. Hamid's nose. Air. Water. Nadia's navel. Music. The sky. Waleed's questions. Newspapers. Reality. And in reality Nadia's infidelity has become a reality. An abstract something that breathes with him this unbearably hot weather. What should he do? Pretty Nadia was still—despite Hamid—pretty; when she winked, flirted, and smiled, all the stones of the pyramids of Khufu smiled— and particularly in those moments which, despite their being repeated, are always newly created and in which the awareness of pleasure mingles with the unawareness of pain, and which at that moment soak up everything in the rose-colored room with the large cracked mirror fixed alongside the window, painted in such somber hue as though suffering a perpetual bashfulness. How many times had he caught sight, from a fleeting glance in the mirror, of the sole of his left foot as it painfully thudded against the bed with the spasms of his body. Had it not been for this cracked mirror he would never have succeeded in knowing that the sole of his left foot was so white. And his friend Hamid is still—despite Nadia—his friend with whom he spends long nights loafing about the endless streets of Cairo, chattering away like a waterfall. Yet he was as light as a feather, one didn't feel him. From time to time he told him some jokes in which brains and thighs were stripped bare, in the manner of an English lord, rolling the words on his tongue in drawling Arabic.

Sweat oozed out incessantly from under his skin, flowing down his broad forehead and pervading the furrows of his face; beads of it rained down, drop by drop, on to his thick eyebrows in a monotonous rhythm, like the sighings of Abdel Wahhab in his song "The Gondola": his eyes would fill up and stop focusing till he was almost unable to see, when he would sluggishly move his hand with the handkerchief, irritably mopping up the sweat. For two years he didn't remember—despite everything he related, guessed and knew—ever using his handkerchief to wipe away even one solitary tear flowing from his eyes. That was true. For two years he had not known tears: the dryness of indifference had befallen him. Most likely this was connected with his twin brother Waleed who had not returned from his ill-fated trip into the desert. It was said that thirst was the cause—and God knows best. No more than six minutes younger than him, he was, nevertheless, stronger. This was neither false modesty nor a stupid desire for futile lamentation. In this Waleed there dwelt the courage of Samson and Socrates, of Saladin, Byron, and Guevara in their love of life and their disdain of death. Waleed used to see millions of things that he himself did not see, and sometimes he would make fun of him because he saw things with his eyes alone—and the eye does not see everything in things. A rose is a rose for all people at all times, even ours, and in every place even in the desert; but a rose in the eyes of Waleed was a-thousand-and-one things: Nefertiti's eyes, the melodies of Bach, the sun's kiss on the sea at its setting on the platinum beach of Agami, the murmuring of "I love you" between a man and a woman. When he used to dream of a morrow in which people would be as equal as the teeth of a comb, his voice would become white. When the three men came and knocked at his door one night as he was on the point of going off to Nadia in the rose-colored room, they entered unhurriedly, lowering their eyelids and softly dragging their feet. This was because they either thought of themselves—rightly or wrongly—as angels of mercy, or because they feared to wake somebody up, though the house was as empty and desolate as a new grave not yet inhabited by the corpse of a man. They cleared their throats more than once in no fixed order, and it was perhaps this that had put them in a state of disjointed hemming and hawing, like the instruments of an orchestra tuning up. They exchanged colorless glances. This it appears was the signal for one of them to stand up. He lifted his body from his chair and surprised him with its great height. Where had he been hiding it? He looked at the man, at the agitated Adam's apple in the middle of his neck with the swelling blue vein. Had Waleed been at hand he would have asked him in no uncertain terms: "What's all this about, my dear fellow?" But Waleed was not present. This man had come with the two other men instead of him. Three in exchange for one. The tallest of them was standing upright in front of him, like an actor on a stage without an audience. Who does he think he is? Most likely Othello, reciting from memory cadenced words that bring to the ear the sound of drumbeats and the blaring of a brass trumpet. Between one moment and the next, the name Waleed was squeezed in without relevance. With a little effort he would have been able to understand something of what the man was saying, but he didn't attempt to. Why? He didn't ask himself. At last, when one after the other they had pressed his hand, they presented him with Waleed's watch, the hands of which lit up at nightfall. Handling it gently, he looked at it hard, and shook it twice to test it before quietly fixing it round his wrist. They were visibly much affected. Why? Likewise he did not ask himself. He shook them by the hand with a neutral glance and walked with them a couple of steps, nay three, toward the door. When the threshold had become a trustworthy frontier between him and them which they would not step across again, he said to them with a smile which, it seemed from the clouds that drifted about their faces, they did not receive kindly: "I thank you. Now I have a watch with hands which light up at nightfall," and they went away. For some moments he stayed where he was. The door was open to the darkness of the street. The light in the house was ravishing the furniture whose anarchy drew out from it, on to the floor and walls, dead, droll shadows. A minute or two of the silence of nothingness, then with firm steps he moved outside, shutting the door behind him on the light with its dead, droll creations, and hurried off to Nadia. That night he enjoyed more than once the sight of the sole of his left foot clearly seen on the surface of the cracked mirror in the rose-colored room. And when Nadia languidly asked him, as she redid her hair which had the color and taste of Italian espresso coffee, about the watch he was wearing and was it new, he didn't know how to answer her. However, in a toneless, enigmatic voice he said to her, "Its hands light up at nightfall." He wasn't sad. Likewise he wasn't happy.

The sun's rays were loitering here and there with provoking slowness, like a policeman on his beat who must return to the station with some customers. Its blazing imprints lay on the fronts of the houses, the branches of trees, the lamp-posts that had not yet awakened, and on some turnings up and down which cars, bicycles, lorries and pedestrians' feet made their way to and fro. Ugh! This life never stops, is indefatigable—and his eyes fell on a compact mass of light reflected from a shop window displaying all sorts of ties. With suppressed irritation he stopped, rubbing his eyes, and without knowing it found himself gazing at the window. Behind the glass stood an elegant man, elegant as a picture in a fashion magazine, examining dozens of ties, gripped by the confusion of having to choose. Choosing is always difficult, sometimes impossible, and in general causes problems. "Any tie's all right," he once said to Nadia when she noticed he wasn't good at choosing ties. Hamid's ties were always very carefully chosen. That day a week ago, when he had met him on the stairs of Nadia's house, hurrying to the street as he finished doing up a couple of buttons of his gray trousers, his tie was hanging down on his chest, the tie with its desert-sand colors and scattered oases of green, and he had smelt Nadia's intimate smell on it. She had certainly tied it for him as she had kissed him and said "Hurry." "Speed is the hallmark of the age," Waleed was always saying. He had asked Hamid nothing; it was Hamid who had asked him with brilliantly contrived surprise, "You! Where are you off to?"

"To Nadia."

"Ah! Nadia lives here?"

Without having asked him for an explanation, by gesture, word, or look, Hamid had voluntarily justified his presence in the house by saying that he was looking for an empty flat and began weaving detail after detail: How he'd known. Where he'd come from. What he'd found. Even the name of the agent he hadn't failed to mention. All the while, he had stood unconcernedly pretending to listen. He had wanted to pat Hamid on the shoulder and whisper to him, "Everything you say is plausible. I believe you. I would believe you even if you were to tell me you were naked with Nadia on the bed waiting to board the Giza train when it came into the rose-colored room through the window," but between wanting and doing lie impassable seas and deserts. Finally, angelic silence had descended upon Hamid. He had heard him swallowing his spittle before asking, "What's the time? I'm late for an important appointment." He had stretched out to him his hand with the watch whose hands lit up at nightfall. Hamid, casting a hurried glance at them and jumping with the nimbleness of a rabbit toward the street, had said, "So long, my friend." Nodding his head without a word, he had begun climbing the stairs, step by step, to Nadia. Hamid had been in every corner of the rose-colored room: on the bed, behind the door, by the window. He had not only been conscious of him when he caught sight of the sole of his left foot in the cracked mirror as the bed gave its traditional tremors, but it had seemed to him that he had asked himself, Did Hamid also see the sole of his left foot? He didn't know what had happened after that because he had sunk into a deep sleep from which he had awoken only when Nadia had roused him in the morning with a cup of coffee. It hadn't been quite hot enough, as at all other times, but he had drained it to the bottom and gone down to the street. In the street, girls, carts, cats, soldiers, old men, dogs, and traffic lights had all been frenziedly propelled into motion with the speed of someone convinced he is living the last day in the life of mankind. On the pavement there had suddenly sprung up before him the fat newspaper seller—as though an enchanted earth had cracked open to reveal him. When he had waved in his face a newspaper crowned with red banner headlines and shouted, "They've got to the moon," he remembered that he should go to his work at the tram company. He went. What could he do? He had to go.

The weather began collecting its forces of cool air and rebelling against the heat. The strong, lofty sun remained the overlord, the ruler, for the whole of the day, its first steps of withdrawal toward its ordained defeat beginning with the counter-attack of the night. Several soft breezes took courage to stir and the small branches of trees shook. Little birds twittered during the moment

when the blood of the wounded sun was spilt across the horizon. Blood—
what is now the color of blood? Is blood still that warm dark red color or has
it changed? He had not yet seen Waleed's blood, so how could he know? But
this thing squirming about in front of him like a snake on the asphalt road,
as though searching out a prey, is it not blood? And this crazy lorry, disappearing with the devilish bend of the road, has thrown to the ground the man
with the white gallabiya and hair and has gone on its way. Inevitably it has
gone on its way, the road being clear and unblocked in front of it. From under
the white gallabiya emerges this red snake that runs toward him with strange
defiance. Everything happens with meticulous method as though previously
arranged. What should he do? The darkness of night falls above his head.
Who is it who calls to him "Help me?" Whence comes that soft husky voice,
reminiscent of Nadia's the day he discovered her infidelity with Hamid? "The
man's blood has been soaked up by the dust." What's this? What's happened?
Where is the man with his white gallabiya and his red snake? The sun too
has fled. The sweat has dried. Those who are running and shoving each other
aside as though the end of the world has come, as though the war of Good
and Evil has broken out, thrust him once to the right, once to the left, the
only word on their lips being "ambulance," while he remains rooted to the
ground unable to move. Millions of ants creep in single file under his skin
with the army of darkness whose moment of victory has drawn near. Bells
ring out jubilantly from afar as though being tolled at the end of the world,
their reverberation growing louder and louder until they seem to be ringing
deep inside him. Has his head changed into a belfry? Voices shout out, "Careful—What's wrong?—The man's gone crazy." Voluntarily or involuntarily,
he was running forward two steps, turning around, standing for a moment
listening, then running, then coming back, then standing, then running. The
voices—and with them an unknown and faceless enemy—were chasing him,
almost catching him. They did actually catch him. He felt a sharp blow on
his right side. The voices shrieked "God almighty!" He opened his eyes to
see what had happened, and he gently brushed against the sky, upright, high
and faraway with the moon. The stars, though, were so close that scarcely a
hand's span separated them from him. What if I were to stretch out my arm
and pluck a star to give to Nadia? No, to Waleed. But where to find Waleed

in the lost desert? Should he ask the three men? They wouldn't know and even if they did they wouldn't say. No. He would give it to Nadia to hang above the cracked mirror or even on the end of Hamid's nose. Certainly not. He would put it in safekeeping to give to the one who would certainly go one day and bring back Waleed. What is that moving above his head? Where is his head? Had the stars begun to have gates that opened and closed? Mouths with tongues were molding words, screwing them up into balls and hurling them into his face. He heard, or imagined he heard, a voice with bent back, leaning on a stick: "What a life! The ambulance came to the rescue of someone and ran over someone else." He understood nothing. Who was the ambulance supposed to rescue? And who had the ambulance run over? And since when did ambulances come? A full, hot hand landed on his forehead, as though it were a left-over from the unbearable heat; in a green voice it said, "How are you feeling?" He wanted to open his mouth to say something he wanted to say, but he only opened his eyes again. He didn't know whether they spoke or not. When he heard another voice like his own asking the time, he moved his hand so as to indicate his watch. Strange, it was not the same movement of his hand as he was accustomed to make whenever he consulted his watch. He saw nothing but total darkness. Where is the watch? He felt for it with the fingers of his other hand. It was there, lying securely round his wrist. At that moment a screaming buzzed in his ears; he felt it issuing from something awakening suddenly deep inside him. Most assuredly it was his own scream. Night has fallen and the hands of the watch do not light up. His shrieks were continuous, like the screaming of a newborn child: "Why, Waleed? Why?" The "why" stuck to his tongue, violently bumping against the wall of night, imbued with every desire to destroy it. When they raised him up on the stretcher to the ambulance, they noticed a tear welling up in the twin lakes of his eyes. A young woman, with a radiant expression and clad in black, who had squeezed her body into the middle of the crowd, whispered, "The young man, poor thing, is crying." No one, though, knew that it was his first tear for two years.

A Murder Long Ago

—∽∽—

Naguib Mahfouz

The Diaries of Alaa al-Din al-Qahiri came out and intruded on the
solitude of my old age, sweeping away its peace and calm and its
isolation from public life. His name came back to stalk me and open
up a wound in my pride. It came, too, as a reminder of a period of being
respected and appreciated, also of a time of being alienated and rejected,
and finally of a time of failure. Having come into the possession of the book,
I became engrossed in reading it. Beginning with the introduction by his
nephew, I learned the secret of why its publication had been put off for a quarter of a century after the man's death in deference to the wishes expressed in
his will. I plunged into the pages of the book, hoping I would come across
a solution to the mystery that had baffled me. From one of the entries there
emanated a glimmer of light that filled me with a sudden rush of insight so
that I leapt to my feet in amazement. "The murderer was right there in front
of me all the time!" I called out, closeted in my room.

Through the mist of memory I crossed to my room in the police station
and saw a man, pale and agitated, rushing in with his tall, sturdy body and
saying breathlessly, "The professor has been murdered in his bed."

With a trained eye I scrutinized him as I enquired of him whom he was
speaking about, and he said, "Professor Alaa al-Din al-Qahiri."

My interest was aroused and I at once realized that the normal routine
would be undergoing a change.

"I'm his servant. I went to his house in the morning as usual and found the door of his bedroom open, so I looked inside and saw him in his bed covered in blood."

In response to questioning, he said, "I leave his house at night and return in the morning, opening the door with a key. As for the other key, the professor has it."

I wasted no more time. Informing the superintendent, I went off to the professor's house with a force of policemen and detectives. On the way I was immersed in memories. I recollected my enthusiasm for his opinions during my student days, an enthusiasm which had then changed to indifference and had ended in rejection. He had been a distinguished university professor and the author of books regarded as the prime sources of propaganda for Western civilization and of bitter criticism of our own heritage. These books had enjoyed the attention of a minority of admirers and the hostility of a great number of people. With the passing of time things had changed and the professor reached the age of retirement. From then on he kept to his house and restricted his contacts to receiving at home certain of his colleagues who held the same opinions as himself, also a number of young admirers. The general intellectual atmosphere in the country became constricted, both at an official and a popular level, and his books were no longer printed. It only became possible, in particular for people writing academic theses, to study them at the Public Library. Despite this, his name continued to be a cultural reality of some weight with the older generation, also with a minority of the young. I was thus not unaware of the significance of the crime and its likely effect.

I studied from the outside the location of the house amid the row of similar ones built by a cooperative: A small, white, neat house, single-storied and with a tiny garden smelling of jasmine. I saw the body turned over on its face, the coverlet rolled back from the upper half and blood covering the back of the head and neck and branching down over the mattress and pillow. He was enveloped in the mute and alien face of death. There was no trace whatsoever of there having been any resistance, for every piece of furniture was in its proper place. I was at once joined by the superintendent and the public prosecutor and an overall search was made of the house and its contents. We were astonished at the meticulous layout of the place with everything spic and span, all except for a tray on a table in the living room that contained a number of glasses of tea in the bottom of which were some dregs, a silver plated metal dish containing the remains of some chocolate biscuits, and an ash tray filled with cigarette ends. The wardrobe had not been touched, nor the watch or the lighter. We also came across an envelope containing a hundred pounds. Preliminary remarks were exchanged between those involved.

"The crime was not committed in furtherance of theft."

"A strong probability, though it requires further investigation."

"There's the possibility of a quarrel or of revenge."

"Does such a possibility include a quarrel of ideas?"

"But the younger generation hardly knows of him—though the inquiry must extend to everything."

"Nothing, too, is known about personal relationships."

I knew the channels by which the investigations would be conducted. Thus, the inquiry began with the questioning of Abduh Mawahib. A man in his fifties, he had worked as cook and general servant for the professor for the past twenty years. The house revolved round him, as happens in the house of a bachelor living on his own. His work ended after serving up the evening meal at eight o'clock, and he would leave the house around nine and take himself off to where he lived in Old Cairo. He would then return the next morning, generally before the professor had awakened. This routine was interrupted on the nights when the professor would receive a group of his associates or his young disciples; his time of departure might then be extended till midnight. In respect of the night on which he had been killed, the professor had had a meeting with four young men who were in the habit of paying him frequent visits. They were graduate students, well known by name and appearance to Abduh Mawahib. However, it seems that Abduh, having had a headache, had taken himself off around ten o'clock. On returning as usual in the morning he had discovered the crime.

"Do you have any suspicions about any of the four visitors?"

"None." Then, emphatically: "None, none at all."

"Why?"

"Because they liked him and he treated them with the affection of a father and the consideration of a teacher. God alone knows, and the final word is yours."

I told myself that here we had before us a crime of murder, with the killer inside the house. We had come across the professor's key to the house in the desk drawer and had found the front door and the windows undamaged, with the windows closed from the inside. As a preliminary step I took Abduh into custody, also the four students, and we set about our investigations.

We examined the sources of the professor's income and discovered that he had nothing but his pension and his account in the bank in which he received the dividends from his saving certificates. There was nothing in his bank statement to indicate that he had drawn out a sum larger than customary to cover his expenses. Our investigations concerning the students and Abduh Mawahib came up with nothing suspicious, and we made a thorough search of their homes. Abduh Mawahib himself lived with his wife in a small dwelling. His three sons were working abroad in Saudi Arabia. When his wife was asked about the time at which he had returned on the night in question, she had answered that she used to go to bed early, and it was evident she had no clear idea about the time. In Sadd Lane, where he lived, there was a café on the corner. The owner of the café gave evidence to the effect that Abduh had called in that night as usual, which in no way contradicted the statements of the man himself, who said that he had gone to the café in order to try to alleviate his headache with glasses of coffee, aniseed, and the like. As for the time, the man was unable to be precise about it because of his having been continually occupied with his work.

It became evident that the students were innocent, so that all I had left was the servant Abduh Mawahib. It was he who was free to enter and leave the house at any time without hindrance. But why should he kill the professor? The fact was—and this was affirmed by experience and studying him—that he was a good, upright, and God fearing man, and in no way did his face give any indication of his being wicked or criminal. I grew angry as I faced this stubborn mystery. The only remaining hope lay in any personal and clandestine relationships he might have had.

"Tell me," I said to Abduh Mawahib, "about the deceased's behavior, seeing that he was a man who never married."

"I know nothing," he answered sullenly.

"Speak. Don't you want to clear yourself?"

"I have God and He wouldn't put the blame on me for someone else's crime."

"All of us have our faults and shortcomings, so beware of protecting the murderer through any sense of goodwill."

But he stuck to his attitude. A plainclothes policeman then brought me the milkman, who stated he had seen at the professor's house, during the time he called on him, a middle-aged woman of some beauty. After bringing the milkman and Abduh Mawahib face to face, I said to the latter firmly, "Let's hear what you know about this woman."

"God has ordered us not to indulge in spreading scandal."

Even more forcibly I said, "And He ordered that a killer should be punished, so talk and clear yourself of the suspicion surrounding you."

"She's a widow who had a long relationship with the professor," he admitted. "She's from a poor family, but they wouldn't be indulgent about anything affecting her reputation. If her secret came out, she'd be ruined."

I promised him that we would be discreet about bringing her in for questioning. I obtained the information I required about the woman: where she lived, her children, her brother who was a mechanic and known for his boorishness. I learnt, too, that Abduh Mawahib used often to act as a go-between, albeit very reluctantly.

I had the feeling that the truth was about to be uncovered after having been inaccessible. When, though, I saw the woman my enthusiasm flagged. I found her to be a woman of such naivety that it bordered on imbecility. She confided in me that she had submitted to the man because of her state of destitution and because of his kindness and nobility of character and that with his death all hope for the future had been shut off. She said that she used to visit him in the daytime so as not to arouse anyone's suspicions, especially those of her brother, and that she had not entered his house for the whole of the two weeks preceding the incident, in which she was supported by Abduh Mawahib's evidence. Things became as mysterious as before, maybe even more so. My imagination worked on rejecting the various suppositions and eventually came to rest on her brother the mechanic. Any doubts I might have had about him were removed when enquiries revealed that the young man had been under arrest at the Khalifa police station on the day of the crime because of having been involved in a brawl. So that was that. With the investigations and interrogations having revealed nothing, the crime was recorded as having been committed by a person or persons unknown.

"These things do happen," I told myself, being in a state of utter frustration.

So here I was, returning to the crime after the passing of twenty-five years from when it was committed and after having quitted the service for five years or more. The publication of *The Diaries of Alaa al-Din al-Qahiri* had brought me back to it. I went on reading eagerly as I came to understand the reasons that had made the professor request that publication be put off for twenty-five years lest it effect certain persons, thinking it best not to divulge their views until after they had died or at least till after they had officially retired. In one of the entries I read: "Abduh Mawahib expressed to me his wish to leave my employ. I was very upset because I am in dire need of him, specially during this critical stage of life and loneliness, also because of his loyalty, integrity, kindness of heart and piety.

"'I treat you like a friend, Abduh,' I said to him.

"'Only an ignoble man denies favors,' he muttered.

"'Then don't leave me. In any case, it is better to work than being idle.'

"'I am not able to do otherwise.'

"'But there's a reason. Don't hide anything from me.'

"He was silent for a time, then said, 'My heart shudders at what I sometimes hear at the gathering of visitors.'

"I answered in astonishment, 'God will not hold against you the sins of others. I promise you I shall silence the discussion when you enter the room.'

"I went on at him until he changed his mind. It appears, though, that he will not stop eavesdropping. Once I caught him up against the door as I was going out for something, and I gave him a severe telling-off. One day when he was serving me my breakfast, I happened to turn round toward the mirror and noticed his image depicted in it, an image that spoke of rage and rancor. A sense of distress came over me and I asked myself whether I should keep on a man who harbored for me such black feelings."

In another place in the diaries, and in a similar context, I read this remark about Abduh Mawahib: "He must be got rid of at the earliest opportunity. I discussed the problem he posed at one of the cultural gatherings and they all praised him and said that he was a model of uprightness and goodness, but I have experience of how such types are capable of acting if their innermost feelings are hurt. I must sack him at the earliest opportunity, whatever the difficulties I may face in replacing him."

And so, at a very late date, I had achieved the breakthrough.

"The murderer was right there in front of me all the time!" I exclaimed.

The time limit for his being punished was come and gone, the investigation had been forgotten, and the senior officials who had undertaken the inquiry were now dead or on their way, and perhaps the killer himself had joined them or even outstripped them to the grave. At long last I had been able to grasp the motive for the crime, something that had eluded me for so long. I wondered had the man died or was he still alive? I could not resist the desire to seek him out even though he had by law escaped the possibility of being punished. I wished to find him, be it only to make known my futile victory though its futility would not be apparent to him until I myself revealed the position, as he was most likely ignorant of the law.

I traveled from Heliopolis to Old Cairo, driven by curiosity and an inner desire for revenge. I found Sadd Lane just as it had always been, with its ancient houses and café standing at the corner, hardly anything changed except for the face of its owner. Abduh Mawahib had several years ago stopped going to the café, so I knocked at his door and made my way into his home. He received me with astonishment. His eyesight had grown weak and he did not remember me. He had a much wrinkled face and downy sideburns that were snow-white protruding from under the edge of his white skullcap.

"You don't remember me," I said.

He spread his palms questioningly.

"But you surely haven't forgotten the murder of Professor Alaa al-Din al-Qahiri?"

There flickered a point of brightness in his cloudy eyes and he frowned warily.

"I am the investigating officer. Both of us are now considerably older."

His lips moved and he mumbled something I couldn't make out, though I read signs of distress on the surface of his face. "At last," I said confidently, "the truth is out and it has come to light that you are his killer."

His eyes opened wide in alarm, but he said not a word. With great effort he rose to his feet, but quickly sank back on the couch. He rested his head against the wall, with his legs stretched out. With the muscles contracted, his face gave out an earthy blueness. He opened his mouth, perhaps to say something which never did in fact escape his lips. Then, surrendering to some unseen power, he allowed his head to come to rest on his shoulder.

In alarm I called out to him, "Don't be afraid. The time when you could be punished for the crime is long past. Regard my words as having been said in jest . . ."

But he had delivered up his soul.

Embarking upon an undertaking in order to realize a futile victory, I had brought about a new defeat that lost me the peace of mind I had been enjoying. From time to time I would ask myself dejectedly, "Am I not also to be regarded as a murderer?"

The Arrival

———ᙏ———

Mohamed Makhzangi

eing the doctor on duty the day Naim died of tuberculosis, it was
up to me to record the instant of death and its cause and to order
that in two hours' time the body be transferred to the mortuary.
I didn't understand why the woman's wailing became more agonized on
hearing the word mortuary. I had noticed that she was pregnant, in fact in
the final months.

Being the duty officer, I was required to see that this hospital was kept
quiet and I therefore ordered Naim's wife to stop her shouting and wailing.
I couldn't understand why she didn't stop, despite the fact that I assured
her that the body would not be dissected but would only be disinfected and
sprayed with sulphur.

When I was unsuccessful at silencing her either by pleading or ordering, I disclosed to her, while pointing to her abdomen that, as a doctor, I
knew that the screaming of a pregnant woman could be dangerous to the
fetus. This time alone did she stop, though her tears continued unabated.
She had spread the palms of both hands under her swollen abdomen as
though gently carrying it.

The Guard's Chair

—⚬ٯ⚬—

Mohamed Makhzangi

A distinguished sculptor who used to work in glass made, for her husband, my friend, a piece portraying a man sitting cross-legged with his head resting on his right hand which was supported on his elbow, creating the shape of a triangle. Her comment about it, which utterly astonished me, was that Ahmad, her husband and my friend, didn't know how to sit as he was most of the time either standing up or stretched out flat.

At first I found this both strange and distressing, but I was startled to discover that I too didn't know how to sit, and that I could bear writing on a slate when I was immersed in an armchair and with my legs extended over cloth stretched across a deck chair.

When I began writing extensively on a computer, I made a habit of choosing very light, portable machines of a small size to suit my reclined sitting position. Also I discovered, without having noticed it before, that I spend most of my time either standing up or lying down stretched out, or sitting in a fashion that is nearer to being stretched out or lying down.

By giving the matter some attention it became clear that there was a common friend who reported the very same condition, and by investigating the matter thoroughly I discovered a second, a third, and a fourth person who behaved in a like manner. The phenomenon, I discovered, existed among many of my friends and acquaintances, then there shone from far off a painful flash that came to my mind.

For all of us had experienced the bitterness of being political prisoners when we were students in the prime of life. The prison we had been put into—like our prisons always—were cells that only had mats made from fiber covered with scraps of threadbare quilts, nothing more than earth covered with asphalt and spread over with thin mats. Possessing no chair, one could only stand, or stretch out, or lie down.

And now I recollect that each one of us, while we were in the prison, would express our repressed yearning to sit on a chair, be it only for a moment or two, and would cast furtive glances at the chair on which the internal guard would sit at the gate to the prison block. But after coming out of prison and having chairs at our disposal, we had, without realizing it, lost the capacity of feeling relaxed when seated on a chair.

A Lover

—∽∽—

Mohamed Makhzangi

vegetarian, he eats neither meat nor eggs and doesn't drink milk, and doesn't have anything to do with milk products. He completely ignores the existence of women and has done so for the past thirty years and has thus remained a bachelor though he is now approaching fifty. No one has an explanation for his exceedingly dapper dress, to which he pays the greatest attention and on which he spends a great deal.

Thirty years ago, while still a young boy, he was in love with a girl of similar age. Two young beings, each one madly in love with the other: the infatuation of the first whisper, the first touch, the first rapture, also the first quarrel and the first making it up after a quarrel, a swift quarrel and likewise a swift reconciliation. They were in the flower of life.

The day came, when out for a walk, they quarrelled. He let her walk ahead of him, in a gloomy, unhappy mood. He turned off into a side street as he moved away from her, though his heart didn't stop leaping about in his chest with the desire to join up with her. He would take a couple of steps, then stop as he thought about catching up to her. But the stubbornness of youth would get the better of him. He'd take two hurried steps in her direction, then stop; he'd resist, then take two more steps, then another two steps and stop. At last he came to a halt, bewildered at the sight that met his eyes.

He saw that the street along which she was walking was filled with cows: a herd of yellow cows racing along in the street that led to the abattoir where the herd was being taken for slaughter. They were rushing toward being slaughtered, overflowing on both sides of the street, leaving pedestrians with no chance but to cling to the walls above the sidewalk.

Stung by a sudden black thought, he ran back till he entered the street to see the extent of the progress of that herd of cattle, and he saw her there in the very middle of the street, wandering astray and unaware of what was threatening from behind. He shouted at her, telling her to get up on the edge of the sidewalk and to stay right up against the wall. Though she heard him she couldn't make out what he was saying, drowned as it was by the roaring sound of the advancing cattle. Taken by surprise by the herd rushing toward her, she became confused and instead of seeking refuge at the far edge of the sidewalk, she screamed and rushed off in her bewilderment continuing down the middle of the street.

She screamed, calling his name as she was drowned in the sweeping waves of cattle, while he called out to her, also shouting her name, and telling her to run forward and make for the sides. Each was calling out the other's name. As he ploughed through the waves of cattle toward her, he employed the point of a pen against the cattle, it being the only instrument he possessed.

He was jabbing it into the flanks of the cattle to try to forge a way for himself, while the cattle pounded against his sides as he stabbed wildly with the pen whose point had become a sharp blade.

He was stained with the cows' blood, feeling the crashing of their chests against him as he went on calling out her name and receiving no reply. Looking across the heads of the cattle, he was unable to see any sign of her.

The herd of cattle went on their frenzied way to the slaughter. The asphalt was revealed ahead of him. He was coughing up blood from the wreckage of his ribs where his lungs had been pierced, so that his blood was mixed with that of the stabbed cattle, and was then mixed with her blood which was also mixed with that of the cattle, as he saw her lying crushed on the asphalt, smeared with mud, blood, and manure.

I forgot to mention that, in addition to his being a vegetarian, and his excessive elegance, and his avoidance of women, it always seemed that he was infused with the strongest and most costly of perfumes.

The Man with
the Mustache and
the Bow Tie

———ᵐ———

Mohamed Makhzangi

H e was standing at the entrance, wearing a white shirt, black trousers, and a red bow tie round his neck.

Quietly, calmly—so much so that it was only by chance that I noticed—the thin hand crept from behind me as I stood in front of the urinal and placed, without any noise being made, the small triangular pink dish in which was a piece of toilet paper folded with immaculate care on top of the porcelain partition, within reach of my right hand—and I withdrew hastily like a frightened mouse.

It had been a rapid movement, cautious and soundless, as are the movements of all who serve, and yet it had alarmed me and had impeded the flow. I felt surprised and resentful.

I resolved, in my resentment, not to leave any money in the plate, as was his objective. However, it being necessary to complete what I had started, I went into the toilet stall and closed the door behind me.

I had scarcely begun before the flow was, for a second time, impeded. I spotted that hand once again, that hand that crept along, under the bottom of the door, to put down the same dish containing the same piece of folded toilet paper.

I turned round, in such a sadistic rage as I had never thought myself capable of, and in a flash trod on that hand.

I sensed the movement of the hand, soft and smothered, under my shoe. My flesh quivered and I trembled, at which the hand was able to make its escape, leaving behind it the small triangular dish.

With impatient rage—as though I were contending with some dumb, inhuman creature—I swung my foot and kicked that hateful triangular dish so that it flew out from under the door.

I was expecting the return of that hand.

The hand did return, even more wary, even more idiotically insistent. As I trod down it dodged away; as I chased after it the hand fled. Finally, with a movement of brilliant importunacy, it succeeded in putting down the dish and making its escape. I gave up in despair.

When I opened the door I found him standing there. The creasing of the cheap cloth of which his bow tie was made caught my eye, as did the frayed and dirtied collar of the shirt and I was determined to convey to him my disdain, be it even by a glance.

But when I looked into his face, where a smile had formed itself on his mouth, a smile which he clearly repeated throughout the day, I froze.

His appearance corresponded to my own—or almost did so. It was as though I were standing before a mirror: the same face, the same shape, except for the mustache he had, the clothes and the bow tie.

I hurried out of the lavatories into the street. One single desire possessed me: to gaze intently at my features in the first mirror I came across.

The Son, the Father, and the Donkey

——〰——

Sabri Moussa

Though Shadwan's body was asleep his head was wide awake. The body was weighed down with the burdens of the long day that had cast the first lock of its glowing hair upon the dark, dew-moistened fields, upon the trees and the rivulets and the southern irrigation canal. The body was weighed down, the muscles in the arms swollen, and the veins in the thighs throbbed with the pumping movement of blood. So Shadwan had squatted down on the bed of palm leaves after supper, when the salt, onions, and maize bread had done their work. Benumbed, Shadwan had stretched himself out, yet his head had remained awake.

The walls of mud and straw could not keep out the howling, nor yet could the bundle of daughters descended from his loins and heaped under a cotton coverlet on a dusty mat. And yet the howling was not all that loud, in fact it hardly resembled howling.

His old father knew what was possible and what wasn't. He was also an expert at knowing what should be kept deep down in a well and not brought out into the open. In any case, pain was nothing new to him. Sixty years was more than enough to train a man in containing his pain when there was no point in upsetting others with it. On the other hand, there was nothing wrong in the occasional groan or moan from time to time.

Yet the groans were like needles, the moans like skewers, all with sharp points that ripped through Shadwan's state of torpor and climbed along his nerves till they reached his ears. And so it was that his head remained awake.

Said Shadwan to himself, "The old man would like to have a doctor, but he's too shy to say so."

These were the words of Shadwan the son, for the branch quivers when the trunk suffers some jolt. But Shadwan, a man hamstrung by life began to think: "What's the use of medicine at the age of sixty?"

For the past few days the old man had been taking his pain off to the general clinic, where he would stand in the queue till his turn came. Never having the time fully to unfold his pain upon the doctor's table, the latter always being in such a rush, he used to give him a mixture that was a 'cure for all ills.'

The old man would return from the clinic accompanied by his pains. While he stopped giving voice to his pain, Shadwan himself was sure it was still there. The old man was someone to endure things in silence. Shadwan's surmise proved to be right, for yesterday the pain had peeped out, had broken through the cordon stifling it and had spread through the house. So the old man went again to the general clinic and again returned with the medicine that 'cures all ills.'

Shadwan was rent in two as he pricked his ears to hear the sounds of his father's pain.

Shadwan the son said, "The old man must have a private doctor," to which Shadwan who was hamstrung by life answered, "For the Prophet's sake, just shut up—where's the fee for a private doctor to come from?"

Shadwan, wanting to shake off his restlessness, sought to move his limbs, but one of his limbs had become numb, so he began massaging it.

Thinking that everyone was fast asleep, the old man on the bench over the stove gave vent to his pain, and the needles and skewers floated about in the darkness, dashing themselves against the walls of mud and straw, collided with the children and thrust their way into the bed of palm leaves where they pierced the ears of Shadwan the son.

"The old man must have a private doctor," said Shadwan the son.

"But where will we get the fee for a private doctor?" answered the man hamstrung by life.

"It's not as if we don't have anything," said son. "I've got a couple of pounds, which are of course needed, but then there's a need for my father too."

"Is a private doctor going to bestir himself at this time of the night?" said the man hamstrung by life.

Said the son, "By the time we arrive he'll have woken up."

So Shadwan the son and Shadwan the hamstrung by life both rose to their feet in one body and stepped over the bundle of progeny to the rear storehouse, where they groped around for the donkey that was tied up there. They woke it up and the donkey got to its feet in a state of rage and began braying. The combined Shadwans led it out of the storehouse, swearing at it as they did so. Carrying their old father, well wrapped up, Shadwan the son set him carefully on the donkey, while Shadwan the hamstrung by life looked on as though in scorn. Even so, he prodded the donkey with his stick and it moved off sluggishly. Turning their backs on the village, they ambled along the dewy track, crossing fields and disturbing the silence. All the while the old man continued to discharge his needles and skewers in the form of moans and groans, though Shadwan had thought that the journey would plunge the old man into a sea of hopes that would dull his pain.

The way was long and the night was cold. At dawn Giza came into view. By the time the donkey had arrived it was broad daylight.

The doctor, having received the two pounds from Shadwan outside took the old man into the clinic and examined him.

Said the doctor, "This old man needs an operation"—and he began to upbraid Shadwan for having left it so late.

Said Shadwan, "We didn't know."

Said the doctor, "You know now. What do you think?"

Said Shadwan, "Do it at once."

The doctor gave a discreet laugh and announced that the fee would be twenty pounds. Shadwan the son stood aghast, his heart thumping, while Shadwan the hamstrung by life said to himself: "For the Prophet's sake, let's just gather up father and take him back."

Said the doctor, "I appreciate how things are—I'll make it fifteen. But make your mind up because the old man hasn't got all that much time."

Said the Shadwan who was hamstrung by life, "By God, man, we don't have a thing."

"That's not my fault," said the doctor, "The responsibility lies with you."
Said Shadwan the son, "I'll sell the donkey."

"Are you crazy?" said he who was hamstrung by life—"we don't have another one."

Shadwan the son cried out, "My father and the donkey are in the scales. What do you think?"

"The old man's of no more use," said the one who was hamstrung by life.

"He's still my father," said Shadwan the son, "and the donkey is his donkey."

The doctor seized the opportunity and ordered that the operating room be made ready.

Said Shadwan the son, "I'll be right back with the money," and he rode off on the donkey to the market where he sold it and returned breathlessly with the money in his hand. He handed the money over to the doctor, who smiled gravely, pocketed the money that had been a donkey, and said proudly: "The operation was successful, but the old man died."

Shadwan, carrying the body on his shoulders, left Giza and went back along the same way.

He who was hamstrung by life stood apart and began scolding him, saying, "I knew the old man well—he wasn't one to depart this life and leave us to benefit from his donkey."

Naked He Went Off

—◊◊◊—

Mohamed Mustagab

The man's naked arm was raised at the entrance to the squalid house. The people were peering into every crack and ant-hole in the front wall of the house in the hope of noticing that anticipated snake-like movement. All eyes continued to strain as they examined the course of bricks and the wood of the façade, the ceiling formed of palm stalks, and the cracks in the walls.

"I'll take a pound as my payment."

He extended his thin, vicious arm upward, so high up that it almost touched the ceiling, then he turned his head toward the people.

"I'll take a pound."

Two lips smacked together and produced a sound of astonishment and an anonymous statement poured out, "You mean you're going to bring out an afrit?"

The man's arm moved back slightly. His eye-sockets grew wider, then closed. He brought his arm down so that it dangled like a piece of rope.

"A quarter of a pound is quite enough, you Southerner."

"A whole pound, without any argument."

Then he stooped down and took up a scrap of cloth and threw it into his basket, and put his stick under his arm, but the hands of the people were all extended to prevent him leaving.

A man famed for his powers of reconciliation said, "Let's come to an agreement, Hagg."

The man was silent for a while, then his eyes blinked and he threw his belongings on the ground and took off his shirt, revealing his thin brown body that was like the trunk of a palm tree that had survived a fire.

"Succour, O Rifa'i."

He took a step into the house and was soon stroking at the darkness with the palm of his hand. Silence crept in and was scattered around.

"I swear by the might of the Prophet and the word of Islam, O strength of honor and light of the Beloved! Succor, O master of might and light of the Beloved! Succor, O Lord of strength and He who silences killers."

The sound of hissing began to flow and eyes stared out without blinking, grasping at hearts, and then the thin, brown naked man was shrieking and trembling, "Enough! Enough, you pimp!"

He drew back, then turned and whispered, "I'll take a pound."

Eyes were freed from the darkness of the entrance and began to inter-weave. A woman recently widowed said, "Where can we get a pound?"

"I'll take a pound, Hagga."

"Never mind about a quarter of a pound," answered the woman, taking a step forward. "We'll give you a quarter of wheat."

The people mumbled among themselves and one of them ordered the woman not to interfere. The man's thin arm was still clutching the stick, with his eyes remaining hidden under their thick eyebrows.

"A full pound."

"D'you think it's the first time we've had a little snake around? The village has lived with disasters. How is it that today a snake should cost us a pound? Man, say God is One!"

"A whole pound."

The crowd went on chewing away at the words spoken, refusing to give in. A brick-maker recounted how he'd woken up a few days ago and found a snake wrapped round his leg and he hadn't been scared of it. The bone-setter told how his wife had killed three snakes all on her own. A man dressed in clean clothes got into a rage and told the people to stop carrying on like that, and he went up to the thin man and whispered, "A quarter of a pound is enough, friend."

The fingers of the nearly naked man were playing with his stick.

Once more he turned round and began walking slowly inside the darkness of the house, with his face to the ceiling.

"Succour, O Rifa'i! I abjure you by the Prophet to swallow your poison and break your fang! I abjure you by al-Hussein, keep calm and rest! I abjure you by Him to whom mankind stretched out his hand and then slumbered! Succour, O Rifa'i. Succour, O Lord of Might!"

The sharp, high-pitched sound of hissing grew less, then was not heard.

"Come down, you pimp! Come down, accursed one! Come down, you who makes the milk go sour, and rusts the cooking pots! Come down, you murderer!"

The hissings came down like thorns, shaking bodies, and the stranger backed off in alarm, then he leaped forward one pace and fixed his eyes on the low roof of the house. He again faced the people, "I'll still be taking a pound."

"I swear by God's grace, the man's a thief!"

The word 'thief' crossed all lines and caused a savage twist to the situation. The stranger closed both his mouth and his eyes and remained steadfast. His eyelashes puffed up and brought darkness onto his eyes.

The hissing of the snake came to a stop and the palm trees stayed towering like afrits. The crowd remained as silent as a wall.

The stranger removed his underwear so that he was completely naked, but the crowd continued to clutch at silence. No one sensed that anything had occurred to cause embarrassment. Not a single glance slithered to his burned, charcoal-colored body. His fingers stretched out for his stick. He broke it and threw it down next to his clothes. Then, with outstretched arms, he moved off calmly. In no time he was swallowed up in the darkness of the entrance and screamed, "Come down! Come down, you criminal! By the life of Abul Qasim, come down! I abjure you by Umm Hashim, come down! Come down, accursed one!"

The man continued to bend over with his two arms plunging into the depths of the darkness, wrenching safety and tranquility from their hearts.

"Come down! Come down! Succor, O Rifa'i . . . . Succor, O Supporter of the Weak! . . . Succor, O Omnipotent One!" And then, with greatly apprehensive slowness, "Come down! . . . Come down!" At that an astounding black coil came twisting along, emerging from great depths, its black hood held erect, grandeur rearing, jerking backward and then drawing after it the savage serpentine body.

"I seek refuge with God!"

The snake continued to sway. While the naked man made movements in its direction with his hand, bowing low and pleading, with the hissing sound entering the skin, the palm trees, the beasts, the crowd of people, the bones, the heart, and the consciousness.

Then the man withdrew slowly. Standing up straight on the threshold, he looked at the people and whispered, "Did you see it?"

He took up his broken stick, wound his clothes around it, and threw them into his basket, which he slung over his shoulder.

He cast a short look at the crowd.

Then, naked, he went off.

The Whistle

—∿∿—

Abd al-Hakim Qasim

A long, long line of children slips between the maize stalks putting under them small handfuls of chemical fertilizer; behind them is an overseer with a long cane and a whistle.

The boy Hasan and the girl Hanim are at the end of the line, each of them holding a pot full of fertilizer in one hand; their hands, brown and thin, move like the pendulum of a clock between the pot and the roots of the maize.

The weather is heavy, overcast; spiders' webs hang between the stalks and stick to forehead and temple; the maize leaves, like pliant knives, scratch at neck and cheek, while the sweat breaks out festeringly on back and under arms.

The boy Hasan is tense: he strikes at the earth, kicks at the stems of weeds that become entangled with the hem of his gallabiya and implant themselves in the sole of his foot.

He is glancing at the girl Hanim all the time. She is slightly withdrawn, looking warily at him. He leans toward her and she moves away sideways, and ever so gradually they put a great distance between themselves and the other children.

The boy Hasan began to breathe more quickly, glancing furtively more often toward her, while her coquettishness deepened in significance and the small handfuls of fertilizer began to fall not exactly on the roots.

The weather became heavier, more overcast. Hasan knocked against a maize stalk; its ear shook, raising a small cloud of pollen whose motes sparkled in the sunlight above the tufts of stalks. Then it sent down a fine rain that stuck to his already wet face and neck, the runnels of sweat bearing the minute beads to his chest and back, while the solution of chemical salt ran from the palm of his hand down his arm and, both hands being soiled, he was unable to scratch his skin that was ablaze with fire.

He moaned. Lowering his head, he rubbed, with the top of his shoulder, at a drop of sweat slowly making its way along the inflamed skin behind his ear. He gazed long at Hanim, breathing heavily, audibly, through his nose, the girl small under his gaze, her face lowered, and the fertilizer falling very far from the roots.

"Hey, Hanim!"

The girl squatted down on her haunches directly she heard the harsh sound of his breathing, planting the palms of her hands in the ground behind her, the pot of fertilizer thrown down at a slant beside her. Her lower jaw hung down and her lips were parted; a lock of dusty hair clung to her moist forehead; her dress was drawn up, revealing her long red underclothes.

Supporting his weight on his knees and hands, the boy Hasan began moving toward the girl Hanim. Her small breasts rose and fell.

Suddenly they heard the overseer's whistle. Quickly they took up the pots and went on placing the small handfuls of fertilizer under the roots.

The weather grew heavier and more overcast. Violently he pulled away a maize leaf that had almost passed through his eyelid and pierced his eye.

He was slightly ahead of Hanim. He looked around him. They were so far from the rest of the children they heard no sound from them.

He turned and found that he had overlooked several plants. He returned to them and gave them fertilizer. Had the overseer seen it he'd have given him a beating.

There were very many plants to be done before they reached the canal and he could cleanse his hands of the chemical salt solution which bit into them like fire, and scoop up water and splash it on to his face and be able to scratch his festering skin.

A grasshopper landed on the back of his neck; its saw-like leg clung to his skin. He placed the pot on the ground and, hunching up his shoulders, moved his neck frenziedly from right to left, his teeth clenched, unable to bring his soiled hand up to his neck lest he set it ablaze. The grasshopper flew off, landing on a stalk, then to another and yet another, heedless of the overseer's whistle.

The only sound to be heard was that of the monotonous repeated movements of their hands between the pot and the maize stalks. Suddenly the boy Hasan froze where he was; the girl Hanim froze too, as though part of him. He leaned forward, inclining his head to one side, listening. There was nothing except for the movement of cicadas; they were completely alone.

Hasan looked round furtively, having forgotten about the pot of fertilizer he was holding up in the air. He stretched out his free hand little by little till he had clasped the girl's hand violently, his eyes exploring between the stalks of maize. Very slowly the girl Hanim flexed her knees, and Hasan too. A long, staccato whispering noise escaped from his lips, and then the two of them were squatting on the ground, their knees joined, their foreheads almost touching. He wanted to stretch out his hand to her, but it was soiled with that chemical salt, and he began to rub it, with quick, violent movements on the ground, to wipe it clean.

Suddenly they heard the overseer's whistle and Hasan rose to his feet. A broken piece of glass must have cut his finger because it was pouring with blood.

The repeated movements of their hands between pot and roots was taken up again. The salt solution trickled down into the wound. Hasan's hand tightened on the pot as he clenched and unclenched his wounded hand.

Hanim was gazing at him apprehensively, her eyes fixed on his back, while her hand moved between the pot and the maize roots.

Blood poured from his finger, his eyes watered, yet he continued to scoop up the fertilizer and place it under the stalks.

After a while there was a gleam of light between the maize stalks, then he found a splodge of sun on the ground and rose to his feet and ran toward the canal to plunge his face into the water.

The Dental Crown

Youssef Rakha

Before walking away from the clinic the dentist will give him something wrapped in gauze without so much as a word. He will place the small sphere of gauze for Zakariya inside the palm of his hand and with gentle resolution will close his fingers over it, like someone rich giving alms to someone poor. He then pats the inverted fist and withdraws his hand.

Zakariya will emerge from the clinic with half a laugh imprisoned there since he had discharged the first half after having kissed the sphere of gauze and rubbed it on his forehead before hiding it in his pocket like a parking attendant taking money from his first customer of the day. Zakariya, before completing his laugh, has noted on the dentist's face a morose look, as though chiding him for his reaction. He has no explanation for the dentist's action other than that it was a humorous portrayal by which he intended to crack a joke after a wearisome session of treatment which caused him to play the role of the beggar receiving a tip to complete the scene. But when the dentist irritably turned away from him as though saying to him, "It's no laughing matter," he went off in a state of frustration, not having understood what it was about.

The clinic was close to Zakariya's house in a dark side street facing a wide square, approximately a thousand paces apart, for he had counted them when on his way there, being scared of having medical treatment for

251

his teeth and wanting to seek a distraction from what was awaiting him. But tonight, with the anaesthetic weighing heavily on his jaw, the return journey would seem extremely long.

Without Zakariya undoing the gauze wrapper or even taking it out of his pocket, he will call to mind the days since the first time the molar tooth gave trouble and he had gone that night to have it treated (and here, he thought, was the tooth going bad for the second time). Approximately ten years ago this same dentist had drilled into Zakariya's tooth. He had dexterously removed the nerve and had then filled up the place where it had been. He had gone on filing it till the tooth had become short and pointed, after which he had installed a crown of porcelain.

Having fixed the crown, he had smiled at Zakariya and said, "It will stay in your mouth for many years."

It now occurs to Zakariya that the sphere of porcelain in his pocket has a connection with the words uttered, but he would not know what that connection was until he arrives at the house. Only that during every hundred paces there will pass through his head a complete year out of his life, and perhaps it was this that had made the route seem so long: he was living once again the last ten years of his life.

He had the strange sensation that the journey of a thousand steps from the clinic to the house was a full re-enactment of ten years, with all its details: the year in which his father had died in penury, and the year in which he had suffered his first nervous breakdown that had caused him to give up smoking hashish; the year when he went with his girlfriend on a journey to recuperate in the countries of Asia, and the year in which he had left his girlfriend to take on another one and about whom he had had a disagreement with her father before marrying her.

The year in which he had visited Lebanon for the first time and read about the civil war there, and the year in which he married, for the third time, a person he found himself unable to live with. Then the year in which he had divorced his wife against her wishes, and the year in which he had gone off to one of the Gulf states to work; then the year in which he had returned to his job in the government, and the year in which he achieved a patent for the first of his technical inventions.

Every hundred steps represented a year, with the anaesthetic paralysing half of his face.

It doesn't occur to Zakariya, until he stretches himself out on the sofa, holding in his hand a cup of sugared tea, that it was as though the anaesthetic was dissolving in its heat, when he stretched out his hand to the sphere of gauze that he had taken out of his pocket and thrown down on the table in front of him. He will place the cup of tea to one side and will take up the gauze packet and will undo it and will see, for the first time, by the light from the table lamp, the cap that the dentist had fixed in his mouth ten years ago.

Will there be registered on Zakariya's face a smile like the one the doctor had given him when he drew his attention to the cap still being in his mouth? Will he feel regret that he had regarded the atmosphere in which he received the cap as a piece of fun? Will he weep?

What is certain is that he will place the cap—without any gauze—inside the palm of his hand, and with gentle resolution will close his fingers over it. He will think that had it been a tooth that had been pulled out he would not have been surprised at finding it in his mouth and that it was—despite its sudden expense—inanimate matter. For the first time, as he was taking hold of that strange body that had lurked inside his mouth for ten whole years without his once having paid any attention to it, he was to comprehend the secret of what the dentist had done.

Another Evening at the Club

Alifa Rifaat

In a state of tension, she awaited the return of her husband. At a loss to predict what would happen between them, she moved herself back and forth in the rocking chair on the wide wooden verandah that ran along the bank and occupied part of the river itself, its supports being fixed in the river bed, while around it grew grasses and reeds. As though to banish her apprehension, she passed her fingers across her hair. The specters of the eucalyptus trees ranged along the garden fence rocked before her gaze, with white egrets slumbering on their high branches like huge white flowers among the thin leaves.

The crescent moon rose from behind the eastern mountains and the peaks of the gently stirring waves glistened in its feeble rays, intermingled with threads of light leaking from the houses of Manfalut scattered along the opposite bank. The colored bulbs fixed to the trees in the garden of the club at the far end of the town stood out against the surrounding darkness. Somewhere over there her husband now sat, most likely engrossed in a game of chess.

It was only a few years ago that she had first laid eyes on him at her father's house, meeting his gaze that weighed up her beauty and priced it before offering the dowry. She had noted his eyes ranging over her as she presented him with the coffee in the Japanese cups that were kept safely locked away in the cupboard for important guests. Her mother had herself laid them out on the silver-plated tray with its elaborately embroidered spread. When the two men had taken their coffee, her father had looked up at her with a smile and had told her to sit down, and she had seated herself on the sofa facing them, drawing the end of her dress over her knees and looking through lowered lids at the man who might choose her as his wife. She had been glad to see that he was tall, well-built and clean-shaven except for a thin graying mustache. In particular she noticed the well-cut coat of English tweed and the silk shirt with gold links. She had felt herself blushing as she saw him returning her gaze. Then the man turned to her father and took out a gold case and offered him a cigarette.

"You really shouldn't, my dear sir," said her father, patting his chest with his left hand and extracting a cigarette with trembling fingers. Before he could bring out his box of matches Abbud Bey had produced his lighter.

"No, after you, my dear sir," said her father in embarrassment. Mingled with her sense of excitement at this man who gave out such an air of worldly self-confidence was a guilty shame at her father's inadequacy.

After lighting her father's cigarette Abbud Bey sat back, crossing his legs, and took out a cigarette for himself. He tapped it against the case before putting it in the corner of his mouth and lighting it, then blew out circles of smoke that followed each other across the room.

"It's a great honor for us, my son," said her father, smiling first at Abbud Bey, then at his daughter, at which Abbud Bey looked across at her and asked:

"And the beautiful little girl's still at secondary school?"

She lowered her head modestly and her father had answered:

"As from today she'll be staying at home in readiness for your happy life together, God permitting," and at a glance from her father she had hurried off to join her mother in the kitchen.

"You're a lucky girl," her mother had told her. "He's a real find. Any girl would be happy to have him. He's an Inspector of Irrigation though he's not yet forty. He earns a big salary and gets a fully furnished government house wherever he's posted, which will save us the expense of setting up a house— and I don't have to tell you what your situation is—and that's besides the house he owns in Alexandria where you'll be spending your holidays."

Samia had wondered to herself how such a splendid suitor had found his way to her door. Who had told him that Mr. Mahmoud Barakat, a mere clerk at the Court of Appeal, had a beautiful daughter of good reputation?

The days were than taken up with going the rounds of Cairo's shops and choosing clothes for the new grand life she would be living. This was made possible by her father borrowing on the security of his government pension. Abbud Bey, on his part, never visited her without bringing a present. For her birthday, just before they were married, he bought her an emerald ring that came in a plush box bearing the name of a well-known jeweler in Qasr al-Nil Street. On her wedding night, as he put a diamond bracelet round her wrist, he had reminded her that she was marrying someone with a brilliant career in front of him and that one of the most important things in life was the opinion of others, particularly one's equals and seniors. Though she was still only a young girl she must try to act with suitable dignity.

"Tell people you're from the well-known Barakat family and that your father was a judge," and he went up to her and gently patted her cheeks in a fatherly, reassuring gesture that he was often to repeat during their times together.

Then, yesterday evening, she had returned from the club somewhat light-headed from the bottle of beer she had been required to drink on the occasion of someone's birthday. Her husband, noting the state she was in, hurriedly took her back home. She had undressed and put on her nightgown, leaving her jewelry on the dressing-table, and was fast asleep seconds after getting into bed. The following morning, fully recovered, she slept late, then rang the bell as usual and had breakfast brought to her. It was only as she was putting her jewelry away in the wooden and mother-of-pearl box that she realized her emerald ring was missing.

Could it have dropped from her finger at the club? In the car on the way back? No, she distinctly remembered it last night, remembered the usual difficulty she had in getting it off her finger. She stripped the bed of its sheets, turned over the mattress, looked inside the pillow cases, crawled on hands and knees under the bed. The tray of breakfast lying on the small bedside table caught her eye and she remembered the young servant coming in that morning with it, remembered the noise of the tray being put down, the curtains being drawn, the tray then being lifted up again and placed on the bedside table. No one but the servant had entered the room. Should she call her and question her?

Eventually, having taken two aspirins, she decided to do nothing and await the return of her husband from work.

Directly he arrived she told him what had happened and he took her by the arm and seated her down beside him: "Let's just calm down and go over what happened."

She repeated, this time with further details, the whole story.

"And you've looked for it?"

"Everywhere. Every possible and impossible place in the bedroom and the bathroom. You see, I remember distinctly taking it off last night."

He grimaced at the thought of last night, then said, "Anybody been in the room since Gazia when she brought in the breakfast?"

"Not a soul. I've even told Gazia not to do the room today."

"And you've not mentioned anything to her?"

"I thought I'd better leave it to you."

"Fine, go and tell her I want to speak to her. There's no point in your saying anything but I think it would be as well if you were present when I talk to her."

Five minutes later Gazia, the young servant girl they had recently employed, entered behind her mistress. Samia took herself to a far corner of the room while Gazia stood in front of Abbud Bey, her hands folded across her chest, her eyes lowered.

"Yes, sir?"

"Where's the ring?"

"What ring are you talking about, sir?"

"Now don't make out you don't know. The one with the green stone. It would be better for you if you hand it over and then nothing more need be said."

"May God blind me if I've set eyes on it."

He stood up and gave her a sudden slap on the face. The girl reeled back, put one hand to her cheek, then lowered it again to her chest and made no answer to any of Abbud's questions. Finally he said to her, "You've got just fifteen seconds to say where you've hidden the ring or else, I swear to you, you're not going to have a good time of it."

As he lifted up his arm to look at his watch the girl flinched slightly but continued in her silence. When he went to the telephone Samia raised her head and saw that the girl's cheeks were wet with tears. Abbud Bey got through to the Superintendent of Police and told him briefly what had occurred.

"Of course I haven't got any actual proof but seeing that no one else entered the room, it's obvious she's pinched it. Anyway I'll leave the matter in your capable hands—I know your people have their ways and means."

He gave a short laugh, then listened for a while and said, "I'm really most grateful to you."

He put down the receiver and turned round to Samia:

"That's it, my dear. There's nothing more to worry about. The superintendent has promised me we'll get it back. The patrol car's on the way."

The following day, in the late afternoon, she'd been sitting in front of her dressing-table rearranging her jewelry in the box when an earring slipped from her grasp and fell to the floor. As she bent to pick it up she saw the emerald ring stuck between the leg of the table and the wall. Since that moment she had sat in a state of panic awaiting her husband's return from the club. She even felt tempted to walk down to the water's edge and throw it into the river so as to be rid of the unpleasantness that lay ahead.

At the sound of the screech of tires rounding the house to the garage, she slipped the ring on to her finger. As he entered she stood up and raised her hand to show him the ring. Quickly, trying to choose her words but knowing that she was expressing herself clumsily, she explained what an extraordinary thing it was that it should have lodged itself between the dressing-table and the wall, what an extraordinary coincidence she should have dropped the earring and so seen it, how she'd thought of ringing him at the club to tell him the good news but . . .

She stopped in mid-sentence when she saw his frown and added weakly: "I'm sorry. I can't think how it could have happened. What do we do now?"

He shrugged his shoulders as though in surprise.

"Are you asking me, my dear lady? Nothing of course."

"But they've been beating up the girl—you yourself said they'd not let her be till she confessed."

Unhurriedly, he sat himself down as though to consider this new aspect of the matter. Taking out his case, he tapped a cigarette against it in his accustomed manner, then moistened his lips, put the cigarette in place and lit it. The smoke rings hovered in the still air as he looked at his watch and said:

"In any case she's not got all that long before they let her go. They can't keep her for more than forty-eight hours without getting any evidence or a confession. It won't kill her to put up with things for a while longer. By now the whole town knows the servant stole the ring—or would you like me to tell everyone: 'Look, folks, the fact is that the wife got a bit tiddly on a couple of sips of beer and the ring took off on its own and hid itself behind the dressing-table.'? What do you think?"

"I know the situation's a bit awkward . . ."

"Awkward? It's downright ludicrous. Listen, there's nothing to be done but to give it to me and the next time I go down to Cairo I'll sell it and get something else in its place. We'd be the laughing-stock of the town."

He stretched out his hand and she found herself taking off the ring and placing it in the outstretched palm. She was careful that their eyes should not meet. For a moment she was on the point of protesting and in fact uttered a few words, "I'd just like to say we could . . ."

Putting the ring away in his pocket, he bent over her and with both hands gently patted her on the cheeks. It was a gesture she had long become used to, a gesture that promised her continued security, that told her that this man who was her husband and the father of her child had also taken the place of her father who, as though assured that he had found her a suitable substitute, had followed up her marriage with his own funeral. The gesture told her more eloquently than any words that he was the man, she the woman, he the one who carried the responsibilities, made the decisions, she the one whose role it was to be beautiful, happy, carefree. Now, though, for the first time in their life together the gesture came like a slap in the face.

Directly her removed his hands her whole body was seized with an uncontrollable trembling. Frightened he would notice, she rose to her feet and walked with deliberate steps toward the large window. She leaned her forehead against the comforting cold surface and closed her eyes tightly for several seconds. When she opened them she noticed that the café lights strung between the trees on the opposite shore had been turned on and that there were men seated under them and a waiter moving among the tables. The dark shape of a boat momentarily blocked out the café scene; in the light from the hurricane lamp hanging from its bow she saw it cutting through several of those floating islands of Nile waterlilies that, rootless, are swept along with the current.

Suddenly she became aware of his presence alongside her.

"Why don't you go and change quickly while I take the car out? It's hot and it would be nice to have supper at the club."

"As you like. Why not?"

By the time she had turned round from the window she was smiling.

Paradise Itself

Mahmoud al-Saadani

Silence and the night reigned over the downward slope of Ibn Tulun and gloomy darkness wrapped around everything in the narrow winding passageway that clung closely to the wall of the ancient mosque. The road was empty of everything but the treading feet of some tired men who were returning to their homes at the top of the slope and a child alongside the wall relieving himself.

But from the top of the slope the light from the café of Ma'allim Sultan shone as brightly as sunshine, and the sound of his radio rang out from afar, and in the light the shadows of those sitting in groups were clearly seen as they passed round the water-pipe between them in a naturally pleasant and relaxed fashion, with the lad Barhouma circling round the clients and the chairs like a wasp, with his voice filling the hunger in those who were empty and those who were full. When Ma'allim Sultan saw him as he approached the top of the hill, he called out as he adjusted his watch to nine o'clock exactly.

"Get chairs, boy, for Ma'allim Radwan and those with him."

As there was no other boy there it was Barhouma himself who would comply with the request. It was nevertheless always his habit, on spotting Ma'allim Radwan coming from afar, to do so.

Ma'allim Radwan had been a regular customer for more than ten years. He was never once late for his appearance at the café every evening at nine sharp, for he worked at the bakery next door to the café, and would start working at exactly midnight, so he would spend three hours in the café without fail. His philosophy, when explaining to anyone who asked about the difficulty of keeping to his set time for arriving at the café, was, "What's to be done when the field's right next door to the house? Isn't it better than going off to the cinema or getting drunk or doing some abominable thing that wouldn't please God?"

The fact was that Ma'allim Radwan never angered God, for he was now fifty years of age, and ever since his wife died he'd lived life in the same manner: from midnight until the morning in front of the fire baking bread, and from morning till sundown sleeping at home, and from nine in the evening until starting work at the bakery at Ma'allim Sultan's café. He didn't come to the café on his own but was always surrounded by a group of friends. He was always the most knowledgeable of them, and always the richest of them, for all the orders that were made were in Ma'allim Radwan's name, and on that evening when he and his group of friends came, they chose a place outside the café and he sat without talking and making a gurgling sound on the water-pipe with a cone of tobacco wrapped in a leaf that never left his mouth. Suddenly, though, he broke the silence that reigned over everyone and acclaimed in a drawn out voice, "I had a dream today—May God make it come out all right."

"All right, God willing," they all called out in one voice.

Ma'allim Radwan continued speaking in the same drawn out melodious tone, "All right! I dreamt that someone came to wake me up and said to me, 'Get up, Radwan.' 'To go where?' I said. He said, 'He who created you wants you.' I said, 'Praise be to God. There is no god but God.'"

Without provocation, one of those sitting with him suddenly called out, "My goodness, Ma'allim! He brings life to bones when they are decayed."

"But of course—it's His power. In short, I went off with him at once. We kept walking along together when we came across a green door, and we went inside."

Another man interrupted. His whole body was shaking in ecstasy as he called out, "God is great. Our Lord promises us that the person in control of this green door brings good."

With confidence and reassurance, Ma'allim Radwan said, "Of course! Well, we entered by the green door and I looked and saw gardens in every color—flowers and plants, and such pleasant greenery, also priceless fruit and vegetables of every sort: guava, green beans, and American apples of the kind that used to come here before the war. I saw the very same kind in the dream, something I'd never seen after the war."

A young man who was sitting with the group crowded round Ma'allim Radwan, replied, "Those who lived before the war were lucky; my father used to say that ten eggs cost just one piaster."

Some of those sitting there made vapid comments about what the young man had said, but Ma'allim Radwan continued right away with what he had to say, "Well, I looked around and saw on the other side animals of every kind: there were gazelles, and there were lions, but all just standing there quiet and peaceful by order of their Lord. I asked the guy who was with me in the dream, I said to him, 'Where are we?' He said to me, 'We're in Heaven, you fool.' As he was saying those few words I looked and didn't find him in front of me. I called out in my sleep, 'O God make it turn out well, O Lord.'"

"Well, God willing," they all called out in one voice.

One of them then said, "Our Lord destined for you a long life. Seeing the person in charge of death in a dream means having a long life. Everything goes the opposite way in dreams."

Ma'allim Radwan gave a feeble laugh and said, "As for death, it's coming to all of us. It will spare no one."

Barhouma the waiter, who had heard a portion of the conversation, said, "Not at all, O Ma'allim, even the mischievous gets a shroud in the end. I hope it will be a long time coming for us."

Ma'allim Radwan took several deep pulls at the water-pipe, then quietly said, "Man, it's something we wish for. Would anyone put off meeting God? But may our Lord make our end a good one and that we see paradise."

He was silent for a while before going on to say, "Paradise is beautiful, my friends. God give praise to the very best of prophets."

Suddenly he raised his hands to the skies and right away called out, "Let us recite the Fatiha on the souls of our dead and all dead Muslims."

Everyone raised their hands in the direction of the sky and recited the Opening Sura in a low voice. Then they passed their hands over their faces and sat in silence. One of them broke the silence, suddenly saying, as though to reassure himself, "Paradise is beautiful, O Ma'allim, but who's going to attain it?"

At once Ma'allim Radwan put one leg over the other and leaned over with half of his body and looked at the person who had spoken to him with narrowed eyes, and said with great calmness, "All Muslims will make it because our Prophet will intercede for us, and in the books of the Hadith there is one that tells us, 'O Lord of the Muslim people, I shall intercede for you.'"

The man who had asked the question opened his mouth in astonished wonderment, and sat down.

"Good Heavens, just look at the power of God, fellows. Then one's going to see Paradise, praise be to God. I used to say that poor folk like ourselves wouldn't be seeing its waters."

Ma'allim Radwan, with the confidence of someone knowing about such things said, "Lies. With our Lord there's nothing called rich and poor. Everyone on the Day of Resurrection is the same. We'll all be standing in a long line in front of two doors, a green door and a red door. The green door, that's Paradise, while the red door is to Hell—may God protect us. He who's destined for Paradise goes through the green door, and he—may it be far from you—who is destined for Hell goes through the red door.

"He who goes through the green door looks around and finds gardens right there in front of him, gardens without limit, and he also finds palaces on either side. Each person takes over a palace, and the palaces in Paradise aren't all that big, just big enough for the owner. They are just a couple of stories. The first floor—forgive me for mentioning it—is just for food, and the second floor for sleeping. They have a system that's absolutely unique. You get up at eleven or twelve with no rush because there's no work to be done. The moment you wake up you go down to wash your face and put on a clean white gallabiya and seat yourself at the dining table just like posh people do. You look around and find on this table everything your heart could wish for of God's good things: beans like pearls pureed in lovely cow's butter, and honey and tahina, and some halloumi cheese, also milk that's just been drawn out of the udder, and some condiment of superb spices, and some bread that's just right, and some cress and radishes from the bounty of our Lord that's growing in the garden. You eat a bit of this and a bit of that, then you walk around for a while in the gardens or sit down at the window that is open and facing north, bringing in a fresh breeze, and the weather over there is always autumn and refreshes the spirit. You don't find any speck of dirt or dust. It just couldn't be cleaner, all by the power of the Almighty."

The group sitting there had listened with full attention, elation, and delight to what Ma'allim Radwan had to say as they sucked at their tongues and scratched between their thighs and went on yawning, without anyone going to look at the oven or attempting to interrupt Ma'allim Radwan who continued, in a delightfully calm manner, to recount his story.

"And so, after that, you go back to sleep—after all, there's no work there, no one coming to look at the oven or the dough or anything of the sort. Everyone's free to do as you like.

"So, right away, you go off to sleep again till around five or six o'clock, just as you fancy. When you wake up you find the food all ready: fried chicken, grilled chicks, rabbits with mulukhiya, liver and kidneys, things that bring the blood coursing through your veins and make your eyes go round as saucers." At this Ma'allim Radwan wetted his lips, and the rest of the people there did likewise.

Someone asked him, "Won't there be any pickles, Ma'allim?"

The Ma'allim answered with the utmost confidence, "These things are a matter of taste. If you want pickles, they'll be brought to you. Anything that you feel like having will be brought to you right away. After all, what are you in heaven for?"

Ma'allim Radwan continued with his lovely story as the others listened with the utmost pleasure.

"After the food you wash your hands. There's no being too lazy to wash your hands—cleanliness is obligatory there. After that the beautiful young houris come to you, young girls as sweet as baqlawa, girls that really set your mouth watering, not like the ladies you see in these streets. These are all matters of taste. Each one chooses according to his taste. Everyone's available to you. And if you've been deprived in this life, you'll enjoy yourself all the more over there. An eye for an eye and a tooth for a tooth."

One of those sitting there called out, "God is most great, Ma'allim! It's really like that?"

The Ma'allim answered at once: "Of course. After all, what's it mean, an eye for an eye and a tooth for a tooth? It means that you'll get what you deserve: you play around in this world and you'll find yourself being fried in hell's fire. You behave correctly and obey God's orders and you'll enjoy things exactly in the way I've just told you."

Ma'allim Radwan was silent for a while, pushing his turban back slightly before saying, "The point is that at twelve o'clock at night supper's all ready in heaven. So down you go and have a light bite to eat: a little milk, a bit of jam, a piece of cheese, a few olives, a piece of French-style white bread, and then you go off for a short walk in the fresh air and under the beautiful moon. The ruler of the moon never hides it away in heaven. It stays lit up all the time, in case you want to see anyone. If you want to visit a group of your friends, any group, you can do just as you wish."

One of those sitting there scratched himself before asking Ma'allim Radwan a puzzling question. "But heaven's very spacious, Ma'allim. How can one visit people there?"

"No, each group that are friends are close together. In any case, if you want to see someone in heaven, all you have to do is to make the wish to yourself and you'll see him right away."

"How can that be?"

Ma'allim Radwan was confused for a while before saying, "Good God! That's in fact what happens. You're paired with your friends."

The man kept quiet, overcome by Ma'allim Radwan's ready response. There was a murmuring among the men, and their tongues expressed various comments.

"That's true, chaps, our Lord is capable of everything."

"Sublime is He. He is the Self-sufficient."

"He cherishes whom He will and He debases whom He will."

"Your Lord is great."

When the voices had quieted down and the Ma'allim was about to continue once again his talk, the boy Barhouma screamed out like a crow, "Ma'allim Radwan, it's now twelve o'clock!"

Ma'allim Radwan plunged his hand into the pocket of his waistcoat and brought out his old huge watch: it was exactly twelve o'clock. He put it back again inside his pocket, and got up and took Barhouma to one side and paid him for the beverages that had been consumed and saluted them from a distance and hurried along the downward slope till he reached the oven. When he arrived at the door he felt the glow of the fire which almost blackened the walls themselves with its scorching heat. Forgetting everything else, Ma'allim Radwan hastily leaped inside. Removing his gallabiya, he hung it up on the nail, then jumped down and opened the oven door and had the sensation of having opened the gateway to hell. Sweat poured down onto his forehead as he handled the loaves of bread so as to hurl them inside the oven, while all the pictures he had drawn for himself of heaven circled around in his brain, that heaven that he would certainly be seeing one day.

For the Love of God

—∞—

Abdul Hamid Gouda al-Sahhar

Fatima sat on the ground. The room that served as her dwelling and which she shared with her chickens and a goat was immersed in dead silence, a palpable darkness. Were it not for the dim light that came from the wick placed above the oven, reflecting on her brown face, one would have thought the place a deserted grave, for the goat lay in a corner out of reach of the light, while the chickens were perched above a large cage, their feet curled round a palm-leaf stalk, their eyes closed. Fatima sat with her head lowered, frowning, pain drawn in the features of her face, sadness in her eyes, burning rancor in her breast. Her husband had been killed some days ago near the bridge as he returned from the field. She knew who had murdered him but had not turned him in to the police as she herself wanted to avenge him. If she'd had a son she would have waited patiently till he grew up, then incited him against her husband's murderer so that he would take vengeance for the blood that had been spilled, for it embittered her life to see her husband's murderer coming and going under her very eyes and she unable to so much as lift a finger.

Fatima continued thinking, her faced overshadowed with loathing. The pupils of her eyes contracted, her jaw stuck out, her lips closed over cruelly. She could not bear to be patient. And why should she be patient? Her husband had been killed and there was no one but herself to seek vengeance for him. She would not find rest, her life would know no peace, till the murderer had received his due and met his end. But what could she, a woman with no son and no money, do? Had she been rich the matter would have presented no difficulties, for a few pounds paid to Sarhan would suffice to have it settled satisfactorily. Fatima clung to the random thought: she had no one but Sarhan, that man who hired himself out for murdering. But what could she pay him when she owned no worldly goods? Wretched and miserable, despair overcame her; she felt restless and got up and took a turn round the room to relieve the burden of sorrow that weighed upon her. Her foot bumped against the goat crouching in its corner, at which an idea flashed to her mind, affording her some comfort. Why should she not sell her goat and give the money to Sarhan for killing her enemy? But would Sarhan agree to do murder for such a paltry price? Seeking solace for herself she began to reason with herself, saying that he would accept, for what had he to lose by killing her husband's murderer?

Fatima desired sleep, but it eluded her. Her senses were keyed up and her chest heaved with a compelling urge that she was unable to thrust aside. She wanted to go out at once to meet Sarhan and to tell him what she had decided and to hear his acceptance or refusal, for she could no longer wait patiently against the desire that tormented her and allowed her no sleep. She tried to prevent the desire from finding expression, but it was too strong for her and she got up and went to the door. As she was about to open it, it occurred to her to take the goat with her, thinking that perhaps Sarhan would accept it from her this very night and so have her hopes realized. Advancing toward the goat, she dragged it away by its tether, and went out into the blackness of the night.

Nearing Sarhan's house, Fatima could hear her heartbeats ringing in her ears and felt a slight tremor running through her body. About to knock at the door, she stayed her hand a while, wrestling with turbulent feelings. But the thought of returning home and waiting till morning broke down her hesitancy. She rapped at the door several times. An eternity seemed to pass before it was opened and revealed a man, short, thin, and ugly, with a ruthless gaze.

"What do you want?" he asked gruffly.

The words of her reply stuck in Fatima's throat. Not knowing how to answer, she pushed the goat toward the man, at which a questioning look took shape on his face.

"What's this?"

"I have come to ask your help," replied Fatima, having calmed down slightly.

"What do you want?"

"Mahmoud Abdel Aati has killed my husband by the bridge as he was returning from the fields. They had had a quarrel. With no one to take vengeance, I have come to you. This goat is all I possess. Would you do me the favor of accepting it?"

She bent forward, eagerly waiting for his reply.

"Take your goat and go away," he said with a frown.

Her eyes brimmed with tears. "Is it because of my poverty that you refuse?" she said in a voice choked with sobbing. "By God, had I anything else I wouldn't hesitate to give it to you, for there is nothing in this world that I want except for the death of Mahmoud."

"Take it and go away."

He was resolved to refuse her. As he scrutinized her, Sarhan saw misery and poverty and that tears were flowing down her cheeks. He was stirred by an emotion that was entirely new to him.

"Take your goat, woman, and go away," he said. "I shall take nothing from you. As for Mahmoud, I shall kill him without payment; I shall kill him for the love of God."

The night passed and the day came. Mahmoud went off to his work, and the hours of the day passed till the sun inclined to the west. Then Sarhan took up his gun and set out, content and tranquil of heart, with the fervor of a man going on a pilgrimage. A sensation of calm and contentment imbued him. Having reached his hiding place, he waited with the patience of a monk secluded in his cell. As Mahmoud approached, he aimed his gun, fired, and found his target.

Sarhan returned home, happy and content, his mind at peace, his soul at rest, joy written on his face, for this was the first time in his life that he had killed for the love of God.

The Snooper

Mekkawi Said

I was a child and she was my neighbor. I was on the threshold of adolescence, while she was at its peak. I claim that I was the first to discover, with her, her body, the first to see its charms at a distance. I became addicted to spying on her as she slipped off her clothes right after she'd returned from school, or as she was about to put on her nightdress, or standing, indifferent to the time, in front of the mirror removing the hair from her armpits with tweezers and taking off her brassiere so as to have a look at the roundness of her breasts. Often, while my eye was on her, my ear would be on the movement outside for fear that one of my brothers would burst into the room that I had safeguarded by placing a chair behind the door and an open book on the desk in which I'd drawn lines in pencil under some of the passages to show that I was busy doing my homework.

She would throw herself down on the bed, then raise each leg in turn while her hand fondled the whole of her body. This would enthrall me, and I risked all that I had in my tin box of savings and hired a telescope from a fellow student at the school who had swiped it behind his father's back. I kept it focused on the mirror and would watch her. My eyes were scarcely able to keep up with the images of her captivating charms, and I would also breathe in the smell of her body and be aroused by her sudden movements as she covered and then revealed parts of her body. When I aimed the telescope at her eyes I found that she was staring at me. Almost dying of terror, I returned the telescope to my fellow student and for a while refrained from walking in the street in case I happened to meet her, and I no longer took an interest in opening the window.

In those days I didn't exactly know the meaning of sex, though I was fascinated by the ideal proportions of her body as the picture magazines I used to steal from my elder brother showed them.

After several months my fears calmed down and I went back again to snooping on her every now and again, until the spectacle changed slightly when an elderly relative of hers used to come to her once every three days. He would explain her lessons to her and would exhibit impatience at her inability to understand them. He looked exhausted with his broad patch of baldness on which were scattered a few white hairs, and with his old pair of glasses with thick lenses. I could almost hear his panting as he leaped behind her when she purposely annoyed him by not repeating the words after him. She would observe his outburst of irritation with a wide smile, while with a thin hand she would check her laughter. Even when he had completely lost his temper and had gathered together what little strength he had to chase after her, she would give a big leap, like a frog, from off the bed to the desk and would throw the pillows at him till he was completely out of breath and his bald patch was shining with sweat. He would then go back to his chair, having accepted defeat. Like a mischievous cat she would watch him; then, being sure that he had calmed down, she'd lower herself to the floor. While cautiously keeping an eye on him, she'd pluck up courage and drag the chair with the tips of her fingers from alongside him so that it faced him; then, she'd put out her hand to the upturned book, would find her place and begin reading to him correctly.

At this he would smile slightly and continue drinking his coffee with a glitter in his eyes.

I would be playing ball in the street, and when I saw him approaching on his broken-down motorbike, I would leave my place in the team, whatever it was, even if I was the striker, and with the speed of lightning would make my way up to our house and would shut myself up inside my room. I would watch the two of them as they started off with a very brief glance at the exercise books, then she'd begin to provoke him into a quarrel and he'd chase after her. At this she would slow down intentionally so that he'd stretch out his hand to her neck, and thence to her breast. With her small hand she'd give him a strong push and leap onto the desk, at which he'd go completely mad. When she saw his bulging veins and his staring goggle-eyed from behind his glasses, she'd make a noise with her feet on the surface of the desk and he'd become completely flustered as he cowered in his chair cautiously looking at the door of the room. She'd calmly get down from the desk and go back to provoking him; despite her being so young, she excelled in keeping him under control. After completely exhausting him, she'd draw up close to him, kissing him on the forehead and thrusting his faded leather case into his chest, signaling to him to leave. Like a well-trained dog he would obey her, but on another subsequent occasion, when she kissed him and seated herself on his lap, she felt hatred for her aged relative, while I hated her very much and left my place at the window.

To this day I don't know why I didn't tell my young friends about her, and why I kept her secret from reaching the grown-ups. The only thing I remember is that I was very happy for some days when I heard that she was going to be married to one of her relatives, and was pleased when I learned that it wasn't him.

The wedding celebration held on the roof of her house was a simple one, though it was exuberant with music and female dancers. I was awaiting his non-attendance with the satisfaction of a stubborn child. He disappointed me when he came along dragging his feet and seated himself on one of the most ancient and battered chairs. With a cloudy eye he contemplated the dancing and those in attendance; not once did I catch him casting a glance at the bride and bridegroom. There was an empty place beside him and I felt myself drawn to him and sat down beside him. I was almost sure that there were tears in his eyes and I leaned forward so as to see him better. At a loss as to what to do, he stared back at me, then stretched out a hand to the pack of food and gave it to me. I didn't reject it and took out a sandwich, which I ate, while I gave him a piece of the cake. Absentmindedly, he took a bite at it, then placed the rest of it back in the pack which was lying in his lap. Suddenly he rose to his feet and I followed him. He shook hands with the father and mother and left. He didn't pay me any attention as he got onto his motorbike. In a low voice he asked me, "Would you like me to take you somewhere?"

I didn't reply. He gazed at me in confusion and started the engine. Smoke from the exhaust flooded over me, cutting off all view of him.

The Lost Suitcase

—⟋⟋⟋—

Abdel-Moneim Selim

I began hunting round for my black suitcase but couldn't find it. While the other cases rested one on top of the other by the door of the flat—one, two and the little one—the black suitcase was nowhere to be seen.

I remembered well that I had had it with me in the train, that the porter at Cairo station had charged me for three suitcases and that I had carried the fourth, the small one, myself. After that I had taken a taxi and had placed three of the suitcases beside me, while the largest had stood alongside the driver. On leaving the cab the driver had carried the large suitcase, while I had taken two of the small ones. This meant that I must have left the black one inside the cab.

I dressed hastily in order to report the loss of the suitcase; then I started thinking: was it possible that the driver had not yet discovered the suitcase? Finally I decided to wait until morning; if the driver had not returned the case by then I would take appropriate action.

As the driver had not made his appearance by morning, I quickly got dressed and took myself off to Roda police station. I went into the duty officer's room, went up to him with extreme politeness, and said, "Good morning."

"Good morning."

As the officer was writing in a ledger I remained standing in silence.

"Yes," he said, looking up at me.

"Please, I'd like to report something," I said with the same politeness.

"Next door," he said abruptly.

"Who to?" I asked.

"The duty sergeant," he said, equally abruptly; "Sergeant Abdel Basit."

"Thanks," I said, and went into the other room where I saw Sergeant Abdel Basit seated at a table, his tarboosh in front of him. On seeing me he put on the tarboosh and looked at me enquiringly.

"Good morning," I said to him.

"Good morning."

"You're Sergeant Abdel Basit?"

"Yes, I'm the duty sergeant."

'Please, I've got something to report.'

"What—a theft?"

"Yes, a theft."

'Certainly, sir, we'll make out a report," and he took up a piece of paper and began to write.

I asked him if I could sit down and without raising his head he answered, "Go ahead."

I sat down to his right and glanced at what he was writing. I read:

This report was made out on today's date at 9:30 a.m. by me, Sergeant Abdel Basit Abu Hassanein, Duty Sergeant. Whereas there attended before us—

Glancing up at me he asked, "What's your name?"

"Ahmad Shafik Lutfi."

He wrote: *Ahmad Shafik Lutfi.*

"What's your job?"

"I work at the Raml Company."

He wrote: *Employee at the Raml Company.*

"Age?"

"Thirty-two."

He wrote: *Age thirty-two.*

"Where were you born?"

"In Edfiena."

"Edfiena? Where's this place Edfiena?"

"In the Rosetta district."

"What province?"

"Beheira."

He continued by writing: *Born in Edfiena, district of Rosetta, province of Beheira.*

"And where do you live?" he asked.

"At No. 28 al-Malik al-Salih Street," I answered.

He wrote down: *Resident at No. 28 al-Malik al-Salih Street, district of Roda.*

"It is in Roda, isn't it?" he queried.

"Yes," I answered.

"Hm—Well, sir, and what do you want to report? Briefly."

"Briefly I would like to report in the following terms—"

"Let's just have it in your own words."

"Certainly. Yesterday—"

"Not so fast," he interrupted, "so I can keep up with you—fine. Yesterday . . . Yesterday what?"

"Yesterday I was coming back from Alexandria with four suitcases, a large one, one for papers, and two medium sized ones—"

"And two medium sized ones—Hm?"

"I took a taxi from the station and when I arrived home I searched around for the black case, couldn't find it and—"

"Hang on a moment for Heaven's sake . . . you didn't find the black one? And then?"

"I remembered I'd left it in the taxi."

"Hm."

"That's it."

"That's all?"

"Yes."

"What sort of a report do you think that is?"

"Yes?"

"Where are you from?"

"I'm from Edfiena, district of Rosetta, province of Beheira."

"Yes, yes, know—And I, let me tell you, am from Gharbiya—meaning what? Meaning that we're neighbors and naturally, being neighbors, I've got your interests at heart."

"Yes."

"You believe in God?"

"There is no god but God."

"Then let me tell you that this report is worthless."

"Why?"

"Why? You may well ask. And how do you think we're going to be able to find the case? We, that is the police—let me tell you—perhaps—maybe, somehow or other—who knows. Tell me about it, sir," and he got ready to write.

"When did you return from Alexandria?"

"I returned on the 4 p.m. train."

"Can you describe to me the cases you brought back with you?"

"Yes."

"Then go ahead and do so."

"The first suitcase was of a dimension of—"

"Let's have it in your own words."

"All right. The first case, the large one, measured about a meter and a half by a meter and was brown; the second was one meter by three-quarters, also brown; the third was half a meter by half a meter, and was black, and the small brief-case was brown."

"And which was the case that was lost?"

"The black one."

"Did it contain clothes?"

"Yes."

"Why not say so? All we're doing is wasting time."

"It contained a thick suit, four shirts, five ties, and some personal papers."

"Bit by bit if you don't mind. What color were the suit, shirts, and ties?"

"The suit was a plain light gray, the shirts were white, and the ties were of various colors."

"What do you mean by 'various colors'? We must know."

"One was plain red; the second red with a blue pattern; the third gray; the fourth yellow and brown with a green pattern, the fifth white."

"White!"

"Yes, white. Well, a sort of off-white."

"Fine, it's fine so far. Now let's get down to brass tacks. You took a taxi?"

"Yes."

"Do you know the make and number of the taxi and the driver's name?"

"The taxi was a Ford."

"Ford?"

"Yes."

"How do you know?"

"I can tell easily."

"And I, my dear fellow, can't . . . how do you know?"

"I read it on the front."

"I see. And the number?"

"4646."

"And how do you know the number?"

"I always note the numbers of the taxis I ride in."

"Whatever for?"

"For fun."

"What sort of fun's that? My dear sir, let's have a sensible reply which we can put down in the report."

"It's just a habit I've got into."

"Have it your own way. This reply isn't in your interests, but have it your own way. And what was the driver's name?"

"I didn't ask him."

"Hm, good. Are you sure that when you left the train you had four cases with you?"

"Yes, I am."

"Did anyone see you with these cases?"

"The station porter carried three of them and I took the small one."

"Do you know this porter?"

"No, but I'd know him if I saw him."

"Good, we'll see about that later. Where did you put the cases?"

"In the car."

"Yes, I know, but where? In the boot? On the roof? Where?"

"I put the big case next to the driver and the three other ones beside me."

"Not so quick—the big case you put next to the driver and the three other ones—hm—where?"

"On the seat beside me."

"And then?"

"And then I arrived home. The driver took the big case, while I carried two and forgot about the last one."

"Hm, and when did you realize you'd forgotten the case?"

"About an hour after getting home."

"Isn't it possible that you forgot the case somewhere else?"

"No."

"Hm, and what else is there to ask? Oh yes—how much do you reckon the things lost were worth?"

"The case I bought for three pounds and the things in it were practically all new. The suit cost me twenty pounds, the four shirts were a pound and a half each, while the ties were a pound each—thirty-one pounds altogether."

"It's quite unreasonable to write down such a sum—thirty-one pounds is too much. Let's say fifteen."

"What! Only fifteen, officer?"

"Let's at least hope we'll find the things. Don't upset yourself. What's it matter—fifteen, twenty, or even more?"

I looked at him without saying a word.

"Well, that's it," he said.

"Can I go then?"

"What do you mean 'go'? You've still got to sign the report. I'll complete it and you can sign."

He wrote: *With this the report was completed at today's date the time being 12.30 p.m. and it was duly signed by the complainant.*

"Please sign here."

I took up the pen and signed.

"No, write your name, don't sign. I mean, just write your name."

I wrote my name a second time, then asked him, "Is that it?"

"That's it."

As I got up to leave I asked, "Tell me, Sergeant Abdel Basit—I mean to say, is there any hope that anything'll turn up?"

"Of course, why shouldn't it? Directly anything happens we'll let you know immediately. Let's all hope that God will be helping."

I thanked him and left. On returning to the Company the manager called for me. I apologized for being late and told him the story. He showed some concern for what had happened to me but did not consider it sufficient reason for my being absent a whole morning. As for my colleagues in the office, they agreed that, as the saying goes, my sole consolation lay in God and that I should expect never to see my suitcase again.

A week passed, then two, and I began to be resigned to the loss of the suitcase. But one morning the manager summoned me to his office. Without so much as a good morning he held out a small slip of paper. I looked at him in astonishment.

"Go on, read it," he said.

I took the paper and read:

Mr. Ahmad Shafik Lutfi is required to attend at the police station for questioning re: Offense No. 215.

Signed: The Superintendent of Abbasiya police station.

I read through the paper a second time but was unable to make anything of it. As I began to read it yet again I became aware of the manager's voice.

"And what offense might this be, Mr. Ahmad?"

"Really, sir, I'm quite at a loss—I don't know what it's all about."

"Well, I certainly don't know. Take yourself off to the police station and come and see me directly you get back. Off you go now. All this nonsense about an offense—off you go."

I left the manager's office, walked glumly to my own, locked it and went off to Abbasiya police station. Was I being accused of having committed some offense? I asked myself on the way there. I stopped a taxi and told the driver to take me quickly to Abbasiya.

On arriving at the police station I jumped out of the cab and hurried into the duty officer's room. I produced the letter summoning me there at which he politely indicated a chair.

"Take a seat."

I sat down while the officer busied himself with an inquiry into a case of assault and battery.

I asked him hastily: "If you could just let me know what it's all about—"

"Certainly, I'll tell you right away—just let me finish what I'm doing."

I fell silent and began watching the scene being enacted before me without understanding it. I heard the officer ask if anybody had anything more to say, after which those present proceeded to sign, and then left the room with one of the policemen. I thus found myself alone with the officer.

Turning over the papers which lay before him, he addressed me with formidable calm, "The question, my dear sir, is one of great simplicity and relates to a complaint lodged by you in regard to the suitcase you lost last month."

"Ah, the suitcase! You've found it?"

"No."

"Then, what?"

"The owner of taxi Number 4646 lives here in Abbasiya and so Roda police station has transferred the case to ourselves for action."

"And so?"

"So the first thing we must do is ask you some questions."

"Right. Go ahead."

The officer took up his pen.

"Your name, sir?"

"My name is Ahmad Shafik Lutfi, I am thirty-two years of age. I am an employee of the Raml Company. I was born in Edfiena, district of Rosetta, province of Beheira, and I live at 28 al-Malik al-Salih Street which is in the district of Roda."

"What is the subject of your statement?"

"But, officer, I've already given all this information."

"Never mind. Everybody has his own way of going about things and I'd like to look into the matter for myself."

"All right, go ahead."

"What's the subject of your complaint?"

"The subject of my complaint is that I was returning from Alexandria about three weeks ago with four suitcases of different sizes, the largest being brown in color and measuring a meter and a half by a meter, the second a meter by three-quarters and also brown, the third a meter by half but black, and the fourth being a briefcase."

"A little slower, if you'd be so good."

"Certainly."

"All right, let's hear the rest."

"I took a taxi from the station and put three of the suitcases beside me and the fourth alongside the driver and on arriving home I discovered that I had forgotten the black one. The taxi was a Ford and its number 4646. The missing case contained a gray woolen suit which cost twenty pounds, four white shirts costing one pound fifty piasters each, and five ties of which one was a plain red, the second blue on red, the third pale gray, and the fourth green on yellow and brown, and the fifth white. The ties cost a pound each."

"You're going too fast."

"The fact of the matter is I haven't got all that amount of time, besides which the whole thing's most annoying."

"I appreciate your position and I also appreciate the considerable loss you've had."

"Thanks very much."

"I'd just like to ask you something else."

"Do."

"Why didn't you report the loss of the suitcase on the same day?"

"The fact is I thought that maybe the driver wasn't free to bring it back to me, that perhaps he was busy taking people about or something. I thought I'd give him till next day."

"Are you certain that the taxi you took from Cairo station to Roda on the day of your return from Alexandria with four suitcases was a Ford?"

"I'm absolutely certain."

"Are you certain that the number of the Ford taxi you took from Cairo station to your home in Roda on the day of your return from Alexandria was 4646?"

"Yes, absolutely certain."

"How can you be?"

"I'm certain because I read the number."

"Have you any other statements to make."

"No, thank you."

I signed and hurried out, jumped into a taxi, and told the driver, "As quick as you can please to Mazlum Street."

Back at the office I rushed off to see the manager.

"Can you imagine, sir, what it was all about?" I said.

He looked at me coldly without answering.

"About the business of the suitcase," I went on.

"What suitcase, Mr. Ahmad?"

"The suitcase I forgot in the taxi—the report has been transferred from the Roda police station to Abbasiya police station because the driver lives there."

But the manager made no reply and returned to his papers. I left the room despondently and went back to my office where I threw myself down into the chair feeling utterly miserable.

A week later the manager called me to his office again and handed me two letters, the first of which read:

Please bring to the notice of Mr. Ahmad Shafik Lutfi that his attendance is required at the police station in order to complete the inquiry into the offense concerning which he was previously questioned.

The Superintendent of Abbasiya police station

The second one read:

Please inform Mr. Ahmad Shafik Lutfi that his attendance is urgently required at the police station.

The Superintendent of Roda police station

I looked at the manager, who was turning over some papers in front of him. I left his room quietly, returned to my desk and locked the drawers, and went out into the street. There I stood outside the main door to the company's offices, not knowing what to do. I held the two letters in my hand; I had in any case to go both to the Abbasiya police station and the Roda police station.

I walked to the bus stop, telling myself that I should go to the Roda police station first in the hope that they had found the suitcase, which would then make it unnecessary for me to go to Abbasiya.

I arrived at Roda police station and went straight to Sergeant Abdel Basit. After wishing him good morning I said to him, "I've come."

"Yes, sir."

I took the summons to attend from my pocket and handed it over to him.

"Don't you remember me?" I asked. "I'm the suitcase man."

He stretched out his hand, read the paper, and said, "Ah—ah—please sit down."

"I hope everything's all right," I said, sitting down quickly. "What do you want me for?"

"It's all right, just take it easy."

"Actually, I've got work to do and still have to go to Abbasiya."

"Why Abbasiya?"

"No reason except that the report was transferred there—I've very little time."

"Ah, certainly—our detectives have found a few stolen articles—among them a pale gray suit like yours."

"In a suitcase?" I asked eagerly.

"Eh? That's hardly reasonable, is it? You don't honestly think the thief would sell the thing with the suitcase. That doesn't make much sense."

"Quite—never mind—can I see these things?"

"Why not? After all, what did we send for you for? Come along."

He got up and went to a cupboard on his right, opened it, and produced a suit.

"Take a look and see if it's yours—no, wait a bit."

He put the suit back in the cupboard, locked it again, and hurried back to his desk.

"Before you see it," he said, taking out his pen, "I must ask you about the cut."

"What cut?"

"The cut of the suit. Not all suits are cut the same way. Just a couple of words will do—your name, sir?"

"My name is Ahmad Shafik Lutfi, I am thirty-two years of age and was born in Edfiena, in the district of Rosetta, province of Beheira."

"Yes, yes, that's right. What sort of cut was it?"

"Single-breasted."

"Single-breasted?"

"Single-breasted—like the one I'm wearing now?"

"Hm . . . and its pockets?"

"Also like these."

"Hm . . . All right, come along and have a look at the suit."

He got up again, opened the cupboard and took out the suit. He began turning it this way and that, but from the first glance I could tell it wasn't mine. I didn't get up from my seat.

"So it's not your suit," said the Sergeant. "That's so, isn't it?"

"No, it's not my suit."

"Right, then let's finish the report."

He returned to his desk and began writing:

The report was begun at the date and time hereof when Mr. Ahmad Shafik Lutfi, employee at the Raml Company, was summoned to attend and after the suit previously acquired was shown to him he stated that it was not the suit he had lost.

With this the report was concluded and he duly signed it.

"Please sign it."

I got up, took the pen, and signed.

"Is that all?" I asked.

"That's all. Sorry to have troubled you. I'm sure we'll find your things, though."

I bade him farewell as I hurried out. "Peace be upon you." But I stopped suddenly.

"Tell me, Sergeant Abdel Basit, wouldn't it be possible to send notices to my home?"

"Of course, why not?"

"Good, in future always send them to my home."

"The fact is one gets a bit lazy and the Raml Company's nice and easy to write and it's a large company and well known."

It was now twelve o'clock, which meant that I would not be able to return to work that day. This also meant a further humiliating encounter with the manager. In any case I had to hurry off to Abbasiya police station so as to catch the officer before he went off to lunch and yet another day was wasted.

I got on to a bus, arrived at the station and went into the duty-room, where the officer met me with a genial smile which boded well. I greeted him and asked permission to sit down.

"Please do," he said.

"You remember me of course?" I asked him.

"Of course."

"And what's it all about this time, I wonder?"

"The thing's got into a bit of a muddle."

"How's that?"

"I'll tell you."

He pulled a file toward him and extracted the report relating to myself.

"It's like this. We summoned the driver of Taxi 4646 who stated that he hadn't been working that day and forwarded a certificate from a repair shop to the effect that his vehicle had been out of service on the day when your suitcase was lost."

"And the upshot?"

"I don't know."

"Isn't it possible that this certificate was sort of forged?"

"To tell the truth it's possible, but it'd be hard to prove."

"And now what?"

"Well, I've an idea."

"What is it?"

"I really do appreciate your position—your loss, so to speak, and I'd naturally like to help you."

"I'm most grateful."

"What I want to say is, isn't it possible that you—muddled up the number?"

"Muddled up the number? Out of the question! I remember distinctly that is was 4646."

"All right, sir, but what I mean is, instead of being 4646, couldn't the number be 6464 or 4664 or 6446 or some such combination of fours and sixes?"

"Impossible. For a start I remember clearly that each four had a six next to it."

"All right, this means that just as the number could be 4646 it might equally well have been 6464."

I kept silent and began to think.

"What do you think?"

"I don't know," I said. From that moment the numbers had in fact begun to get mixed up in my brain.

"It's possible," I said.

"What's possible?"

"What you say's possible."

"Which is the most likely number?"

"I don't know anything any longer. Let's say 6464 and try it out."

"All right, I'll take down these statements from you and we'll look into it all. After that certificate forwarded by the driver I'm really supposed to close the report and file it away. However, I appreciate your position so I'll open it again on the basis that you want to amend your statements in respect of the number of the vehicle."

"Fair enough. It's possible—it's possible I really did make a mistake."

The officer began to write.

"What statement do you wish to make?"

"With regard to the number of the vehicle which I took on the evening of my return from Alexandria and which I previously said was Number 4646, I would like to state that I have remembered that the correct number of the vehicle was 6464."

"Is there any further statement you wish to make?"

"No."

I left. The time was past two o'clock, which meant that the Company had closed its doors and there was nothing for me to do but go home.

I woke early next morning wanting to arrive at the office in good time so as to get through some of my work which was in arrears. All day long I succeeded in avoiding the manager. Neither did I meet the manager during the following week nor did he send for me. Gradually I dismissed the business of the suitcase from my mind.

However, one morning he did call for me.

When I entered his office I found him standing in front of his desk. At once he burst out angrily, "What I want to know, Mr. Ahmad, is where all this is going to end!"

I looked at him mutely.

"Where are all these police stations, questionings, and offenses going to end!"

In dread I asked, "What police stations, sir?"

"Read it," he said and handed me a small slip of paper. I stood rooted to the spot, too scared to step forward and take it from him.

"Go on, read it!"

I stretched out my trembling hand and took the piece of paper without looking at it.

"Read what it says—go on."

At last I read:

Imbaba police station.

Please note that Mr. Ahmad Shafik Lutfi is requested to attend urgently at the police station for questioning in Offense Number—

I was unable to go on. I stood up, not knowing what to do and looked beseechingly at the manager.

"What about it?" he asked sharply.

"I don't know," I answered.

"How do you mean you don't know? The suitcase was said to be at the Roda police station, then at Abbasiya, and now it's found its way to Imbaba."

"But, sir, it's not as if I've been a thief or done anything wrong!"

"You'd better go off to the police station. I'd dearly like to know where it's all going to end. Everything must have an end somewhere. Off you go."

With difficulty I dragged myself back to my office and sat down at the desk. I felt unable to move, unable to think intelligently. I then became aware of the piece of paper in my hand. Imbaba police station—Roda police station—whatever police station it might be at, I no longer wanted the suitcase.

However, there was nothing to do but get up and go to the police station. It was 10 a.m. and I had a mass of work in front of me. It was a long way to Imbaba. What had I to do with Imbaba police station?

I left my office and, feeling that I shouldn't waste any time, I signaled a taxi.

"Imbaba—the police station—as quick as you can, please."

When I got there I dashed into the duty officer's room and silently handed over my piece of paper.

"You're Ahmad Shafik?" he asked me.

"The very same."

"Please sit down."

I sat down and waited.

Opening the file in front of him, the officer said, "Last month you made a statement at Roda police station?"

I was getting impatient.

"Yes! What else?"

"And you said that the number of the taxi was 4646?"

"Hm," I said quietly, looking at him.

"And then at Abbasiya station, the station for the district in which the taxi driver lived, you said that the number of the taxi was not 4646 but 6464?"

"Hm."

"The driver of that taxi's called Mustafa Humeida and he lives here in Imbaba."

"Yes."

"That's why I've got you to come along, so that I could ask you about the whole business."

"I've told it all before."

"Never mind. The thing's now in our court and I'm never happy about an investigation unless I've done it myself."

"Hm, and what would you like to ask me about? Shouldn't you question the taxi driver first?"

"Look here, my dear fellow, I can't ask him till I've made sure."

"Made sure of what?"

"Once you said the number of the vehicle was 4646 and on another occasion you said it was 6464. I must make sure. Maybe you'll be saying yet some other number."

"So you want to ask me about that?"

"I'm going to start from the very beginning. I always like to do all my own investigations."

"Right. Go ahead. And what would you like to ask me about?"

"I'll tell you right away." He produced several sheets of paper from the drawer of his desk and began to write:

On today's date there appeared before us, the Duty Officer, Mr. Ahmad Shafik Lutfi who stated—

The officer leafed through the previous reports, and then went on writing.

My name is Ahmad Shafik Lutfi, I am thirty-two years of age and was born at Edifena in the district of Rosetta, province of Beheira. I am an employee of the Raml Company and live at 28 al-Malik al-Salih Street in Roda.

He turned to me. "What exactly was the subject of your statement?"

I sat up straight and said, "Officer."

"Yes?"

"Officer, I have lost nothing."

"What's that?"

"I haven't lost any suitcases."

"What do you mean?"

"What I mean is that I returned from Alexandria with all my suitcases complete and intact. I lost nothing."

"I don't understand what it's all about."

"I am telling you that I haven't lost a thing."

"Not quite so fast, my dear fellow! First of all, your name is Ahmad Shafik Lutfi, is it not? And you were born in Edfiena, district of Rosetta, province of Beheira, were you not? And you are, are you not, an employee of the Raml Company?"

"Exactly."

"What then are you talking about? Previously you made certain statements in a police report at Roda and Abbasiya to the effect that you had lost a suitcase on—"

"It isn't true."

"What? Isn't this your signature?" He thrust the reports I had previously signed into my hand.

"Yes, that's my signature," I said.

"Then the suitcase was stolen from you?"

"And I, as owner of the suitcase, tell you that nothing was stolen from me."

"And these statements?"

"A mistake."

"Forged?"

"No, a mistake."

"Didn't you read them before you signed them?"

"Yes, I did."

"Sir—officer, my four suitcases are all safely at home and nobody's stolen anything from me."

"Fine, we'll just write a couple of words to that effect."

The officer began to write. In complete silence I watched the pen racing across the paper. At last he looked up at me and said, "Please sign here."

I signed.

"Well, that's it," I said, getting to my feet. "If you'll excuse me."

"Where do you think you're going?" the officer asked.

"To my work. That's the end of the matter, isn't it?"

"The end of the matter? What do you mean? Sergeant Mahmoud!" he shouted at the top of his voice. "Hey, you standing by the door!"

The policeman appeared and saluted.

"Take this gentleman away," the officer told him.

"Take me where?" I asked in alarm.

But the officer was again writing in the report. I glanced at the policeman standing behind me; straining forward as far as I could I managed to read:

The said person is to be transferred back to the police station at Roda where he is resident so that he may be questioned in respect of a charge of being a nuisance to the authorities and dealt with under Section 135 of the Criminal Code.

The Clock

—ᴠᴠᴠ—

Khairy Shalaby

I was walking along a dazzling, crowded street—I think it was Suleiman Pasha or one like it. I was pushing aside great multitudes of humanity at every step in order to make my way. All the women of Cairo were naked and gave out a smell of kerosene. There were men who looked like gas cylinders licking the backs of the women and placing money between their breasts and their thighs. Suddenly I saw my younger brother in his peasant's gallabiya and white skullcap. Shoulders, thighs, and breasts separated me from him. Delighted to see him, I began stretching out my neck so that he might see me.

He too was stretching out his neck. As we drew closer, it seemed as though we would both be going our own ways. However, each of us prepared to greet the other. When I stretched out my hand he did the same by reaching out between the many obstructions. Our hands met in a quick touch that earned us many rebukes and curses.

Then I don't know where he went. I immediately recollected that I hadn't seen him for years. I remembered that I had wanted to ask him about all sorts of things. My question presented itself: Do you know anything yet about our younger brother who didn't come back from the war? But the question did not come out.

All at once I found myself in a funeral procession. I asked who the dead man was and was told it was the husband of my eldest sister, that he had died in the war, and that there had been news of this. I thought those around me walking in the funeral would blame me if they found themselves alone with me, but I didn't know exactly what I was to be blamed for. Then we arrived at a place that I thought was the cemetery. One thing convinced me that I was right—this was the ancient sycamore tree that was in the center of our village cemetery.

While I was standing far off from those who were making their prayers over the body, I saw my younger brother who hadn't yet come back from the war and about whom we had been unable to gather any information, though we had asked everywhere. His long face with its fair complexion was just as I had known it, ever smiling. He was wearing a gallabiya, over which he had put on an army belt. I hugged him and wept.

When I told him we'd had a terrible time trying to find out what had happened to him, he laughed as usual and said that we shouldn't have bothered. Then the procession went off again to enter into the cemetery. There was a certain air of reverence enveloping the mourners, although we come from a family scarcely deserving of acts of courtesy. I said to myself, "Such are the funeral processions of righteous martyrs"—and I had a feeling of jealousy for the deceased.

But suddenly I discovered that Dr. Henry Kissinger, President Nixon, and President Ford were walking at the front of the procession and that they were also receiving condolences. The folk from my village had turned out in gallant fashion and were greeting them and smiling just like them. All of a sudden there was no one there at all. I saw nothing in front of me except for a vast expanse of desert that gave off scorching heat and the smell of kerosene. From somewhere came the voice of a reciter chanting the Quran, while the sun, suspended in the sky, was sinking down into the far horizon like a clock without hands or dial.

The Man and the Farm

Yusuf Sharouni

At ten o'clock in the evening Munira felt the first twinges of pain and at eleven her husband, Badawi Effendi, went off at a run—in spite of his size—to call the doctor.

Badawi Effendi's luck was in: the doctor had no other delivery to deal with that evening, though he was not in his clinic when Badawi got there. One of the nurses telephoned him at the club where he was on night call, playing Coon-can with his friends. So he told the nurse to go and find out how urgent it was and to judge for herself as to when he would be required.

Panting, Badawi Effendi got back to the house with the nurse to find that his mother-in-law—whom he had sent for—had come to sit through the hours of labor with her daughter. At midnight the doctor arrived.

It was a somewhat cold March night, with the moon not yet up. The doctor and Badawi Effendi sat on the balcony which was just above ground floor level, sipping coffee, gazing at the stars, and listening to the rustling of the trees in front of them. Spring had covered their branches with green and the wind carried the scent of blossom which had not yet revealed its fruit. Meanwhile the two men strained their ears toward the woman within who was suffering the pangs of childbirth. The doctor had given her some drops of medicine to assist her during labor and an injection to guard against the risk of hemorrhage; after that he had left it to nature to complete her work while he merely acted as watchman and assistant. The woman herself gave out an almost continuous low moaning sound which was intensified from time to time.

Though the first experience of its kind in the lives of Badawi Effendi and his wife Munira, it was one that was being continually repeated in the life of the doctor. While for him cases of childbirth—like the human creatures he treated—possessed a certain similarity, each none the less possessed its own uniqueness.

Badawi Effendi and Munira were no newlyweds, however: they had been married for seven long years without having either sons or daughters and during these years they had come to feel that their marriage was like a barren fruit tree.

Badawi Effendi was a farmer or, to put it more exactly, the owner of a market garden near the city of Cairo. On marrying he had left the market garden to his brother and had settled with his bride in one of the suburbs of the capital. Though Munira was his cousin, she had spent her life in the city. She was as white as milk, as plump as a duck, and rather short of stature, especially when measured against the tall, hefty frame of her husband. Quite possibly she herself would not have objected to living in the country, but Badawi Effendi, ever-watchful for her comfort (a feeling resembling love had existed between them since childhood) had moved to a small modern home. His share of the work consisted of looking after the transportation of the produce and selling it by auction to the traders in the city markets; from time to time he also advised his brother about bringing on a certain crop so as to make it available before the market became glutted, or keeping back some other produce so that it could be sold out of season at double the price. Badawi Effendi's spare-time hobby was reading: papers, magazines, and the occasional book, for he had had the opportunity of studying up to secondary school level and had also learnt how to sport a European-type suit; his brother's education, on the other hand, did not extend beyond the village school and he continued to wear either gallabiya or jubba.

One month of their marriage, then another, passed in expectancy. The earth had taught Badawi that he should wait, that he should allow time, after sowing and watering, for it to produce its first small green shoots in due course; these shoots too, should be given time in which to grow and flower, and these blossoms in their turn should be accorded time to wither and give place to fruit.

They began to be perturbed. Badawi Effendi did not wish to upset his bride, though he knew she was in fact already apprehensive and that her mother— who was now standing beside her as she suffered her labor—had also begun to share their concern. Their need for a child was an instinctive one, the need for the next step in the natural order of things. Each began wondering: Is there something abnormal in this? Which of us is it—the seed or the soil?

A year passed, a second year began. Whenever night came and bed brought them together, Badawi Effendi would feel that the spark of passion within him burnt as brightly as ever. Before marrying he had heard from certain of his friends that this spark would wane, that frequency, habit, and the ease with which it could be satisfied would all serve to quench the flames of passion. But he had found that the opposite was true, and that sex was like food: no sooner had one had one's fill at one meal than one was looking forward greedily to the next.

Badawi Effendi was by nature skilled in the ways of love. He knew how, little by little, to awaken in his wife the deepest of her dormant emotions so that she responded to and with him, while he rejoiced in his manhood and the passionate desire it kindled within her. Why, though, was it, he continually asked himself, that each failed to give the other a proof that they had done all in their power, that they had both played their parts to perfection, he as a complete man and she as a complete woman. These poignant moments passed, yet the seed did not grow, the vegetation did not flower, the blossoms bore no fruit.

It is not, however, in the make-up of a farmer to resign himself to the infertility of his land. The soil which Badawi Effendi and his brother now cultivated had been regarded as barren more than fifty years ago. His grandfather, buying it for next to nothing, had begun to till it, at first planting it with rice, then with lucerne and beans. Then his father had taken over and, doubling his efforts, had treated it with chemical fertilizers until he managed to make it yield a fine crop of vegetables both summer and winter. And thus it was that the idea began, little by little, to grow in Badawi Effendi's mind, timorously at first, yet with ever-growing insistence.

Munira's sister had married several months after them and not a year had passed before she was delivered of a child who had filled the house with his crying. His mother had told Badawi Effendi, just before she died, that one shouldn't let such matters rest without doing something, while his mother-in-law had pointed out to her daughter that children gave a wife a certain standing in the home, that they were a comfort in one's loneliness and gave an atmosphere of warmth and gaiety to a house.

And thus Badawi Effendi and his wife came to have experience of doctors as they went from clinic to clinic, from laboratory to laboratory, being examined and analyzed. They came to know other childless couples, entering a world of doctors, of women and men and their troubles, a world in which women struggled to attain the pangs of childbirth. Badawi Effendi felt that he was like the branch of a tree and that he did not want this tree to be felled; he wanted it to be handed on after his death in the same way as he had taken it over from those before him.

They went away from the doors of these clinics and laboratories with a verdict of 'not guilty': the seed was fertile, the soil was fertile, yet somehow no plant grew. And so they abandoned medicine, more bewildered than ever, feeling as though accursed by some unknown hand.

For a little while Badawi Effendi considered the suggestion, made by one of the doctors, that his wife should have recourse to artificial insemination. However, he rejected this idea absolutely; in fact he expressed such disgust at it that the doctor, who had suggested it in a most delicate and indirect way, felt quite embarrassed. Badawi Effendi wanted to have a son of his own, a sprig that would grow from his own branch; he wanted to enjoy seeing his own features coming to life in the growing child. He wanted him to be sturdy, intelligent, and full of energy like his father. He had no desire to import the seed—he wanted to till his own farm by himself, otherwise it might as well remain barren.

Two years passed, and his mother-in-law insisted more and more that medicine was nothing but humbug and robbery. Otherwise why did they not have children when neither of them was in any way to blame? Despite the fact that Badawi Effendi had studied up to secondary school level, despite his reading of the magazine *The Doctor* and his being well aware that it was chemical fertilizers which gave life to the land and not charms, magic, or incense, he still fell back on a childhood filled with superstition in his moments of despair. So he left the whole thing to his mother and mother-in-law, between whom there had been a kind of reconciliation when they received the doctors' reports, where before there had been something closely akin to furtive recrimination, as though each was responsible for her son or her daughter. The two of them agreed that the spirits, who were clearly casting their spells between Munira's thighs, preventing her from becoming pregnant, must be placated.

And so it was that the outside lavatory—where the spirits had their home—was thoroughly cleaned, sprinkled with sand, and adorned with roses and other flowers; at the same time a bottle of sherbet, another of rose water, and several pounds of sweets were strewn on the ground. Incense was burnt, drums were beaten, and no one was allowed inside; Badawi Effendi, Munira, or any others in the house had to use the neighbors' lavatory. These rites were carried out for a whole twenty-four hours. The old woman who had been called in also ordered that a sheep be slaughtered and that by dawn no single piece of it should be left; every scrap of meat had to be eaten before midnight and the bones buried before daybreak.

Badawi Effendi and his wife were told to wait for a month for the results of these endeavors. The month duly passed and there was indeed a pregnancy. The trouble was, though, that it wasn't Munira who became pregnant but her mother, who was nearly forty-five and whose youngest child was ten years old. In explaining this away it was said that the spirits must have lost their way.

This disaster had a bad effect on Badawi Effendi and his wife, for having previously tried out scientific methods with scientific calm they now took to superstitious methods with superstitious zeal. It came as a terrible shock to Badawi Effendi to see his mother-in-law's stomach swell up when she already had no less than seven children—it was as if she had stolen his child from him. From the very beginning Badawi Effendi had not seen eye to eye with his uncle's wife; when, therefore, she became pregnant in place of his wife, his hatred of her grew only too evident and the mere sight of her irritated him. As for Munira, she felt real jealousy of her mother. It was as though she faced one of Fate's enigmas: why should it bestow something on someone who didn't want it while denying it to someone who yearned for it?

An atmosphere of tragedy settled on the house. The hot weather had spoilt the tomato crop of which Badawi Effendi had had high hopes. Though Munira was in no way responsible for this, her husband became sullen, quick-tempered, and rude toward her. Sometimes Munira would bend to the storm, at others she would flare up. When at her wit's end she would burst into heart-rending tears and say, "I know the reason, it's because I haven't given you children. You know it's not my fault, though!" to which he would reply furiously, "Well, it certainly isn't mine." But before long, little by little, his heart would relent and he would wipe away her tears. It was no easy task to calm her, and he would have to fondle and caress her, draw his big fingers through her soft, flowing hair, and over the uncovered parts of her body and kiss her as she lay in his strong arms, supine as a frightened cat, and all too soon, like the most passionate of lovers, their bodies would be joined and serenity would reign.

The previous summer Badawi Effendi's mother had died at the farm. She had been brought up there, and had seldom left it, though she would pay visits of several days to her son Badawi when she would ask how they were getting on and deliver herself of advice to both sides. After hearing the news of her death Badawi and his wife were obliged to attend the funeral and receive the usual condolences. On the night of the funeral ceremony, after the flood of wailing and weeping had died down, Munira learned from the women who came to pay their condolences that a strange Bedouin woman had arrived at the village three days earlier. This woman claimed to have the power of finding lost things, curing the sick, and quickening the barren. Though Munira's faith in such matters had diminished considerably since the episode of the spirits, she was like a drowning person clutching at any straw. On the following day, therefore, she sent for the Bedouin woman and told her of the thing for which she yearned. The woman asked for a gold ornament of hers on which, as she expressed it, "she could pass the night," and said she would return it at dawn the following morning. She also gave Munira two small rolls of wool, telling her to place one of them between her thighs; at midnight she was to substitute the other one and keep it there till morning and, with the help of God the One, she would become pregnant.

In an agony of hope Munira had given the Bedouin woman one of her gold bracelets—worth no less than twenty pounds—and had then carried out her instructions to the letter. The next morning she had waited for the woman to return with her bracelet as promised. But the woman never came back, and on enquiring about her Munira was told that she had left the village on the previous evening for an unknown destination. Realizing that the whole business was a sheer swindle, Munira opened the two rolls of wool and found that one contained what looked like lucerne seeds together with some white powder, while in the other there was a piece of paper written on in such a small and poor hand that she was only able to make out a few words such as "At your service . . . ." Bemoaning her bad luck more than the loss of the bracelet, Munira threw the lot away. Some women who heard her weeping came to console her, thinking that she was crying for the old woman who had departed this life—and who had also been her uncle's wife—and were both surprised and impressed at such loyalty.

The days of mourning passed and Munira returned to Cairo with her husband. On one of their nights together, outwardly laughing at her stupidity but with the heaviest of hearts, she told her husband of the story of the Bedouin woman. Despite this unfortunate experience, Munira's period was overdue. She waited a few more days in disbelief and then informed her husband.

Badawi Effendi had toyed with the idea of divorce but had found it distasteful and had therefore rejected it, just as he had rejected the suggestion of artificial insemination. Munira was his cousin; she had become a habit and he was not one to change his habits. Besides, they loved one another, and just as the fault was not his so, too, it was not hers. More than once he had been told that if he were to marry some other woman children would be born to him, while she, by marrying someone else, would bear children. His feelings on the matter were those of a peasant who refuses to sell any of his land however hard pressed he may be. More than once his friends had urged him to take a second wife. This, too, he knew was impossible, for it would hurt Munira to her very depths. Moreover this would be a new departure in his family, neither his father, grandfather, nor—he had heard—his great-grandfather ever having taken more than one wife.

These thoughts had given place to even more dangerous ones. At a certain period a desire for death had stirred within him—the death of one of them so that he could marry someone else and have children, or she some other man and bear him children. These somber thoughts did not come to him merely as a wish but in the form of an obituary, of people offering their condolences, of funeral rites. He would imagine one of them mourning the other, and many other details came to him with the utmost clarity. Badawi Effendi did not allow such pictures to take root in his mind but fought against them, thrusting them away from him one by one, believing—as did his wife—that everything was ordained by fate. This faith of his brought Badawi Effendi to a state of mind not far removed from mysticism.

When his wife, who was determined to continue the struggle, informed him of her state of health, a ray of hope sprang up within him, but most warily, for this was not the first time her period had been delayed. Once, in fact, it had stopped altogether for two months, at which they had gone off to a famous woman doctor who had advised them to have an analysis made at cost of two pounds. The victim of this analysis was a rabbit which was injected with some of Munira's urine and was then slaughtered on the following day for an examination of its ovaries. On returning to the doctor to learn the result of the analysis she informed them that there was no pregnancy. They didn't believe this doctor and accused her of not knowing what she was talking about, though it was not long before the truth of her words became apparent. And so it was that this time Badawi Effendi waited in trepidation for several more days.

Eventually, Munira confirmed the good news, for she and her mother had gone to a doctor who assured her that this time she really was pregnant—after six years and three months of marriage. Badawi Effendi, in spite of his huge size, had literally danced with joy; he had caressed her stomach, fondling it with fingers and lips; he had placed his ear against it as though to hear the pulse beats of the embryo which was as yet no more than a mere sperm. Now Badawi Effendi's manhood was fulfilled: the barren land had been fertilized just as his grandfather before him had made fruitful the waste land he had bought. Now it was up to him to guard it, nurture it, care for it, until in the fullness of time its fruit was born, live, warm, real.

Arrangements for welcoming the baby were begun and the two of them gave much thought to the question of a suitable name. Would it be a boy or a girl? Munira started to make baby clothes, a small mattress, a small pillow, a small coverlet—everything small became a part of their world.

But still Badawi Effendi was nagged by a slight feeling of doubt. He had often heard (especially in his bachelor days) of women with husbands who, deprived of their most cherished dreams, nevertheless continued to love their wives more than their dreams and thus found themselves torn between two conflicting desires: love for the wife who existed and for the dream which did not. Torn between love and sympathy for her husband and the desire to fulfil herself as a woman and a mother, such a woman would go with some young man just once, so that she might experience motherhood and her husband fatherhood; having achieved this, she would never see the young man again. Badawi remembered that Munira had become pregnant during the days of his mother's funeral and had come to him with the story of the Bedouin woman at that time. Could it be that she had been preparing the way for what happened later? Could it, for instance, have been his own brother? His brother was the one who actually cultivated the farm, while he merely had the job of selling the produce. Could it be that his brother had cultivated his farm for him in another fashion? He banished the ridiculous idea from his mind, knowing full well that neither his wife nor his brother was capable of perpetrating such a thing—it was merely a stupid thought that had come to him in a moment of weakness, just as other stupid thoughts had done in the past. Perhaps those two rolls of wool, with that white powder in one of them, had been responsible after all? Perhaps one of them had contained the seed of some other man?—No, it was his own seed, he was sure of it. After all, he was not the only man to whom such a thing had happened. It had, for instance, occurred in the case of the former omda of their village after ten years of marriage, and to Sheikh Maihoub after no less than twelve, and both their wives were above suspicion.

He remembered the first night of the funeral when all the mourners had left and Munira, in the living-room on the flat roof of the house, had exhausted herself with weeping and wailing, while he, too, despite the fact that his mother had been a lady of advanced years, had been much saddened by her departure from this life. It had been a chokingly hot, clammy July night and each of them had gone to sleep without feeling desire. At dawn, though, he had woken up and left the room to relieve nature; he had felt the early breezes on his face, had breathed in the odour of the countryside, a mixture of earth, greenery, and animals, and it was as though this smell, charged with the memories of childhood and youth, had revitalized him and kindled within him a flame of desire. He had returned to the room on tiptoe, but his movements must have disturbed her, for she opened her eyes momentarily as he drew near to her. It was as though he wanted to bury his sorrows within her body, and the desire that burned between them had never been stronger.

Now here she was—nine months later—suffering the pangs of labor. Being his first experience of such matters, it was quite impossible for him to know whether the sufferings of his wife were peculiar to her or were in fact experienced by every woman in such circumstances. Several times he had looked for the answer in the doctor's eyes, unwilling to reveal his fear and feeling of helplessness. Six hours had elapsed and the cocks had begun to call like muezzins from the neighboring roof-tops as his wife continued her cries and groans. He had slipped into her room for a moment and had been confronted with the frightful spectacle of her lying there bathed in sweat in spite of the cold weather, moaning softly. The six years' struggle had become focused into these hours. He said a few tender words of encouragement before being ordered out by the doctor who saw no point in allowing him to witness such a scene.

Badawi Effendi had the highest respect for the doctor, for his calmness, gentleness and experience; he was like some small deity, holding in his hands the keys of life for his wife and child. Badawi was also struck by the doctor's great humanity; and the fee he would be getting seemed to Badawi quite inadequate for being kept up so late and for all the care and attention he was giving. Furthermore, the doctor's cheerful manner and smiling face inspired boundless confidence in Badawi.

They were of similar age, each being about thirty-five. The night, the solitude, and the silence had created a sort of friendship between them. Badawi Effendi knew certain facts about the doctor, for instance that he was a government doctor by day and that he had his own private clinic in the evenings. He both earned and spent a great deal, his spending being largely at the gambling table and on his mistress, despite the fact that he had a wife who was an object of desire to others.

The doctor talked to him about his two children, a boy and a girl. The girl, though the younger of the two, was the cleverer and was in a higher form than her brother. Badawi Effendi talked to him about his farm, methods of fertilization, the seasons for the various vegetables, and the way prices rise and fall. The doctor spoke about the government hospitals, their lack of equipment, and the general muddle they were in, and about a woman who had come to him at the government hospital with a hemorrhage: no sooner had they put her on the operating table than she had died and an investigation had been made to determine the extent of his responsibility. Badawi Effendi told him about his long struggle to produce a child, about the doctors he had met, and the data he possessed about the pregnancy, as though wishing to make quite sure that it was genuine.

Once again, as a faint sickle moon appeared in the east, they drank down a couple of cups of coffee. While the doctor reassured Badawi Effendi about his wife, the first light of dawn unfolded, the first early morning breeze stirred. The doctor then went inside to see how things were progressing. A matter of minutes before sunrise—at 7:30 a.m.—Badawi Effendi heard the crying of his newborn child and was himself moved to silent tears.

The Mother

—✺—

Ibrahim Shukrallah

Nagiya awoke at dawn to the dull echo of stabs of pain rising up from her body to her sleep-befogged brain. No sooner was she completely awake than her whole body was racked by the full force of these stabs which came from her side; long stabs of piercing pain which, now that she was quite conscious, followed one another with regular precision. With each separate pang, preceded as it was by an interval of quiet, came the hope that it would be the final one, and she would find herself listening, waiting. But the period of quiet would not last long; all too soon it was followed by another stab, more quiet, another stab, quiet, and yet another and another.

Nagiya stirred uneasily on her bed. The coldness of dawn shook her body lying on its mattress of straw over the dead stove. A sharp cry of pain broke from her, but no one answered. She kept silent, and once again the pain quivered in her side. In anger she renewed her cries.

"Hafiza . . . Come here, girl! . . . Where are you? . . . Come to me!"

She listened. From outside she could hear her husband's voice swearing angrily at the donkey: "Come on with you, you son of a bitch!" Then the sound of Omran, her father-in-law, slowly gnawing at a piece of dry bread; also the voice of Hafiza's child, crying listlessly, without anger—as he always did when he awoke in the early morning—and of Hafiza herself, rocking him, her voice heavy with sleep.

Pain again seized hold of her body. In fury she began thinking about the piece of bread Omran was gnawing. In her mind's eye she saw him chewing it slowly between his toothless jaws, his face wearing an expression of engrossed contentment, scarcely aware of his surroundings. "Have you got nothing better to do than eat, the first thing you get up?" She muttered angrily, and once again pain twisted her body.

"Hafiza, you little wretch!" she cried in a voice choked with the pain that had come on with renewed vigor.

"What's wrong, mother? Pain's come again?" Hafiza slowly approached, wiping the sleep from her eyes.

Directly Nagiya heard these words spoken in such a gentle, conciliatory tone, she burst out at her daughter:

"Your mother! I'm no mother of yours. If I were it might mean something to you that I'm lying here dying, with the pain tearing at my side."

Hafiza bent over her, her breasts pointed and youthful, a smile on her round, full face and moist lips.

"It's all right, mother," she said, speaking in a slow, gentle manner; "the child was crying and I was feeding him."

Nagiya's heart softened at the deep, kindly voice of her daughter. She remembered how fond she was of her, how much more she liked her than the others. She was about to smile at her when the pain returned, rending her exhausted body. She recovered from it and turned to Hafiza, her face convulsed.

"You and your father are leaving me here to die . . . Why should you care so long as you've got your husband and child? Why should you care whether your mother lives or dies? . . . Ah! Shame on you! . . . You've turned out just as brutal as your father."

"But what can we do, mother?" she said softly, turning away her head, wounded by her mother's unjust accusation. "Who can father leave the field to? . . . Anyway, here I am, sitting by you."

Nagiya did not reply, and Hafiza squatted down on the stove, silent, her head lowered, hearing nothing but the occasional groans that broke from her mother; from time to time she passed her tongue over her lips in an anguish no words could express.

Then the monotonous, unchanging noise of the child's crying reached them, sounding like some meaningless phrase committed to heart and repeated by a schoolboy. Hafiza stirred uneasily and her mother turned to her.

"Go and see to the child, Hafiza,"

Her body waited, as though with eager expectancy, for the next stab. She followed her daughter's footsteps as she left the room, and her heart went out to her. She could also hear Omran's voice as he sat with Muhammad and Zaina round him, both of them chewing bread, while he told them in his broken voice: "It's much better with salt." Then, after a while, she heard him give a short laugh. "Eh . . . don't you agree it's better with salt?" The blood rushed to her head with inward rage. Then came the mounting screams of the child, vibrating from the rocking, and a little later she made out the voice of Hafiza's husband addressing her sharply: "If she's all that ill why doesn't she go to hospital?"

Suddenly Nagiya turned away from it all, her body alerted and ready to meet the next stab that clutched at her bowels, causing her to stretch straight out on her back. "Hospital . . . hospital." The one word echoed through her head, unaccompanied by any sort of emotion. For a while she continued shaking her head to right and left as she repeated the word, until Hafiza returned and squatted down on the stove by her side, the child in her lap, his mouth at her breast and his eyes tightly closed. She bent over him, wrapping him round with her black milaya.

"Take me to the hospital," her mother said.

"Why, mother? Do you think we hold you so cheap we'd pack you off to hospital?"

"Hafiza, take me to hospital," she continued, in a voice choked with self-pity. "Take me to hospital, Hafiza."

She was repeating these words when Khalifa entered.

"Yes, . . . now you're talking sense," he said in his loud, self-confident voice. "Go to hospital, then they'll make you well again and you can come back cured. . . . Tomorrow, Hafiza my girl, you take her to town and put her into hospital."

Accompanied by her daughter, Nagiya went to the Qasr al-Aini hospital. Of the train journey and the tramp through the wide streets, of the crazy traffic

and noisy, merry, and quarrelsome inhabitants, of the towering, defiant buildings—of all these she was oblivious, existing as she did behind veil of pain,
hemmed in by colorless, undefined impressions. The sharp stabs had now
passed, to be replaced by a dull ache that permeated her whole being. She had
submitted to this pain had immersed herself in it to the exclusion of everything
else. All worries had disappeared and there moaned only fear and images of
death. In evoking these vague thoughts Nagiya's brain derived a vague yet
subtle pleasure. She took her mind back to the past, to days that had long
gone by, to as far back as she could remember, and found that every minute
of her life had been nothing but worry and toil: wrenching her body at dawn
from amid the clinging clouds of gentle sleep, spending her entire day running
between the house and the field till, at night, she threw herself down in exhaustion. When the illness had come, she had fought and struggled against it for the
sake of that life of hers which, in spite of her everlasting grumbling, she was
unable to conceive as ever being different. Now that her body had yielded, her
mind too experienced the pleasure of complete submission.

Hafiza walked by her mother's side, her hands holding the black milaya
wrapped round the child, who, at first, disturbed by the noise of the train, had
cried, then, between his sobs, had smiled and fallen asleep to his mother's
rocking. Occasionally he woke up to let out his listless, monotonous crying
for a while, but would soon be asleep again. At length, after asking the
way a number of times, Hafiza and her mother reached the gate of the Qasr
al-Aini hospital.

"What shall we do now?" Hafiza turned to her mother.

Nagiya made no answer, for she had found a new and unexpected pleasure in the worry that her daughter now bore. Why should *she* go on thinking
and striving? Her whole life she had done so, not only for herself but for
others, so it was high time somebody else did the worrying.

Hafiza stopped a passerby. Awkwardly she inquired how she could get her
mother into hospital. He showed her the place where the names were registered, then added, "But they're not taking anybody now."

Hafiza continued on her way, terror and anxiety blinding her to everything. On reaching the office she began explaining her case in halting words,
her face pleading and imploring, but she had no sooner finished speaking than

the clerk burst out at her, "Well, what's wrong with her—she's standing on her two legs, isn't she? . . . We haven't got any beds."

Hafiza renewed her appeals, calling to mind all the expressions used in such circumstances: "Please, sir . . . May God reward you for your kindness . . . May the Prophet . . . She's a poor old woman with many children . . . She's been suffering a long time from this illness of hers . . . May God protect you, sir."

But he only snapped at her again and turned to someone else. At this Hafiza was overcome with shame, humiliation, and embarrassment. She stood sheltering by her mother's side, a sense of complete helplessness engulfing her.

They stood thus for a while: the mother speechless yet experiencing a subtle joy at Hafiza's helplessness, while Hafiza bent over her child with her sad, round face, her mind a void. When a policeman ordered them to leave, they went out. On reaching the door they were met by the man who had first directed Hafiza to the office.

"Didn't I tell you they weren't taking anybody now?" he remarked, an exultant ring in his voice. "You see," he rambled on, "they only take people who have some sort of influence, and they don't care a rap about poor folk. Now, when my aunt fell ill, and we wanted to have an operation done, only Dr. Hussein Bey could get her in . . . you see, he's a very decent fellow and has a high regard for me." He bent over Hafiza confidingly. "You seem to be poor folk—listen, I'll tell you of a good plan. Get your mother to lie down on the ground and sit by her side and scream for all you're worth, then they'll fetch an ambulance that'll take her right off to Qasr al-Aini where she'll get a bed and everybody'll be happy."

These words fell on Hafiza's ears like magic. She glanced at her mother's silent face, but found no reply there.

"Thank you, sir," she said to the man.

"Well, there it is," he answered as he made off. "I'm telling you, there's no other way."

A period of silence followed between the two women, after which Hafiza said: "What shall we do now, mother?"

Nagiya turned to her, her face an expression of deep misery and self pity.

"Begin screaming, Hafiza!"

Directly she had said these words she threw herself to the ground, covering her face with the edge of her milaya. For a moment Hafiza stood confused, overcome by grief. Then she heard the weak voice of her mother saying: "Begin screaming, Hafiza!" so she started sobbing softly, then, gathering together her strength, she burst out into wild shrieks and wails that steadily increased in volume. The child, woken by the noise, opened his eyes; his face trembled, then he began crying loudly, his small features contorted, his eyes closed in temper.

The passersby collected round the two women. They stood by inquiring in loud voices what had happened and offering explanations. Most of them wandered off again, but a small number remained, curious to see what would be the outcome. A policeman came up and asked what the trouble was. For a while he stared frigidly at them, then telling some of those standing by to help him, he carried the woman into the hospital, with Hafiza following after him, her voice having now died down to a mere succession of choked mutterings: "May God bring you back to health, Mother."

The policeman explained the position to the official, who glared suspiciously at Hafiza, while she lowered her head; asked about her mother's name and what was wrong with her, she answered as best she could. The official ordered the mother to be taken into the hospital, but when Hafiza tried to follow, he roughly stopped her, ordering her outside. When her pleading availed nothing, she slowly went out into the street, her head filled with an overwhelming sense of bewilderment and futility in the face of everything. Exhaustion welling up within her body, she seated herself cross-legged on the ground and, taking the child to her warm bosom and arranging the ends of the milaya round him, she leant her head against the stone-work of the wall behind which her mother lay in one of the large, lonely buildings.

Her eyes closed. She endeavored to find, within the recesses of her mind, some clue as to what she should do and where she should go. No answer presented itself; all she felt was anger, anger against everything, but especially against her husband whom she could now picture with his broad, cheerful face and boisterous laugh. She imagined him returning from his round in the village where he worked as a barber, carrying his razor blade and soap, and sitting down to his dinner without so much as asking about her. Then perhaps, as he often did, he would start playing with Hosna, her young sister. How he loved Hosna! It sometimes seemed that he preferred Hosna to her and to her own poor child. She hated him and wished that she could inflict on him the very aguish that now surrounded and threatened to engulf her. Sadness surged up inside her; but soon, for no particular reason, she found herself thinking about Hussein, the son of the village omda, who had once smiled at her as he cycled along a country lane. Now studying here in Cairo, he dressed in European clothes and led a happy, luxurious life which was so above all that ugliness, filth and hate which was her lot. Yes, why shouldn't she go to him this very evening, go to him and ask him what she ought to do. Maybe he'd invite her to spend the night with him at his house. Her face flushed with excitement and shame at this daring idea. She wandered on in her dreams, imagining herself knocking at his door, his opening it to her, his greeting her with joyful smiles, while she stared at the ground, smiling yet embarrassed. Then he would have all kinds of tasty food prepared for her and served on a large high table, after which she would experience the marvelous warmth of a soft bed . . . . Plunged in these happy dreams, sleep crept upon her, rising inside her with a delicious stealth. She yielded to it, having curled herself round the child so that her whole body covered him.

The Country Boy

—mm—

Yusuf al-Sibai

This story has four main characters and of these only one is, in all probability, still alive today. Of two of them I can say with certainty that they have departed for the other world, and as to the third the good Lord alone knows what has happened to him.

I know not what has prompted me not to change the name of the characters and so spare myself the trouble of thinking up fictitious names for them; perhaps it is laziness, or maybe the certain knowledge that none of them would be upset if the story were to be published. More than all this is my confidence in these characters, for one of them was my late father, Muhammad Sibai, and I am sure that had God granted him a longer life he would have forestalled me by publishing the story himself, as he did in the weekly *Balagh* with most of the incidents that happened with the late Sheikh Abdel Rahman Barquqi. As God did not give him the opportunity of writing it, let me do so on his behalf, and if it is true as they say that the departed see us and are aware of what we do, I dare say he will read it and that his loud guffaws will ring out in the heavens as they did in his lifetime on earth.

The story begins a very long time ago—I am positive it was before 1917, which is to say before I was born—in a bookshop in Ghaith al-Idda Street which joins up Bab al-Khalq with Abdin.

Two men are sitting in the bookshop: the owner and the owner's friend. The first was a religious sheikh with a turban, while the second, my father, was dressed in European style. Both men were well-known literary figures of the time.

I can well imagine my father with his bulky body, broad shoulders and full red face, seated in a cane chair with one leg crossed nonchalantly over the other, as though seated at Shepheard's, and alongside him Sheikh Abdel Rahman on another chair with his flowing gibba and elegant kaftan over his extremely tall body, and with a face no less pink and white than my father's, also with one leg crossed over the other as he pulled at the mouthpiece of a shisha that gurgled beside him.

The two friends were joined by Sheikh al-Fakk, who was leading his son Imam by the hand.

I do not know very much about Sheikh al-Fakk, but I do know that he was a good God-fearing man, clean-living and extremely pious. He had spent his life in the country, and his son having finished his primary education, he had brought him to Cairo to go to secondary school. Whom should Sheikh al-Fakk have recourse to other than those two eminent educationalists and men of letters, Messrs Sibai and Barquqi, with both of whom he was very friendly?

And so it was that the good man brought his son to Cairo and began asking about his two friends till he ran them down at the bookshop. After the usual exchange of salutations, the man began explaining the purpose of his visit.

"I won't hide from you, Mr. Sibai, that I'm frightened about the boy in Cairo. I hear it's all depravity and immorality and I'm afraid the lad's eyes will be opened and he'll be corrupted. I told myself there was no one better than yourselves to look after the lad. I'll leave him in your hands, knowing that it's as if he's in his own home, isn't that so?"

"My dear Sheikh," the two answered with one voice, "the lad's like our own son. Relax and don't worry about him."

"That's just what I told myself—who better to come to than you?"

"You're very kind."

"God bless you both."

And so Sheikh al-Fakk took himself off, leaving his son in the care of his two friends.

It remains to introduce the fourth character in the story: Imam al-Fakk.

The reader may well imagine, having learnt that Imam the son of Sheikh al-Fakk had finished his primary education and that his father was frightened his eyes would be opened to the depravities of Cairo, that he was some naive young child. Imam, though, was no such thing. At that time primary schoolboys were often as old as the fathers of today, with some of them sprouting beards and mustaches. The student Imam al-Fakk was a hulking man. Though he looked silent and quiet, it was a case of still waters running deep. With closed eyes and lowered head, all shyness and diffidence, he would sit beside his father, oozing innocence, when all the time there wasn't a brothel or hashish den in Tanta he hadn't patronized.

This was the pure, God-fearing, upright, and inexperienced son whose father feared would be corrupted by the depravities of Cairo; this was the person entrusted to the care of my father and his friend. Now, I happened to know from personal experience that my father did not have the time to see about the bringing up of his own children, let alone other people's, and the same was true of Sheikh Barquqi.

The first thing this God-fearing young man did was to go off to the headmaster of a national school and strike a bargain with him whereby he took a quarter of the fees in exchange for merely registering him at the school: he wouldn't trouble him with attending, taking books or anything of that sort, all that was required being that the headmaster should register him as a student for a consideration of five pounds. Having registered at the school, Imam al-Fakk then proceeded, with the remainder of the fees, to wreak havoc in Cairo.

Days, weeks and months passed and Imam, as the saying goes, went the whole hog, his fame spreading throughout every brothel and house of ill-repute in the city.

News of what his son was up to began to get back to his father from fellow villagers visiting Cairo. At first the sheikh would not believe it and thought it was all some plot engineered out of envy. At last, though, his suspicions were aroused and he thought it best to go to Cairo to see for himself the real state of affairs and set his mind at rest.

He descended on his son and confronted him with the accusations and rumors, at which the son closed his eyes and began expressing his grief at the wickedness of people and their love of spreading false rumors and slanderous lies.

The father calmed down a bit and his misgivings lessened. Wishing, however, to do away with all his doubts, he took his son and went off to see Sheikh Barquqi and Mr. Sibai.

Leading his quiet, gentle son by the hand, the sheikh arrived at the bookshop which was the favorite meeting place of the two worthy men of letters.

"I'll make no secret of it, friends," began Sheikh al-Fakk after exchanging greetings, "I've been hearing some very bad things about Imam."

"Nothing wrong, I hope?"

"I was told his conduct was disgraceful, that he was misbehaving himself all over the place, and that he's not paying the least attention to his lessons or the school—that he's really kicked over the traces."

Great astonishment was expressed on their side. "Imam? Who said so, my dear sheikh? Who could say such things? God forgive us! Imam's like a kitten whose eyes haven't yet opened."

The kitten whose eyes had not yet opened made himself look even more innocent and self-effecting.

"By God, you'll pay for this, Imam, you dog," said my father to himself, "putting us in this position." Then, addressing himself to Imam's father: "Imam? His conduct disgraceful? Why, with him it's from home to school and straight back home again. He's killing himself with studying and we had to tell him to ease up a bit—isn't that so, Imam?"

Imam lowered his head in agreement.

The two friends began reassuring the father, enumerating Imam's good qualities and holding him up as a paragon of virtue. The sheikh was duly convinced and hung his head in shame.

"By God, that's just what I said to myself but the way people were talking aroused my suspicions, God curse their father's."

"My dear sheikh, they were jealous of you, envious of you for having such a successful son."

"Never mind, may God forgive them. The journey was not in vain as I've had the pleasure of seeing you both."

The sheikh arose to go—his mind completely at ease, and stretched out his hand to take farewell of his friends. At that very moment, a cart drawn by a donkey and carrying a cargo of women hove into sight. Their voices were raised in song, while one of them, wearing a tarboosh and holding a stick, was standing up in the cart and waggling her belly and hips. The madame, with her fat, flaccid body and red kerchief, with her milaya hanging over the edge of the cart, was beating away on a drum, with the rest of the women clapping in time.

The spectacle could well have passed without incident. There was nothing special about it to attract attention and many such carts had passed by the bookshop. However, calamity struck when one of the women caught sight of our friend Imam standing behind his father, his hand outstretched to bid farewell to Sheikh Barquqi.

Striking her breast with her hand, the woman called out, "Tafida girl, isn't that Imam over there?"

"By the Prophet, it looks like him."

Several voices exclaimed, "Yes, that's Imam all right."

"And what," shouted the madame, "brings him among all these sheikhs?"

The women asked the owner of the cart to stop and one of them got off, shouting:

"The good-for-nothing's been owing me twenty piasters for the last month. Hey, man, where's the money?"

After this incident the sheikh took himself off with his son and neither my father nor Sheikh Barquqi ever laid eyes on them again.

Useless Cats

———ॴ———

Bahaa Taher

From the very first day my colleagues in the company treated me as though I was a spy: I had no place either in their homes or in their hearts. While I wasn't a spy, the circumstances under which I had arrived from the company headquarters in Cairo at the desert mine certainly gave the impression that I had come to keep an eye on them, especially given the fact that the director-general, who was disliked by both the workers in Cairo and at the mines, was the person who had deputized me to write a report about the productivity of the workers and the impediments they faced. This was the exact task I was charged with, but the actual interpretation of it in practical terms, as understood by the workers at the mine, was the proposition that the workers who were not performing up to standard and meeting the required amount of production should be punished and that increased loads be placed on those who were to be kept on.

I hated this assignment from the very beginning and had my misgivings about it from the day the general manager asked me to meet with him. Mr. Hamdan greeted me with a smile and stood there shaking my hand warmly, and this unusual friendliness merely increased my apprehension, especially when he began telling me, "The company must recompense you before you are retired. You are an exemplary employee with a spotless portfolio stretching across thirty years. You really deserve to be promoted but there are no positions available." Now he is trying to make it up to me by sending me to the mine for a period of two months where I'll earn a decent sum of money in the form of a travel allowance and a special increment for working in a remote part of the country.

I muttered, "I've got blood pressure and gall bladder trouble—I pay a visit to my doctor practically every week."

To this he replied jubilantly, "That's great—the dry desert climate will do your health good."

I was never to know how the dryness of the desert would benefit high blood pressure and inflammation of the gall bladder, and the matter was made even more obscure when he explained his medical philosophy: a human being, having been created from earth, would benefit whenever he was in contact with the land. In the clean, virgin desert to which he was sending me, it would be enough for me to take up a handful of earth or sand and to breathe it in deeply and then to rub those parts of my body that were giving me pain. It would also be best for me to sleep directly on the sand whenever possible so that I was in direct contact with the earth.

I didn't understand a word of what he was saying, though I was aware of one thing: There was no way I could escape carrying out his instructions.

My wife disliked the assignment as much as I did and she counseled me with the words, "There's no point in making the journey and being treated this way. Arrange for your pension and leave the job. The four months that are left till you reach retirement won't make any difference." I told her she was right but that I was afraid of what Mr. Hamdan might do, even if I had reached my very last day at work. He was a person who couldn't take someone not accepting his orders, and no one knows how he's going to react, though it's always exceedingly unpleasant: an enormous deduction from one's salary, constant assignments to investigate misdemeanors, actual or imaginary; a sudden transfer to some place far away from anywhere habitable where there are no schools for the children. His reputation in the company was the denier of good, the aggressor, the wicked. Among the workers he was given the abbreviated form of "Mr. Denier," so who was I to challenge him?

My wife wasn't convinced. She said, "You can refuse to go. All your life you've been in the legal department, so what's your connection with inspecting and production?"

Even so, I didn't refuse to go.

However, my colleagues in the company revenged themselves on me once I'd arrived at the oasis.

In the morning I turned up at the company in a white summer suit that I had had specially made for the desert climate. On returning at noon I found that the white suit had turned red.

With a consoling smile the man at the hotel who looked after the laundry said to me, "God help you, sir. This here is rust. No amount of washing or cleaning will get rid of it. God help you, sir."

I understood right away the secret of the furtive smiles exchanged between the fellow workers who had made up their minds that I should accompany them right away so as to become acquainted with the mine and the debris that secretes the metal and which is full of the red dust that had attached itself to my suit and ruined it forever. I then understood why it was that I was the sole person wearing a white suit.

I was nonetheless surprised at my colleagues' reaction to this misfortune the following day. They were all coming up to me singly and slyly, each one of them confirming to me that he had not been a party to what each one described as "the cheap plot" against me and my suit. Each one put the blame on unspecified plotters who were impeding the work in the mine while he himself had been resisting them for a long time.

Each of them terminated his conversation with me by expressing the hope that my final report would commend those who were devoted workers and that he himself, one of the devoted workers, would provide me with the names of the bad workers who were obstructing production and who deserved to be punished.

I told myself that no wonder they were regarding me as a spy seeing that all of them were ready to be spies.

But how could I explain to them the difference between investigating and spying?

Was I not in fact secretly spying on them in their work and following up the reports of those who had come before me? As well as uncovering all the secret papers that were buried in their work dossiers?

Of course I had nothing to gain or to lose in respect of any reward or punishment that came to them. Could I therefore be heard to say that the spying

I was doing was honorable or innocent? No, for I would be presenting the results of the investigation to a person who was neither innocent nor upright at all and would find pleasure in signing the punishment to be handed out. I was a claw of this wicked aggressor, whether I liked it or not, so why was it that I hadn't insisted on refusing the assignment? I don't forgive myself nor those colleagues who were so ready for betrayal. I avoided being in contact with them and confined my work to examining the papers and production reports relating to the mine.

Thus I was forced into isolation, even from myself. After a few days in the oasis I had the sensation of having been exiled for decades to this bleak land. I forgot the sound of my own voice. Hours would pass without my speaking to anyone or doing anything other than sorting through the workers' files and jotting down notes before going back to the hotel.

I was almost on my own in the summer with its heat in that desolate hotel in the heart of the desert. From time to time passing foreign tourists would come and spend a night or two, though the hotel still looked empty and deserted. The workers would say to me sadly that there was hardly an empty room in the winter season.

As for now there was no one there for them other than myself and they knew that I was Egyptian and an employee of the company. There was therefore not the slightest hope that I would treat them as the tourists did, yet even so they took good care of me, maybe because of my age. I almost felt embarrassed when I saw them all surrounding me during my three meals; I was put off by the way they looked at me as they stood far off, ready and waiting. I'd make a movement with my hand and their boss—Said, dressed in a black suit—would come forward with attentive steps, followed by at least two men wearing white kaftans, even if all I was asking for was a glass of water. The two who had been following him would then disappear for several minutes to return with one of them carrying a bottle of iced water that he'd give to Said, while the other one would be carrying a glass on a metal tray. Said would take a long time opening the bottle, frowning as though from the effort he was making. Having opened it, his companion would place the glass in front of me and Said would carefully pour out a small measure of water, while he stared into my eyes. I would take a sip and say, "Fine . . . icy cold," after which he would fill the glass, leaving the bottle on the table and retire from the scene. I had seen them practicing these rituals with the foreign tourists, but in respect of drinks other than water.

There was no way in which the servants at the hotel could avoid dealing with me or I them. I was accustomed to spending most of my day in the air-conditioned restaurant in order to escape both the heat and the loneliness.

Said noticed that I was suffering from loneliness and he suggested to me that I should change the environment, proposing that on the weekend I should undertake a journey into the desert to have a look at the ancient Pharaonic temples and see the white sands that were the goal of tourists from distant countries.

He said that they were soft sands that spread out, resembling a great sea, with their vast white dunes looking like advancing waves, and if you listened carefully you could feel, when the breeze blew, the surging of the waves, and that when I saw that great white sea I would want to stay there all the time. Said aroused my curiosity, but when he told me about the costs of the journey by car to that white sea and putting up for the night on its shore, I felt wholly satisfied with the yellow sands that stretched all around me and the view I had from my room and through the window of the restaurant: a jungle of palm trees in a deep depression of land, whose leaves touched the dwellings built on top of the hillock.

As for my other source of enjoyment, it was discovering the cats, or, rather, the cats discovering me.

I was in the habit of having my dinner in the hotel garden when the evening breeze was cooling down the day's heat. It was a beautiful, well laid out garden surrounded by casuarina and eucalyptus trees interspersed by beds of strong-smelling flowers. I was told that the wife of the owner of the hotel had brought these flowers from her country and that she had instructed the gardener as to how they should be watered and trimmed. Although she and her foreign husband jointly owned the hotel and ran it together, I noticed that she inspired much greater respect from the staff than her husband. They usually spent the summer abroad and I hadn't seen either of them since arriving.

It was this lady who was also the owner of the cats that roamed freely around the garden night and day. There were seven cats of different colors with the magical eyes that all cats have; they were also very clean and moved with great elegance. No sooner had I seated myself in the garden than they would surround me from all sides. They would gaze at me in silence as they waited for me to throw them some food. What astonished me from the start was how quiet and strictly disciplined they were, quite unlike those cats that draw attention to themselves by scratching at one's clothes or meowing and scrabbling about under one's feet to attract attention. These merely sat in a circle round me, and if I threw some food to one of them, the others wouldn't pounce on it but would remain gazing at me in silent supplication. My favorite cat was a ginger one with yellow eyes and all the other shades of coloring that ripple in cats' eyes, and it was she who would come forward when I signaled to her. The others were also beautiful and were mainly gray with white stripes and with thick, furry coats. I was in the habit of touching their backs and plunging my hand into their soft fur. As for my favorite cat, she was entitled, on being given the signal, to jump onto my knee and to submit happily to my petting her. There was also a male cat with a bulky body that would stand at a distance and strut about, stretching its legs to the maximum as it gave me a sideways, indifferent glance; however, when its turn came for me to throw it something, it would be quick about hurling itself at it.

I formed a friendly relationship with these gentle cats. However, one evening, during dinner with the cats circling round me, Said came and began chasing them off and kicking out at them so as to keep them away from me. I told him to let them be as I liked having them for company and that they were doing me no harm. He had a bad nature and he gave me a glance that was almost one of rebuke, as he said, "Why do you like them? I hate cats."

"And why do you hate them?"

"Because they kill the chickens in the coop."

In astonishment I asked, "Cats kill chickens? Are you sure it's not a weasel or perhaps one of the desert foxes?"

"I've seen the cats with my own eyes. I wait for them at night and when they come near the chicken coop at my home I fire at them with a shotgun and they scatter."

I wanted to terminate my conversation with him, so I said, while looking at the cats, which had distanced themselves, "So long as you're sure about it."

The cats had collected under one of the nearby trees, while looking in our direction and moving warily as they prepared to flee at any moment were Said to renew his attack. It was clear that there was mutual distrust between them and him. But instead of taking himself off he suddenly gave let out a loud laugh and said, "Do you know, sir, if the lady owner were to see me harming the cats, she'd cut my head off!"

I tried to win him over to feeling better about cats by saying to him, "The lady's quite right, Said. You know, there's a saying of the Prophet's . . ."

"About the woman who imprisoned one," he interrupted me. "Who do you think I am, sir? I'm not an ignoramus. I've got a degree in philosophy. And don't ask me about what brought me to take up this job."

I didn't ask him, so he gave another laugh and completed what he had to say, "We don't imprison the cats here, sir. As you can see, they are as free as can be, running around and eating and drinking till they've become like mules."

This wasn't in fact true because the cats were actually quite slim and seemed to me to be perfectly content with the food they had. But I too didn't comment, while he went on to say, "It's we who are imprisoned here, sir. The lady imprisons us even when she's somewhere else. Can you believe it? She is now out of the country but she knows everything that happens here. She knows what each one of us does from the moment he starts off his working day. When she returns she'll say to me, 'Said, where did you go on such-and-such a Tuesday at such-and-such an hour and leave your work?' Then she'll deduct half a day from my salary."

"For sure there's someone who's letting her know what's going on, for sure there are one or more spies among you."

Unconvinced, he nodded his head, "Maybe."

I laughed and said, "For sure, Said, for sure, not maybe! There are spies among you who are conveying news to the lady. She can't be a witch who knows the unseen."

With a certain bitterness he said, "By God, sir, her actions are more painful than magic. Today, when receiving my monthly salary, I found that a whole week had been unfairly deducted, and every one of the workers had a similar unfair deduction."

"And why do you tolerate this unfairness? Why don't you refuse . . ."

I stopped in the middle of the sentence. I had noticed something. But, anyway, Said didn't answer my question.

In his complaining tone he concluded what he had to say, "And what's the salary anyway? If it weren't for the piasters paid to me by the clients and the piasters and money made from the tips, this job of mine would work out at a loss. What a salary and a half! The money the lady spends at the vet for the cats is twice my salary. Can you believe that she takes them to a vet at least once every month?"

"And what's so strange about that, Said? I know that they give cats injections against different illnesses."

"Yes, and she also has them operated on so they won't have kittens."

"Both the males and the females?"

"To a one, males and females."

He went back to looking at the cats with a kind of satisfaction.

"All of them are rotten cats."

"All are cats that are . . . what exactly?"

"I said that they are rotten cats. Don't you believe me?"

I gave out a loud laugh as I said, "When it comes down to it, Mr. Said, we're all rotten cats."

"How's that?"

"Think about yourself. You've taken a degree in philosophy, have you not?"

"I haven't just forgotten philosophy, sir, in this place—I've even forgotten how to read and write!"

I turned toward the cats as I enquired, "Are these operations the reason for their being so strangely quiet and have they been injected with something else that has made these cats lose their cattiness? And what about us?"

I made a sign to the cats gathered under the nearby tree for them to get close, but I was conscious of Said addressing me in a tone of voice quite different from the one he used when talking of the cats. He was asking of me with extreme politeness, "Is there anything else Your Excellency requires?"

While I continued signaling to the cats, I said, "Said, I didn't ask for anything in the first place for me to be requiring something else. But what are your thoughts about our refusing?"

"Refusing what exactly, Your Excellency?"

"Nothing, Said. You can go now, thank you."

When the cats saw him departing they slowly began to come nearer. I whispered to them as I held out my hand toward them, "Come along, little brothers and sisters."

And obediently they came.

The House of the Spinster

—∿∿—

Sahar Tawfiq

hat has caused your face to invade my dreams tonight?

I haven't seen you for ages and haven't dreamt of you, so what brought you into my dreams tonight?

Sometimes you might go out early to enjoy the morning and the air cleansed by the aroma of dew, along the canal in which horses take their bath, with boys leaping around them as they washed them while playing about in the water on warm summer mornings. The leaves of the trees still carried drops of dew, cradled gently lest they fall down.

As you stand at the bridge regarding the rising of the sun your eyes continue to follow the tranquil red sphere, until, after a while, they find themselves facing an unbearable brightness; so, defeated, they avoid it, while you go down to the road that will take you back home so you can sleep during the whole of the day's heat.

As for now, I can watch neither the horses nor the sun, for I must go and bring some bread and wrap myself up against the cold of early winter. By the time the feeble golden threads of light make their way with difficulty between the clouds, I shall be on my way to work.

And now, what has brought this small strange bird that is flying close to the ground in search of bits left behind by the cleaners? A bird with a split tail flying with its eyes to the ground so that it would have collided with my feet had it not taken a sudden turn. Did it, at the last moment, see the movement of my foot? Or was it that its ears had heard them moving?

And you, you stupid tree, what has made you blossom into flower in the month of Touba? Your boughs are devoid of leaves yet their ends are full of strange, large red flowers. Why don't you have the patience to wait, like other trees, for spring to come?

All classmates in the same school, yet you are always stirring up trouble, picking continual quarrels, and yet even so you are always welcomed. I have never understood how you manage it.

I was sitting over there in the far corner surrounded by hubbub. I was reading and in a world of my own, but the moment you enter you begin to pick on someone, "What's up with you today—did your father's wife beat you?"

"No, I met up with your handsome face!"

Loud laughter breaks out. You also don't forget to have a dig at my being alone, "Have you been sitting over there forever?"

They take the opportunity to mock me. "Let her be—she's not paying you any attention. Leave her alone—she's busy with this book she'll not be finished with for another year!"

There's nothing for me to do but to appear calm. I give the smile of someone in retreat and once again immerse myself in my book, yet I don't read; I watch them from afar, dreaming of some other world.

We were also living in the same house, and I would see her slipping out through the openings in the garden's rear fence, laughing as I watched her.

"Don't tell my mother that I have come back so late."

"You're drunk!"

"Drunk? That's not true, I just feel slightly dizzy. I drank down a full glass at one go."

"You're joking."

"I swear to you, I took a bet that I'd do so and I won the bet."

"Listen, why don't you come along so we can talk for a while in the garden?"

"What were you doing in the spinster's house?"

"Oh, she was showing me an album of her photos."

As for me, I was never able to intrude.

In class there would be a debate and the school would be quiet. From my place in the class my eyes would concentrate on a single tree whose branches were bare of leaves but were full of large red flowers although we were still in the month of Touba.

"What were you doing in the spinster's house?"

"Oh, she was showing me an album of her photos."

"Really, an album of her photos?" I said jeeringly. "And how did you like it?"

He laughed, "You all look alike!"

Angrily she answered, "Certainly not. You can't say that she and I are alike."

He gave an enigmatic smile, at which I became more angry. "Who do you think you are? You've become so conceited," I said.

"I deserve to be," he said gently.

"You're all the same."

"Men? Yes, of course."

"Conceited and stupid."

"Conceited maybe, but not the other."

"But this is always with our volition—believe me!"

"Women rule over us."

"And we rule the world."

"A rule of destruction and ruin."

"And yet we rule the world."

"Only in appearance; it only seems that man is ruling."

"Listen here, man rules and is in charge. You, what's your name?"

He has begun to change. I say, "What do you mean?"

"After whom are you called? Isn't it your father's name?"

"Oh, these are appellations, the real extension is to the mother."

"That's not true. We are called by our mothers' names only on the Day of Resurrection."

"This is the proof. The true extension is the extension of the womb from the womb."

A moment of silence followed. Once again he was quiet, then he answered, "This is only an organic extension, not a material one."

"What's organic and what's material? You've answered yourself."

Then I remembered, "What were you doing in the spinster's house?"

I was never able to break through.

I used to come here to make small purchases, but for a long time I'd not come and made any such purchases. But I was never concerned about that, not at all.

I didn't see you going off and I didn't want to see you going off, and now I ask, I ask you, overcoming a feeling of regret. Why did you move off at that time? And why have you come back once again?

What shall I say except to hug the sole thing that still concerns me, and I ask: What is it that has brought you to my dream this night?

I look toward the tree.

In the garden of the small, old house is a large mango tree that used to cast a shadow over the garden, and several other small trees, and when you stole your way in the evening from the rear garden fence, I'd always see you entering your house through the back window that leads into the bedroom you share with your brother. While I'm at my window, I always see you, but it would seem that you never saw me.

You would steal your way into the spinster's house. As for today, no one steals into my house, no one.

Abu Arab

———∿∿———

Mahmoud Teymour

I n a humble hair-tent near the estate of Imad Bey lived Suleiman Wida
and his wife and children. They belonged to those Bedouin Arabs who
gain their living by tending sheep, and roam about from place to place
in search of pastures. This Suleiman, whom people out of fear and respect
called Abu Arab, was a giant of a man, with broad shoulders and a dried-up
face, over which the skin was tightly drawn. As he walked along, wrapped
in his great white shawl, he was like a swaying camel, and if you heard him
chanting his monotonous song over his shisha, you would imagine yourself
listening to a howling wolf. He was quick to anger, and if anyone provoked
him, he would become like an enraged bull; yet he was easily calmed down,
and, when humored, became as gentle as a lamb: all smiles and good-will.

He bore great love toward his six children and treated them with the tenderness of a mother. He also had a dog named Dahab, which had an equal place
in his heart with his children. He had found the animal by chance, when it was
still a puppy, almost dying of hunger. He had taken good care of it, till it grew
up, and became the guardian of his flock, the protector of his tent. Dahab was
a black, shaggy, ferocious-looking dog, which had grown to be like its master
in character—fierce when the occasion demanded, gentle at other times.

Imad Bey, the owner of the estate, lived with his wife and Hamid, his only
son, in his old house, which the peasants called 'The Manor.' Hamid was a
spoilt lad of ten, whose parent's love for him bordered on worship. He spent

his time with his servant, Mabrouk, trying to catch birds and fish, or playing on the hills at the edge of the canal, from which the two would hurl down stones at the dogs. As a result of the boy's teasing, bitter enmity grew up between him and Dahab. Whenever the dog divined Hamid's presence—even a good way off—it would prick up its ears and sniff the air, glaring savagely in the boy's direction and preparing for attack. Then it would begin to bark loudly. If Hamid, when with his friends, caught a glimpse of Dahab, he would rain down a shower of stones on the animal, and then seek the protection of his companions against possible retaliation.

One day Hamid went out as usual with Mabrouk to play on the hills. They were alone. The dog chanced to come along, and as it was busy drinking from the canal Hamid threw a sharp stone at it, which drew blood from its head. Dahab swung round furiously, looking for the culprit, though knowing it could be none other than Hamid. The boy had sought safety with his servant on the peak of a high, steep hill; but the dog, instinctively aware of this, rushed up the slope, barking and taking no heed of the hail of stones it encountered. The boy, perceiving that he was in danger, began shouting in a choked voice for Mabrouk to come to his help; but the other, to save his own skin, had taken to his heels. The dog found its path clear, and rushed forward with additional strength and courage. It had almost reached the summit of the hill, and only a short distance separated it from the boy. Hamid saw his enemy drawing near, its eyes blazing like fire, its hair bristling, and he trembled. But suddenly he was conscious of a strange power entering him, and, like a soldier with his back to the wall, he took up a desperate stand. The dog, too, paused, glaring at its adversary with blazing eyes, preparing for the mortal attack. A moment passed thus, with the two enemies facing each other, motionless as statues. At last the dog sprang; but the boy was quicker, and, hurling a stone, cut the dog's head open. The animal staggered and recoiled. It tried to muster its strength to renew the attack, blood pouring down its face and making a red mist before its eyes. Then it lost its balance, tumbled over, and went rolling down the slope.

At the bottom it stopped and lay still. The boy stared horror-stricken at the corpse, and his eyes followed the trail of blood right down the hill. Suddenly he felt strangely faint; he sat on the ground, shaking all over, his face deathly pale.

On his way home Abu Arab heard sounds of wailing and lamentation coming from his tent. He was puzzled, and feared that there had been an accident. He entered hurriedly.

"What's wrong?" he asked.

They all bowed their heads in silence. Abu Arab glanced round and saw that everyone was there. He hastened out to where his flock was grazing; he found nothing missing, but, noticing that Dahab was not to be seen, he returned to the tent.

No one answered.

"It—it was for him you were wailing?"

One of the boys nodded.

"How did he die? Was he killed, or was it an accident?"

His wife softly approached and began to tell him the manner of the dog's death. He listened without interrupting; but soon his face paled, and he was seized by ungovernable rage.

"By the head of my father," he shouted, "I will kill him! And in the same way as he killed Dahab."

Several months went by, and people forgot the incident of the dog's death. But when darkness and the silence of sleep descended on the estate, Abu Arab would prowl like a wolf round Imad Bey's house, waiting for the opportunity to carry out the vengeance he had sworn.

One night he left his tent and made his way toward 'The Manor.' He was muffled in his great shawl, and carried a lot of sharp and heavy stones, which weighed him down as he crept stealthily along. He wriggled over the fence, jumping down into the garden with the agility of a cat. Then he climbed a tree very near the window of the boy's room, and hid himself in the dense foliage. Here he waited and watched, with eyes of a predatory hawk.

An hour passed, during which time Hamid kept coming into the room and going out again into the hall, never settling anywhere. Abu Arab began nervously fingering the stones that lay in the folds of his gown.

At last Hamid's mother came in with her son, carrying him to his bed, where she laid him down to sleep. The child clasped her round the neck, smothering her with kisses; so she took him in her arms again, hugging and kissing him, and gazing at him with tender adoration.

Abu Arab sat tense, watching as the mother lovingly fondled her son and listened to his merry, childish laughter. She rose with the boy in her arms, and walked slowly round the room, singing in a gentle voice, the child hanging round her neck, his eyes closed in sweet content.

A strange numbness, coupled with a feeling of deep depression, took possession of Abu Arab; a stone slipped from his hand. At last, when the mother perceived that her darling was asleep, she approached the bed and laid him in it. Covering him up and kissing him softly on the forehead, she tiptoed from the room.

For a long time Abu Arab gazed at the sleeping, blissfully smiling child. He, too, gave an awkward, embarrassed smile, as if in reply. A sudden pain, like a dagger-thrust, pierced his heart; he leapt to the ground, and began running along the road to his tent, filled with self-loathing. As soon as he reached his tent, he hurried to his son, who was the same age as Hamid, and, taking him in his arms, began eagerly hugging and kissing him, while the tears streamed from his eyes.

Thirst

Mahmoud Al-Wardani

The oppressive smell woke me from my sleep. I went on combating sleep without succeeding in overcoming it. I shook off successive nightmares till it seemed to me that in the end I had the sensation of having a burning thirst, while hearing the barking of distant dogs. On the way to the bathroom I came to a startled stop, for the neighborhood to which I had finally moved in preparation for building a conjugal nest was "free of dogs." I remembered that it was precisely this remark that I had repeated over and over again in order to persuade my fiancée Magda of this fact and to begin right away realizing our dream and savoring a stabled married life crowned with love and tenderness.

The sound of the barking of dogs grew louder. Feeling frightened, I stretched out my hand along the wall so as to put on the light. The light didn't come on, so I began feeling along the walls with my fingers, trying out the rest of the switches without avail. Though I knew my way to the bathroom well, I was frightened, especially as the fighting of the dogs outside did not let up. I recollected that for some time I had had a candle hidden away somewhere. While feeling my way along with the palm of my hand, the oppressive smell that had woken me from sleep was growing stronger as it gushed forth from everywhere and increased my fear. Though the flat was sparsely furnished, I had not accustomed myself to wandering around in it on my own in the dark. I bumped into a chair, bringing it to the floor, and bumped my leg against the sole worktable until I found my way to the kitchen, with my hand stretched out in front of me and arrived at the small table. How happy I was when my fingers knocked against the old candle. Nothing remained but to find the matches, though luckily enough I had my lighter in my pajama pocket. Finally I succeeded in lighting the candle.

Returning to the large room, I set the candle on the table. Thirst was burning my throat so I ran to the bathroom and opened the tap so as to drink down the water that was falling into my palm. I was alarmed at the stickiness of the water flowing down. On fixing my gaze at it in the little light that was issuing from the sitting room I saw that the water was dark colored, and all of a sudden I understood everything, while also distinguishing the smell. The smell was that of blood and without a doubt what was coming out of the tap was blood. I stood there, confused and alarmed. Should I close the tap and take myself off to the living room to have a drink from the fridge, for I was still attacked by thirst? What was going on with me? The barking of dogs was almost turning into a howling, blood was flowing and my hands were sticky and stained, and there was no electricity! Was I asleep or awake? Noticing the towel that was hanging up, I seized hold of it and wiped my sticky hands, then dried my fingers well, and immediately went to the sitting room.

Opening the fridge, I took up a bottle of water. First of all, I brought it up close to the light from the candle and almost called out in terror: it too was full of blood. The burning sensation of thirst grew worse and I imagined that I was screaming with pain. Then, because of a strong gust of wind that came from I know not where, the candle was blown out.

I sensed darkness in front of me. Crossing the bedroom, I was able to reach the bed where I covered the whole of my body and head with the blanket. I was trembling all over, shuddering from the touch of my fingers and the palm of my hand, also the obscure odor of blood that still gushed forth noisily from the tap. After a while it seemed to me that the barking of the dogs had died down; perhaps I had gone to sleep.

The smell was still strong and had perhaps increased, was more tenacious and was hanging in the air, though daylight was showing itself beyond the closed window. Thinking quickly, I speedily donned my clothes and within minutes was at the door of the flat. On looking at my watch as I was crossing the street I was horrified to see my hand stained with blood. I tried to hide it in my pocket as I got into the microbus that would take me to work. I told myself that there was something mysterious about it all, especially when I saw that the palms of the hands of the passengers, also those of the driver, were stained. In addition there was the smell of it, which invaded my nostrils and brought on a sensation of being thirsty.

The solution was to contact Magda by telephone at home before she left for work and to tell her what was happening to me. While I was taking out the money from my pocket to pay the fare, I noticed that my right hand was also stained and that the blood had dried. The fingers of the man sitting next to me, to whom I handed the fare, were also stained. I also glanced at those of the driver as they held the steering wheel and found that they too were stained.

We were approaching the stop for the organization in which I was employed and I called out to the driver, "Please, driver—this is the place . . ."

I turned to the right and walked along at a leisurely pace along the main street that led to the organization's building. It occurred to me to smoke a cigarette during the few minutes it would take me to arrive at my work early as usual. Yes, I am the first to arrive. I don't remember ever not being the first and beginning my day by greeting Magda and whispering words of passionate love in her ear. Thus I meet the day, prepared for all the vile treatment of my bosses.

On crossing the street to enter the organization, I was about say a good morning to Amm Khalifa the gardener, but I stopped in my tracks, seeing that the man was holding gardening hose spewing out bright red blood that gleamed in the first light of day. This was certainly a ghastly day—and it had been a ghastly night. But even more ghastly was the stench of blood bringing on a sensation of thirst that made my body tremble violently.

Passing through the door, I greeted the security men at the entrance, then went up the marble stairs to my office on the first floor. As usual I was the first to sign in and the first to take his seat. I rang Magda's number but the telephone went on ringing without anyone answering. I lit up another cigarette, then rang the canteen and asked Amm Hashem to send me my coffee.

Once again I tried to get Magda, this time on her mobile, but she didn't answer. I answered Amm Saleh's greeting as he brought me my coffee on a small yellow tray, and with it a glass of blood. I almost screamed, but controlled myself and decided to ignore the matter and to deal with it as though nothing unusual had occurred. In fact I raised my face to him, wresting from him what I took to be a smile.

I redoubled my efforts not to show the disgust I felt when I looked at the cup of coffee and found it to be full of warm blood.

How could I escape from all this? Magda wasn't answering and the house, work, the microbus were all soaked in blood, so what was I to do and where was I to hide? I tried to get to my feet but my legs failed me, so I kept to my chair in front of the desk, greeting my colleagues who had begun to arrive, bringing with them the hubbub of office hours. Then they drank tea and coffee consisting of blood without turning a hair, so I decided to be equally crafty by showing no concern. They read the papers and chatted and laughed, but I felt the danger of their asking Amm Hashem to bring them their breakfast sandwiches. I said to myself, "If they've drunk glasses and cups of blood right here in front of me just minutes ago, what sort of breakfast will they be having?"

I found myself getting to my feet. Certainly I was almost staggering, but I could no longer bear the sensation of thirst. When I was sure everyone was busily engaged with something, I made my way quietly outside. More than once I almost tripped up and fell to the ground, but I would right myself at the last moment. Going out by the gate, I gazed around me in the wide street in front of the office. The street, as usual, was peaceful. The world became blurred in front of me. I didn't know where to go with this painful thirst burning at me. I felt that my tongue was swollen and my lips cracked. Should I, for example, take the first taxi and go to Magda at her office? The important thing, first of all, was to cross the street, but I was suddenly confronted by a car going in the wrong direction. For some moments I was unable to understand how a car could be going at this crazy speed in the wrong direction. I was thrown into confusion by hooting and a sudden clamor as cars came and went in every direction. I realized that I wouldn't be saved: I was in the center of the road with cars crossing in front and behind me. I surrendered completely and, with eyes closed, continued to cross the road.

The Picture

—✺—

Latifa al-Zayyat

mal's eyes came to rest on the spray that left behind it, against the horizon, a zigzag thread of sunrays in the colors of the rainbow: a marvelous spectrum which could scarcely by seen unless one tilted one's head at a particular angle and looked hard. She pointed it out to her husband facing her across the table in the cafeteria overlooking the meeting-place of sea and Nile at Ras al-Barr. He could not see it. If only he could have. The spectrum disappears when it's really there, then one imagines it to be there when in fact it has disappeared with the waves rolling away from the rocks of the promontory known as The Tongue which juts out at this spot. The waves of the sea start butting against the rock once more and the spray resumes its upward surge.

"There it is, Izzat," Amal shouted in her excitement, and her son Midhat grasped the hem of her dress and followed her gaze.

"Where?—Mummy—where?" he said in disjointed words that didn't ripen into a sentence.

The look of boredom faded from Izzat's eyes and he burst out laughing. An effendi, wearing a tarboosh and suit complete with waistcoat, shouted: "Double five, my dear sir, double five," and rapped the board with the back-gammon pieces, at which the fat man swallowed his spittle and pulled aside the front of his fine white damascene gallabiya to mop away the seat. An old photographer wearing a black suit jogged his young assistant, who was taking

338

a nap leaning against the developing bucket. The seller of tombola tickets, brushing the sand from his bare feet, called out: 'Couldn't *you* be the lucky one?' Amal gave her shy, apologetic smile and then she was so overcome by infectious laughter that she burst out laughing without knowing why. Suddenly she stopped as she realized she was happy.

"Daddy—food—Mummy—ice cream!"

Izzat turned round in search of the waiter. His gaze became riveted to the cafeteria entrance and he smiled, turning down his thick, moist lower lip. His hand stretched out mechanically and undid another of the buttons of his white shirt, revealing a wider expanse of thick hair on his chest.

The table behind Amal was taken over by a woman of about thirty who was wearing shorts that exposed her white rounded thighs, while her blonde dyed hair was tied round with a red georgette handkerchief decorated with white jasmine, and another woman of about fifty, the front of whose dress revealed a brown expanse of wrinkled bosom. Izaat clapped his hands energetically for the waiter who was actually close enough to have come at a mere sign.

"Three—three ice creams!"

Amal was horrified at her husband's sudden extravagance.

"Two's enough, Izzat," she whispered, her face flushed. "I don't really want one."

Izzat gave no sign of having heard her. He kept repeating, "Three ices— ice creams—mixed—got it?" in an excited voice.

When the waiter moved away, Izzat called him back again and said stressing every syllable:

"Make one of them vanilla. Yes, vanilla. Vanilla ice cream!"

Amal relaxed, smiling triumphantly. "Where is it all coming from?" her mother had asked her. "Surely not from the fifteen pounds a month he earns? Have you been saving? No wonder, poor thing, your hands are all cracked with washing and you're nothing but skin and bone. What a shame he doesn't understand and appreciate you properly. He's leading you a dog's life while he gallivants around."

Amal pursed her lips derisively. She and Izzat together, at last, really on holiday at a hotel in Ras al-Barr! A fortnight without cooking or washing or polishing, no more waiting up for him, no more of that sweltering heat.

She bent her head back proudly as she swept back a lock of jet black hair from her light brown forehead. She caught sight of Izzat's eyes and felt her throat constrict: once again the fire was in those eyes that had become as though sightless, that hovered over things but never settled on them. He had begun to see, his eyes sparkling anew with that fire that was both captivating and submissive, which both burned and pleaded. That glance of his! She had forgotten it—or had she set out intentionally to forget so that she would not miss it? The fact was that it had come back and it was as if he had never been without it. Was it the summer resort? Was it being on holiday? Anyway it was enveloping her once again in a fever of heat.

Amal noticed Izzat's dark brown hand with its swollen veins and she was swept by an ungovernable longing to bend over and kiss it. The tears welled up in her eyes and she drew Midhat close to her with fumbling hands and covered him with kisses from cheek to ear, hugging him to her, and when the moment of frenzy that had stormed her body died down she released him and began searching for the spectrum of colors through her tears as she inclined her head to one side. She must not be misled: was that really the spectrum, or just a spectrum produced by her tears? . . . "Tomorrow you'll weep blood instead of tears," her mother had told her, and her father said: "You're young, my child, and tomorrow love and all that rubbish will be over and only the drudgery will be left." Amal shook her head as though driving away a fly that had landed on her check and murmured to herself: "You don't understand at all . . . I . . . I've found the one thing I've been looking for all my life." Her eyes caught the spectrum and she awoke to a metallic jarring sound as the glass of ice cream scraped against the marble table.

"Three ice creams, two mixed and one vanilla."

"I'll look after the vanilla, old chap. Vanilla will do me fine," said Izzat, carefully enunciating his words and giving a significant smile in the direction of—which direction? A suggestive female laugh came back in reply. In reply to the smile? Amal cupped the iced glass in her hands and turned round as she watched him. *White—vanilla—strawberry—pistachio—and the yellow ice? Would it be mango or apricot? Coloring, mere coloring. It can't be—it can't be.*

"Why don't you eat it?" asked Izaat.

She took up the spoon and was about to scoop up the ice cream when she put it down and again cradled the glass in her hand.

Izzat spoke to his son.

"Ice cream tasty, Midhat?"

"Tasty!"

"As tasty as you, my little darling."

A second laugh rang out behind Amal. Her hands tightened round the iced glass from which cold, icy steam was rising, like smoke. She raised her eyes and reluctantly turned her head without moving her shoulder, slowly lest someone see her, afraid of what she might see. She saw her, *white as a wall, a candle, white as vanilla ice.* For a fleeting moment her eyes met those of the white-skinned woman in the shorts. Her lower lip trembled and she looked back at her glass, drawing herself up. She sat there stiffly, eating. The woman in the shorts took a cigarette from her handbag and left it dangling from her lips until the woman with the bare expanse of bosom had lit it for her. She began to puff out smoke provocatively in Amal's direction, but Amal did not look at her any more. She was a loose woman. Izzat hardly said a word without her laughing. Obviously a loose woman and he wasn't to blame.

Midhat finished eating his ice cream and began glancing around him listlessly, his lips pursed as though he was about to cry.

"The pier, I want to go to the pier."

Amal sighed with relief: a great worry had been removed. This loose woman would be removed from her sight forevermore. She bent her head to one side, smiled, and said carefully as though playing a part before an audience,

"Certainly, darling. Now. Right now Daddy and Mummy'll take Midhat and go to the pier."

She pushed back her chair as she gave a short affected laugh.

"Where to?" said Izzat with unwarranted gruffness.

"The child wants to go to the pier."

"And where are we going after the pier? Surely we're not going to suffocate ourselves back at the hotel so early?"

Midhat burst out crying, trammeling the ground with his feet. Amal jumped up, clasping the child to her nervously. *Izzat? Izzat wants to—it's not possible—good God, it's not possible—*Midhat, irked by the violence with which he was being held, internsified his howling.

"Shut up!" Izzat shouted at him.

When Midhat didn't stop, his father jumped up and seized him from his mother's arms, giving him two quick slaps on the hand. Then Izzat sat down again and said, as though justifying himself:

"I won't have a child who's a crybaby!"

Amal returned to her chair, and the tears ran silently from Midhat's eyes and down to the corners of his mouth. As though she had just woken up, the woman in the shorts said in her drawling husky voice:

"Come along, my sweetheart. Come along to me." She took a piece of chocolate wrapped in red paper out of her pocket.

"Come, my darling! Come and take the chocolate!"

Amal drew Midhat to her. The woman in the shorts put her head to one side and crossed her legs smiling slightly, she threw the piece of chocolate on to the table so that Midhat could see it. Amal cradled Midhat's head against her breast, patting his hair with trembling hands. Midhat lay quietly against his mother's breast for a while then he lifted an arm to wipe away the tears, and, peeping from under his arm, he began to steal fleeting glances at the chocolate. The woman in the shorts beckoned and winked at him, and Amal buried his head in her breast. *It's not possible, not possible that he would go to her—Izzat—Midhat—it's not possible that Izzat would want her.* With a sudden movement Midhat disengaged himself from his mother's grasp and ran to the neighboring table. The lewd laugh rang out anew, long and jarring.

"Go and fetch the boy!" Amal whispered, her lips grown blue.

Izzat smiled defiantly. "Fetch him yourself!"

"We're not beggars," she said in a choked voice.

"Where does begging come into it? Or do you want the boy to turn out as timid as you?"

Amal didn't look at the table behind her where her son sat on the lap of the woman in shorts eating chocolate and getting it all over his mouth and chin, hands and shirt. She wished that she could take him and beat him till he—but what had he done wrong? The fault was hers, hers alone.

"Good for us, we've finished the chocolate and now—up we get and wash our hands," the woman in shorts drawled in her husky voice.

Amal jumped to her feet, white-faced. The woman in the shorts went off, waggling her hips as she dragged Midhat along behind her.

Putting a hand on his wife's shoulder, Izzat said softly, "You stay here while I go and fetch the boy."

Amal remained standing, watching the two of them: the woman with Midhat holding her hand, the woman and Izzat following her. She watched them as they crossed the balcony of the cafeteria and—through glass—as they crossed the inner lounge and were lost behind the walls of the building, the woman's buttocks swaying as though detached from her, with Izzat following her, his body tilted forward as though about to pounce. For step after step, step hard upon step, lewd step upon lewd step. "No, Izzat, don't be like that. You frighten me, you frighten me when you're like that, Izzat." She had spoken these words as she dropped down exhausted on a rock in the grotto at the Aquarium. Izzat had been out of breath as he said: "You can't imagine—you can't imagine how much I love you, Amal," with pursed lips and half-closed eyes, heavy with the look of a cat calling its mate, a look that burned and pleaded. *Izzat and the other woman—and the same look that burned and pleaded . . . It can't be—It can't be.*

"A picture, Madam?"

Amal had collapsed exhausted on the chair, waving the old photographer away. "No, Izzat—no, don't put your hand on my neck like that! What'll people say when they see the photo? They'll say I'm in love with you—No, please don't." "Here you are, Milady, the picture's been taken with my hand on your neck and now you'll never be able to get rid of me."

"A postcard size for ten piasters and no waiting, Madam."

"Not now, not now."

The man went on his way repeating in a listless, lilting voice, "Family pictures, souvenir pictures," while behind him the barefooted tombola ticket-seller wiped his hand on his khaki trousers. "Why shouldn't yours be the winning one? Three more numbers and we'll have the draw. A fine

china tea set for just one piaster. There's a bargain for you!" "I'm so lucky,
Mummy, to have married a real man." "A real man? A real bounder, you
mean. Work! Work, he says—funny sort of an office that's open till one and
two in the morning!" That's what Saber Effendi, their neighbor, had said,
and Sitt Saniyya, pouring out the coffee, had remarked, "You see, my poor
child, Saber Effendi's had forty years in government service and there's not
much that escapes him."

Lifting Midhat on to his lap, Izzat said softly, "The child went on having
tantrums before he would wash his hands."

Amal gave him a cold searching look as though seeing him for the first
time. She bent her head and concentrated her gaze on a chocolate stain on
Midhat's shirt. Izzat appeared to be completely absorbed by teaching the
child to count up to ten. Midhat stretched out his hand and put it over his
father's mouth. Izzat smiled and leaned toward Amal.

"You know, you look really smart today—pink suits you wonderfully,"
he said.

Her throat constricted as she gave a weak smile. Again the old photographer
said, "A picture of you as a group, sir. It'll be very nice and there's no waiting."

"No thanks," said Izzat.

Amal spotted the woman in the shorts coming toward them with her
swinging gait.

"Let's have a picture taken," she said in a choked voice.

"What for?"

Aloof, the woman passed her, looking neither at her nor Izzat. She sat
down and started talking to her woman friend.

Amal leaned across to Izzat, the words tumbling from her mouth:

"Let's have a picture taken—you and me—let's!" she pointed a finger
at him, a finger at herself, and then brought the two fingers together. With a
shrug of his shoulder Izzat said, "Take your picture, old chap."

When the photographer had buried his head inside the black hood, Amal
stretched out her hand and took hold of her husband's arm; as the photographer gave the signal her hand tightened its grip. Waiting for the photograph,
Izzat did not look at the woman, nor she at him. When the photographer came
back with the picture, Izzat stood up searching for change.

Amal snatched eagerly at the photograph. She held it in her hand as though afraid that someone would seize it from her. *Izzat at her side—her lover—her husband—*The woman in the shorts pushed back her chair violently as she got to her feet. Passing near to their table, her eyes met those of Amal for a brief instant, fleeting yet sufficient—Amal let the picture fall from her hands. It dropped to the ground, not far from her. Without moving from where she sat she propped her elbows on her thighs and her head in her hands, and proceeded to gaze at it with a cool, expressionless face. The picture of the woman looking up at her was that of a stranger, a feverish woman grasping with feverish hand at the arm of a man whose face expressed pain at being gripped so tightly. Slowly, calmly, Amal stretched out her leg and dragged the toe of her shore, and then the heel, across the photograph. Drawing back her leg and bending down again, she scrutinized the picture anew. Though sand had obliterated the main features, certain portions still remained visible: the man's face grimacing with pain, the woman's hand grasping the man's arm. Amal stretched out her leg and drew the picture close to her chair with her foot till it was within arm's reach. She leaned forward and picked it up.

When Izzat returned with change the picture had been torn into small pieces which had scattered to the winds. The spectrum had disappeared and the sun was centrally positioned in the sky, while people were running across the hot sands to avoid burning their feet. Amal realized she had a long way to go.

Notes on Authors

IBRAHIM ABDEL MEGUID (born 1946) has established his name as a writer of novels. *The Other Place,* translated by Farouk Abdel Wahab, was awarded the Naguib Mahfouz Medal for literature and was published in English translation by the American University in Cairo Press in 1997. Several of his novels are set in Egypt's "second city," Alexandria.

YAHYA TAHER ABDULLAH was born in Karnak near Luxor in Upper Egypt in 1942. Despite having had little formal education, he quickly made a name for himself as an outstanding individual voice among the writers of short stories in Egypt. A volume of some of his short stories was published in translation under the title *The Mountain of Green Tea*, and more recently a translation of a novel entitled *The Collar and the Bracelet.* He was killed in a car crash in 1981.

YUSUF ABU RAYYA was born in 1955 in the village of Hihya in the Nile Delta and studied journalism at Cairo University. After working on various newspapers and magazines he was awarded a period of three years to concentrate on his creative writing. His novel *Wedding Night* was awarded the 2005 Naguib Mahfouz Medal for Literature and has been translated into English by Neil Hewison.

MOHAMMED AFIFI (1922–81) was the author of an outstanding book that appeared on 18 June 1946 under the title *Anwar* (Lights). Among his many other publications is the short and delightful *Taranim fi zill Tamara* (Little Songs in the Shade of Tamaara).

In typical fashion, Afifi wrote his own obituary: "Dear reader: I regret to inform you about something that might sadden you slightly, and that is that I have died, and of course I am not writing these words after my death (something slightly difficult), but did so before that, and I enjoin that they be published after my death, it being my belief that death is something personal and doesn't require that others be inconvenienced into sending telegrams and crowding around the Omar Makram Mosque where ceremonies of mourning are usually held at night."

ABBAS AHMED (1923–78) was a prolific writer and published widely in magazines during his lifetime. The only work to appear under his name in book form was the short and highly acclaimed *The Village*. The story included in the present collection was taken from a volume of short stories by him assembled and published by his friends after his death.

AHMED ALAIDY, born in 1974, has written satirical stories for young people and currently writes a political comic strip for an Egyptian weekly. His novel, *Being Abbas el Abd,* was published in English by the AUC Press in 2006.

RADWA ASHOUR was born in Cairo in 1946 and graduated from the Faculty of Arts at Cairo University. She later took her doctorate in African-American Literature from the University of Massachusetts. At present she occupies the chair of English and comparative literature at Ain Shams University. She has published five volumes of literary criticism, also several novels and collections of short stories. Her novel *Granada*, translated into several languages, won the Cairo International Book of the Year award in 1994; she was also awarded the Constantine Cavafy Prize for Literature in 2007.

IBRAHIM ASLAN was born in the Nile Delta in 1939. Though largely self-taught, he is regarded as one of Egypt's top writers. He is the Cairo correspondent for the prestigious Lebanese newspaper *al-Hayat*. His early novel *The Heron* was made into a highly successful Arabic film, *Kitkat*, in 1991.

HANA ATIA, born in Cairo, took a degree at the Pyramids Academy of Arts in cinema techniques and has written several screenplays. She has made a name for herself as a writer of short stories, of which she has published three volumes. She is also the author of a novel. Several of her stories have been published in French and Norwegian translations.

SHUKRI AYYAD, born in 1921, studied Arabic literature at Cairo University and also took his doctorate there. He was later appointed professor of Arabic at the same university. He wrote several volumes of short stories and also published a number of translations of fiction from the English, also works of literary criticism.

SALWA BAKR, born in Cairo, made her name with her first book of short stories, which she published at her own expense. A selection of her stories translated into English by Denys Johnson-Davies has been published under the title *The Wiles of Men*. Also available in English translation is her first novel *The Golden Chariot* and a recent novel entitled *The Man from Bashmour*.

REHAB BASSAM took a degree in English from Ain Shams University. Having worked writing advertisements and translation, she now devotes her time to publishing children's books. The present story is taken from a collection of stories published in 2008, which has gone into numerous editions.

MOHAMED EL-BISATIE was born in 1938 in a Nile Delta village overlooking Lake Manzala. Though many of his writings are about his childhood home, he has never felt the desire to return since coming to Cairo to attend university. He has published several volumes of short stories and novels, many of which have been translated into English and other languages. A representative volume of his short stories translated by Denys Johnson-Davies was published under the title *A Last Glass of Tea*. His novels available in English are *Houses Behind the Trees*, *Over the Bridge*, *Clamor of the Lake*, *Hunger*, and *Drumbeat*.

MAHMOUD DIAB was born in Ismailiya in 1932 and took a degree in law. He is best known as a playwright. His play *The Storm* was chosen to represent Egypt at a UNESCO competition.

SHEHATA AL-ERIAN was born in 1961 and began his writing career as a poet, writing in both the classical and vernacular forms of Arabic. His first novel earned him the Egyptian National Merit award in 2000.

MANSOURA EZ ELDIN (born 1976) studied journalism at Cairo University and published her first collection of short stories in 2001. She then published two novels. Her novel *Maryam's Maze*, written in 2004, was published in an English translation by the AUC Press in 2007. Her second novel *Behind Paradise* was short-listed for the Arabic Booker Prize in 2010. She is fascinated by the relationship between dreams and reality.

SHAWQI FAHEEM took a degree in psychology from Ain Shams University, after which he worked as a translator and program presenter for Egyptian radio from 1962 until 1998. He has translated many short stories from the English, also plays by such modern writers as Harold Pinter. He also writes short stories and critical articles that are frequently published in Egyptian and Arab periodicals.

ABDUL RAHMAN FAHMY was born in 1924 and studied Arabic literature at Cairo University, after which he worked as a teacher of Arabic. He published several volumes of short stories as well as plays.

HOSAM FAKHR has published three volumes of short stories, the first of which appeared in 1985 with an introduction by Yusuf Idris. In 2006 he published a novel; this was followed in 2007 by a volume of short stories from which the story in this collection is taken.

IBRAHIM FARGHALI was born in 1967 in Mansoura, Egypt, but grew up in Oman and the United Arab Emirates. He took a degree in business administration from Mansoura University in 1991 and worked for a time as a journalist. He then worked at the literary magazine *Nizwa* in Muscat before returning to Cairo and working with *al-Ahram* newspaper. He is now an editor with *al-Arabi* magazine in Kuwait. He has published two collections of short stories and two novels, one of which, *The Smiles of the Saints*, was translated into English by Andy and Nadia Fouda-Smart and was published by the AUC Press in 2007.

SULEIMAN FAYYAD was born in 1929 in a village in the province of Mansoura. He has published several volumes of short stories and has worked as a teacher of Arabic, previously having taught in Saudi Arabia. He has also published a novel that has been translated.

HAMDY EL-GAZZAR was born in 1970 in Cairo. In 1992 he took a degree in philosophy from Cairo University. He has published numerous short stories and articles in the Arabic press and has also written and directed three one-act plays. His first novel *Sihr aswad (Black Magic)* was first published in 2005. The novel was awarded the Sawiris Foundation Prize for Egyptian Literature in 2006 and translated into English by Humphrey Davies and published in 2007. It was also published in a Turkish translation. His second novel *Ladhdhat sirriya* (Secret Pleasures) was published in 2008.

FATHY GHANEM (1924–99) was a novelist, short-story writer, and literary critic. Having graduated from Cairo University in law he started working for the Ministry of Education, then as a journalist with the magazine *Rose al-Youssef*. He wrote novels including *al-Gabal* (The Mountain) and *The Man who Lost his Shadow*, which was translated into English by Desmond Stewart and published in 1966; the novel was also translated into French.

GAMAL AL-GHITANI, born in 1945, is the author of *Zayni Barakat*, *The Mahfouz Dialogs*, *Pyramid Texts*, and *The Zafarani Files*, all published in English by the AUC Press. He is editor-in-chief of the literary review *Akhbar al-adab*.

Yᴏᴜsᴇғ Gᴏʜᴀʀ was born in 1912. He took a degree in law and worked for several years as a lawyer. He published no less than 250 short stories, which appeared in Cairo's leading magazines; more than seventy of them were turned into films. He was awarded several prizes for his writings.

Nᴀʙɪʟ Gᴏʀɢʏ was born in 1944 in Cairo. He studied civil engineering at Cairo University and later worked as an engineer in the United States. Upon returning to Cairo he began writing short stories under the influence of such writers as Borges and Kawabata; he also read widely in the writings of the Sufis. He currently resides in Paris. A book containing a selection of his short stories was published under the title *The Slave's Dream,* from which the present story is taken.

Aʙᴅᴏᴜ Gᴜʙᴇɪʀ was born in 1950 in a small village in Upper Egypt. For many years he worked as a successful journalist in Cairo and a freelance creative writer. Recently he spent several years in Kuwait as the editor of a periodical, but has now returned to Egypt and has settled in a village outside Cairo. He has published several volumes of short stories, as well as four novels.

Yᴀʜʏᴀ Hᴀᴋᴋɪ began his career as a lawyer and then entered the diplomatic corps. Upon resigning from government service, he devoted himself to literature; together with such figures as Taha Hussein, the playwright Tawfiq al-Hakim, the short story writer Yusuf Idris, and, of course the novelist Naguib Mahfouz, he made up that group of exceptionally talented figures who laid the foundations for the literary renaissance in Egypt midway through the last century. He is best known for his short novel entitled *The Lamp of Umm Hashim,* the first of several works in Arabic dealing with the way in which an individual tried to come to terms with two divergent cultures. The novel is available in an English translation by Denys Johnson-Davies.

Gᴀᴍɪʟ Aᴛɪᴀ Iʙʀᴀʜɪᴍ was born in Cairo in 1937. He graduated from the Faculty of Commerce at Cairo University, then took a diploma in art appreciation and worked at the Ministry of Culture. For two years he taught in the northern costal town of Asila, giving the name of the town to a novel published in Damascus. He presently lives in Switzerland where he works as the correspondent for several Arabic publications. He has published several novels and volumes of short stories.

SONALLAH IBRAHIM was born in 1937. He studied law and drama at Cairo University and then took up journalism. In 1959 he was imprisoned for his leftist writings. Released in 1964, he then moved to Berlin where he worked at a news agency. He later moved to Moscow, where he studied cinematography. In 1974 he returned to Cairo, since when he has dedicated his time to writing fiction, concentrating on novels, many of which are available in translation. In 1998 his novel *Sharaf* (Honor) received the national award for best Egyptian novel, although the author declined to accept the prize.

YUSUF IDRIS was born in 1927 and died in London in 1991. He published his first collection of short stories in 1954 with an introduction by the eminent man of letters Taha Hussein. He was later considered the undisputed master of the Arabic short story. Having qualified as a doctor, his experiences as a private practitioner and a government health inspector provided him with rich material for many of his most famous stories. A concern for the underprivileged underlies much of his writing, whether it be short stories or plays, a genre in which he also excelled. Two volumes of his short stories have been published in English translation, as well as his novel *City of Love and Ashes*, translated by Neil Hewison. A selection of his writings is to be found in *The Essential Yusuf Idris* edited by Denys Johnson-Davies.

SAID AL-KAFRAWI was born in the Nile Delta in 1939. A formidable creative writer, he has confined his talents to the short story, of which he has published some fifteen volumes. A representative collection of his stories, translated by Denys Johnson-Davies, appeared in 1998 under the title *The Hill of Gypsies*. Individual stories by him have appeared in most European languages. He has made a reputation for himself as Egypt's leading writer of short stories, most of which deal with life in the Egyptian countryside.

EDWAR AL-KHARRAT was born in 1926 in Alexandria and studied law at the university there. His first volume of short stories was published at his own expense in 1959. Since then he has written prolifically and has produced a large number of novels and volumes of stories. He has also been an active translator from English and French. Two of his early novels, *Rama and the Dragon* and *Stones of Bobello* are available in English translation, as are two more recent novels, *The City of Saffron* and *Girls of Alexandria*. He was awarded the Owais Prize in 1994–95 for his contribution to Arabic literature, and the Naguib Mahfouz Medal for Literature in 1999.

LUTFI AL-KHOULI was born in 1928 and studied law, practicing for several years. He was in and out of prison in the 1960s on many occasions because of his left-wing activities. In 1965 he brought out the socialist magazine *al-Tali'a (Avant-garde)*. Besides publishing volumes of short stories, he has also written plays and film scenarios and a book on Bertrand Russell and Jean-Paul Sartre.

NAGUIB MAHFOUZ (1911–2006) is the only Arab author to have been awarded the Nobel Prize for Literature; the award was made in 1988. He wrote nearly forty novels and a dozen volumes of short stories. Among his most well-known novels are his early *Midaq Alley*, his short novel *Miramar,* and the monumental *Cairo Trilogy*. A selection of his short stories was published by Denys Johnson-Davies under the title *The Time and the Place*. Many of his novels have been made into successful films and his work has been widely translated into more than forty languages.

MOHAMED MAKHZANGI was born in 1950 in the town of Mansoura in the Delta of Egypt. He studied to become a doctor and later specialized in psychology and alternative medicine in the Ukrainian capital Kiev. Having worked for some years as a doctor, he later turned to journalism and creative writing, working for several years in Kuwait on the magazine *al-Arabi*. Besides several volumes of short stories, he has published a literary examination of the Chernobyl nuclear disaster, which he himself lived through. The book is available in an English translation under the title *Memories of a Meltdown*. Translations of his stories have appeared in English, French, German, Russian and Chinese. He is represented here by four very short stories selected from many such stories that he published several years ago. He divides his year between Egypt and Syria.

SABRI MOUSSA was born in 1932 and has published several novels, collections of short stories, and film scripts. His works have been widely translated. One of his best-known works is his novel *Fasad.al-amkina* (The Corruption of Places), which won the Pegasus Prize for Literature.

MOHAMED MUSTAGAB was born in 1938 and was largely self-educated. For a time he worked on building the High Dam in Aswan. His first novel was published in 1983, winning a prize and being translated into several languages. He later wrote other novels for which he won several prizes. A novel and other stories were translated and published in English by Humphrey Davies. He died in 2005.

ABD AL-HAKIM QASIM was born in 1935. Having gone to school in Tanta in Egypt's Delta, he then attended Alexandria University. Because of his political activities he was sentenced by a military court to five years' imprisonment in 1960. On his release from prison he completed his novel *The Seven Days of Man*, which was published to great acclaim in 1969. He later published several other novels and a number of short stories. For some years he lived in Berlin, but returned to Cairo in 1985 where he died in 1990.

YOUSSEF RAKHA was born in Cairo in 1976. Having taken a degree in English and philosophy from Hull University in England, he then worked as a reporter and editor at *al-Ahram Weekly*. He has published five books in Arabic, a collection of short stories, and two books of travel writings.

ALIFA RIFAAT was born in 1930 and spent most of her adult life in various parts of the Egyptian countryside as the wife of a police officer. It is largely from this period that she has drawn the material for her short stories. In English she is best known for the representative volume published under the title *Distant View of a Minaret*.

MAHMOUD AL-SAADANI (1928–2010) wrote plays, novels, short stories, and travel books, although he started his career as a journalist. In his fiction he wrote about the middle and lower classes of society in Egypt with sympathetic humor and in his own blend of the literary and colloquial languages.

ABDUL HAMID GOUDA AL-SAHHAR (1913–74). After taking a degree in commerce from the Egyptian University, al-Sahhar became a novelist and screenplay writer, though he began his career writing short stories for magazines. He also wrote historical novels and several successful movie scripts. His last post was editor of *Cinema* magazine.

MEKKAWI SAID was born in 1955 and has published a number of novels and volumes of short stories, many of which have gone into multiple editions. Among the literary prizes he has won is that of the Dar Suad Al-Sabah Literary Competition for his novel *Ship Rats* in 1991; in 2007 his novel *Cairo Swan Song* was short-listed for the Arabic Booker Prize. He has also written widely for various Arabic television programs.

ABDEL-MONEIM SELIM was born in 1929 in the province of Rosetta. He studied law at Cairo University and worked for a time as a tax inspector. He has published several volumes of short stories and a collection of plays.

KHAIRY SHALABY (1938–2011) was one of Egypt's most prolific writers. He published more than ten novels and half a dozen volumes of short stories. Among his best-known works is his novel *Wikalat Atiya,* which was translated into English under the title *The Lodging House* and has also been translated into French. Individual stories of his have been translated into Russian and Chinese.

YUSUF SHAROUNI was born in 1924 and studied philosophy at Cairo University. After spending several years as a teacher in Sudan, he returned to Cairo and worked at the Supreme Council for the Arts, Literature, and Social Sciences. He later spent several years working in Oman. He is known for his considerable contribution to the short story in Egypt.

IBRAHIM SHUKRALLAH (1921–95) worked with the Arab League for much of his life, at one time being in charge of their Indian office and later their London office. He is the co-author and translator of the seminal book *Images from the Arab World,* which introduced to readers of English much of Arabic literature, starting with the poetry of pre-Islamic times up to the writings of early twentieth-century authors like the playwright Tawfiq al-Hakim. He is also the author of a distinguished volume of Arabic poetry. As far as is known, he wrote only two short stories.

YUSUF AL-SIBAI was born in 1917 and was assassinated in Cyprus in 1978 because of his support for Sadat's peace treaty with Israel. He headed the *Al-Ahram* newspaper and was then appointed minister of culture in 1973. He was a widely popular writer of short stories and novels, with many of his writings adapted for the cinema.

BAHAA TAHER is the author of *Love in Exile* and *As Doha Said,* both published in English by the American University in Cairo Press. In 2008 he was awarded the first International Prize for Arabic Fiction (the 'Arabic Booker').

SAHAR TAWFIQ is a writer of short stories and novels and an English–Arabic translator. She has received several awards, among them the Award of Arkansas University Press for Arabic Literature in Translation. She worked for many years as a teacher but now devotes her time to writing and translating.

MAHMOUD TEYMOUR was born in 1894 into an aristocratic Egyptian family of Turkish origin and is today regarded as the pioneer writer of the Arabic short story. A collection of his stories was published in Cairo in 1946 under the title *Tales from Egyptian Life*, translated by Denys Johnson-Davies—the first volume of Arabic short stories to appear in an English translation. The story "Abu Arab" is taken from that volume.

MAHMOUD AL-WARDANI was born in Cairo in 1950 and worked for many years as a journalist. He is also an accomplished writer of short stories of which he has published several volumes, in addition to more than half a dozen novels. Several of his stories have appeared in English and German translations.

LATIFA AL-ZAYYAT was born in 1923 and died in 1996. Having taken a doctorate in England, she became professor of English at Ain Shams University. The short story reproduced here is taken from the first representative volume of Arabic short stories in English translation published in 1967 by Oxford University Press. She also wrote two novels, *The Owner of the House* and *The Open Door*, both of which are available in English translation. Her writing was unusually modern for its time in that she employed the colloquial language in much of her dialogue, something that is being increasingly done by today's younger writers.

DENYS JOHNSON-DAVIES has produced more than thirty volumes of translation of modern Arabic literature, including *The Essential Tawfiq al-Hakim* (AUC Press, 2008), *The Essential Yusuf Idris* (AUC Press, 2009), and *The Essential Naguib Mahfouz* (AUC Press, 2011). He was described by Edward Said as "the leading Arabic–English translator of our time." Johnson-Davies received the Sheikh Zayed Book Award in 2007 for Personality of the Year in the Field of Culture.

Glossary

———

Abu ———: father of ———.

Abul Qasim, Umm Hashim, Rifa'i, al-Hussein: Holy figures in popular Islam, often appealed to for intercession.

Antar: A traditional hero of Arab folk tales.

al-Azhar: A district of historic Cairo.

bango: A form of hashish.

Bulaq Abu al-Ila: An area of Cairo.

the Companions: The revered Companions of the Prophet Muhammad.

gallabiya: A man's gown-like garment.

goza: A makeshift water-pipe, often used for smoking hashish.

Hagg/Hagga: A Muslim who has been on the pilgrimage to Mecca; also, a general term of respect for an older man or woman.

Hours of Pride: A collection of short stories by Edwar al-Kharrat.

al-Hussein: A district of historic Cairo.

jubba: A long outer garment for men.

kofta: Grilled fingers of minced meat.

Ma'allim: Term of respect for a businessman in traditional society who is of some standing but little or no formal education.

milaya: Wrap worn by women.

Mosque of Ibn Tulun: A ninth-century mosque in Cairo, the city's oldest.

omda: Village chief.

Say: Let us not be stricken other than by what God has decreed for us:
Quran 9:51.

Sayyid Ahmad Abdul Gawad, Zubayda, Kamal, Yaseen: Characters in
Naguib Mahfouz's *Cairo Trilogy.*

shisha: A traditional water-pipe.

taamiya: Fried patty made of beans.

Umm ———: mother of ———.

Umm Kulthum: Twentieth-century Egyptian singer, widely admired
throughout the Arab world.

Throne Verse: A well known and favorite verse from the Quran 2:255.

Modern Arabic Literature
from the American University in Cairo Press

Betool Khedairi *Absent*
Mohammed Khudayyir *Basrayatha*
Ibrahim al-Koni *Anubis • Gold Dust • The Puppet • The Seven Veils of Seth*
Naguib Mahfouz *Adrift on the Nile • Akhenaten: Dweller in Truth*
Arabian Nights and Days • Autumn Quail • Before the Throne • The Beggar
The Beginning and the End • Cairo Modern • The Cairo Trilogy: Palace Walk
Palace of Desire • Sugar Street • Children of the Alley • The Coffeehouse
The Day the Leader Was Killed • The Dreams • Dreams of Departure
Echoes of an Autobiography • The Essential Naguib Mahfouz • The Final Hour
The Harafish • Heart of the Night • In the Time of Love
The Journey of Ibn Fattouma • Karnak Cafe • Khan al-Khalili • Khufu's Wisdom
Life's Wisdom • Love in the Rain • Midaq Alley • The Mirage • Miramar • Mirrors
Morning and Evening Talk • Naguib Mahfouz at Sidi Gaber • Respected Sir
Rhadopis of Nubia • The Search • The Seventh Heaven • Thebes at War
The Thief and the Dogs • The Time and the Place • Voices from the Other World
Wedding Song • The Wisdom of Naguib Mahfouz
Mohamed Makhzangi *Memories of a Meltdown*
Alia Mamdouh *The Loved Ones • Naphtalene*
Selim Matar *The Woman of the Flask*
Ibrahim al-Mazini *Ten Again*
Yousef Al-Mohaimeed *Munira's Bottle • Wolves of the Crescent Moon*
Hassouna Mosbahi *A Tunisian Tale*
Ahlam Mosteghanemi *Chaos of the Senses • Memory in the Flesh*
Shakir Mustafa *Contemporary Iraqi Fiction: An Anthology*
Mohamed Mustagab *Tales from Dayrut*
Buthaina Al Nasiri *Final Night*
Ibrahim Nasrallah *Inside the Night • Time of White Horses*
Haggag Hassan Oddoul *Nights of Musk*
Mona Prince *So You May See*
Mohamed Mansi Qandil *Moon over Samarqand*
Abd al-Hakim Qasim *Rites of Assent*
Somaya Ramadan *Leaves of Narcissus*
Mekkawi Said *Cairo Swan Song*
Ghada Samman *The Night of the First Billion*
Mahdi Issa al-Saqr *East Winds, West Winds*
Rafik Schami *The Calligrapher's Secret • Damascus Nights*
The Dark Side of Love
Habib Selmi *The Scents of Marie-Claire*
Khairy Shalaby *The Hashish Waiter • The Lodging House*
The Time-Travels of the Man Who Sold Pickles and Sweets
Miral al-Tahawy *Blue Aubergine • Brooklyn Heights • Gazelle Tracks • The Tent*
Bahaa Taher *As Doha Said • Love in Exile*
Fuad al-Takarli *The Long Way Back*
Zakaria Tamer *The Hedgehog*
M. M. Tawfik *Murder in the Tower of Happiness*
Mahmoud Al-Wardani *Heads Ripe for Plucking*
Amina Zaydan *Red Wine*
Latifa al-Zayyat *The Open Door*